# Venus
# Mons
# Iliad

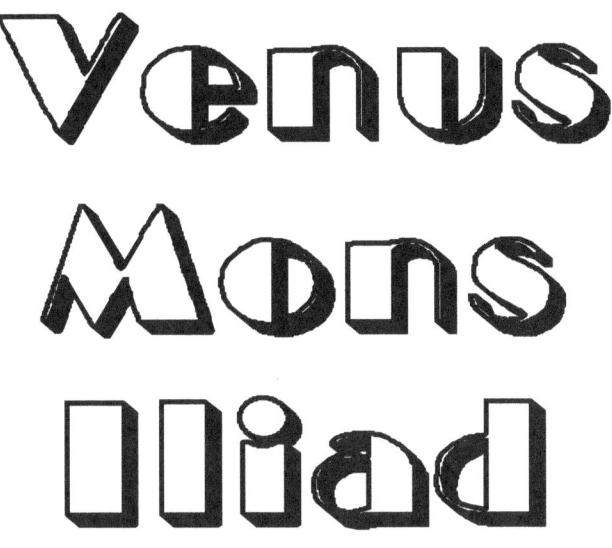

# Venus Mons Iliad

## William R. Burkett, Jr.

**The New
Atlantian Library**

# Dedication
# To All the Girls I Loved
# Before

I love the song *To All the Girls I Loved Before* as rendered in duet by Julio Iglesias and Willie Nelson. Iglesias' suave, exotically accented tones evoke night trains to Paris and the haunting echo of high heels on cobblestones. Nelson's hard-living whiskey and smoke-roughened voice recalls roadhouse sex, long American road trips and tangled sheets in cheap motels. The song is a true anthem for a ramblin' man, his longings, and his gratitude for restless women.

Long before I heard them sing it, I heard another song authored and sung by Dory Previn. She was called from the audience to sing it in a Southern California jazz joint called the Lighthouse. Hers was the ballad of a lonely woman asking a new man if he cared to stay till sunrise – *it's completely your decision ... it's just that going home's such a long lonely ride.*

I did not stay till sunrise with the woman who took me to the Lighthouse, on what amounted to an unacknowledged first date. She didn't invite me to stay that night. Sometimes luck mends such mistakes. We were lucky.

But all beginnings have their endings already written somewhere in time. New love spirals into loss and melancholy – and bittersweet gratitude – as in the song Julio and Willie perform flawlessly. Life moves relentlessly on. A jaded woman told me once men and women should always live separately with occasional conjugal visits. It was her solution to the fundamental rift between two sentient species compelled by biology into symbiosis.

Love nonetheless endures, whether with a proper or improper stranger. This book is my heart's gift for ramblin' men and restless women everywhere.

*"There is no greater agony than bearing an untold story inside you."*

- Maya Angelou, *I Know Why the Caged Bird Sings*

# Venus
# Mons
# Iliad

# Venus Mons Iliad
## Table of Contents

# Prologue

CALL ME ISHMAEL. Ish will do for short. I was not christened Ishmael. But the name has not been used for an epic character for a couple hundred years, so why not? The best-known Ish is the narrator of *Moby-Dick,* a fictional character of "mystic and speculative consciousness," as some would have it. So I believe Ishmael and I share some traits. The Genesis Ish was banished to wander in the desert. Melville's Ish was self-exiled at sea aboard a doomed whaling ship. Did Melville intend sand-to-seawater irony? The kind of question critics ponder.

"I alone am left to tell the tale" is one of the most resonant sentences in fiction.

I don't do well in deserts. *Mal de mer* is a lifelong affliction. But call me the third Ish anyway. Ish has been a nickname of mine for over half a century – from the German Ich, pronounced with a sibilant C. A literary friend compared my *roman a clef* about my perambulating career to Ishmael wandering after the mythic whale. He suggested an untold Iliad of mythic proportions threaded my own rambling life. I saw his point. And I saw the coincidence of name and nickname, which appealed to my own mystic and speculative consciousness.

I looked Iliad up: defined lately as (1) a series of miseries or disastrous events; (2) a series of exploits regarded as suitable for an epic; or (3) a long narrative in the Homeric tradition. Close enough.

*Venus Mons Iliad*

Venus Mons is my mythic symbol for the alien species with which men coexist in uneasy symbiosis on this planet. From an early age I was preoccupied as an exobiologist by this alien species. A once highly popular book cemented the notion of alien cohabitation with the facile suggestion that men are from Mars, women from Venus.

No alien invented in science-fiction or by Hollywood was to me more terrifying – more beguiling – more difficult to know – than Venusians. I alone am left to tell my tale.

# Chapter 1:
# The Early Days

I WAS BORN IN A TIME OF WAR. The first smell I remember is the distinctive odor of canvas duffel bags in the front hall, deposited by khaki giants leaving for and returning from war. The war meant I lived the first years of my life almost exclusively among women. The only males around were my often-absent grandfather and my mother's teenage brother who was home only long enough to eat and sleep. Eventually I knew the old man was a fireman, absences due to long firehouse shifts. By the time I knew that, one war ended and Korea took my teenage uncle to his own war. I remained mostly alone among women, a situation that continued through high school.

The central authority of my life was the family matriarch. In those earliest days there was also my mother, her cousins and girls she went to high school with, and a steady trickle of older female visitors, the matriarch's friends from her flapper days. Whatever a flapper was. What I envisioned from their tale-telling visits was a period of high-stepping gaiety when anything went.

Most of these older women had moved on to big Northern cities, kept by doting, well-heeled husbands – who never accompanied their sentimental journeys home, or anywhere else they cared to ramble. They always were deferential to the matriarch, as if she were the natural leader. Since she *was* the matriarch I never found that strange, though they provided kaleidoscopic contrast to her tired clothing and care-worn features. Always well-dressed and perfectly made-up, they dripped expensive furs, glittered with jewelry and wafted delightfully exotic perfumes. The term that comes to mind when I remember these birds of paradise is wicked big-city ladies.

They thought I was cute and liked my mother, though the matriarch said none had children of their own and certainly not grandchildren. They teased my teenage uncle but avoided the old man. Nights the old man was on duty they would stay long past my bedtime, leaning in to the matriarch with *Soto-voice* stories and knowing laughter. I heard enough to know sex, romance, or a combination of the two were almost exclusively their topics. Thus my earliest sense of wonder about the wide world was linked inextricably to the great mystery of sex.

The ancient, ill-tempered crone who lived with us during the war – and kept telling me to run over her with my tricycle because nobody gave a damn about her – was my widowed great-grandmother. Her words on sex provided a stark contrast to the merriment of the big-city ladies. Even her bitter memories of lost Southern grandeur during Reconstruction paled beside her cold rage at men, beginning with her dead husband.

*"A stiff dick ain't got no conscience,"* she would mutter against the happy banter of the visitors. As for romance, *"When a man gets that soulful look in his eye, just means he has to pee."* Stinging indictments I did not quite understand, but her rage was plain. Perhaps she was marked by the stress of fourteen live births and unknown number of miscarriages that ruined her illusions of Southern belle-hood.

Happy or sad, amused or bitter, this house of women talked incessantly of sex, the practice of sex, the happy or unhappy myth of romance and the intransigence of men in their relationships with women. Classic little pitcher with big ears, I heard without comprehension but sensed a world of freighted meanings. The old man grumbled they were turning me into a fairy by talking so openly around me. The matriarch said her friends avoided him because she had married beneath her, unlike them – deliberately selecting a virile bull to give her strong children. Romance had been no part of her calculation.

Without vocabulary to ask about this three-letter word laden with mysteries the old man thought better left unsaid, or how a boy could be turned into a fairy, I noticed visiting females halted all such talk when he or any other male interloper was around. I suppose I didn't count as male – which probably was the old man's point.

After the Hitler war ended my father and tall khaki uncles came home. My infantry uncle scored an Army truck from the local military camp to move the bitter crone to an old-folks home, freeing up sleeping space for returnees. I got to ride in the high open cab between him and the old man during the move, glad to be rid of her.

My father wasn't home long – banished by my mother when her brothers caught him screwing a fellow veteran's wife. A man I was told to call my step-father showed up from the Pacific Theater after the Japanese surrendered, married and impregnated my mother. I disliked him. He was a horrible, clingy suck-up who tagged after her like a puppy. I was glad when he worked her last nerve and she kicked him out. She was a divorced mother of two before it became a national trend. My brother was on the leading edge of the post-war baby boom.

The returning uncles loved a Christmas story about me, tinged with sex of course, the year I was three. In the midst of an uproarious highly inebriated party, adults found me with a little girl my age behind the living room couch, clothing pulled asunder. A drunken woman burbled oh how cute, they're playing doctor. The old man corrected her: *don't look like he's playing to me.*

Family sex tales, to me, proved my childhood was colorful. Decades later my baby-boom brother shared his darker view: we were a white trash family obsessed with sex as the characters of Erskine Caldwell's *Tobacco Road.* I wondered if he subconsciously remembered how the family women loved that book. Their favorite part was where a naive Road girl visits the city and falls under the influence of a corrupt hotel porter who sells her favors to guest after guest all night. Returning home sore and satiated she remarks of the hotel: *"they sure know how to treat a lady."*

My brother was bothered so much by the sense of being trapped in a white-trash family he fought to escape that orbit, and did, marrying into a family of college professors with quiet, conventional lives, eventually becoming a patriarch in his own right.

The main story that disgusted him was a women's favorite: before my birth, my soldier father, living with my mother in the front bedroom when he could leave post, bragged incessantly about the size of his "hammer." His teen bride had nothing to compare but she was skeptical. So they called in the matriarch with a yardstick for an objective measurement. The image of the matriarch applying the yardstick to his erection while her daughter looked on was one my brother wished he could un-see. Hard evidence, excusing the pun, of white trashiness.

White-trash family. A harsh judgment. I was too ignorant to get it. Among the women surrounding me, sex was everyday conversation. I had no real idea what sex was. Boys were eternally different from girls, who grew up into men and women. Then sex would occur, a deep mystery. Another oft-told story: the newspaper delivery boy taken in hand, so to speak, by a hot older woman. Deflowered, he pedaled his bike home, entered the house unspeaking and went to bed fully clothed – with his shoes on.

"It was the shoes that gave him away," the matriarch would say dryly, and visiting female laughter would cascade.

A third story concerned one of the matriarch's six sisters who married a career GI. Their yardstick pegged him at a full twelve inches fully engorged, described dismissively as too much for comfortable intercourse. They sent away for a leather harness for the beast that blocked the final five inches from penetration. With no concept how that might work, I credulously accepted it without doubt or judgment. For my brother it was another horrid image best forgotten.

Humor was frequent in women's sex tales, but not constant. My infantryman uncle married the girl he dated before he went to war, and moved out. The matriarch had expected him to give her back the years stolen by Hitler. After my cousin was born, another boomer, his wife said no more children. Ever after, the matriarch would bitterly mutter, his wife made him ejaculate into a towel, emasculating him as surely as Delilah shearing Samson's locks. Nobody could make this stuff up.

My oldest uncle, recipient of a field commission and staff officer for Eisenhower, came home *already married* to a woman he met while waiting for orders to the Pacific after V-E Day. The matriarch was icily furious. This was the son whose teenage romances were grist for her stories. She was as high on romance as she was down on raw sex.

To spark one girl, he "hitchhiked to Bethlehem on a snowy Christmas Eve." Bethlehem, Pa., but the way she pronounced the phrase made me see shepherds and creches. How a Georgia boy knew a Pennsylvania girl is lost. Details were irrelevant – as long as he returned to the nest, sparking done, as he always had before the war.

To marry a stranger without prior approval – and bring her home – was betrayal. Evidence supporting the crone's assessment men were weak-minded when their lower head was rampant. This was magnitudes worse. Because – a great tragedy of the matriarch's life – while her son was still an enlisted man he had received both the Army's and her permission to marry a sweet English girl in London. The matriarch approved war-time romances. I was a product of one. So was my English cousin born before D-Day.

The matriarch already had invited his war bride to America to live, hoping to have her home to greet him when Japan fell. She confronted him about his betrayal. He coldly said his past marriage was a dead issue. She hoarded the few loving letters from her forsaken daughter-in-law all her life. All I knew as a boy was her contempt for the bigamous second wife and refusal to forgive his trespass. Only a whore with the skills of Babylon could have destroyed his moral fiber. The great mystery of sex could turn dark and twisted, destroying romance. It was a lot for a male child to assimilate.

With my mother twice-divorced and living at home, the matriarch said I was her second chance, her shining hope to raise a man-child right. Before I reached puberty her views metamorphosed into dire warnings against conniving females who would use sex to destroy me, as they had her sons. But secretly, with considerable trepidation, I yearned toward the great mystery.

# Chapter 2:
# Episcopal Day School

AFTER THREE VIOLENT YEARS in grim public grade schools, the family matriarch decreed transfer to Episcopal Day School more suitable for my fragile soul. Seldom has a road to hell been paved with better intentions.

It started out okay. My first recess the third-grade class bully tried me out. He wouldn't have lasted a day in public school; one punch and I bloodied his nose and wrecked his dominance. Like every good thing that happened in day school, the event came with baggage: my fists earned me the friendship of an eerie kid who turned out to be the real monster. But that was for later.

The second good thing was my drawing was recognized as talented, unlike public school teachers who ridiculed my notebook doodles. I participated in a mural contest: crayon on brown butcher paper. My depiction of an Indian village, tepees and a war-bonneted chief warming his backside at a campfire, was scissored out, mounted, and submitted to a Women's League art show. I won the blue ribbon. Predictions of my success as an artist were frequent by fourth grade.

Aptitude testing by some national firm returned results pegging my IQ above 150. Classes were very small and each student got plenty of attention. I took for granted the attention my score got me from the principal, a silver-haired woman with almost the authority of my matriarch. Of *course* I was special.

But there was the issue of Sharon.

In the relaxed atmosphere of this strange new school, the girls ran in packs during free periods. Their fun was to gang up on a boy and tickle him, because of course boys were honor-bound not to fight back. Perhaps their behavior was a rebellion against all the genteel training on table manners and cotillion dancing. Every student but me was from wealthy Old South families where even grade-school training presaged debutante balls and college. The girl-packs were ignored by the teachers.

Sharon was the leader of the pack. I was fresh meat. The day they closed around me I was horrified. Grimly determined to defend my ticklish ribs. But I couldn't bring myself to hit a girl. Despite my struggles they swarmed me and wrestled me to the floor. One on each leg, one on each arm, one with an arm around my head. Where the hell were the teachers?

That left only Sharon free, standing over me. Smiling like a devil as they told her to get on with it. She knelt over me and said I know something that will make him crazier than tickling. And she took my face in her hands and kissed me. Right on the lips. I jerked worse than if she tickled me, shocked almost senseless by her boldness. Even more shocked that I liked it. She pulled away, got up and told them to let me go.

Immediate chant: "Sharon's got s boyfriend!" They let me go without a single tickle. I was never attacked after that. In Cotillion training, Sharon always seemed to be my dance partner. Lolly, the cute blonde from one of the wealthiest families, was named Queen of the Cotillion for the formal winter dance. She selected me for her processional escort, and stuck her tongue out at Sharon. But there was no other poaching. Sharon filled my dance card that night. My eerie buddy Stewart predicted I would be sorry when the sixth-grader who figured Sharon belonged to him found out. I heard but could not comprehend. From the long perspective of old age it seems incredible so much quasi-adult emotion filled those pre-pubescent days. We were a precocious bunch.

Christmas break, I was home amid Christmas baking and decorating and grown-up partying with highball glasses, school the farthest thing from my mind. A strange car stopped in front of the house. A poignantly familiar girlish figure stepped from the passenger seat and came up the walk alone. Sharon.

The matriarch, observing and apparently all-knowing, ordered me to the door alone to greet her. As we stood there, Sharon's mother came up the walk with a wrapped Christmas present. Sharon took it and shyly presented it to me.

To say my emotions were in turmoil is understatement. I literally didn't know what to do as grownups spoke over our heads. The paper looked expensive and the box was weighty. Sharon insisted on a present for me, her mother told the matriarch, wasn't that just precious? Did I even thank her? Don't remember. Remember praying for the embarrassment to end. Soon as they were gone I was hissing at the matriarch we had to get Sharon a present *right now!*

The women of my family made the selection, something a little girl would like as much as I liked the big red magnetic racing car Sharon gave me. Whatever it was is lost forever in my embarrassment as they simpered and fussed about the cuteness of young love. The matriarch dispatched my grandfather to drive me to Sharon's house where the rich people lived. I made that long walk alone, just as she had. Men like the old man didn't participate in such silliness. I dealt with my reception alone. Christmas passed without further incident.

But the very first day after Christmas break, a fat furious sixth-grader cornered me outside the school lunch room. He pinned me to the wall and threatened to kill me because I gave *his girlfriend* a present. Here was the first ugly twist to my psyche at that damn school: I learned I was a coward. Feeling totally helpless before the larger boy – gigantic in memory – I crawled. Oh, I crawled. I whined it was not my fault, I *had* to give her a present. She gave me one first! The shame of that lives, ever-raw.

He screamed like a wounded animal *she gave you a present*? He smashed his fist into the lunch room wall. Then he hurt me. Before he could beat me to death – which I believed imminent – grownups intervened. I didn't throw a single punch for fear of making him madder. No memory of blood or bruises survives. Just bitter shame I was a coward.

I believe he was expelled. I know the matriarch got involved. The school principal, a trained psychologist, counseled me when it was clear I was traumatized, starting at shadows and sudden noises, though the sixth-grader was gone. I got through the year and the summer following unscathed. My eerie friend Stewart was not so lucky. His unmentionable summer experiences led to my second traumatic twisting. He took me into the bathroom to show his secret treasures: graphic photographs of naked people having sex.

The images not only rocked me, they caused a strange heat that suffused me and left my pulse pounding. Here was photographic evidence of the great mystery so much discussed in my family. He sniggered and touched me in a disturbing way. Said he could show a lot more if I came home to meet the family chauffeur.

Of course I could not go home with anyone unless I cleared it with the matriarch. That was beyond question. Which may have saved me from who knows what. But not from being harassed by Stewart, as if crawling to the sixth-grader signaled he could now bully and dominate me, and he did.

The relaxed teaching staff assumed our wrestling matches were friendly. They weren't. He liked to jump me and ride me down when the recess bell went, hold me down and grope me as teachers disappeared from the yard, laughing at my fear of being late to class, whispering his chauffeur could teach me things class could not. I was a nervous wreck. I remember twirling locks of my hair around and around obsessively. It was inevitable my fascination guided my hand in art class.

The blow from a steel-edged ruler across my drawing hand came out of nowhere. The pain was shocking.

We had a substitute teacher that day. She snatched my pad. I had been drawing a naked woman in profile. The line the teacher's slashing blow interrupted went out at an angle from the woman's hips. Terrified and in pain I was thankful she struck before I completed the erect cock I meant to intersect the woman's groin. The woman's hair and face were complete, but only her front profile from neck to hip. I meant to sketch the cock first, then a man.

Dragged to the principal's office I could argue, and did, that the silhouette was of a clothed woman, the line the beginning of her skirt. The shrewd old principal nodded and tapped the engorged nipple. *And this?* The pencil slipped I said. I was going to erase the bump. The substitute teacher snorted and demanded punishment for nastiness. The principal sent her back to class, tended swelling cuts on my hand and gave me an aspirin. The rest is a blur. Someone came and took me home.

There was no choice but to spill my guts to the matriarch. She was coldly furious. But not at me. At the teacher who struck me. At Stewart's parents who permitted their chauffeur to corrupt their child. There was a lot of grown-up conferencing and telephone-calling. I went back to school unpunished. And I will be damned if a girl on playground monkey bars didn't complain to the teacher on duty – the substitute with the ready ruler – that I tried to look up her skirt. He's a nasty little creep, the teacher said loudly, but it's no good to complain – you'll just get in trouble like I did.

I never saw her again. She would never teach again, the matriarch reported with grim satisfaction, having reached out to church hierarchy and school licensing authorities. Stewart was sent to military boarding school. The pedophile chauffeur vanished. I had more sessions with the shrink-principal to the effect I was not "bad" and it was important to continue my artwork. But my sketches turned to knives and guns and violent combat. I never drew a woman again. Day School heritage was that I was a coward. Worse, a coward who could not draw the alien creatures that were the fountainhead of the great mystery of sex.

# Chapter 3:
# Florida

THE OLD MAN RETIRED from the fire department. He sold our house to a chiropractor who was going to turn it into an office on a street whose other houses already had been razed for businesses as 1950s commercialism swept into the neighborhood. We moved to a North Florida garage apartment two doors from the ocean. It had none of the charm of houses the matriarch tried to persuade him to buy in St. Augustine or St. Petersburg over a two-year search.

My fourth and fifth-grade years were spent on Greyhound buses and in Florida schools, with brief appearances in Georgia schools where I was treated as an outsider. The matriarch led my mother, brother and me on the long house hunt. We rented apartments, my mother waitressed in Walgreen's in St. Augustine and legendary Webb's City in St. Pete, to supplement money from home. We got to know a lot of real-estate men. Orlando was a bust; a sudden polio outbreak threatened quarantine before we found an apartment. The matriarch instantly got us out of there on the first bus. I remember a sick fear as if the very air was contaminated with the dread sickness.

Winter in St. Augustine, the landlady had to clean our oil heater, complained kids burning stuff clogged it. The matriarch fished in the boiler with a poker and produced twisted half-melted condoms – I thought they were toy balloons – and said sarcastically: *"Kids* didn't do this." She explained later, another fragment of sex data. I read *Of Mice and Men*. Steinbeck's story seared my brain with poor simple Lenny, led fatally astray by a seductive woman. The matriarch used Lenny as a teaching moment, warning darkly that could be my fate if scheming females got hold of me.

St. Petersburg's endless sunny weather was next. The afternoon paper was free when it rained. Real estate men carried grocery sacks to fill with oranges and grapefruit from orchards doomed by new subdivisions. My mother's waitress friends called Central Avenue *Rigor Mortis Boulevard* for decrepit Yankee retirees. I broke a collarbone playing baseball and lost a Little League season, but discovered my mother's paperback romance novels in a drawer. The characters engaged in more sex – not graphically – than most 1950s books. Reading, I saw plain as day the naked-sex snapshots my corrupted classmate showed me. The confluence of words and images stirred something wild and hot in my blood: men and women having sex, loving and losing and finding each other again. It fueled a rebellious yearning to defy the matriarch's warnings if I got a chance. Not that I ever told her.

The old man traveled to each city to examine houses selected – disapproved them all. Then sale of our home closed. He took the matriarch on a plane ride to North Florida into the teeth of a hurricane, *Howling Hazel*. Came back and said start packing.

We settled into a palm-shaded beach neighborhood where raw sexual energy blossomed like oleander under the Florida sun. There was the Jewish liquor wholesaler whose oceanfront house hosted perpetual parties. The hard-drinking radio exec with the horny nurse wife the old man fixed up. The nubile teen across the lane with her boyfriends. And Blondie.

Blondie was quintessential Floridian, a beach dweller and sun lover. She raised Dachshunds instead of children and owned many nice things. She named her dogs for a Broadway show. You could hear Colonel Pickering and Eliza barking as the three of them came up the lane. The Colonel was the only Dachshund I knew of to run off a Doberman that invaded his back yard. Some sausage dog, the Colonel.

Blondie was in her fifties but her breasts were firm and tip-tilty as a girl's. I knew this because she stood naked in front of her boudoir mirror next door and daily combed her hair the obligatory strokes to keep it beautiful. I had a perfect line of sight from our upstairs bathroom through the branches of a giant palm tree. As I achieved fumbling puberty I admired her body often.

When you saw her clothed in the lane, walking saucily away from you with that cloud of bright gold hair whipping in the sea wind, you'd swear she was a slim young woman. She worked very hard at staying blonde and beautiful. Her fitness regimen was vigorous yard work in shorts and a sleeveless top under the brutal Florida sun. She did all the yard work for a rich lawyer's oceanfront spread. Waggish neighbors said she did the bed work too, because Mrs. Lawyer was sick all the time. My personal hero was the lawyer's rake-hell son who seemed to have a bevy of beauties on call. I was too naive to wonder if Blondie doubled down with the son.

The Beaches legend was that she started as an upstairs maid for one of the rich inland families that kept a beach house and worked her way up. Screwed her way up. She spent time as a paid traveling companion for wealthy men who took trips to Miami and Havana and preferred a blonde beautiful traveling companion.

It should not have surprised me Blondie and the matriarch of my family hit it off. Before long they had their heads together telling secrets. She was a Florida embodiment of the expensive older women who visited the matriarch in Georgia. The matriarch said wryly Blondie spent more money on her body than she spent raising four kids and two grand-kids. Their affinity, so like that with the well-dressed perfumed women of her past, confused my teen-age brain. Blondie was Florida sex appeal walking. The matriarch was dried out by the sun and bent from a lifetime of toil. Her friends stopped coming to see her in Florida. Perhaps Blondie reminded her in their absence of her lost flapper youth.

Blondie shared the secrets she knew about anybody on the Beaches worth knowing secrets about. The matriarch told me that's why nobody in authority troubled her about the stable of young women she groomed to go on the road as she did. *Nobody gonna raid that cat-house* is the way she put it.

As soon as brief winters ended Blondie hosted one long, continuous yard party I could only compare to the Alabama Tiger's boat in Travis McGee novels. The matriarch would sarcastically say, "The Ha-Ha Season has started." Curvaceous young women came and went with hard-drinking city executives and Naval officers. Sex was the social mixer. I understood, but the act itself remained cloaked in mystery. The McGee books had a lot of sex but in indirect language.

The years slipped by in long summers and autumn Northeasters, with occasional hurricanes passing offshore which made great body-surfing in the angry ocean. High school was a largely unpleasant experience. But one day when I was fourteen, Blondie told she would like a ride on my new motor scooter.

Holy smokes. I had never had a girl on the jump seat. "Then it's about time," she said. She was wearing jeans to avoid getting burned by the hot exhaust; she had come prepared. I wished furiously my scooter could magically become a blazing fast BMW cycle like one of my friends had. But no; it putt-putted away at walking speed, then running speed, finally up to thirty mph, absolute top end.

Her long lean legs were snug around my hips. She leaned those often-ogled breasts into me and tightened her work-toned arms around my middle. When we passed plate glass windows and I saw that glorious blonde hair streaming behind while she hugged me, I almost had a religious experience. She rode well, leaning with me on turns. I wished I could ride forever or at least until everybody on the Beaches saw us. When we got back I didn't know what to do with myself.

"You took me for a ride on your motor scooter," she said. "It's only fair I take you for a ride in my MG." Holy smokes twice. Was there anything cooler than those little MG convertibles? If there was I couldn't think of it. I clumped behind her trim figure like a plow-boy jumping furrows. She flipped me the keys. "You drive," she said.

Oh god. How humiliating to admit I had never driven a stick shift. I waited for ridicule. "You drive and I'll shift," she said. Back in those dark sexually repressed days before the sixties, I had read movie reviews about celluloid symbolism for sex: Robert Mitchum releasing a stallion into the paddock with a mare while his hooded gaze held the heroine motionless – fade to black. A woman kneeling in front of a seated man playing a saxophone between his legs. That kind of thing. You drive, I shift was a new one. I worked the clutch while her left hand engulfed the short gear lever so close her knuckles rubbed against my right thigh.

She would say "Punch it. Now!" We got into a rhythm. That little MG flew. Having a good-looking woman's hand rubbing my leg so close to my groin, the spasmodic leaps of the car and her exclamations as I learned the clutch, gave me a painful erection. When we got back, I had to sit for a while before I could climb out without embarrassing myself. Blondie just smiled and said we'll have to do that again sometime. We never did. But I knew I would never forget that ride.

Some indeterminate time later, the matriarch informed me Blondie requested my overnight presence in her home. One of the Naval fliers had become possessive of one of her resident girls and threatened mayhem if he caught her with someone else. He had to go to sea soon and Blondie feared it would make him desperate. She needed a man around and I was it. She would pay me of course.

"Didn't say how she would pay." The matriarch was grinning! For all that she counseled against wiles of teenage girls, she exempted women of a certain age. Said I had to start somewhere – and like the newsboy of family legend, where better than an experienced older woman? If not Blondie, she added, then the cute brunette I would be protecting. I reminded her I was a confirmed coward.

She said I could take my Jimmy Foxx Louisville Slugger in case the guy showed up, but not my shotgun. She didn't want me to shoot a Navy officer. She didn't get it that I didn't know if I was more afraid of the lurking sailor or the sexy women. I don't know what she told Blondie. There was no ugly confrontation. The brunette went off to Miami with her latest business executive and it was never mentioned again. It would be decades before I understood that marked the first instance in a life-long string of missed opportunities to get laid.

# Chapter 48
# Literacy and
# Self-Discovery

READING WAS MY FIRST LOVE. And will be my last. I have been reading almost seventy years, can't recall a time I could not.

Preliterate memory offers a few isolated sense-memories: smell of coal fires in open Georgia fireplaces is in my DNA. When I hit Germany as a GI, and earned my nickname, they burned a lot of coal. I immediately felt home despite alien gutturals and cold blue neon instead of hot red and yellow. Coal smoke raises a dark silhouette of my old man coming in the front door, framed in blinding white outdoor glare. There was a rare Georgia snowfall when I was six months old. I was a toddler in my mother's lap when a chair rocker broke. The bottom dropped out of the world. Then impact, safe in her arms; she laughed like crazy.

The matriarch and my mother read to me. My favorite was "The Owl and the Pussycat:

*The Owl and the Pussycat went to sea*
*In a beautiful pea-green boat,*
*They took some honey, and plenty of money,*
*Wrapped up in a five-pound note ...*

My mother was a perpetual calorie counter, so I knew weight was measured in pounds. Thought for years their supplies weighed five pounds.

Transition from them reading to me, to reading myself, was swift. I read my first entire novel at age six. *Bronco Apache* by Paul Wellman. A far cry from Owl singing to *Pussy my Love*. The matriarch said my paternal grandmother *was* an Apache. Quoted as proof a letter: "High water come. Turn radio on." She wrote like Hollywood Indians talked. So I sided with the lone warrior escaping a train bound for a cell at Fort Francis Marion to ghost back to Arizona.

Oddly enough the one episode in the book etched in my brain involved sex: the Apache hidden in a barn watching an amorous couple head for the hayloft. The boy instantly aroused when his girl lifted long skirts to reveal slim ... *ankles.* I jolted with recognition. The matriarch's one vanity was her delicate "patrician" ankles. In all the women's sex talk around my house I dimly grasped that exposed ankles were a big deal early in her life before hems migrated north in the Roaring Twenties. The unforgettable thing was oblivious vulnerability of the amorous boy. The lethal fugitive did not strike, but it planted a kernel of paranoia to germinate decades later in my own amorous episodes.

I read voraciously. Mostly Westerns, where romance was often a *leit motif*. Zane Grey for instance offered a "happily-ever-after" smooch once gun-play concluded. The matriarch did not censor my reading. We often discussed books. She liked the woman's answer to the gunfighter asking should he start an avalanche to trap them in a box canyon, safe from vengeful Mormons: *"Roll the stone, man, I love you."*

As I entered puberty on the Beaches I scoured books for the mystery of sex. My body was changing. The public view: I was shooting upwards, putting on weight. Five-foot-five and 150 at fourteen; 6'2 approaching 200 pounds three years later. Size twelve shoes, feet still growing, XL gloves too tight in brief winters.

Privately: constant hard-ons and obsession with sex, frustrated by abysmal ignorance. Micky Spillane, Raymond Chandler, Richard S. Prather – the hard-boiled mystery writers I began to read had *allusions* to sex. I flipped pages at the newsstand looking for sex. Unknown to me, mysterious censorship forces were fighting a furious rear-guard action against graphic sex in books.

Back when the sun never sat on the British Empire, writers of explicit-sex books provoked an 1868 British court censorship ruling, *Regina v. Hicklin,* banning writing that would "deprave and corrupt those whose minds are open to such immoral influences." By which the court meant *everyone who could read.* Balzac, Flaubert, Joyce, D.H. Lawrence were banned *because they might affect impressionable children.* As if they foresaw my prurient interest.

In the door-less rooms of my beach home, my tumescence was a source of fun. Adults trekked through the sleeping porch to the TV room saying: *"The circus is in town."* The matriarch had to explain they referred to my tented sheet. Visiting uncles: *"One day you'll regret those piss-hards. You only get so many hard-ons in a lifetime."* They gossiped in the TV room while I tried to sleep: *"He's got plenty to satisfy a woman."* I had a morbid fear the measuring yardstick would appear. It didn't.

I was on my own to confront the rampant monster. Like an alien possessing me. I caged it in a jock strap at school to avoid embarrassment. When my jocks were in the wash – I couldn't justify buying a week's worth – I cradled my books awkwardly in front of my groin. Especially after a girl behind me in English class decided to give me back rubs to imitate her friend rubbing her boyfriend's back in seats beside us, and blowing in his ear. I was afraid that was next. She terrified me. I avoided her outside class.

I was shocked between classes to see another "good girl" openly stroke the bulge in the jeans of the meanest juvenile delinquent, right in front of everybody. She looked hypnotized, in her own world. He smirked at everybody, like see what I can make her do? *Everybody* knew about sex but me.

Dressing out for gym, one of my classmates proved to own a prodigious flaccid cock. Never saw its like until seventies pornographic movies introduced the world to John Holmes. Mine you might call labile, a two-inch bud until awakened. Some perverse competitive circuit tripped in my brain: *I can match that.* I unfurled as I went to the showers. The red-haired weightlifter coach – naked, a squat hairy orange orangutan with a little bud of his own in a dense copper nest – crowed: *"Don't anybody drop the soap! Ish got a serious hard-on!"* I almost died amid raucous laughter. Never took another gym shower.

Meanwhile in the wide world, censorship crumbled. *Peyton Place* by Grace Metalious was published in 1956 and leaped onto best-seller lists. In 1957 the U. S. Supreme

Court in *Roth v. United States* decreed obscenity means the "dominant theme taken as a whole appeals to the prurient interest ..." but any writings with the slightest redeeming social importance "have the full protection of guaranties."

This was the first real leak in the dike of what were called Comstock Laws after a guy ironically from the same Brooklyn that spawned Henry Miller. Yin and yang. An 1873 Act of Congress for "Suppression of Trade in, and Circulation of, Obscene Literature and Articles of Immoral Use" essentially codified the 1868 British court view. Comstock thought it not enough, and led further suppression.

Until *Roth* (not Philip Roth of *Portnoy's Complaint* fame; that brouhaha was later.) the Supreme Court had not extended First Amendment protection to sexy writing. When it did in 1957 I had a paperback copy of *Peyton Place* to inflame my prurience. But I still was ignorant as the day is long. Alone in the upstairs bathroom that afforded my view of Blondie's breasts next door, the beast often reared its unrepentant head.

It occurred to me to scald it into submission. I shut off the shower and knelt, holding it under the faucet. Turned up the hot water until it hurt so bad I had to pull back. It would not deflate. I rubbed it to ease the burn. Something physically shifted in my groin, like furniture being moved. When I pushed the foreskin back, there was a milky teardrop on the hole pee came from.

I had no clue. *Portnoy's Complaint* wouldn't be published for another ten years. Rough teenage joking about beating the monkey, choking the chicken and other such terms were nonsense to me. I wasn't about to ask what they meant. That little bathroom was the only privacy I had to come to grips, excuse the pun, with an erection that refused to go down. I finished that bath and strapped it down with a freshly laundered jock. Noticed a strange mumps-like ache in my balls. Wondered if I damaged something. *Nobody* could be that ignorant you say? Up yours, and the horse you rode in on.

Memory suppresses how long it took to figure out. What remains are bathtub images of further experiments with warm water where the white teardrop appeared without scalding. When I squeezed it, pressure in my balls eased. Sooner or later I decided a few strokes might help – and was stunned by copious blasts of viscous white liquid against shower tiles. Relief poured through me. The swelling subsided. Finally I'd found a way to tame the beast.

It was an obvious progression to bring *Peyton Place* to the bathroom to rouse the sleeping beast so I could stroke it back to sleep. Remembering sex pictures a fourth-grade classmate showed me that got me in trouble, I wondered where to find some now. I searched, but all I found were artful nudes in a Peter Gowland photo book. They lost their punch quickly, unlike the written word.

In 1959 I scored a first-edition paperback of *Lady Chatterley's Lover* after a federal judge threw out an attempt to halt American distribution. Maybe the best thirty-five cents I ever spent. I visited the upstairs bathroom between showers now. Always with a book. Grateful for the matriarch's incessant cleaning which offered a pristine toilet bowl. Because when I sat and shoved my erection between my legs for concealment in case somebody opened the door – no lock – the head dipped in the water.

As for visuals, *Playboy* was out there in the wider world. High-school chums said it was available under the counter at the bus station magazine stand. I finally got the nerve to ask. The newsstand guy didn't even blink. Times, they were a changin'. I scored my first Playmate calendar and hung it in an unused upstairs cubbyhole. One Playmate, hands stretched above her head, her sweater-bottom caught in her teeth to bare one perfect breast, was my favorite. The family women shrugged it off as boys will be boys.

If only they had known. The calendar was my secret log. Each month's days bore my cryptic numbers. Lots of numbers. If I was particularly charged up, the number was seven – for each spurt. Days I had the house to myself had several numbers: seven, maybe four, three, two, two and a half, one-half. Diminishing returns. A day was all it took to recharge. With no one to ask, I fretted until Agnar Mykle's *Lasso Round the Moon* reached town in paperback. His Ichabod Crane protagonist found that masturbation prevented the dreaded premature ejaculation that left a woman lying there "smoking and looking at her watch" waiting for you to be ready to go again and maybe please *her*. Hah! Not only would that have solved the problem plaguing Lawrence's effete Englishmen that drove poor Constance Chatterley into the gamekeeper's arms, now I had a rationale. If I ever conquered my fear of real-life females, I would have staying power to show them something ... .

# Chapter 5:
# Curriculum Change,
# Part One

HIGH-SCHOOL JOURNALISM CLASS: Putting the school newspaper to bed, typing last-minute stories late into the golden January afternoon. Strange it took a session with a shrink over thirty years later to bring that day to vivid life.

Once more I see palm trees on the edge of the school grounds thrash in the onshore breeze. The breeze would cut like a knife through my denim jacket on the way home. My Cushman motor scooter leaned on its kickstand by the hurricane fence at the school's north gate beside the journalism teacher's Nash Metropolitan.

I liked that the school paper was named *The Northeaster,* because I loved autumn Northeasters that blew in after Labor Day and flushed away summer's muggy heat. The tourists vanished, the Beaches belonged to the locals again. But I never wanted to be a journalism student. It was forced on me by a curriculum change this second half of my senior year.

My senior art class was canceled over the Christmas holiday. Blond, lanky soft-spoken Mr. Lundquist, with a passion for art and a strange soft lisp somebody said was Scandinavian, was gone as if he had never been. The art classroom was stripped and dark, the students scattered. Nobody seemed to know what happened to him. No teacher would talk about it. If I tried to ask, they got funny strained looks and their eyes got shifty.

I wasn't happy about journalism class. I didn't think highly of newspapers and magazines, or the men who wrote for them. One and all, they dragged my mother's name through the ink after the state attorney said a seafood cook murdered a cab driver because of her. But I already was trying to write fiction, influenced by the matriarch of my family, herself a disappointed writer. My English teachers said my short stories showed I was a good writer when I applied myself. I needed the semester credit to graduate.

"But I want to be an artist," I told the counselor. "Mr. Lundquist was going to get me an apprenticeship with his friend in Jacksonville who runs a studio. Drawing and painting all day, every day. I can't draw women. He said his friend would fix that, there were live nude models to study."

"Yes, well..." The counselor pursed her mouth at the word 'nude' and her eyes got shifty like the others.

So now I was under the supervision of petite, spare Miss Bensen, she of the slightly protuberant blue eyes, nondescript pageboy haircut and passion for snappy paragraphs. All the other journalism students had been together since September, so I was odd man out. Miss Bensen liked my writing right away though. And I knew most of my new classmates. The one I knew best was Sharon from Sunday school, ironically named the same as my third-grade girlfriend in another state.

This Sharon, and this long-ago January day, is why my 1990s shrink directed my thoughts backward, deep in time's well. I saw Sharon almost every Sunday for six years since my family moved to the Beaches. But being with her in a small high school class was different. Sharon had blossomed without my noticing. But I noticed that long-ago January.

She had developed softly rounded curves to go with her ink-black hair, smooth olive skin and those dark glowing eyes that always brimmed with secret amusement. Her unplucked crow-wing-black eyebrows met above her strong nose without a break, symmetrical as the lifted wings of that crow. To my fledgling artist's eye, the effect was a reverse negative of the white wings of flying seagulls Mr. Lundquist had required me to paint repeatedly. Finally he allowed I might become a Boardwalk painter good enough to impress Tobacco Belt tourists.

Sharon's body had caught up to her dramatic face. She was like some exotic feline creature among the other teenage girls our age with their faded tans, pancake makeup and plucked brows. I was fascinated and uneasy with Sharon's changed appearance, and with her familiar-strange nearness in journalism class instead of Sunday school.

The matriarch had warned me for as long as I could remember to beware the wiles of girls. She had me scared of girls even as I lusted hopelessly. So far the result was stalemate: no dates, no kisses, no clumsy groping in a movie theater. Teenage girls at this stage of their lives were after boys for one of two reasons the matriarch would lecture, creaking back and forth in her old Georgia rocking chair in our garage-apartment home. Their first motive was to seduce you into showing interest and then yelling rape if you touched them. The second motive was related to the first, but more deadly. They would trick you into doing more than touch, getting them pregnant, and rope you into an early marriage. Then you can kiss your art career goodbye she would say, let alone any hope of being a writer. And pause in her rocking to unload a brown stream of Butternut snuff into her spit can. She remained bitter about the marriages of all her sons, and hoped to teach me better.

Shameless hussies always go after the honorable boys who would do the right thing for the wrong reason, she warned. By her lights every single female my age was a shameless hussy. For proof she offered a member of my Sea Scout squadron: a star athlete who dropped out to marry and get a job to support an impending child. He rode a real motorcycle and the blonde always seemed glued to his back, both of which I envied. Our sarcastic squadron-mates asked where the baby would ride – on the headlight?

I could never reconcile the matriarch's contempt for women with my mother's evident role as the object of jealous gun-play. Her involvement with the seafood cook left me terribly confused. My brain flatly denied sexual inference – despite salacious hints in newspapers and magazines.

The shrink thought my confusion stemmed from an absent mother spending time with men like a seductive single woman. I rejected that. She wasn't absent; she was working to put money at the house. She hoarded tip money to purchase my scooter. The matriarch and her husband ran the household, but my mother was always there for me.

The shrink's sudden interest in the seductive absent mother theory (*"Every session you reveal another layer, like peeling an onion."*) diverted her momentarily. Professional that she was, she bookmarked my mother for another time and got back to Sharon. Sharon liked me well enough all the safe Sunday-school years. She seemed to like me in journalism class. The day the shrink dragged out of painful memory unwound behind my eyes like a movie reel ...

I was on one of the class's three big Royal typewriters, finishing an editorial about the evils of driving drunk. Timely and relevant, Miss Bensen said – but don't be too specific and cause fresh pain. On Christmas Eve a drunken college kid had slaughtered the longtime high-school shop teacher and his wife out on Beach Boulevard. This was the first *Northeaster* since the event. I remembered an old Roy Acuff song on the Grand Ole Opry: "... I heard the crash on the highway, but I didn't hear nobody pray ...When whiskey and blood ran together, I didn't hear nobody pray ..." and used some of the words. Miss Bensen liked it.

Then I finished a sports cartoon, using left-over India ink and sketch pens to draw a catcher suspended high above a baseball diamond, gloving a Soviet Sputnik, while tiny figures below stared up at him. The caption: "Nothing gets by that boy." Sharon arched her left eyebrow, amused. Asked if I could find typos as well as I drew. Complimenting and teasing me at the same time, strangely exciting. I found more than her. She allowed I possessed many talents.

Even my shrink's gentle prod could not release how it came up the last school bus had departed and Sharon faced a three-mile walk home. "Let me drive you home." I plunged before I could think.

Her eyes were full of immediate mirth. "I'm not riding behind you on *that*." Head toss toward my scooter out the window. "What? Hike my skirt clear up – I don't even know how high! – and show my legs and who knows what to everybody on the Beaches? No, thanks." In this land of the endless swimsuit, a high-hiked skirt was instantly inflaming. Particularly if such suddenly bare legs would be around my waist. But I was shocked she thought I would compromise her dignity that way. "Your ears are turning red." She giggled.

"I didn't mean the scooter. I meant my car."

"What car?" She didn't believe me for a second.

"My 1955 Mercury sedan." Before I could stop myself.

She cocked her head, considering. "Does this car of yours have a heater?"

"Of course it has a heater!" I was sunk. I didn't have a car. My grandfather had not let me drive the Mercury three times. Maybe she'd turn me down and I could save face...

"Well, okay," Sharon said. "Where's your car?"

"At home. Students can't park cars on the school ground." That at least was true.

"Oh." Her mouth turned down. "Too bad. The scooter or nothing, huh?"

*My shrink stopped me there. Didn't I know Sharon accepted the idea of my scooter? Never crossed my mind.*

I told Sharon I would go get the car. Digging myself deeper. "Well – Okay," she said. "But I'm not going to wait here for you. I'll start walking home. You can pick me up on Third Street when you get back."

She didn't want anybody to see her waiting for me. That was really smart of her. That's how rumors start in high school. It took four kicks for the cold engine to sputter to life. Then the choke caught and held. When the Cushman plodded up to speed my eyes streamed; only sissies wore goggles. Then I was home, wondering what the hell to do now.

# Chapter 18
# Curriculum Change,
# Part Two

THE MATRIARCH WAS ENSCONCED in the TV room watching "Dark Shadows" on the old B&W Muntz. A soap opera about Barnabas the Vampire. The strange details you recall decades later. "What's got you in such a state of high dudgeon?" I never knew what a state of high dudgeon was till that minute.

*The shrink thought it amusing about Barnabas the Vampire. What did you tell her? she asked.*

I managed to convey poor Sharon was running a bit of fever from hard school work and might catch her death walking home in the chilly afternoon. The old man was napping when the matriarch nudged him. The old fire horse rolled over and started to put on his shoes almost before his eyes were open. Quick as he was, his wife was back with Barnabas before he got them tied.

"I'll go take the poor child home." He was yawning and scratching under his arms. My life flashed in front of my eyes. I would die if he went. But he smirked, more comprehending than I could have imagined. "You told her you'd come get her yourself," he said.

My throat locked, but I nodded.

He flipped me the keys. "Those are cloth and suede seats in that car, you hear? If they get anything sticky on them, they still better come home clean as they leave."

I fled. The old man had a way with women – any woman, anytime, anywhere – that gave the lie to his wife's fierce portrait of a male's vulnerability to treacherous witches one and all. It never crossed his mind I wasn't going to try hanky panky – any more than it crossed hers that I would. I sternly controlled my rioting emotions as I guided the big Mercury out of its narrow garage. If I dented a fender, might as well never come home. No one wanted to awaken the old man's titanic temper. Before I knew it I was cruising grandly past the high school, eyes raking Third Street sidewalks for Sharon. Would she walk on this side or the other side? I wasn't about to drive past her focusing just on one side.

Three miles to her cross street at the end of town twisted time's pace. It had been racing like a stopwatch before I got the Mercury. Now it slowed to a torpid crawl. I was all the way south before I could grasp Sharon wasn't on Third Street. The heater was throwing out too much heat. I was sweating through my shirt. I cranked down the window and turned off the heat. The deepening chill off the ocean dried sweat. I could start warming the car up when I saw her.

Maybe she stopped off for a Penny burger and a Coke. I drove north, trying to look everywhere at once. She wasn't there. Maybe she changed her mind and waited out of the cold. Maybe Miss Bensen made last-minute changes and kept her even later.

Maybe some crazed rapist from New Jersey snatched her off the street in broad daylight.

The journalism classroom was dark. It felt weird to drive the Mercury around the school-bus loading loop.

Maybe I heard wrong. Maybe she said First Street and I heard Third. What an idiot! I drove toward the ocean and turned on First Street, rolling slowly through lengthening shadows past motel after deserted motel. Not a tourist to be seen. The motel pools were empty as the parking lots. Most motels had their Vacancy signs turned off. No sign of Sharon.

That only left Second Street, lined with cottages and small apartment buildings, one of which was where the cook ambushed the cab driver. A few locals were out in the cold, some walking dogs. Every female form triggered a rush of relief followed by deepening dread when it wasn't Sharon. She had vanished from the face of the earth. All because I offered her a ride home. It was my fault.

Finally I accepted enough time had passed for her to walk home. But I didn't believe it. If newspapers were to be believed, people – children or attractive girls – walked away from home or school and vanished. Sometimes their brutalized bodies were found, sometimes they were simply – gone. Fear crept through my unwilling brain.

Sharon's big two-story home sat just behind the seawall. Smoke puffed out of a chimney, shredded by the onshore breeze. Long shadows cast by her big house reached across the seawall to the beach. Not details I shared with my shrink, but unrelentingly clear in memory. I trudged up the wide front stairs and rang the bell. A smiling woman answered and invited me out of the bitter wind.

I introduced myself in the wood-smoke-smelling hall as Sharon's Sunday-school classmate. Her mother said how nice! Oh too bad you've missed her! She works late on the school newspaper. I said I knew. Then my words came in a rush. The proffered ride, the agreement to pick her up on Third Street, my search. Maybe Sharon had called? I was afraid I sounded like an idiot until I saw worry.

"No, Sharon hasn't called." Her husband came to the door, still in suit and tie from the city.

"This isn't like Sharon. Is it?" he said.

"No it isn't."

They thanked me almost formally. For the offer of a ride, for looking for Sharon and finally for letting them know something must have happened. I drove home in a daze. Later the matriarch was watching the six o'clock news and I was sitting on the dark downstairs porch close to the old Duo-Therm oil heater when the phone rang. The old man yelled from the kitchen.

"Ish. Some girl." He handed me the phone. "First time for everything," he grumbled. "Now they're calling you at home. Where's it gonna end?"

I turned my back, ears burning. "Hello?"

"Hello." Sharon sounded like she was suppressing a laugh. I felt my stomach flip-flop. "My mother made me call you. She said you were all worried about me."

The amusement in her voice cut. I didn't know what to say. "I looked everywhere for you," I said finally. "What happened to you?"

"Nothing happened to me, silly! I just decided to walk home along the beach. Feel the cold breeze in my hair. Winters are too short in Florida, don't you think?"

I did. Any other time I would have been thrilled Sharon and I saw eye to eye on that. But I couldn't shake the emotions of the afternoon. "You walked home along the beach," I repeated mechanically. "But you said you'd like a ride home!"

"No." Laughing openly now. "*You* said you'd give me a ride. I just changed my mind and decided to walk on the beach."

"But I looked for you all over." I hated the whine.

"I knew you probably would. I didn't want to be bothered. So I took the beach."

At that precise instant, the old man went into the tiny downstairs bathroom on the other side of the kitchen wall to urinate. The sound of the heavy flow came clearly into the kitchen – it was why no one could use that bathroom when there was company. I thought I would just go ahead and die if Sharon heard that, sitting in her big warm house with a real fireplace burning real wood.

"What's that sound?" she asked right away.

"What sound?"

"You sound dopey, Ish," she said. "Did I wake you up? What's that roaring sound? It sounds just like an electric train going round and round. Do you still play with electric trains, Ish?"

After her casual cruelty about ducking me, I couldn't imagine being much more miserable. What on earth had the old man been drinking? He never drank beer and stopped drinking corn liquor when he retired. Finally he was done.

"I don't play with electric trains anymore," I said.

"You just turned off the transformer and stopped your little Lionel train when I caught you!" Sharon was having fun. "I never knew you were so silly, Ish!"

Words stuck in my throat. The matriarch went on and on about girls who yelled rape or trapped you into marriage.

She never warned they could make you feel like an utter moron. I hated this so bad I was grinding my teeth.

"I think playing with an electric train is cute for your age," Sharon said. "Maybe I'll come over someday and help you play with it."

*Thirty years on, commenting on my near-total recall of an ancient conversation, my shrink was surprised by my answer that as a child I was told I had a photographic memory. ("Another layer of the onion!") Then she said if my recall was accurate as that, Sharon was trying to make amends. Didn't see it then. Still don't.*

"I don't have an electric train!" I said. "All I wanted was to give you a ride home."

"Well, I just decided that I didn't want you to."

How could I ever face her in class after being such a dupe? Would everybody know? "You could have just told me you didn't want a ride."

"I didn't want to hang around on the street where you could bother me about it."

Bother. Second time she said it. Such a simple word. Such a dagger in my heart. I was crushed. If this was how it was going to be with girls I wanted no part of it, or them.

*But you must have been angry, my shrink said. You had a right to be angry. To speak up for yourself. Try it. Tell her now. Right here. An exercise. Immediate angry words jammed together in my head. I didn't mean to bother you, your Highness! Kiss my pimply Georgia ass, Princess! Not on the left side and not on the right side, but right in the middle. It'll be a cold day in hell before I bother you again, you heartless bitch! There, the shrink said. Don't you feel better?*

Maybe. Maybe not. The shrink was surprised one "trivial" incident poisoned my trust of the female species so thoroughly. She didn't have the back-story of the matriarch's conditioning – another onion layer I suppose. She said Sharon liked me, who knows what would have happened if I spoke up for myself? But I didn't. The humiliation festered. I could barely stand the rest of the semester in journalism class. I armored my soul against her dark laughing eyes. It got easier but no less painful. The last time I saw her was in cap and gown at graduation.

I never found out what happened to Mr. Lundquist. I never got my apprenticeship with an art studio to paint live nude models. My fledgling art career died unborn. My mother used her contacts to find me a job as a newspaper copy boy. To the amusement of jaded newsmen, I avoided any slightest possibility of intimacy with females. I blamed it all – loss of my art, my pathological distrust of girls – on the unwanted curriculum change.

# Chapter 7:
# Ugly High School
# Incident

ALMOST HALFWAY TO MY EIGHTH DECADE I am home at last thanks to my brother, in a snug cottage older than me with a glass-front gas furnace whose flames wake nostalgia for fireplaces of earlier homes. Without the need to saw, split and haul firewood. That frees me to write like mad after creativity was bottled up by a year of motels and succession of failing computers. I gladly returned to my Iliad.

My brother, in his words, is now a patron of my art. He secured me this home. He exhibits kindly interest in my work. Even thinks my Iliad might sell. His own Iliad lately has been one of fitness and weight loss. He took the occasion of his seventieth birthday to report he's down to his ninth-grade football-playing weight of 235. I watched those games. He loomed like a White Hulk at left linebacker in his white JV uniform. He looked bored. No opponent ran plays to his side of the field.

Three years ahead of him, in my final school year, I weighed 208 and stood 6'2. This made me fifth heaviest in my graduating class. Fourth tallest. At least two of the bruisers heavy as my brother were under six feet. But for height there was Murphy the basketball center. So I was fifth and fourth. The odd details brought to mind by my brother regaining his playing weight.

The four heavies of my class created the ugliest memory of my senior year. They invaded my homeroom class one bright morning, confronted me and threatened to beat the crap out of me.

For about thirty seconds I thought it was a joke.

But the varsity fullback was so mad his spittle hit me in the face. Two were so angry their faces were bright red. Biggest of them all was impassive. Six years before, already bigger than anybody else, he rammed me so hard when I tried to block him in a tag-football game that I landed on his teammate cutting behind. I lay there with all wind knocked out. His teammate was no better off. I swore off football.

Now he was varsity center. I pitied opposing linemen.

The fullback and the linebackers backed me into a corner, spitting curses. The center waited, a dangerous Buddha. Classmates stared in shock. Where the homeroom teacher was I have no idea. I could not get my mind around it. They kept calling me a dirty pervert, a sneak and worse, inarticulate with rage.

They scared me. Badly. My gaze locked on the fullback's prominent Adam's apple. He was grade-school class bully when I moved to the Beaches six years ago. Jumped me to show me my place. I bloodied his nose. So I knew he could bleed. My mind was racing like a rat trapped in a maze. But even rats fight when cornered. My grandfather always said, when outnumbered destroy the leader, jump the next one and the rest would run. I didn't believe it that morning. A straight right to the throat should disable the fullback, but his thick throat looked like cement. I resolved to hit him with all my might if they closed in.

They didn't. Just stood at arm's length ranting. I was so scared I would have tried to punch clear through him. Maybe killed him. We formed a quivering tableau of poised violence. Their accusations became intelligible. That was even more terrifying. They said I was making obscene phone calls to their girlfriends! Talking dirty about what I'd like to do to them. When the girls said they'd tell their boyfriends on me, I said I'd whip the bunch.

"Well, here we are!" the fullback said. "Gonna whip us?"

They were so *sure*. Their absolute conviction gave me a horrid sick feeling outside fear. Had I gone off the rails so far in my frustrated virginal lust that I blacked out and *did* those things? The matriarch always warned me about associating with teenage girls. I never had. Not one date, not one kiss, no phone calls back and forth. But somehow the mysterious sex thing had reached out to grab me. Girls were accusing me of nasty things anyway.

I began to talk. Deny. Appeal to reason. The accusers decided to march me out of class and through the halls to their football coach, a sloppy giant of a man they revered. I wouldn't dare lie to Coach! Not one teacher intervened. On the walkway to the coach's gym office, one of the asshole linebackers shoved me hard, intending to put me down. Who knows what would have happened if I fell? I shrugged him off. His throat cartilage did not look as armored as the fullback's ...

The fullback intervened, saying save it for Coach. To his eternal credit the coach was shocked at their behavior. Said they courted expulsion. Worse, suspension from the team. The team would be a shambles without them. He did not care what I had or had not done, the team came first. That was the tipping point. Violence became unlikely. He ordered us all to the vice principal's office to sort it out.

The vice principal was a brutal asshole who believed them and called me a dirty pervert. I was beginning to half believe it myself. All I could say over and over was call my home, like a mantra. He sent the others to class and pushed me to confess. Finally he called.

The matriarch and the old man arrived like avenging angels. When the asshole accused me, she almost stripped skin from his bones with her coldest drawling contempt. He goggled and sputtered. The old man picked up the big flat paddle with holes punched in it to raise blisters on backsides. This guy used it for corporal punishment. The old man sneered: You use this on boys' asses? Give you a thrill? Who's the real pervert here? The man shrank before my eyes. The matriarch supplied the finisher: if you *ever* touch our grandson I will personally kill you.

They took me home. Whether the four were expelled I don't know. I was terrified to go back to school for fear they were laying for me. The matriarch gave me a medicine bottle full of her Butternut snuff. What she carried in her wild days as a rum-runner's girl. Throw it in their eyes she said, it will blind them. Then beat them to death.

The vice principal's paddle gave the old man an idea. He came in from the garage with the oak arm of a wrecked rocking chair, electric tape around the small end for a grip. Leave it in your book bag on the scooter, he said. If they jump you it will probably be there. This won't break, but their heads will. Say you were repairing it in Shop Class if anyone asks. I was to carry the snuff in my pocket. If they struck inside the school, douse them and run for the scooter. Ready as I could be without the old man's .45 or my hunting Bowie.

The first day back, when I parked my scooter by the hurricane fence to chain it, Cricket and Jay and Kenneth were there. We'll walk you in, Cricket said. Words cannot convey my emotion. None of them were fighters. None of them were in the weight-class of my pumped-up enemies. The courage that took! None of them of course had the shotguns they hunted with (Cricket and Kenneth) or Mauser K-98 (Jay). Not even a switchblade.

By fifth period I had a switchblade of my own. Leon, member of the Flat Top gang, had been a loyal friend since I refused to rat him out for bad behavior. From his leather motorcycle jacket he produced the blade, red plastic pearlized handle, razor-sharp. Where I couldn't carry the knife he recommended a banker's roll of quarters to hold in my fist. He used one to knock teeth out in a gang rumble. Over the course of fifty years I lost the switchblade (and my original Bowie knife) but never forgot the quarters trick. Not even airport security objects to a roll of quarters.

Meanwhile my first novel stalled. I told the matriarch I could not finish it because I was writing about heroes but was the worst kind of coward. She said don't be silly. Do you think writers are brave as their heroes? Why do you think they write? It's wish fulfillment.

The ambush I feared never took place. The fullback arranged with his girlfriend to listen on an extension when the obscene caller continued his harassment. Then he called me. I expected more threats and did not want to talk. The matriarch said I must. First thing he said, "It's not you. Don't sound anything like you. We gonna find this asshole and mess him up. Since he screwed with you too, you want a piece?" I said no – in case you're wrong again. He didn't know what to say to that. So we left it there.

Just to put the cherry on top of this craziness his girlfriend called. She didn't believe him, wanted to hear me on the phone herself. Said damn, he was right. I said of course it wasn't me, I don't call girls. Her answer floored me. She said all us girls noticed that. Why don't you? You could you know. I really thought it was you making those sexy remarks. I wouldn't mind if it was really you …

Suffering Christ on a crutch. I got off the phone quick as I could. Then the girls who got calls began stopping by my table in the lunch room to say hello and *invite* me to call, to prove no hard feelings. I wanted to say *I'm* the one with hard feelings. But I didn't.

I watched with jealous envy as my young Leviathan brother cut a wide swath through what the matriarch called his beach bunnies. He was too young to drive. I had to chauffeur! Once at a beach bonfire one of the moms – I got to sit with the moms while the younger teens snuggled in the shadows – asked which of the twins he dated was with him out in the dark. Another mom: "Knowing him, both!" Ha-ha-ha. I was never gonna get laid. Hell I probably was never gonna get kissed!

The ugly incident fed my paranoia. And my self-disgust for failing to fight. Just like third grade when I crawled to a sixth-grader, who hurt me anyway. Girls were at the root of both third and twelfth-grade troubles. Wasn't sure what to make of that.

There was an absurd, implausible postscript graduation night. Cricket scored liquor from a fish camp operator. Jay drove his dad's wide-track Pontiac while I topped up his drive-in Coke with bourbon. Cricket and a weird kid named Duane rode in back. We cruised the parties. I was amazed how many drunken "good girls" were openly comparing their fucks with football players. A brainy scholarship recipient, flushed with alcohol, rolled her eyes at me: "Ish, grow up!" My companions got so drunk they were afraid to go home. So I took them home with me to sober up.

The matriarch perked coffee and held Cricket's forehead over the kitchen sink while he was sick. He owlishly said he was not drunk. He could read cans on the shelf. "A-J-A-X – Ajax! See?" Jay went to the beach – and walked right off the seawall. We rushed behind – he was on the sand, still walking. Did not even notice his fall.

Ah, but Duane ... Duane in his cups was remorseful. Confessed he was the one who called girls saying he was me. Why did he *do* that? Because he could not get a date. The football players had all the cool chicks. And it was exciting how girls reacted to his dirty talk. He couldn't help himself, but needed a name they would believe. I was the only one the football team would fear. If they tried anything I would hurt and humiliate them, maybe free up girls for him to date ...

I felt like feeding him to the hammerheads patrolling the night surf. But high school was over. I was free. I would never see any of them again. When Jay sobered up he just took Duane home.

# Chapter 8:
# The Houser Theory
# of Women

ARCHAEOLOGIST OF MY OWN DISTANT PAST, I delicately separate ancient well-browned pieces of copy paper. These were chopped from rolls of left-over newsprint, flattened, and guillotined several times down to 8 1/2x11, then carted to the newsroom for the use of reporters. Newsprint is not the highest quality paper and didn't need to be. News stories spun out of rattling manual typewriters only survived long enough to pass through copy editors' hands, pick up a headline, and move to the typesetters. Carbon copies littered reporters' desks until galleys were proofed and the presses rolled. Both original and copy were discarded. By the dictionary definition of ephemera, stories on copy paper certainly qualify. Unless you were a teen-age copy boy using copy paper and a battered newsroom reject of a typewriter to teach yourself to write.

I carefully preserved my writing on that cheap paper through the decades, thinking there might be good stuff for later. In my seventh decade it was a shock to realize this *was* later. Time to excavate. Larry Houser stepped out of the shadows of forgetfulness to espouse his theory of women.

Larry was the bawdy old Associated Press traffic manager for Northeast Florida, slovenly of dress, macabre of humor, and cackling of laugh. He was only man I ever saw who wore carpet slippers to work. He introduced me to bootleg copies of Henry Miller's Paris books, still banned in most of the U.S. He spoke knowledgeably about the happy sexuality exuded by the Brooklynite's writings. Sex was neither dirty nor sacred, he informed me, gazing up at overhead fluorescents reflected in the thick lenses of his glasses; it was *fun*. He warned me to get in on the fun as soon and frequently as possible or I would rue my failure when I was his age. And he was right.

But at eighteen, sex was a holy mystery. Even more, I did not trust any slightest indication of interest from a female. These always raked up still-raw emotional pain inflicted in what most would consider a trivial incident. It made me nervous when every single good-looking woman on the newspaper staff found her way to the wire room to engage me in conversation week after week. Houser noticed of course and issued sardonic commentary that embarrassed me dreadfully. So I listened and banged on the typewriter.

First entry on that aging copy paper: "You're too serious a young man to offer 'em a good lay. You're like a damn Boy Scout. Loyal, true-blue, pure – and virginal."

No way I could confess my fear of humiliation to him. I hated it that what he said was true. Especially the virginal part. Despite my fear of females I was transfixed when they parked their cute butts on my desk, hiking skirt hems above attractive knees. They sat loose-hipped, yakking at me, swinging their feet idly back and forth like a kid on the edge of a swimming pool. This afforded glimpses of soft thigh above stocking tops and sometimes even more: the shadowed grottoes where Henry Miller disported himself with the self-described happy innocence of a porpoise nuzzling a coral reef. I was paralyzed, unable to stand and reveal my obscene tumescence. I had a notion they were laughing at me. I admitted I was afraid of them.

"There's that too," he said with that awful cackle. (This directly from the copy paper.) "I've never seen a copy boy in my life that got so much of it rubbed all over him. I've never seen such a shrinking violet either. It must be a natural law."

He said all copy boys that had gone before were horny little devils that lusted openly after anything in skirts – but had to chase it down if they wanted to nail it. Here, it was offered to me on a platter. Directly from the copy paper: "You may as well go ahead and get it over with. Hell, one of them's gonna get your cherry no matter how hard you try to hold onto it."

This comment came right after I declined an especially sexy female reporter's request to go home with her to move some furniture. She said her husband was out of town and I was big and strong. Houser told me a lot more was on offer than pushing furniture around, and I was a fool to turn it down. My secret shame was that I wouldn't have the faintest notion what to do if he was right. Fear of failing to perform made my teeth ache.

That wasn't the only overture or the only woman making one. They spoke openly in front of old Houser, as if he were just another undusted fixture like the noisy teletypes. He had the veteran wire service man's ability to freeze into invisibility in plain sight to hear things they're not supposed to hear. In years to come I noticed it more than once when I became a reporter; it was almost an AP trademark. I never asked if he worked stories before he moved to Traffic, responsible for the care and feeding of teletype machines that moved the news. Traffic managers were the techies of their time.

If not up to their greasy elbows in the guts of misbehaving teletype machines, they swapped typed backchat and jokes with their opposite numbers all over the country before the internet was a gleam in DARPA's eye. Or they keypunched Braille-like symbols onto spooling ticker-tape. The tapes were the primitive precursor of computer disks. When it was time to transmit, they fed the tapes through a mechanical gadget that translated the punched holes back into words that printed out on every teletype on the circuit. Houser could read the tape with his fingertips without taking his eyes off the young women or his mind out of the gutter.

From my old copy paper: "You really should go." (About the woman with furniture) "That one is hot as a two-dollar pistol. Go on, get it over with. Then they'll leave you alone."

"What?" I was startled. "Why?" I didn't get it. If I was such an attractive quality, why would they start leaving me alone if – hard as it was for me to envision – one of them did initiate me into the mysteries and, even harder to imagine, I managed to perform?

Houser's answer, immortalized on copy paper: "Because then you'll know what you've been missing and want some more, that's why. The natural balance of the universe will be restored. You will be just another dirty-minded, grabby, pimply-faced copy boy."

It was all too much to take in. "How do you know I'm not dirty-minded now?" I asked him.

"Oh, I know it," Houser said, smug as only an old and successful lecher can be smug.(I was typing his words down like dictation.) "I know it, but they don't. They can't think of but one thing at a time. They can all smell your cherry and that's what's driving them crazy. It's like a cat. Ever see a cat sit in a bathtub for hours and watch the faucet drip? No? Well, cats do that. Know why?"

"Cats are curious?" (I didn't record his snort but remember it well.)

"It's that a cat can't figure a dripping faucet out." (I typed) "It keeps on dripping. It just keeps on and on dripping. That's you. You're the faucet. I have never seen so much instantly available pussy in my life. I can speak with perfect authority because I have never got one piece of it and probably never will. I am too old and smelly."

I didn't record my answer but it was to the effect that I bathed regular.

"But you can't wash that cherry smell off," the copy paper says. "Why don't you go ahead and get it over with, so I can say I told you so? I ain't gonna last forever, and saying I told you so is one of life's few remaining pleasures."

He named another woman on the staff. All these decades later, I remember my ears burning hot as fire. She was my favorite. And she did come around a lot. Houser grinned like a crocodile.

"She's a good one to start on. Old enough to know better and too young to care. Married, too, so there's no worry about getting trapped young. And she really eats you up. Or would, if you'd give her half a chance."

I recorded his soliloquy as a defense against my embarrassment. And a half-formed notion that copying actual spoken language was good writing practice. I wanted to be outraged at his irreverence toward the girl of my fevered dreams. But I couldn't get mad at him. He made his pronouncements like God. God with a prurient streak.

"Might as well get it while it's hot," he concluded. "It ain't in you to be a eunuch."

I told him he was the dirtiest old man in the world.

"Thank you," he said. "I like to think I have certain qualifications in that line." The fluorescents burned in his glasses, but not as brightly as his false teeth in a happy grin.

# Chapter 9:
# Seawall Code

SHE WAS A LEGGY OLDER WOMAN with long raven-dark tresses who rented an apartment across the lane and wore tight black pants and men's white dress shirts with the top buttons unbuttoned over the swell of large firm breasts. She was the first woman I knew who never wore a bra. She was very proud of her ability to whistle shrilly through her teeth louder than any man. The odd things you remember. Her husband was quite ill and seldom seen outside. She was fairly plain as far as looks but to a horny teenage virgin she exuded sex like an aroma. I was nineteen and terrified of her.

I was out of high school, working days as a copy boy at the city newspaper and nights at home on my first novel. Of course my family had to tell everybody I was a writer. The mother of a buddy of mine, who trained for the diplomat corps before she married and spoke fluent French, asked me point-blank: does it have any sex in it? I remember blushing and saying no. "Then it'll never sell," she pronounced.

So I was careful who I spoke to about my writing. I didn't want to talk about writing, I wanted to write. We lived two doors from the beach. The ocean was my muse. When I got stuck I walked up to the seawall to think and watch waves. After she learned I was writing, when I walked to the beach the leggy lady from across the lane would show up to talk about writing. She evidently read quite a lot. She said I was so young I should get out experiencing some real life so I could write about it.

Now, as she said this, she was sitting on the seawall bench leaning forward, elbows on knees covered by the long shirt-tails of her men's shirt with the three top buttons undone. It was hard not to stare at her abundant breasts. Was it a come-on? How the hell do I know?

The cool sea breeze – I was sure that was what caused it – created two symmetrical tents the size of my thumb in the oxford cloth of her shirt. I felt my face burn. I was sure if she noticed the instant bulge in my pants she would be so offended she might call a cop. Or worse, report me to the family matriarch. I turned my back and said I needed to go for a walk on the beach. I politely declined her offer to go with me, explaining I needed to be thinking, not carrying on a conversation. She just smiled and nodded and didn't even act offended. I walked far enough for the swelling to subside and then a little farther. I didn't turn back until I saw her vacate the seawall.

The next time I was on the seawall staring out to sea I heard someone come down the path behind me. Then I didn't. Nobody came past me to the steps down to the beach. When I turned, there she was, sitting with black-clad knees demurely together under the shirt-tails and her chin in one palm, watching me silently. I said hi. She said I didn't want to interrupt your thinking, I like watching you think. Did she smell the cherry on me, as old Houser said female reporters at work did? She scared the hell out of me.

Another neighbor was a hard-drinking construction contractor who traveled the Southeast and told everybody I reminded him of Robert Ruark, a North Carolina writer who was in his heyday. I knew Ruark's writing from *Field and Stream* and liked it, and was secretly flattered. But the leggy lady disagreed. She said he had the right state, wrong writer. She said my stormy expressions and long-legged walks on the beach reminded her of Thomas Wolfe. Had I ever read Thomas Wolfe? I had not. You should, she said. I think you will see yourself in him.

The days drifted by and it became her common seawall question: had I yet read *Look Homeward, Angel* or any of Wolfe's other books. I had not. I was closing in on my last chapter with no interest in extraneous reading just then. She said Wolfe writes about his experiences as a young man and you could too. I reminded her I didn't have any experiences to write about. You will, she said; Wolfe's young man meets this one female character and you could learn a lot from her.

And there she let it lay. Sometimes it seemed she was speaking in some kind of code. Her presence on the seawall across the summer was disturbing, but not in a bad way. I covertly enjoyed her attention and missed her when she didn't show up. There was a humming tension between us on the seawall I had no idea how to interpret, but it felt nice.

When I finished my book I spent a lot of time editing and retyping a clean draft, a grind that kept me off the seawall with my nose in the typewriter days on end. Our chance encounters became less frequent and then stopped. The first editor I sent the manuscript bought it immediately. In the ensuing excitement I forgot all about Thomas Wolfe. I didn't read him until after the leggy sexy lady with the sick husband had moved on. I discovered

Wolfe's principal female character, Esther Jacks, was an older experienced woman who initiated the young writer into the erotic mysteries of womanhood. I experienced a jolt of recognition followed instantly by regret. I finally had cracked the seawall code, forever too late.

# Chapter 10:
# Virgin Flight
# on a Whisperjet

WORKING SINCE BEFORE I GRADUATED high school as an apprentice in the news business, by the age of twenty I was awarded journeyman reporter status. I had my own desk and Royal office-model typewriter near the city desk. I already had been on the front page with a byline. My news features got half-page displays inside, illustrated by the best photographers we had. I was on a roll. So the city editor awarded me a perk: a media junket aboard the inaugural flight of the Boeing Whisperjet.

Complaints from the public living under flight paths of noisy jet aircraft had filled newspapers almost since the first passenger jets were put in service. This was Boeing's response: quieter engines, hence Whisperjet. A plane-load of reporters would be treated to a wide circuit over the sea and eventually home, enjoying plentiful free booze and snacks along the way. I asked what I was supposed to write.

"Not a damn thing," the city editor said. "This is a freebie. Enjoy it."

Wow. I couldn't wait to tell my folks I was truly in the big time now. The matriarch of my clan predictably burst my bubble. A new jet plane? Didn't I know those things crashed, especially experimental ones? If I died without a will, my divorced father might try to claim rights to my intellectual output to spite my mother. But she would take care of it, contact an attorney to draw up a proper will – writing my absent father out – before I flew.

I pretty much forgot her dark mutterings. Especially when the tall, nubile red-headed city-desk clerk asked me for a ride home. To say I had a crush on her would be to understate. But the way she flirted with older men and ignored me gave no hope. Now, suddenly I was doing well, and she wanted a ride home. I stifled the memory of the high school humiliation I suffered around an aborted ride home involving a girl I liked. Maybe this one would be different.

We walked out together. I had excellent hearing in those days and heard the boss's executive secretary say don't they make a cute couple. I was flustered and pleased at the same time. But the redhead disrespected my ten-year-old Chev. Now you're a hotshot, you should buy a car with air-conditioning she said. We opened all the windows and I drove fast across the big river to drive out humid summer heat. Cooling river breezes whipped her glorious mane of hair. I was amazed I was in a car alone with an attractive girl. It was exhilarating and scary in one. I still was a virgin with no idea how to behave with females.

When we got to her house she invited me in, saying her mother would like to meet me. But her mother wasn't home. She offered me liquor though we were both underage. I declined, fearful of the Highway Patrol, so she made coffee. Then, as God is my witness, she said she was going to get into something a little more comfortable.

My head spun. Women in novels said that before showing up in sexy nightwear as a preliminary to seduction.

I berated myself immediately. This was real-life, not a story. She just wanted to lose the painful high heels and sleek sheath that comprised her work attire, probably for jeans and tennis shoes.

But no; she emerged in a pale-blue satin night dress with the top three buttons unbuttoned, no bra, revealing significant cleavage. The hem stopped just below the juncture of her pale thighs. I almost spilled my coffee. She smiled brilliantly and said by the way, her mother wouldn't be home for four hours. Why didn't I take off my tie and get comfortable. We could spend that time getting to know each other.

It shames me still that my first reaction was a dutiful teenager's. I said I better call home so they won't worry. She seemed a little put out but knelt to show me the phone on the floor beside a chair. I could not help but notice the short night dress rucked up to expose the lovely globes of her bare butt; no panties. I knelt and dialed home though that vision almost made me forget the number. The matriarch soon was on the line. Her directive: *you have to come home right now! Our appointment with the lawyer to sign and witness your will is in one hour.* I had utterly forgotten in my infatuation. The Whisperjet ride was tomorrow.

The redhead still knelt beside me, following my conversation. She put her hand on my back--*no, no, you can't leave now! I want you to stay*, she whispered urgently. *Can't you put off whatever she wants?* But I simply did not have the fortitude to defy the matriarch's command. It was embarrassing to explain. Her disappointment turned to irritation. I stupidly said I can meet your mother some other time. Her tight-lipped response was *I don't think so.*

The signing and witnessing of the will is lost to memory. I remember a restless, unhappy night. I was dog-tired when I boarded the Whisperjet and then nervous when it seemed to jump into the sky, pressing me back in the seat. Then it was up and cruising over the ocean. For the first time in my life I saw the planet from high up.

The cabin was quiet enough for conversation. Soon as the seat belt sign went off, Boeing PR guys worked the aisles, lobbying a score of reporters. Some were ushered up front to see the flight deck. I was glued to the window watching the world pass below. A young PR guy plopped down beside me, nose already red from imbibing, to ask what I thought. I mumbled complimentary noises as the drinks tray arrived. He asked what I'd have and I said bourbon which seemed safe enough. He laughed and said he really *was* in the Deep South, handed me bourbon on the rocks and asked the stewardess for another Scotch. Nobody asked me for a driver's license to prove my age.

The bourbon smoothed down my throat and lit a fire in my belly, as he described the long arc the Whisperjet would take to bring us back home. He surprised me by knowing who I was; I was unfamiliar with the preparations good PR men made for these junkets. We had more drinks. I developed an unfamiliar buzz. When the stewardess came back I asked if she had coffee. She did. I switched to coffee because I had to drive home after the flight.

The Whisperjet performed flawlessly. Landing was routine. I thoroughly enjoyed my first airplane ride, not least because I had been drinking like a real reporter and could tell the matriarch she had worried about nothing. The next day at work the redhead again was ignoring me while others quizzed me about the new jet. I had missed my moment. She never asked for another ride home. I never did meet her mother.

# Chapter 11:
# Disillusion

THE FIRST TIME I SAW PARIS, four of us GIs on a three-day pass from Germany rented rooms in a hot-sheets hotel in Pigalle, agreeing we were so horny we should go straight to the famous wellhead of sex. I thought them more experienced. No male of twenty-two could have been *less* experienced.

I was sitting next to Goldman in his beat-up '50 Volks when I saw the Eiffel Tower framed between two banks of roofs down a twisting market street. Morgenstein and Novak crowded forward from the back seat to see too. For me the sight evoked a powerful emotion akin to coming home.

Goldman took charge of our little band and designated the morning of Christmas Eve for sightseeing. The four of us left our Pigalle hotel in a mad rush that I found silly: Goldman and his Instamatic, Morgenstein and his Leica, Novak and his Polaroid. They thought I was crazy without a camera. We covered La Tour Eiffel, Notre Dame and L'Arc De Triomphe in a steady drizzle. It was like Parcheesi with cameras. The muddy, crowded carnival of Pigalle seemed a brave, pathetic, hopeful tourist trap to me. I liked it a lot. I grew up around Florida tourist traps.

At early dusk the lights of Pigalle began to sparkle, footlights for an amazing, erotic parade of prostitutes, revealingly clad even in the damp cold evening. To my dazzled view they offered a sexual cornucopia of every hair color and skin tone and feminine shape in the world, shivering in flimsy attire under awnings and doorways. I couldn't help gawking. I was a twenty-two-year-old virgin and ashamed of it. Here I was, a real GI, a graduate of Military Police school with a NATO Secret Clearance and a serious Cold War job. But still a virgin. I was determined to do something about it.

I was disillusioned when my allegedly experienced companions failed to take the lead. They never approached one single prostitute. Eventually I realized they were not as seasoned as squad-room bravado suggested. Aching with frustrated lust, I tried to persuade them into one of those live-sex venues that lined the street, each promoted by carnival-like barkers who swapped friendly backchat with the prostitutes between pitches to the throngs of tourists.

What I said was I wanted to prove it was all a hoax and nothing sexual would happen on stage. But my secret hope was just the opposite. Filmed pornography had not yet flooded the world. I needed technical guidance to illustrate the erotic words of Henry Miller, Grace Metalious, D.H. Lawrence and Agnar Mykle.

My companions refused to go. They balked at the required price of admission: an expensive bottle of purported champagne for each stage-side table. I didn't have enough money to buy one by myself and was afraid to go in alone anyway.

Next I wanted to get in one of those sidewalk boxing rings on Pigalle, featuring club fighters who promised you 500 francs if you could stay in there with them for two minutes. *Juste Deux Minutes*. Work off some of my frustration and earn enough money to brave the fleshpots alone. I had my hands on the ropes and one foot on the edge of the canvas when Goldman clamped me in a damn MP come-along hold and marched me off surrounded by the other two. I don't know what they were afraid of. I knew how to handle my fists and take a punch if I didn't know the first thing about getting laid.

I sulked. One of my favorite novels, *Lasso Round the Moon* by Agnar Mykle, said for every Norwegian trying to have an adventure, there was another Norwegian running after him to stop him – for his own good. I thought sourly Goldman would make a pretty good Norwegian of the second type. When they began debating whether to go see *Mary Poppins* or *Thunderball,* opening in theaters that evening on the Champs, I screwed up my courage and left them. I almost waited too long.

Most of the whores had been swept off the streets by the weather. The one I finally approached had a transparent dome umbrella to protect her hairdo from the sleet and one of those European string shopping bags full of groceries: loaves of bread, a wheel of cheese, a bottle of wine. She wore a sleek dark sheath with a hem just above the knees that showed off nice legs, but her attire was far more conservative than the flimsies I saw earlier. She walked like her feet hurt in those high heels.

The way she cocked her head at me, unsmiling, when I said "Combien?" gave me an ugly turn. Maybe I had picked on a civilian headed home from an office job.

Then she sighed, and named her price: twenty francs. I thought that was five bucks, and I had five bucks. She offered to make change! When I declined, she gave me a real smile. She led me to a Pigalle hot-sheets hotel. I gave ten francs to the concierge for a room key and towels.

The great mystery finally was about to unfold.

What a letdown. She folded her plastic bumbershoot and slithered out of her dress, shucked her bra and knelt in front of me before I had my belt buckle undone. With the efficiency of an Army medic, she unzipped and examined me, a literal short-arm inspection. I passed muster and she went to the little bidet every French hotel room had. She lathered a wash cloth and wriggled out of her silk panties, demonstrating by sign language she was washing just for me.

Then she beckoned me over. Like magic, her soapy fingers went from clinical to erotic. My cock responded with alacrity. At a virginal twenty-two with a nude, attractive woman cupping my laden balls and smiling up at me, my brain couldn't catch up with my body. I kept thinking there should be more to it.

She patted me dry, led me to bed, pushed me onto my back, straddled me, and inserted tab A in slot B. No condom; for the first time I felt the liquid clench of vaginal sheathing. Before I could appreciate it, she impaled herself fully and then was off to the races. She rode like a maniacal jockey, with what sounded to my jaundiced ears like phony groans of gasping passion.

Before I could complete the metaphor she had me in the final turn. I crossed the finish line in a blaze of sudden heat from my groin. She slumped on me, panting.

A deep, unreasoning sadness rose like a dark tide. Was that all there was to the grand mystery? My disillusion was complete. She levered herself off, still breathing hard, and posed fetchingly at the bidet, one foot up on it, to clean up. When she glanced back at me, her eyes widened comically. She came back and took hold. I *was* only twenty-two after all.

"Encore?" she inquired. "Maintenant?"

"Non, merci." The engorged flesh was willing. But my brain wasn't.

"C'est ça." She was dressed and gone before I sat up.

I walked nearly vacant streets in the bitter wind for a long time before I wandered back to my hotel. The great mystery had unfolded, and I was bitterly disillusioned.

# Chapter 12:
# Snowing a Little
# in Paris

IT WAS SNOWING IN GERMANY when we fell out for guard mount and mail call. We read our mail in the back of a three-quarter-ton on the way to our posts. I had one letter. It had a Paris postmark. My heart began to bump hard. Her handwriting flowed across the page like music from a desert flute. Some of the words defeated me. She begged forgiveness for her clumsiness attempting to write in an alien language, which she spoke much better.

*"It's snowing a little in Paris and it's very cold outside. Me too. I have the impression I am snowing in my heart and is cold. Thanks thou for been a little fire comes from far away just thank you for been existed for me..."*

The cold in Paris Christmas Day had been a still quiet cold. The rain slipped through the streetlights with hardly a sound, trying to turn to sleet. The holiday crowds provided all the noise – the laughing, toy-horn tooting crowds – and the bleating horns of the traffic.

I slept in all Christmas day, refusing my companion's urgings for another round of tourism. From time to time I heard high heels click up the stairs outside my room accompanied by a heavy male tread; feminine giggles, male murmurs. It appeared our hotel did a booming daytime business of the hot-sheet variety even Christmas Day. I had accomplished my goal of surrendering my virginity to a working girl the night before in another such hotel. The unveiling of the great mystery of sex was bitterly disappointing. Could that really be all there was?

Eventually hunger drove me to a cafe for a jambon avec beurre et fromage – so tasty I had a second – then sat in the café with black French coffee, nursing my disillusion. Through fogged-over windows I watched lovely French women, cheeks reddened by the cold, ankle by in svelte winter coats. My thoughts turned again to Agnar Mykle. I tried to dissipate my disillusion with the thought the evocative English translations of his love scenes were so vivid they could guide real lovemaking now I understood the mechanics of the thing. If there was such a thing as real lovemaking.

It was already dark when I stumbled across the USO on the Champs. America closed around me inside. They were having some kind of dance there. To my newly sensitized state it was awful. The French girls were lovely and animated, dressed to kill, radiating sensuality. But the American soldiers left them sitting alone and acted like it was their first junior-high formal, clustered together and laughing like teenagers. I thought later they'd go spend a mille for a blow-job or twenty francs for a screw up in Pigalle. Maybe they would. Or maybe they'd go see *Mary Poppins* like my companions. Everything was colored by my disillusion.

Until the lithe dark-haired woman in the little black dress asked to sit at my table. She was with another guy, a German-Canadian. As soon as she sat next to me, he was out of it. She knew it, and he knew it. I didn't know it until a lot later. When she finally flat-out told me, we had only a few hours to be together. We didn't waste any of it.

She loved that old flop-brim fedora of mine. When cigarette ashes fell on it, she would pick it up and carefully wipe them off. After I stamped my postcards I told her I liked her perfume. It interrupted the Canadian's discourse about how being a man and a soldier amounted to the same thing, and how his German father had been with Rommel before migrating to Canada. The wrong thing to be telling someone with a Russian-Jewish heritage who lived in an Israeli kibbutz.

But she didn't much like the U.S. either, calling us imperialists who dominated Israel as the price for our support against the Arabs. That irritated me. Out on the Champs, an Army three-quarter-ton truck with its white star on the olive drab door rolled by amid bleating taxis and Citroens. I told her I was an imperial security policeman, and pointed dramatically. Change the color of that star from white to red and see how freely you would criticize Moscow if Israel was a Soviet satellite, I declaimed. And if I was, for instance, a Russian security policeman instead of an American one. It was an indelicate point, but she smiled at me as if I had imparted the wisdom of ages. Her dark eyes glowed. I noticed her hair in the indifferent USO lighting had the sheen of the midnight Seine under city lights.

When the GIs and the girls finally got together to dance and laugh, the USO got noisy. The three of us ducked out and walked around the Etoile to a cafe on rue Grand Armee, next door to of all things a Ford dealership with American cars under bright showroom lights. It was too cold to sit on the sidewalk but warm and cozy inside, where the pimps played the pinball machines and waited for their girls to come back from assignations. She ordered peppermint tea. The Canadian and I drank coffee.

The Canadian kept after her to promise him a date next weekend. She wasn't buying it and it was so obvious she wasn't that I was embarrassed for him. When he excused himself for a bladder break I told her I'd better be going.

"No," she said. "Don't go now." The way she said it did peculiar things to my insides.

"Why not?" I said. "You two have some things to work out."

"No." She shook her head imperiously. "He and I have nothing to work out." She leaned forward, holding me in her dark eyes. "You," she added. "You and I have things to work out."

When the Canadian came back, his growing desperation was explained. He had to catch a NATO bus in less than a half-hour to go back to his post outside Paris. He was running out of time to secure a date. And no way he wanted to leave her with me.

He had no luck at all. She tucked her arm under mine with complete familiarity and smiled at him and said we would walk him to his bus. Suddenly we were the couple and he was the outsider. The very idea caught me so by surprise I could hardly breathe. The NATO bus had a regular stop right around the Etoile from the café. It was already loading when we got there. She shook hands with him and said goodnight and tucked her arm back in mine. I will never forget the forlorn expression on his face framed in that bus window.

But I forgot it then, instantly and completely. Because she was right there in front of me in that snug black coat with the fur collar, her hair tucked up in a scarf against the cold rain. Her eyes were bright as stars in the reflection from spotlights on the Arc. While I was no longer technically a virgin I wasn't sure what to do next. We walked kind of aimlessly and looked at Christmas displays and the derelicts. The bums on their park benches all seemed to have a jug of 50-centime skull thumper and they all looked happy. She danced away in front of me, moving lightly backwards, gazing at me, smiling gravely.

"What?" I asked.

"I am memorizing you," she said.

I felt my ears burn in the cold and said something foolish and grandiloquent to the effect that in the Old South where I was born, gentlemen always walked their ladies home. She said home was all the way across the city. Furthermore, she lived in a girl's hotel. I took it for dismissal of my clumsy attempt but she showed no inclination to leave me.

We walked some more and paused at a map shop. Lighted world globes were on display, and her delight was infectious. We pressed our noses to the window side by side, trying to find our respective spots on the globes. And there was Florida, easy to see. On the adjacent globe, Israel. She linked her arm with mine, pressing close. "An omen," she said.

"Ships that pass in the night," I said.

Our reflected faces were very close. Mine was shadowed by my hat. I saw her turn to study my profile. "Explain."

So I told her it was a phrase the matriarch of my family used to describe chance encounters, like ships from different ports en route to different destinations exchanging Morse signals at sea. She hugged my arm more tightly. "But sometimes ships can sail along together for a brief time, yes?'

My throat tightened. "Yes."

She led me happily down the street, not letting go. Couples were running and dancing from the sheer exuberance of being alive and together. Our shadows moved together as one beneath the streetlights, the shadow of a couple. I felt like I should be running and dancing too. But I still didn't trust it. Paranoia about women instilled by the matriarch blended seamlessly with plots of spy novels. The glue was my situational awareness of my military role in the Cold War. The USO approach, the handoff by the alleged Canadian, her ostensible infatuation with me. Was my lowly spear-carrier role as keeper of military secrets of enough interest to the Sovbloc to spring a classic honey trap on me?

It was almost midnight. The last Metro trains ran at one a.m.

We passed winter-dormant gardens. There were gendarmes in black cloaks walking almost invisible in the gardens. Walking their posts. I had to leave 10:30 the next morning to get back to walking my post and keeping my secrets in Germany. Make my excuses and walk away? Avoid risk? Or go with my heart's rebellious urging against my doubting brain?

*All girls should have a poem*
*written for them even if*
*we have to turn this goddamn world*
*upside down to do it.*
*                    - Richard Brautigan*

*Stoic philosophers identified the term (logos)*
*with the divine animating principle pervading the*
*Universe.*
*                    - Wikipedia*

# Chapter 13:
# Snowing a Little
# in Paris,
# Part Two

HER HEELS RANG ECHOES out of the blank walls. My old crepe-soled shoes were soundless. I held onto myself tightly. She mentioned the outer logos of the universe invented by Greeks to crush illogical emotional man in its patterns. I said the Metro was my logic then, tearing me away. She said she had to take the Metro too, but would walk all the way home before she would be the one to leave.

I knew Goldman would leave without me. He was scared shitless of AWOL. I didn't have nearly enough money on me for the train back to Germany. Combinations on the bunker locks I kept the lists for would be changed the minute I didn't show. The January password list I drafted would be scrapped. The alarm would go out to pick me up, sooner rather than later. The watch on the Czech border would be intensified.

She led me into Place Victor Hugo because I said I was a writer. There was a Metro station there. She let out a little cry and said she had forgotten it was there. She didn't want it to be there. Because now I had seen it I would leave her. I said see what? All I saw was her. She faced me beside the Metro steps, gloved hands in mine, and said the outer logic must be honored in some things. A woman, she said quietly, cannot say take me in your arms and love me.

"That is for the man to do."

To say your heart stops is only a saying until it does, on a frozen midnight *Place* in Paris, waiting for your answer. I had never even kissed a girl before. But I took her in my arms, and kissed her.

I felt her cold lips move under mine, and grow warm, and part. For the first time in my life I felt a woman's tongue caress mine. It was like being electrocuted. Then my tongue responded as if it had known how all along. My heart was back in full operation, banging my ribs and thumping in my ears. When we could speak again, she murmured it was time for me to take her home. I mumbled a question about the girl's hotel. She smiled and said she meant I should take her where I was staying.

At that moment, I hated Morgenstein desperately. A prudish Midwestern Baptist with a German name who would never surrender his sleep of the righteous for us. I suddenly felt as desperate as the Canadian as I tried to explain. But she placed her gloved fingers over my lips and said we would find a way. We must.

She paid for a taxi to her side of town, pointing out government buildings and monuments as we passed. She said Parisian architecture was so beautiful it soothed a deep ache, like hunger. I believed her. I would have believed anything. When the taxi deposited us at a cafe for coffee to chase the chill from all the walking, she cautioned me against speaking English, which wasn't popular in that quarter. From the number of bandy-legged little Asians wandering drunk with fresh mosquito bites on their faces, I wondered if the Viet Cong got R&R to Paris. The way the world was going, it would figure.

She ordered for us. It was one of those small warm brightly lit places in a dark cold city. A clean well-lighted place as Hemingway would have it. One whole wall was mirrored to create an illusion of spaciousness. We were not the only couple letting coffee cool as we held each other and kissed, long, slow, learning kisses. It was almost an out-of-body sensation to see, over her shoulder, our joined reflection. Never having known how alone I had always been, until I wasn't.

We have to find a room, she said softly. She would do the talking. She smiled radiantly and said I looked like a *flic*, a cop, in my fedora and overcoat. She would be my trollop, paying her Christmas bribe to me. And laughed delightedly at my expression.

The search took an eternity in dark echoing streets. We would step into small lobbies. I would stand silent while she queried. We had pooled our francs and she said we had enough together for a room. But that late on Christmas night there were no rooms. Finally we found a dwarf desk clerk with an oversized head who had to stand on a high box to reach the counter. A giant Alsatian that shared his night vigil stood up and looked me over, wagged his heavy tail once, and settled back into a comfortable curl.

Beneath the dwarf's impressive skull, one vivid blue eye, the left, and one green eye appraised us carefully. I wondered if the dog's approval influenced his. He reflected for a long moment and then rented us his own room, far up under the eaves, interminable flights of narrow stairs above the narrow street, leading us up there personally to turn down the covers. Romance and commerce in a perfect Parisian blend was my secret cynical thought.

Eyes locked on the sway of her dancer's hips and flex of her calves, I never saw the low dark beam at the head of the stairs. The dwarf, and she, passed easily. The passage was not friendly to a distracted man over six feet tall. I rammed my head so hard I staggered and saw stars. I thought I would black out – had time to think what an outlandish thing to happen following this woman to a bedroom – and then, instantly, just...dismissed it. The shock, the pain, the dizziness. Gone. I *would not* permit it to deter me.

The dwarf left us. She got me seated in the single chair beside the low bed and went into the bath down the hall. Alone, I listened to echoing footsteps and laughter of late revelers down in the street. Before I had time to panic she was back, barefoot, wearing only her dress. She had taken down her hair. It floated around her shoulders in a dark cloud.

She knelt before me and put her arms around my neck and kissed me. Then leaned back, and the dress slipped off her shoulders to her waist. She had removed her bra. As Mykle and Grace Metalious and D.H. Lawrence wrote, her dark nipples were engorged. When I kissed the left, it was a hard nub. She arched her back and made a low, murmuring sound in her throat. The first time I ever heard that primeval almost-growl of female need. It vibrated in my bones--not something I recalled from erotic writings, but somehow instantly known and understood.

By then there weren't very many hours left. But somehow there was time enough. Time enough for slow, urgent lovemaking that seemed to unfold as naturally as breathing, just as Agnar Mykle wrote it would. There was not much in the way of foreplay; our time in the cold streets and the cafe had taken care of that.

 I simply mounted her as she opened to me, warm and wet and ready, and covered her with my chest as her arms came around me and her heels found my hips. I was lost in her warmth and response, moving with her and in her on the low bed atop the worn quilts with no tomorrow and no yesterday in a cramped warm cubicle in a half-frozen city.

One of Mykle's passages about the necessity of holding back until a woman found her climax flamed in memory. I slowed even more. We melded into a single pulsing organism. I experienced her first powerful shudders through my whole body with a feeling approaching reverence.

There came an unforgettable moment when her dancer's legs left my hips and drove into the mattress, lifting my whole bulk. She held me like that, and held me, and suddenly my entire buried length was caressed by hallucinatory forceful waves as if a seawall had burst. Then she subsided, lax, eyes closed, inert. It scared me senseless. I held perfectly still not knowing what to do, and gazed down at her slack evidently unconscious face for a hundred years or so.

She came back to me all at once, with a gasped inhalation. Her arms and legs tightened around me while she breathed in surging billows.

"I knew it would be this way with you. Knew it would be wonderful." Then her eyes widened. "But you're still...you didn't..." Those marvelous, slippery internal muscles squeezed and massaged me. "Ohhh..." and we were into it again, slowly and piercingly sweet and lingering. Beyond all doubting, here was the great mystery I despaired of finding just last night.

We rocked that old bed, squeaking, as our rhythm became wild. Her orgasms intensified again. My need gathered like a thunderstorm. She demanded "You must! This time you must!"

I did. The storm broke over us simultaneously. Maybe I passed out a little, too. It was my first experience of afterglow, whispering together like children, telling our life stories, being utterly lost in her eyes, touching, exploring. I remember the amazement in those eyes when she discovered I was not circumcised.

"Does it matter?" I said.

She never really answered, but became fascinated with the hood, touching, stroking, sliding it back and forth like a new toy. When she took me in her mouth I thought I would have a heart attack. I was only twenty-two so within moments it was time to go again. And we did. And we did. And we did.

In those few hours that seemed magically to stretch into enough time for it all, she led me from one delight to another, from one plateau to another as if she had choreographed each movement. That seemed an appropriate term somewhere deep inside my amazement, because she was in Paris studying the dance. Her lips and fingers and body offered wordless cues and my body hit its marks and moved right into the next thing as if I had been dancing this particular *pas de deux* forever. Even when we spooned on our sides and I entered her from behind, amazed all over again at her tightness, until I began to suspect...my god! But I was too shy to learn for sure, and just surrendered to it completely. By now I had staying power and drove on and on through her convulsions until my fifth or maybe sixth orgasm of the night.

When finally sated and snuggling, she complimented me as a lover. In the intimacy of the moment I was moved to confess I had been a virgin, with a mental asterisk for the foot-sore prostitute of Christmas Eve. She called me a liar. I swore it was the truth. She resisted the notion with undisguised delight. We both were laughing at the absurdity of life and wonder of having found each other in Paris.

Finally she grew grave. "If this is true," she said. "Only if, you see, then you were born to make love to women. You will have an interesting life. But I still don't believe you!"

I never wanted to leave her. But the clock was ticking. She knew about duty she told me. She had been a sergeant in the Israeli Army, which I couldn't quite get my mind around. She said in her native tongue there was no term for individual rights, only for duty. It was the outer logos thing again. I could cheerfully grow to hate the damn Greeks.

# Chapter 14:
# Snowing a little
# in Paris,
# Part Three

WE TALKED AND KISSED and caressed and held each other until a phone call from the dwarf at the hotel desk, as agreed, put a period to our magic interlude. It wasn't raining when we got out on the street. The roofs were grey with frost. The sky was pink with a cold new dawn.

There was an empty, lost-feeling time while I stood around the corner from her girl's hotel, shivering uncontrollably, while she got ten francs from her room to cushion me on taxi fare to my hotel. The Metro was running again but I couldn't risk getting lost. When she returned and put her arms around me I stopped shivering instantly.

Her arms felt right as anything in my life. We didn't say much. We had said everything there was to say. We knew each other as if we had known each other all our lives. We huddled in each other's arms, prolonging the moment. The sun was just up, the city still sleeping. I had to go. I didn't want to. I held her very tightly and kissed her goodbye on rue de la Gregoire de Tours. We said shalom. But it was goodbye.

She walked away from me, head down, shoulders slumped. Her heels rang on the cobbles in a slow knell. I wanted to run after her and take her in my arms, to hell with outer logic and duty and everything else in this sorry world. I didn't. She turned the corner and did not look back. A vast aching emptiness opened inside me.

The Gauloises-smelling cabbie professed astonishment an American would name the Moulin Rouge as a *morning* destination. Tried to convey it was *ferme*, closed. I waved him off and said just go. I couldn't remember the name of our hot-sheets hotel but it was one block from the Red Windmill, my landmark. Don't remember the taxi ride or packing my AWOL bag or a word my companions said about my overnight absence.

When Goldman pointed his old Bug north I slept like a dead man. He stopped at a village before the German border and they had a hard time waking me so the two in back could get out. I fell asleep in the cafe while they tried to order a meal. I grew impatient. My exuberant high school French teacher stepped out of the shadows of my exhausted brain. I had thought childhood eidetic recall long lost but suddenly I could repeat Miss Burge line for line and with her accent.

"J'ai beaucoup faim," I told the waitress, "et tres, tres fatigue." One of Miss Burge's favorite sayings.

"Pourquoi?"

"Une affaire de coeur dans Paris. Je t'aime Paris!"

I ordered for us but don't recall the food or the French I used to convey my Paris miracle to the curious waitress. But she approved with warm smiles. Her approval eased my awful loneliness. I slept through the border and almost all the way back to post. It was very hard to fit myself back into dreary Army routine. I was a changed man and my heart was still in Paris. Even the little German dry-cleaner who did our uniforms knew: "When you came back from Paris you were so full of love," she said wistfully.

Most lifers were home with their families the holiday week leading to New Year's. The duty was desultory. I couldn't concentrate. Among mail waiting in Germany was a Christmas card from my newspaper editor who tried to save me from the draft. Knowing my maverick ways he was surprised I had not yet taken on the Army "with a Gatlin gun." Against the memory of my utter helplessness when she walked away from me, his reminder that back home I was considered a force to be reckoned with was bitterly ironic. But it got me thinking.

My most effective weapon was a typewriter not a Gatlin gun. I couldn't shoot my way back to Paris but maybe I could type my way back. I was still very angry with the Army for making me sign a non-disclosure document saying our work was so secret we must never discuss it with a newspaperman. Could anything be more idiotic for a newspaperman to sign?

So during that dead-slow week between Christmas and New Year's I buried myself in Army regulations stored outside the post JAG office. The duty JAG was a Specialist Six and sympathetic. There was a little-known provision allowing a solider to petition for change of duty if his assignment would cause undue burden to his civilian life. I copied the pertinent parts and retreated to my typewriter in MP Operations.

I did not of course stake my petition on my aching need to return to my lover. I waxed eloquent about my newspaper career, interrupted by the draft, and expressed that my military obligation should not lay on me the absurd burden of not talking to newspapermen when I *was* one. The Army had plenty of slots for information specialists where my newspaper training could be put to use; military cops were a dime a dozen. Transfer me to an information slot in Paris and find another sucker to guard nukes in Germany.

I mailed carbon copies to certain addresses State-side and submitted my petition to my hard-nosed MP first sergeant when he returned to work. He laughed at me and said it would stay in his in-box; get out of his orderly room. I said I hate to think of ramifications to your career if that is still on your desk when the Congressional inquiry comes through. He sneered. But I was remembering my kindly executive editor who, when my Gatlin-gun editor complained about my draft notice, dialed a number in front of me. "General," he said, "Another of my boys has been drafted. Can you set him up in the reserves?"

Of course the general could. The general always did. The general would be happy to. But when I learned that escaping the draft meant a lengthy reserve commitment that would coincidentally require me to stay with that newspaper for a long time I chose to accept the draft and get it over with. Not that I had plans to leave. I just didn't like not being able to. My maverick streak. The boss understood. He was a good man. He said if the Army messes you up in any way let me know and Charlie will fix it. Charlie was a senior member of the House Armed Forces Appropriations Committee who owed his seat to the support of our newspaper.

My carbons bore fruit. The First Sergeant got yelled at from headquarters when Charlie's official telex arrived. My captain gave me his personal driver for a visit to headquarters where a major and a colonel expressed admiration for my writing skills as evidenced in my petition. The Army was nothing if not reasonable. The Army respected and admired the Congressman for all he had done for the Army. It was a shame the Congressman even had to be bothered by something like this. That bone-headed First Sergeant needed a tour in a war zone to round off his rough edges.

I was polite and deferential and secretly amazed they would say such things to me about my sergeant. I was given coffee. I was treated with such deference other MPs saluted me, probably assuming my private's uniform was cover for one of the spooks who used the same HQ.

The brass had scoured the NATO command in France. The closest information-specialist position to Paris was Fontainebleau, a short train ride outside the city. Would that do? It would. My utter helplessness as she walked away had been illusion. Back on post I tried to compose a letter to let her know I was coming. I wanted to describe my efforts to return to her but wondered how well she read bureaucratic English. I endured guard mount without complaint because my orders were being cut. I would be in Fontainebleau by Presidents' Day.

Too late. Forever too late.

I had known she was going home but not when. Her letter I read that guard-mount mail call said she was leaving. By the postmark, she was already gone. *"Come soon to see me in Israel"* is how she closed.

The ponderous wheels of Army bureaucracy ground on. I had called in all my favors to get to her. But the target had

93

moved. Israel was a puzzle I did not know how to solve. Paris would be a haunted city. The clash between DeGaulle and NATO was in full swing, but all the sound and fury seemed childish. My letter telling her I got myself reassigned to Paris, to get back to her, was never answered. Maybe she thought me unhinged. Maybe she never got it.

The Greek logos had the last word after all.

*Intermezzo: noun; a movement coming between the major sections of an extended musical work (such as an opera).*
                                        - Merriam Webster Dictionary

*Poetry has nearly everything that music can give – melody, rhythm, sentiment – but it has this advantage: it can come closer to the heart...*
                                        - Allen, *Best Loved Poems*

*Trying for prose to emulate poetry in reaching the heart, my affectation has been that my Iliad is a prose opera; hence the occasional intermezzo.*
                                        - Ish's writing log

# Chapter 15:
# First Intermezzo
# Absence of poetry

"WHERE ARE YOUR POEMS?" the sultry librarian asked me with the firm assurance of her kind of woman that I would have written poems. Woman with liquid dark eyes and long black hair and a kind of sad facial beauty unillumined by her wry smile. Mediterranean? Hebrew? I never knew. We never consummated the unspoken attraction that hummed through all our conversations.

This was on an old Army garrison post beside the Seine in Fontainebleau. I had arrived at Headquarters Company out of nowhere to assume editorship of the garrison newspaper, still wearing MP crossed pistols on my lapels. The first night, the orderly room clerk told me where to find the EM Club after assigning a bunk. I walked over still in Class As for a burger and beer. An obnoxious loudmouth with slicked-back blond hair, his face reddened by whiskey, saw my brass and immediately braced me, grinning like a shark. A lousy MP off-duty in his bar? By god he was going to kick the shit out of me. He stepped close to my bar stool: *and what do you have to say to that?*

Hell it was like being a kid all over again where every time I changed schools the bully had to try me out. Except for two instances – one the guy was twice my size and the second I was outnumbered four to one – I won those fights. Those instances I knuckled under rather than fight convinced me I was an arrant coward. But breaking boards under the informal guidance of a karate brown-belt, followed by MP judo training, taught me a few things. And this loudmouth was no bigger than me.

"Go ahead," I said, channeling a favorite line from Hoss Cartwright on *Bonanza,* "start in, do your damndest. Let me know when you're done – and I'll kill you."

The drunk blinked. Shook himself slightly. And busted out laughing like a loon. Slapped me on the back. "By god they finally sent me a partner with some balls!"

It was one of those Alice in Wonderland moments. The drunk told the bartender whatever his new partner was having was on him. Korsaw – the drunk – was an MP. He read my pistols and jumped to a conclusion. He had waged a one-man battle against drunken Engineers who treed a civilian bar off-post – after his partner skipped when the broken beer bottles came out. Saying he was going to call for reinforcements.

My new best friend pistol-whipped an Engineer lieutenant wielding a broken beer bottle and waded in with nightstick and clubbed .45. He broke heads and restored order. Said his complaint got his yellow partner transferred out. The bartender added respectfully there were bruised and battered Engineers lined out the dispensary door at sick call next day.

Korsaw was incredulous I was the new editor, not his expected partner. Hell, we could have had more fun than since he hung up his Hell's Angel leathers when drafted. Had I ever rode a hog? I said only a little Cushman scooter. He laughed his ass off. *Anybody here gives you a hard time, you let me know.*

Word of Korsaw's endorsement got around, because everybody was curious about my sudden arrival. There was a lot of illegal activity in the incestuous relationship between NATO allies and locals, including a thriving black market that drained the American exchange warehouse of liquor, smokes and luxuries. It was widely assumed my assignment was a CID cover story. Through some osmosis I did not understand, that made me sexy to the women on post. Which was only enhanced when they learned I was a published writer.

The librarian's assumption about poems made me feel badly lacking. I told her I had no poetry. I considered poetry beyond my ability.

"No poems?" Perplexed. "I thought you would have poems. The way you talk sometimes has poetry in it."

97

A pretty compliment. Perhaps an invitation to intimacy. But I was in mourning for the woman who left Paris before I could manipulate the military system to get back to her.

As for her compliment, I already knew the difference between the discipline of poetic expression and spontaneous discourse between men and women, where words exchanged feed upon and enrich each other until they fly away into silence like wild birds escaping any chance of written captivity.

# Chapter 10:
# Bush Bunnies and
# Other French Fauna

*CASERNE:* FRENCH FOR MILITARY BARRACKS or garrison. When I used political influence to extract myself from what amounted to the Cold War front line in divided Germany, I wound up in a NATO caserne outside Paris. "Garrison soldier" was a term my World War Two uncles used with contempt. One of my MP sergeants in Germany warned me "garrison duty" deserved its shady reputation. Corruption would be the order of the day.

Specifically he cautioned me against the caserne supply sergeant. All supply sergeants knew how to work a seam in operational procedure requiring reassigned line soldiers to take their entire combat load-out with them, even to garrison-duty. Since there were no garrison line-item numbers for combat gear, garrison supply sergeants confiscated and sold it on the Black Market. My MP mentor prepared two crates for me. One with winter parka, pile cap, over-boots, insulated mittens with trigger fingers, anything I thought useful for back-home hunting season. The second held helmet, gas mask, pack, canteens, atropine syringes, 7.62 NATO magazine pouches and such. The first crate I mailed home.

I enjoyed the garrison supply sergeant's suspicion he had been out-played. No parka, no pile cap? Hot tickets on the black market. I played dumb. "All they sent, Sarge." He had to settle for unmarketable stuff. Which may have fueled rampant caserne gossip I wasn't a real transfer from the line but a CID impostor sent to stanch bleeding of the European Exchange System. Their warehouses were on our caserne.

The red PI stamped in my 201 to explain my surprise arrival was viewed as CID cover. No one would believe I used political influence to get to Paris for love of a woman. I let them assume the worst.

Before too long a local GI attached himself to me under the guise of showing me the ropes. Sold me a new battery-powered wristwatch for half the PX price. Arranged my invitation to an off-post party hosted by a dissipated non-com, marijuana and hash thick as cigarette smoke, zoned-out partiers, available women. Paranoia made me leave early.

He decided I must prefer simple working girls and checked out a Jeep to show me bush bunnies. I did not believe him, so he showed me. We drove one of the Paris ring roads to an unimproved rest area. It resembled a motor pool: three-quarter-tons, deuce-and-a halfs, Jeeps, even olive-drab Army sedans. Uniform pants dangled out more than one window. There were girls in the vehicles. Glimpses of naked forms engaged in sex. "Told you," he smirked. "Looks like we have to wait. All the girls are busy."

As we sat, a dirty old *deux-chevaux* Citroen pulled to the shoulder. Douchebowl in GI vernacular. A man and woman exited – civilians. He opened the back and handed her a folded partially inflated air mattress. They kissed. He drove off waving. She hugged her mattress and went into the ... well, bushes.

"Aw," the Chicagoan said. "Hubby kisses her and sends her off to work. Ain't that sweet?" A demented chortle I would come to know. "Drives some of these young GIs crazy, those kisses. Specially when hubby picks 'em up at the end of the day after a few blow jobs." I had absolutely no idea what to say.

He asked if I wanted the new girl. I said no. "Prefer one already warmed up and sloppy?" I may have shuddered. That chortle again. He told me about a wrecker operator high in his cab getting a blow job. Finished, the bush bunny blew sperm bubbles at him. He vomited down the side of his truck. She thought that cute and tried to kiss him. He bailed with her right behind him, half naked and giggling. "How do you say kiss me in French? *Embrasse-moi, m'embrasse?* Something like that. Chased him twice around the truck."

I had to say something. "If they do it in the vehicles what's the air mattress for?"

"Hell you can't do it in an open Jeep like this. For comfort. And a place to sit waiting for customers." He said every Paris ring-road turnout featured bush bunnies, some favored by civilian long-haul truckers for whom he felt kinship. That was his civilian job. "Truckers always know where to eat and where to fuck. No bush bunnies at home, but plenty pussy at truck stops."

Of course he entertained the caserne rumor mill with my finickiness. Headquarters-company squad mates were an eclectic bunch: chaplain's assistants, bus drivers for the dependent schools, orderly room clerks, the gamut of garrison duty. All bush bunny fans, all amused by my fastidiousness. Two of the bus drivers had chaste love affairs going with lifer dependents. After a kiss and a grope in the post theater riled them up, they would head for the bush bunnies in the old Buick one of them owned. Sex and smuggling seemed the whole purpose of the garrison, Army duty a distant third.

Shadiest thing an MP in Germany did was sell his cigarette ration – four cartons a month – to locals at inflated rates. American smokes were highly prized. At the caserne, whole pallets of cigarettes vanished despite MP searches of outbound vehicles. Cases of liquor too. My Chicago friend hinted he touched a piece of the profit but was arrest-proof because he only *advised* on fool-proof schemes to move contraband. No audit trail.

I deduced his smuggling trick: a vehicle *below* suspicion, a rusty fertilizer-smelling old sidecar-motorcycle used by gardeners who kept the caserne pretty. Crammed with garden tools and fertilizer bags, the sidecar featured a hidden compartment that held a couple dozen cartons. Or two cases of Scotch. He was unwillingly impressed but unworried; he had orders stateside, tour complete. Other operations were bigger and badder. Easier to go after them than try to prove his involvement. I knew he was right when the CID dragooned me to shoot raid photographs of big Black Market caches along the Seine.

I hoped my MP buddy Korsaw, former Hell's Angel pulling white-hat duty, wasn't involved. Didn't really want to know, he was so colorful. Christine, Queen of Pigalle, was in love with him. Periodically she left Pigalle to set up shop at an *auberge* two blocks away so she could see him every night. Days she plied her trade in comfortable beds. No roadside air mattress for the Queen.

I tried to conceal plebeian shock when my assistant, a mild little clerk, extolled her prowess. *She fucks GIs from Korsaw's garrison?* He shrugged. It's just business. Always free for Korsaw. She even buys *him* stuff, he said admiringly.

Much as I learned in Paris about sex, I was never going to understand the race I came to call Venusian.

# Chapter 17:
# Innocently Abroad
# With the Colonel's
# Daughter

I HAD ONLY MET SUE, the colonel's daughter, at noontime. But we spent every hour the rest of the day together, talking about everything under the sun. She was a large-framed girl, long-legged, lanky and coltish, with lustrous black hair in a French roll, a pert nose, mobile lips and I-dare-you eyes – and she was an unmitigated nut. I liked her a lot.

I was her guest for lunch at the NCO Club – previously and subsequently off-limits to me – for a pre-event interview. I was a lowly Private First Class in the U.S. Army, stationed just outside Paris the last days before DeGaulle kicked NATO out of France. My claim to fame was that I was a published author. Her father was a NATO staff officer. She was a civilian employee of the library system, who wanted me to give a talk about writing.

That evening at the library, she plied me with cups of pretty good French coffee and prepared her introduction. Only five suckers initially showed up. Sue and her boss went through the library, frog-marching innocent victims to fill the chairs. Sue gave her little speech and a couple of prearranged questions. I opened my mouth, disengaged my brain and commenced to talk.

The chaplain's assistant at Fontainebleau, ironically a former Hell's Angel like my MP buddy Korsaw, said I had a speaker's voice that would reach any cranny of a large room. Maybe he was right. People drifted over and asked questions. I told jokes. People laughed, people talked back. It was supposed to go half an hour. After an hour and a half I was just getting warmed up. Coffee and sandwiches were passed around, and a copy of my novel. When the group broke up I was hemmed in by, I guess the word would be admirers, who wanted a personal word.

The library closed. Sue vanished. When she came back she had exchanged her librarian's uniform for a little black dress and svelte heels. Duty done, it was time to party. The military hierarchy would pick up the tab for entertaining the guest speaker. I was oh so young, but not born yesterday. My newspaper reporter's eye noted the entertainment committee had grown to include two of her bosses and a Special Services captain before we reached Cheval Noir, an exclusive little bistro on the Seine. Everybody was riding the expense account for a good time.

Enjoined to eat heartily I had a very good steak, an odd but tasty cucumber salad, and helped kill two bottles of a *très* expensive red wine. The French waiter, evidently noticing a subtle deference paid me by the others, tipped the bottle into my glass and stood back and waited. I had no idea what was going on until the Special Services captain told me I had been selected to approve the wine. I certainly flubbed that test for sophistication. It didn't disturb my appetite or taste for the wine. I topped off with orange sherbet served in a frozen, hollowed-out orange. The rest chose *the desire of the king* which for the life of me I could not describe, large and flamboyant, most expensive thing on the dessert menu.

The other two library staff called it a night back at Hotel Henri IV. Sue and the captain and I wound up at an old barn converted into a discotheque palace where drinks cost $2.50 a shot. The hidden music player blared out *jerk* and *frug* tunes, seven or eight in a row, while dancers went crazy in softly spinning colored lights. They resembled rubber duckies in a carnival ring toss bobbing in a tin tub while rubes tried their luck.

To prove we were still in Paris, many patrons ignored everything but each other, snuggled at their tables, whispering and making love, perched on wicker chairs at tables where red Dutch shoes supported red candles. The noisy music stopped. A string of soulful French love ballads began. Lovers took their act to the floor, mouth to mouth, moving like sleepwalkers in an erotic dream. Athletes retired to perspire and drink.

I had been alone at my table as the colonel's daughter and the captain went out of their minds leaping, jerking, and flailing. She had blisters on her feet the next morning from dancing so hard. When the love ballads came on Sue wanted me to dance with her. I said I haven't danced since Cotillion. But she marched me out and took me in her arms and by God I danced. If that was dancing. Moving slow and dreamy against a good tall woman who murmurs things about how comfortable it is in your arms and lies about what a good dancer you are. I was peering over her shoulder to see steps of the other dancers to imitate.

She was fragrant with some subtle French perfume activated by her frantic earlier dancing and in that silly stage of drunkenness delightful in some women, intensely desirable and intimately aware of her effect on me, pressing closely to ensure I knew that she knew.

But my damned brain wouldn't shut off.

In our conversations over the day she said she didn't go in for all that romancing stuff but enjoyed flirting as long as it was understood flirting would go no farther. Knowing myself, such an understanding meant it would go nowhere at all. And there was the captain to remember. I thought he assigned himself along to make sure the enlisted man knew his place and stayed in line. That would justify his inflated expense voucher.

Depression raised its ugly head. I was in Paris, but the woman who made me a man was not. But here I was experiencing lust for a seductive, goofy American girl. Sue sensed my mood shift because she didn't ask me to dance again. And I didn't ask her. But we stayed the night, drinking and talking during the quiet music. The fast sets, I sat alone brooding. Why was I strongly attracted, despite guilt about my missing Israeli love? And why was I so afraid of rejection on one hand and military protocols on the other to do anything about it?

Sue took me home with her – part of the deal that brought me to the library was a place to stay. If Edgar Allen Poe built a three-story chateau on the outskirts of Paris this is what it would look like: gables, spooky statuary in the gardens, fountains, servant's quarters, garages that had been stables. She drove her VW inside, we closed the iron outer gates and sat in the kitchen.

She made me a cup of hot tea and drank fruit juice. We talked of shoes and ships and sealing wax, and cabbages and ... my lost love and her almost-lovers. Like a Frenchman she propositioned in a café, then told off when he quite logically took her arm and started for his hotel. We strayed into abstract philosophy by four am. and decided to hang it up.

She put me in the guest room next to her parents' bedroom and cautioned should I come out *for any reason* the hall floorboards squeaked. Her father was a light sleeper. In my room I laughed at myself in the full-length mirror, drunk and depressed, wondering if that was an invitation, too timid to find out. I slept as soon as my head hit the pillow.

I awoke to a beautiful clear day and the sound of a gas mower. I showered, shaved and dressed, and wandered downstairs. Through French doors to the garden a pleasant gray-haired lady was leisurely combing out the fur of a fat complacent white cat. It was a perfect snapshot of a way of life. I knew I would always remember. As if I had stepped into a movie and Cary Grant and Kathryn Hepburn would come through the front door any minute. When she noticed me I introduced myself.

She led me to the kitchen for a large glass of orange juice, the perfect hostess. She had been briefed her daughter's guest was an author, so she settled me in a wing chair with books to read while she went, as she put it, to drag Sue out of bed. Mom reported railway and electric workers were out on a wildcat strike. Sue would have to drive me back to my post. She fixed us a big wholesome American breakfast, first home food since I went overseas. She seemed to approve of me at her kitchen table with Sue the nut. The food helped my hangover. But what I really needed was a drink. Sue was cool and debonair in a svelte Navy outfit with bright orange silk scarf.

She drove like an angry Frenchman. I saw cars back off in respect as she rode the Bug's gears on narrow French roads. No traffic lights; workers turned them off before they went out. Rains returned at Versailles. We picked up her sister at SHAPE HQ, suffering a hangover, furious Sue made her ride in back, deferring to "another one of your *men*." I felt the cold weight of disapproval on my neck until she fell asleep.

My Sergeant Major and the adjutant were looking out the headquarters window when we pulled up. The S-M asked me who those two were. I said oh, two colonel's daughters. Sue came in to be introduced and tell him thanks for "borrowing" me before giving me a quick peck on the cheek and departing. His eyebrows climbed halfway up his bald cranium.

"M'sieu Ish, it appears you have moves we never suspected."

I felt like a fraud in the old warrior's eyes. "Not guilty," I said.

He slapped me on the back. "That's my boy. Always plead 'em not guilty." But I wasn't guilty then, or guilty later. I never got laid by the colonel's daughter. The female telegraph in NATO establishments around Paris relayed word from convivial parties that Sue was always there, always expecting to see me. I sent word back I didn't go where not invited. No invitation ever arrived. And I never saw her again.

*... But I was desolate and sick of an old passion*
*Yea, all the time, because the dance was long:*
*I have been faithful to thee, Cynara! in my fashion.*

-Ernest Dowson

# Chapter 18:
# A Haunting
# Resemblance

I KNEW SHE WAS NOT IN PARIS ANYMORE. But svelte women among thronging crowds along the boulevards, whose heels rang on the pavements as hers had, haunted me. If a woman was a similar height with hair dark as the Seine under streetlights, my foolish heart would lurch. If she walked with a dancer's grace it was worse.

This particular raining night – it always seemed to be raining that spring – a woman fit so closely I stumbled when I saw her. Dark hair around her shoulders, tossed by an errant breeze, though I only saw my vanished lover's hair that way when she took it down and took me to bed. But the resemblance arrested me mid-stride.

Frenchwomen always were acutely attuned to attentions of men. She made eye contact. I averted my gaze. She closed the space between us gracefully. Peripherally it was a ghost walking. She spoke to me. In French of course. Her teasing voice broke the spell – the voice was different.

I heard *pourquoi* but not why she asked *why*. I guess my raincoat, old fedora and soft suede shoes looked native. She said something else. I gave it up. "Parlez vous Anglais?"

She cocked her head. *"Americain?"* When I nodded, she said "I 'ave *un peu* Anglais. *Porquoi* you stare, *Américain*? I am pretty, *non*?"

"Oui," I said. "You remind me very much of someone."

She puzzled it out looking up at me. Her face lit: *"Une copine!* Oui?" Saw my bewilderment. "Votre amour? Comprenez-vous?"

That I could get. "Yes – oui."

"Où est-ce qu'elle est?" She paused. "Where – is – she?"

"Far, far away."

Her lips formed a cute moue. *"Au loin*? Pauvre de vous."

I could get most of that. "Merci."

Lights along the Champs made rain drops sparkle in her dark hair. Taxis bleated. Crowds parted around us. She said *un peu soul*. Small soul? Poor soul? I shrugged. "Lonely," she said slowly. "A little, n'est pas?"

"A lot," I said. "Beaucoup."

She winked. *"Je pourrais vous aider."* I shrugged again. "I – can – 'elp." She smiled brilliantly, took my arm. "Vingt francs."

For God's sake, she was a hooker. The ratio of working girls in female *pietons* always seemed high even on the Champs amid airline offices and movie theaters, not far from *Le Figaro*. I had just left The Blockhouse on the Etoile, the NATO photography office that processed film for me. She arched her brows and tugged.

"Alors? Allons nous amuser!" Suddenly we were walking. She threw her laughing face to the rain, almost skipping. Right size, right shape. Right hair. It felt eerily familiar. Lovely features not the same, but her exuberance was. She happily dragged me against a flashing don't-walk light at a *passage pieton,* free hand up imperiously to stop traffic. Amazingly, rain-wet cars braked with a sibilant hiss of tires. A taxi objected with blaring horn. She flipped him off insouciantly.

She chattered and clung, smiling up at me. One of the strangest walks of my life. I was in Paris, walking with a professional doppelganger of my lost love. My first visit to a working girl had been all business, depressing. This was like Henry Miller ramblings about happy whores. Was I really doing this? My dead great-grandmother whispered in my head: *A stiff dick ain't got no conscience.*

She led me down a side-street to a discreet hotel. Exchanged banter and air kisses with the towel-keeper. I forked over the requisite ten francs for towels. One time and I knew the drill. What was different was his friendliness. He shook my hand! In the room with its inevitable bidet, she took my face in still-gloved hands and kissed me. I was astonished but kissed her back, now I knew how.

She murmured approval, divested her gloves and raincoat. Tousled her thick hair, shaking out water droplets. Then reached for my tie, expertly slipped the knot and lay it aside like I was a gift to be unwrapped. Unzipped herself, slithered out of her dress and gestured for me to undress. I complied. She removed her black bra and panties and kicked off her heels, leaving just garter belt and black

113

nylons like something out of a men's magazine. The effect was visceral.

My boxers could no longer contain my tumescence, rearing through the slot like a cobra. She knelt. I expected the brisk short-arm examination of my previous working girl. But no; she hefted it admiringly. Gave me a squeeze. Pre-orgasmic fluid leaked from the stretched foreskin. She pushed it back and gave me a quick lick. I trembled. She laughed with delight.

"*Elle a de la chance,* votre amour!" She stripped my boxers. "Maintenant, *aller au lit avec moi.*" She led me to bed, not by the hand. I hadn't been drinking so didn't understand *lit (leet). G*ot the *with me* part. She tugged me into bed. Whispered "Il est grand!" I'd not been in France long enough to expand my high-school French. She wrapped arms around my neck. Murmured, "*Faire l'amour* avec moi." I understood *with me* and *love.*

My brain buzzed without benefit of alcohol. Dazed by how ready I was, enchanted by her demeanor, her form superimposed on a vision of the woman who made me a man in this city. She was wet and hot and ready. She groaned when I bottomed against her cervix. My neck hair lifted. Four months ago I learned that sound past all forgetting. She wrapped legs clear around me. Held me to prevent withdrawal. Relented just enough to permit slight lifting, pulled me deep again, laughing and gasping, nibbling my neck. We found the primal rhythm: nipping teeth, cascading laughter, gasps. And below, squeezing little convulsions each time I paused on the down-stroke.

My pauses seemed to make her crazy. She bucked, pulled my hair, murmured a steady stream of French.

Trying to trigger me. No, no, sister – I been to the mountain. Learned Agnar Mykle was right. A man delays to satisfy a woman.

She got wilder. Bounced me around like 190 pounds was nothing. Dug fingernails in my back. In a distant corner of my mind I made a note my skin was chafed by nylon-clad legs; get rid of them in future. The chafing stopped when she opened her legs and drove heels into the bed. Almost lifting me, not as powerfully as my lost dancer. The move was my unequivocal signal. I unloaded. She cried out. Felt like she drew blood from my back. If she was acting, she deserved an Oscar. Where had the sweat come from that stung my eyes?

I stayed sheathed, twitching with aftershocks. Her cunt gripped each time I twitched. She reached up to caress my eyes free of sweat. She was breathing hard, eyes bright, no longer laughing. She looked content. Had I held long enough? Had those spasms been orgasmic? No way to know. No way to ask.

From my one previous working-girl experience I expected her to disengage, clean up and dress. Instead she put arms around my neck and kissed me, slow and strangely intimate. It was like closing a circuit. I still was twenty-two, after all. My cock swelled in her. She was awash in our bodily secretions, slippery, friction reduced. No deterrent to John Thomas, as Lady Chatterley's lover named his cock. Being me, I was embarrassed. Wasn't the going rate twenty francs a fuck? Wasn't this like sneaking through the chow-line twice for another glass of milk?

She murmured and shifted. I must be crushing her while I built a new hard-on. I moved onto my side, almost coming loose – but she came over with me, pushed me on my back, straddled and drove down. Just like that my erector set was complete. She leaned her hands on my chest, hips pistoning, laughing again through the swirling curtain of her hair – her breath caught when I took her breasts. Her nipples nudged my palms like hot flint.

Despite copious lubrication I didn't last as long this time. Lifted her like a bucking bronco when I came. No idea if she did. Finally caught my breath as she curled up beside me, head on my shoulder, petting my sweaty face, giggling and murmuring. Most went right over my head. "Votre *copine* est ... *une femme chanceuse.*" I had to look it up.

She was in no hurry, unlike the previous working girl. We were not annoyed by an impatient towel-holder as other GIs had warned. She went to the bidet and brought back a warm soapy cloth to wash my finally diminished cock. A quick fond kiss made it twitch. She giggled. One way or another I got dressed – remember her refastening a rumpled stocking after she cleaned herself at the bidet – and she tucked her pretty self into clothing with economic speed. Made a pass at makeup and lipstick in the mirror. Ran a comb through her tangled hair. Good to go.

Downstairs I got European air kisses. She bid *au revoir* and slipped behind the counter with the towel-holder, who took her coat and patted her shoulder. Looked like she was in for the night. I trudged back up the Champs toward Rue Marbeuf's NATO establishment. There was a cheap snack bar and a shuttle to the *Gare* where I could catch the Fontainebleau local.

Looking for a ghost, I fell in with a living woman full of irrepressible *joie de vivre* who restored my faith in Henry

Miller's tales about happy Paris whores. My body – even the light sting of scratches on my back – felt vibrantly alive. My brain tried to rationalize. Best I could devise: a happy working girl was to real lovemaking as target practice was to hunting big game. You got to feel the gun go off. Verify accuracy. But neither paper nor prostitute plumbed your soul.

# Chapter 19:
# Orleans Operator
# Number 2

I REMEMBER HER as Orleans operator number two because that's how she introduced herself at the end of a call I made from Fontainebleau. At first I thought she just liked to eavesdrop because she commented on the story I told the Army newspaper editor in Orleans. But she wanted to flirt. She said she found my Southern accent delightful. This in the most charming French accent. So I returned the compliment.

She complained very soon about her Air Force boyfriend who "has to be drunk to have enough courage to sleep with me." Then she said from the deepness of my voice she inferred I would not require liquid courage. Her obvious attraction to me, and that remark particularly, provoked a welter of thoughts.

I remembered an old wire-service man telling a virginal copy boy that as soon as I got laid and realized what I was missing, the natural balance between male and ever-mysterious females would be restored. Once I knew what I had been missing I would want more. Women previously drawn to my virginity like bees to honey would achieve their ordained upper hand, and play hard to get. In a way his prophesy reflected a lifetime of dire warnings by the matriarch of my family to beware the wiles of designing women.

I was emphatically no longer a virgin. I had outmaneuvered Eisenhower, to adopt a favorite phrase of the matriarch, to return to Paris for the woman who made me a man beyond any unmaking. But Fate always had the last laugh on me. Before I could goad Army bureaucracy to act, her time in Paris was up. It was her duty to go home to Israel; she told me her native language had no word for individual rights, only for duty. My letters went unanswered, leaving me bereft in the City of Light, haunted by her memory.

These tangled thoughts drifted through the back of my mind in the first and subsequent conversations with Operator Number Two. Like switchboard operators the world over she could work the phone system like a virtuoso. I was seldom in my office for long before she dialed through. I wondered how that worked, but a Fontainebleau operator, herself possessed of an erotic French accent but who assured me she was old enough to be my mother, confessed to aiding and abetting her switchboard sister by calling her when she knew I was in the office.

This allegedly motherly woman – I never saw her – was a pure romantic in the wonderful way of the French. She said she sensed the same masculinity the younger woman did and predicted a glorious affair if I would just make an excuse to go to Orleans. It appeared European women were unlike Americans, who would lose interest once I was no longer virginal according to my wire-service mentor. Instead they had radar that locked on men who knew what to do in bed. I still was kind of amazed I was now that man.

But the woman I ached for every day was long gone.

So when Operator Number Two came right out and said come see her, we would do lunch and see what developed, I created a business reason to go so I could have a military car and driver. Almost felt like heading for an audition to see if I lived up to my voice and verified her instincts.

Man, the odd situations sexual attraction leads you into.

My business was with my opposite number, the Orleans garrison newspaper editor. Always cordial before, he became instantly uptight when I mentioned lunch with Operator Number Two. Didn't tell me until after he invited himself to lunch with us that he carried a torch for her. The glance of casual contempt she gave him when we got to the restaurant should have doused it. But he squirmed like a puppy, happy just to be noticed.

Ah those French lovelies with their chic dark hair flipped just so and form-fitting dresses of soft supple material that hugged their bodies like a lover. Number Two was a fine example, wine-colored jersey knit showing a hint of perfect knees beneath a peekaboo hem, a soft scoop neck that accentuated her elegant neck and a subtle swell of milk-white cleavage. European air kisses for me, which inundated my senses in a drift of exotic French perfume. I had one of those random thoughts that the tradition reminded me of animals sniffing each other, and accomplished the same thing.

No air kisses for him. Right in front of him, she questioned my bringing him along. A co-worker I said, I honestly didn't know how to get out of it without being rude. I added I had not realized she was so popular with all the locals. All right in front of him. Didn't bother him. Like Minnie Pearl he was just so proud to be there.

But she reacted as if slapped. Her face reddened. So did fresh whisker rash in her cleavage. The fresh hickey on her neck darkened to plum. Her makeup had masked these stigmata until she blushed. Well I knew she had at least one lover, the liquid-courage air force guy.

My fellow editor was a sap. No kinder way to say it. He wriggled in his chair like a schoolboy. He went on and on about how gorgeous she was, everybody thought so, especially him. She rolled her eyes at me and leaned across the table, excluding him from conversation with body language clear as a stop sign. She asked me why strong men are so cruel and boys so needy. Hell, she thought I brought him along to torture him. There was nothing I could say to that.

But I did have a perverse pride. If she was interested in seducing me, she should have chosen a turtleneck top. Advertising amorous escapades on her pale flesh quenched my interest like seeing merchandise marked down for a quick sale. To say lunch was uncomfortable puts it mildly. The other guy kept trying to divert her attention to him with increasing desperation. She angled for me to stay in town overnight – with her. I was wondering if I could catch my driver before he returned to Fontainebleau to punch out for the day.

I did catch my ride. For days thereafter, a sad little voice hung around in the background when I conducted telephone business with Orleans. Or she would call, tipped by her co-conspirator, and we would have brief shallow conversations that trembled on the edge of previous intimacy. I felt bad that she felt bad. My local operator lobbied for her gently. I couldn't tell her the stigmata of earlier lust had turned me off; a Frenchwoman would find that juvenile. Fifty years later, so do I. A real man would have rebranded her with his own mark.

But I never went back to see her or mend my unintentional cruelty. All too soon I was shipped out of France with the rest of NATO. Now, reading notes penned by that priggishly self-important young man, Operator Number Two springs to sensual life vividly as yesterday. She was mine for the taking. Instead she became another in my life list of near-misses. Tired and old, nearing the end, I wish I could apologize to her.

*If you are lucky enough to have lived in Paris as a young man, then wherever you go for the rest of your life it stays with you, for Paris is a moveable feast.*

-Ernest Hemingway

# Chapter 20: Soixante Neuf in 1966

I TOOK A WEEK'S ANNUAL LEAVE to say goodbye to Paris. The day before I was scheduled to leave I was in a hot-sheets hotel just off the Champs-Elysee, learning pronunciation and practice of *soixante-neuf* from a slender young blonde who had recently come up from Brittany to make her fortune on her back.

I hadn't been certain I had enough ready cash for a final lay, but when I saw her diffident approach to a well-dressed businessman near the Etoile, and how disappointed she looked when he turned her down, I asked "Combien?" Lo and behold, her asking price was within my limited means.

When we got to the hotel, a bit of comedy ensued. It developed I still had been converting dollars to marks and she quoted francs. Damned if she didn't ask the towel-keeper for change so she wouldn't overcharge, second time a Paris working girl was so considerate. Second time I said keep the change.

She was so fresh and attractive and innocent-looking, so thrilled to have made the sale – so honest! And I was still very young and inexperienced. No longer technically a virgin. my education was sadly lacking. I fixed on one gift I had not known how to give the woman who loved me to manhood in this city. I mustered my nerve and my high school French to ask for instruction in *soixante-neuf.*

"Soixante-neuf?" Her voice ascended the register in astonishment.

"Oui, s'il vous plait."

In stumbling phrases, I conveyed my ignorance. She did not make fun of me. But she was incredulous an American would admit ignorance in anything. I gathered Americans weren't big on cunnilingus either, not with a working girl.

She was sweetly solicitous as we began my lesson and she saw I was deadly serious. It was my first dive into what Henry Miller, in Paris before me, likened to a coral reef where a porpoise could nuzzle with delight. I imagined a sea-tang in the wetness beneath her Venus Mons. She was patient with the language barrier. Patient with my clumsiness when I was distracted by her oral ministrations at the other end of the known universe. We switched to straight cunnilingus before we fucked. Ultimately, I got the hang of the thing. She became unprofessionally ardent, grinding her Mons against my mouth so hard she bruised my upper lip.

She spent a lot more time with me than the usual working girl did those days. The towel-keeper eventually tapped on the door to make sure she was all right. And I suppose to remind her other customers were waiting.

As we dressed, she embraced and kissed me tenderly, like a lover. She invited me to meet her at a nearby sidewalk café for breakfast. That was certainly out of the ordinary. I was immensely flattered. Her face fell when I told her I would be on a plane to America tomorrow. She seemed genuinely sad.

I had known GIs who relished their prostitute girlfriends, most notably a former Hell's Angel who commanded the devoted affections of the so-called Queen of Pigalle. The Queen was a local legend, known to have scratched and clawed other women who made a play for him in some bistro while Korsaw leaned back and enjoyed the show. She was a working girl, and even screwed other GIs in our unit, but that was just business. The Queen of Pigalle loved only Korsaw.

Just my luck, on my last day in Paris, to find an honest working girl so unjaded she took pure pleasure in her work, and might like to have a GI boyfriend. But I had a plane to catch. I would have to deploy my new-found intimacy with Venus Mons in another country. I knew whatever transpired, my gentle teacher would remain a sweet memory of youth in the City of Light.

# Postscripts
## Trying to leave Paris

*As it turned out I could have had breakfast with the cute blonde. I had another whole day plus in town due to military mismanagement. Directly from 1966 notes:*

Situation Normal – All Fucked Up. Here we go again. The inefficiency of the Army's attempts to evacuate France under DeGaulle's edict have conspired to leave me stranded in Paris with my cash running low. They checked me out of the transit hotel and had me cooling my heels all day until they finally concluded they could not shoehorn me onto today's flight stateside.

I wound up pre-processing for another flight tomorrow and wondered if I would be sleeping on a park bench with the winos and their fifty-centime bottles of skull-thumper. But the Army found me a room in the Hotel de Paris – one of many Hotels de Paris. This one at 51, Avenue Du Maine, a two-star establishment with clean rooms and private baths.

The salon is spacious with couches and chairs and an escritoire, all done up in red and black leatherette beneath a quaint bronze chandelier. The hunting prints on the wall include riders and Walker hounds baying a European elk … A wide picture window opens onto the tree-lined boulevard, beyond which a massive multi-story building is being constructed.

Paris seems to be building everywhere – and building upward, above the old low skyline. Jackhammers and rivet guns and rumbling cement and gravel trucks form cacophonous counterpoint to the incessant bleat of taxi horns and click of high heels. The fresh raw odor of new construction blends with old stale ozone from Metro gratings. Paris roars and thunders and beeps and clops and laughs and propositions twenty-four hours a day. I stood in the doorway with the petite chien belonging to the proprietaire to watch le passage des pietons: bearded students, chic women, many hommes serieux in tailored business suits with the self-important comportment of men involved in building and running this new Paris.

Then there are the whores, icons of old Paris. I am developing a special fondness for these. Down here in Mont Parnasse they go to work early, 1600 hours, and shout their wares like fishwives to the serious men. These are not nearly as slender, well-built and lovely as the ones assigned by their pimps to patrol the Etoile for tourists, but some of them compensate with sheer Renaissance size, proportion and laughing enthusiasm. But I fear I am too low on funds to consider a farewell fuck.

No matter how many times I count my money I have only thirty-four francs to my name, for a taxi to the Littrez embarkation center tomorrow and the twenty-five-franc head tax France charges to permit you to leave the country. After Paris has had her way with you for a week the big electric board at Orly that reports departing flights loses its appeal.

That large-framed redheaded whore on the corner is very stimulating. One imagines a delightful Henry Milleresque romp. She quoted me twenty francs. Would the

Army pay to get me out of France and take it out of next month's pay? I wish I had the courage to find out.

Tomorrow is scheduled to be my fourth airplane ride, second ocean crossing. Tomorrow my soul could be required of me and I will die screaming, frightened beyond sanity by a dizzying plunge into infinity. I am not so much afraid of flying as I am of *crashing*. Placing myself totally within control of scientific theories of lift and propulsion inside an aluminum tube, umpteen thousands of feet above umpteen fathoms of shark-filled salt solution, scares the hell out of me.

You cannot help but imagine the unendurable shock of metal falling on solid water, human paste along crumpling bulkheads; searing flame that you feel crisp you into charcoal. Or swimming clear in a daze, only to feel a tug and see your leg disappear into clenched ripsaw teeth in a hellish snout. It is a form of whistling past the graveyard to avoid these things by envisioning them. But I sure wish I had an extra twenty francs ...

# Chapter 21:
# Harvey Hill,
# Part One

WHEN I CALLED HOME FROM NEW JERSEY to report I was back in the U.S., it was immediately clear how I had changed overseas. When the family matriarch answered the phone her voice sounded stuck on a slower RPM. I impatiently talked over her a couple times because she spoke so slowly. She resented it: "How-uh come you-uh speak-in' so *fa-yust*?" It appeared I had lost a lot of my Southern accent.

It was confirmed when I strained to catch the nationality of the strange accent of the announcer calling my Atlanta flight and finally realized she wasn't foreign, she was Southern. Takeoff scared me as always. I was convinced the flight from France depleted some finite pool of luck that would run out one day in flaming wreckage. I sweated out an endless aerial promenade in clouds above Atlanta before the plunge to earth.

In less than an hour I was airborne for the short hop home and survived that. I took a taxi to the Beaches. A sea wind was tossing palm trees shrouding the lane where I grew up two doors from the ocean. My soul expanded like a balloon. "Nice little beach house," the cabby said. "Wish I could afford one."

My mother and the aging matriarch came out to greet me. Our home seemed to have shrunk while I was gone. In an unusual public demonstration, my mother kissed my cheek. The cabby gave her an appreciative up-and-down as most men did, and me a thumbs-up. He thought she was my slightly older girlfriend. My mother had that effect on men. When she casually hefted my duffel bag in one hand and B-4 in the other, the cabby's eyes widened. "Slinging mail bags in the Postal Annex agrees with you," I said. "You've developed some muscle."

"Pshaw! I always been strong."

"Your granddaddy is inside," the matriarch said. "We made the living room his bedroom. He cain't climb stairs no more."

The old man was sitting up in bed where my typewriter used to be in what suddenly was a tiny room. I had braced for what he would look like and felt a flood of relief. He looked like himself, tanned and grinning, showing off perfect false teeth. His triceps writhed with coiled muscle when he hitched around to shake hands. Only evidence of the missing leg was a dip in the bed sheet; not even diabetes and amputation diminished him.

"You got my old room upstairs," he said. "Yore mama put yore typewriter and pipes and books up there."

"What's that I smell in the kitchen?"

"I fried a mess of shrimp earlier," the matriarch said. "I know you like 'em cold, and they're ready now."

"I made tartar sauce like they did at Strickland's," my mother said. "And Mama baked biscuits for you."

"Biscuits is breakfast food but I did it," the matriarch said. "And you know how I hate to make biscuits anymore."

"Git out of that hot ol' uniform and let's eat," my mother said. "Your clothes is upstairs in Daddy's room." She eyed me with the calculating eye of a life-long calorie counter. "They'll be loose on you now. Maybe tight in the shoulders."

As I started for the stairs I noticed a framed painting above the old man's head. A well-done portrait of a sad carnival clown. Not an imitation of Emmett Kelly; the makeup wasn't sad, the clown was, behind his translucent happy makeup. I had spent an afternoon in the Louvre a couple of days ago, not easily impressed. But the portrait was arresting. "That's new," I said.

The old man was grinning like the Cheshire cat. "Glenda bought it to me in the hospital when they cut off my leg. Said it was how she felt."

The matriarch put her hand on my arm. "She's been coming out to visit a lot since you been gone. Said she must miss you most as bad as we do." Her mouth twisted; she did not approve feminine interest in me. She had warned me against designing women for as long as I could remember. I felt dizzy. Too many changes, too fast. The slow drawls, the shrinking house, the old man's missing leg, biscuits at midday – and now Glenda.

"Guess you're more like me than I thought," the old man said. "Got one o' them 'come-back' peckers they keep comin' back for."

The matriarch punched the old man on the arm. "Shut your foul mouth, you embarrassed him." It was true.

He chuckled. "Wait till she gets out here this evenin'."

"She said you had a date with her tonight." The matriarch fixed me with her ice-blue eyes. "Was she makin' that up?" I was suddenly sixteen again and she was protecting me from women's wiles.

"I didn't know she could get away," I said.

135

Not really a lie but not the truth. A date? It was true our correspondence had become more intimate while I was in Europe. Equally true I sent a telegram from Paris American Express telling her when I'd be home. But she was married to a possessive asshole. My mother cocked an eye. "Oh, she'll get away all right – for you!" She never shared her mother's fear women would take advantage of me. "Expect her at seven. I'd put money on it."

"No takers," the old man said.

"Oh she'll be here all right," the matriarch grumbled.

And she was, driving up the lane in a new gray Mercury that looked big as a battleship in the narrow lane. The old man, out on the front stoop in his wheelchair, directed her to park in the neighbor's yard. They were talking when I got to the front door. She planted a peck on his bald head. Then here she came in that rapid heel-clicking walk of hers, wearing a simple sleeveless lime-green shift with a nice V above her perky breasts. She walked right into me and wrapped her arms around me, tipping her head up to give me her laughing eyes.

"Welcome home, stranger." I couldn't seem to find my voice. She went up on tiptoes and whispered. "You better hug me back, you big lug. And if you don't kiss me, your grandfather will!"

I had never hugged or kissed her in my life. Thought about it a lot, never had the nerve. Never had the nerve to kiss any woman for that matter. Paris and my amazing lover there changed me forever. Now it seemed this was the purpose of the change as her tongue invaded my mouth and found mine. The height difference was such it took a subjective eternity to realize the twin points of fire against my lower rib-cage were her nipples through the thin fabric of her frock. She released me suddenly and pulled back. I dropped my arms, thinking she'd been shocked by the bulge that swelled my pants. But she grabbed my hands tightly and stood looking at me with swollen lips and sleepy eyes.

"Ready for our date?" I gulped and nodded. She cleared her throat. "Can we take your car? I'm in no shape to drive!" Like I was. I led her to my Barracuda and handed her in, admiring the tidy way she tucked in her tidy body. When I drove away, she waved gaily. "Your grandmother thinks I'm corrupting you."

"I certainly hope so," I said. "After that kiss."

Her laughter was a happy silvery sound. I drove south, not really knowing where I was going. When I reached Beach Boulevard the choices were turn down onto the sand or west toward the city. Old beach-dwellers' habits sent me west. I had surprised too many incautious lovers in cars while beach-walking, seen too many cars taken by the returning tide. Besides, sand rusted the undercarriage. She was turned to face me, knees drawn up fetchingly. She had kicked her pumps off. "We're not going to make out on the beach?" She sounded disappointed.

"The tide," I said. "Can't risk being distracted down there."

"Oh!" Her hand trailed gently up and down my leg. "Nice slacks. Are they European?"

"The slacks are PX. The shirt is German."

"I don't think I like bucket seats. I can't get close enough."

I reached behind the seats. "Before my brother went in the Navy – ah!" I brought out a thickly rolled beach towel and pushed it down between the seats.

"Trust your brother. Your folks told me all about his string of beach bunnies." She swarmed across the towel to snuggle. I drove off the highway onto San Pablo Road and turned into an ancient sand logging road through scrub pine and cypress hammocks, nursing the car until I felt the sand was firm. I drove slowly out to the Intracoastal Waterway until we could see yachts passing. When I shut off the engine, she came into my lap. We kissed and held and whispered things we only hinted in letters. At some remove, I couldn't believe the unattainable married beauty was in my arms whispering words I had only dreamed.

When I finally palmed her breasts the nipples almost burned my hands through her frock. She groaned. I thought I'd hurt her. I still was very young toward women. Did not recognize that primal sound of need in the confusing context of Glenda. She removed my hands and pulled back to her seat. For an eternal moment my eyes refused to convey an image to my brain, as if struck blind.

In that moment she reached behind, unzipped and shucked her frock onto the floorboards and came back into my arms stark naked. No panties, no bra. The inference almost more than the bare fact nearly made me ejaculate in my pants. "Remember when you told me the Barracuda's back seat folds down like a station wagon?" she said against my mouth.

I mumbled something that might have been yes.

"Show me," she whispered.

By the time I had the seat down, the beach blanket under her hips on the uneven carpet, my shirt off and pants around my ankles, the sometimes-hated part of my brain that stood apart and kibitzed woke up. Reminded me my long-absent father told me when I was 18 to always get a room; car sex with your clothes bunched around you was for amateurs. Yet here I was in that very position with a woman I was hopelessly in love with.

*So I knelt there at the delta, at the alpha and the
omega, at the cradle of the river and the seas. And like a
blessing come from heaven for something like a second
I was healed and my heart was at ease.*
- Leonard Cohen, *Light as the Breeze*

# Chapter 22:
# Harvey Hill

TOO LATE TO THINK ABOUT A ROOM. She opened to me
and I went into her, and her bare heels dug into my rump,
lifting her hips to tug me deeper while she writhed and
sobbed under me. Now my brain recorded the damn gas
tank was half empty. Every thrust caused a hollow boink
below the carpet. My brother had warned me. What kind of
moron designs a car for fucking and puts the gas tank in
such a stupid place? My brain short-circuited my cock. I
softened slightly. I thrust deep to gain friction, but lack of
friction was not the problem.

Then I realized her sobs had become actual tears. She
was clinging to me like a limpet, crying as if her heart were
broken. I stopped thrusting and held her. "What is it?
What's wrong?"

"I love you, goddammit!" First time she'd ever said it.
Before I could say anything she sobbed into my shoulder
like a hurt child. "I love you and I can't come! I love you in
me and I can't come. Goddammit, what's wrong with me!"

"Darling," I said. First time for that too. "Darlin', stop fretting. It's okay." My cock softened quickly. "We just got started. It's okay."

"I wanted you so bad," she wailed. "Now I've messed it all up."

"Hush now. Hush. Everything's okay. Everything's okay." The big rear window was totally steamed over. I was slick with sweat. But I still felt her scalding tears against my neck. The only thing I could do was keep gentling her like a spooked horse. "You said you love me," I said. "Do you realize you said it?"

She shifted under me. "Of course I love you, you idiot. But why didn't you say it back?

"Oh, shit, Glenda, I've been in love with you since the first day I saw you back when I was a copy boy."

She sniffled. "Really? But you never..."

"I was too afraid."

"Oh Ish, really?"

I raised her tear-wet face, a pale blur, and realized dusk was falling. "Really," I said. "Glenda, I love you."

"What are we gonna *do*, Ish? I mean..."

Before she could finish the thought, bright headlights flared against the steamed-over window. I heard a truck engine. "Oh god! It's Marcus! He followed me!" She began to emit a low wailing terrified sound. But I could hear voices now, Cracker voices, above the truck engine.

*–Somebody rippin' him off a piece. –Sumbich blockin' us getting' to the houn's.–Gonna lose that 'possum, shore.– S'all right, let's go take a look, maybe get a taste our own selves.–Hell, yeah!*

142

My rage was instantaneous. I never remembered later how I got out of the car, pants around my ankles, my Colt from under the front seat braced on the tail-light housing. Neither woods-runner had even opened a door. "Shut off your lights!" I sang out in my best MP voice. "Do it now." I was peripherally aware of Glenda behind the steamed window, scuttling for her dress.

"Hey, nowww," came the drawled response. "Ain't no need..."

"Shut 'em off or I shoot 'em out. The next rounds are through the windshield."

"We got shotguns in here, you asshole!" But the headlights went out.

"You'll never get to use 'em." I had never been so coldly, killing furious in my life. "Back out of here. Now."

Heard them muttering. Didn't care. They were already dead. All that remained was the formality of dying. "Aw right!" An aggrieved redneck whine. Backup lights went on. "But this here is a public Goddamn road an' you're blockin' it."

"You leave and I'll leave and you can have the damn road."

The pickup ground backwards out of sight. One final remark – had to have one to save face – drifted through the humid twilight: "Must be *some* piece of ass, you ready to kill for it."

I pulled up and belted my pants, ears strained to the sound of the truck in case they stopped. They might get their Cracker danders up. In the dark with shotguns, two on one, they'd have the edge. But the truck went onto San Pablo, tires on pavement, then through the gears and away.

Time to get out of here before they changed their mind and came back. I stuck the Colt in my belt, not bothering with my shirt. Backed the Barracuda around. Couldn't bear to look directly at Glenda in her unzipped dress, one bare knee tucked against her breasts, hair in disarray. In dashboard lights her eyes were enormous and fixed.

I made the road trying to look everywhere at once, and floored it. No pickup was going to catch the Barracuda. I took back roads toward the city before heading east in brooding silence from the other side of the car. Knew we couldn't show up at home like this. I cut off on a road remembered from high school. Had to stop somewhere to pee. Parked on top of Harvey Hill where you could see traffic coming for miles from either direction.

"I didn't know Florida had any hills this tall." Her first words since the possum-hunters showed up.

"This is the only one I know. Harvey Hill. Be right back."

When I was back in the car she gave a kind of laugh. "Men have all the advantages that way."

"You can leave the door open and go behind it. I won't look."

She laughed with a little more feeling. "Too late. You've already seen everything I got."

I took her hand. "I love you."

"I was scared to death back there, Ish."

"Just possum hunters. Probably half-drunk on 'shine. They were scared too."

"No wonder!" She squeezed my hand. "You moved so damn fast! And your voice! I got chills. You always pack a gun?"

"If you ever need one, it's usually too late to go home and get it." I kissed her hand. "That wasn't the kind of chills I meant for you to have."

She was gazing out the windshield again. "I hate being a failure as a woman."

"What the *hell* are you talking about?"

"You know what I'm talking about."

"We were interrupted. That's all."

"But before that, I couldn't – you know."

"We're neither one teenagers anymore making out in a car. That damn gas tank bonking every time I..."

"Oh god!" She buried her face in her hands. "I wanted your homecoming to be the sweetest thing, and I ruined it completely."

I pulled her hands away from her face and forced her to look at me. "Listen to me: you know what the most important thing is that happened tonight? For me?"

"What?"

"You said you love me."

"Oh, Ish. I *do* love you. I even tried not to for a long time. But I do. And now it's just ruined."

I was exasperated. "Nothing is ruined." I kissed her. She was inert for a long heartbeat and then kissed back. We snuggled across the bucket seats without the towel. We kissed and touched until she pulled back gently. Her lips curved up.

"I just have to say this." I heard a return of life and humor. "I absolutely know you're glad to see me." She squeezed my resurgent erection. "So can you put the pistol in your belt away? I know it's not the classic Mae West line, but the metal hurts my boobs."

145

We were both laughing when I came back into her arms from tucking the Colt away. I kissed her nipples through her dress to apologize. They hardened instantly. When my fingers worked under her bunched-up hem she was soaking wet. "I told you it was going to be okay." I scrunched down, raised her legs and put my mouth against her feather-soft pubic thatch. Her fingers laced in my hair. Her hips began a slow, intense tidal roll. I didn't know if it was my pulse booming or hers, as she clamped her inner thighs against my ears.

She came with a galvanic shudder, pressing her Mons against my upper lip so hard I knew it would re-bruise atop the one left by the little blonde from Brittany. Her whole body seemed to melt around me. Then she jerked with alarm. "Oh, my *God!*"

I opened my eyes to blinding white headlights – again – and pushed upright. Into the beam of a big flashlight behind which an official-sounding voice was saying: "Are you all right, Ma'am ... Oh, I'm *terribly* sorry, Sir!" The flashlight beam was snatched away. Between high beams behind and the rising moon I made out a Florida State Trooper by the door. He actually tipped his Stetson. "My apologies, Sir. I thought the lady might be stranded alone out here..."

"Thanks. But we're fine." I felt her moisture on my lips and chin.

"So I see," he said dryly. He saw plenty before he diverted the flashlight. "May I suggest getting a room?"

"Same thing my father told me."

"Wise man. Y'all take care now." And he was gone.

"Are you okay?" I asked her.

"I sure *was* – for about a second." She shook her head. "I don't know what to say, Ish. We've wasted all the time I have. I'm at an Arts Council meeting, just so you know."

"We haven't wasted a minute, far as I'm concerned."

"But what about you? A man gets so *frustrated* when he's – uh – when he can't..." I had no idea then how cruelly her asshole husband had conditioned her to feel guilty for his failures to perform. I took her back in my arms.

"Will you relax?"

"I'm such a failure as a woman!"

"And knock that off." I felt a laugh building inside. It escaped. "This isn't you. This is Fate, making fun of me. Offering with one hand, taking away with the other. Like I got drafted just when book royalties were rolling in and things were going good at the newspaper." I didn't mention rushing back to Paris too late, the woman already gone whose loving made me adult enough to handle this crazy night. "You honest to God love me?"

"God help me," she said. "Honest to God I do."

"Then the rest will work out – however it works out."

"God, I don't want to leave you! But..."

 But she had to get home to face her life. I released her and keyed the ignition. "I know an all-night gas station that keeps clean restrooms. We can get cleaned up."

She rearranged her dress. "Good," she said briskly. "I kept my panties and bra in my handbag so they'd be clean when I went home. I had this crazy idea..."

I was laughing with open delight that she had arrived stripped for action. So to speak. "Nothing crazy about your idea. You got to admit, though, this has been some first date."

She jabbed me lightly. "Are *you* okay? Truly?"

"Finer that frog's hair."

She broke out laughing too. "I love you, you nut!"

I took a huge breath and let it out. "And I love you."

"Somehow, someway, we're gonna try this again before you leave," she said. "But I will never, ever forget Harvey Hill."

# Chapter 23:
# Sad Love Letter,
# Unsent

SHE DID NOT SEND THE SAD LOVE LETTER she wrote after the events described below. She gave it to me after a lot more water under the bridge. I found it fifty years later in a Rubbermaid tub full of notes, manuscripts and correspondence from a life lived on paper. The ink was faded. The words were fresh, as if sadness has no shelf life. How did Faulkner phrase it? The past is not dead. It isn't even the past.

*Dear Ish,*

*Although you have said goodbye, not shalom – not wait for me – but goodbye, I still think of you constantly. A song, a scene, a wisp of smoke from a passing pipe sends me into melancholy daydreams. Nothing seems to be able to stop the memories, the hopeless wishes, indeed the fantasies, from shouldering their way through whatever I am doing or saying or thinking.*

*Sometimes I am in Paris with you, walking down the Champs, or in a cozy café drinking something warm and sweet; sometimes – many times, and I can't explain it – we are in London, hatted and coated snugly against the chill dampness. At times we are walking in a sun-spattered forest and I*

*breathe deeply to savor the freshness of the air.*
*Sometimes we are sitting before a fire. I am very*
*quiet while you read or work and I would not*
*disturb you for any but the utmost emergency.*
*So many times you spoke of things that might have*
*been. These are some of the things my dreams are*
*made of. Even now ...*

She had been unable to find another free evening after our first chaotic date when I was home on annual leave. Best she could do was a poignant lunch. I was committed to another year of military servitude far away. She said she dreaded my departure. I felt empty when I left her, a feeling too familiar from my lost love in Paris. These heartaches at parting were something the matriarch never told me about in her warnings against women.

Glenda's devotion had finally softened the after-all romantic heart of the matriarch, usually suspicious of women interested in me. My mother already was on her side. Unknown to me, the women in my life hatched a plot: she would leave her husband, child and job and follow me Northwest. My mother would come with her, two women who loved me driving my Barracuda cross-country. The matriarch would ensure my favorite uncle, a big wheel in Southern politics, got my mother's Post Office transfer expedited to a Washington city. Meanwhile she could waitress while Glenda found an art-studio job. But best-laid plans of Venusians, as well as mice and men, gang aft aglay.

I was sequestered in the rainy Northwest, absent for the storm of Southern Gothic melodrama that burst in Florida. She planned her escape like a convict because her domineering husband treated her like one. Fifty years ago I had never heard of abused-wife syndrome or whatever it's called.

He had acquired a boat for commercial fishing in South Florida. Her presence aboard was required when she could get off work. She told him she had to drive to town for supplies, left the car and took a bus home to pack and flee.

He caught up with her at home, packing. Like a canny warden he had smelled something brewing. Did she leave the car keys for him? Did he have spares? Hot-wire the car? Anyway, he caught her. She never told me what he did when he caught her. But he forced confession of her putative road trip – and naming of her co-conspirators.

Then he made what should have been a fatal mistake.

He drove her, trembling and terrified, to my beach home to raise hell about them helping her. He was lucky. First because my mother was at work slinging mail bags. She was perfectly capable of beating him to death with her bare hands for hurting a woman who loved me. The second lucky break was due to the matriarch's unwavering iron code of conduct. Which takes explaining.

When he literally dragged his cowed wife into our living room to confront the matriarch, it was now my old man's bedroom. One leg gone, he sat ignored in his wheelchair. The asshole had no conception his life hung by the proverbial thread. He stormed at the matriarch for aiding his wife and announced she had recanted her travel plans with my mother. Had forsworn anything more to do with me. He was there to put my family on notice to back off.

"Let her speak." I can hear the coldness in the matriarch's voice without having been there. A rum-runner chieftain's girl before she married a stronger and meaner man, blowhards left her contemptuous.

The old man sat boiling. He had a soft spot for Glenda. She painted him a sad clown picture after his surgery. He had permanently injured better men with his fists. The old 1911 Colt tucked in his wheelchair saw him through gunfights he walked away from but enemies did not. Most often told tale of his power was about an armed gangster in a barbershop ranting because the old man married his boss's squeeze, saying he would punish such insolence. Not knowing who slept in the next chair under a hot Turkish face towel. The barber whipped the towel away like a conjurer. The old man grumbled awake and sat up. The hoodlum ... fainted. The old man eyed the prostrate guy with the shoulder holster: *What the hell's wrong with him?* The barbershop exploded with laughter.

But while the old man was titular head, the matriarch governed our family. No violence at home without her command. He waited, coiled like a broken-back old rattlesnake.

"Let her speak," the matriarch repeated.

The idiot shoved his diminished wife. "Say it!" Never looking up, she said it: no road trip, no more contact with me, no separation from him, no divorce.

"Are you sure?" the matriarch said. "This is your decision?" Perhaps not the exact words. But fifty years later I still can hear that diamond-cutting tone.

"Yes," Glenda said humbly, eyes down.

When she described the scene later, the matriarch told me the idiot *preened*. His preening almost tipped her decision to unleash the old man. But her iron code held.

Glenda twice denied her favorite grandson. And betrayed the matriarch, for trusting this woman with my affections. The matriarch gave no Biblical third chance. "So be it," she told me flatly. "Forget her."

I was astonished by the road trip the women who loved me had cooked up. Incredulous Glenda crawled before my old man and the matriarch, safest place on earth she could be. That had to mean I was just a fling despite her vows of love. Which hurt badly as anything I can remember.

Glenda had a diametrically opposed version of the incident: that she had to protect that nice old couple from her brutal keeper. She wrote to explain that she lied to save them, of course she loved me. I followed the matriarch's decree and said goodbye. The letter she gave me later was proof that in her heart of hearts no goodbye was final. The Southern Gothic storm was just a blip in our love affair. I kept it as evidence, given circumstances preceding its composing, I would never understand women.

Intermezzo: *noun; a movement coming between the major sections of an extended musical work (such as an opera).*

# Chapter 24:
# Second Intermezzo –
# Distractions

*From 1966 Army notes in the Pacific Northwest after the bizarre confrontation between my family and an angry cuckold. I still pined for my lost Paris love, and was in shock about what happened in Florida with Glenda. So I distracted myself with observations about the Northwest – usually involving women.*

## The GI's Tale

WE HERE IN THE STATESIDE ARMY this Vietnam era have been reduced all the way back to Chaucer, sitting on drawn-up foot lockers in a rough circle as before a fire in an ancient inn, passing an illicit jug of Irish whiskey from hand to hand, each of us in turn telling his tale.

Some of them accuse me of trying out story plots and dialogue on them for my writing, under the guise of recounting actual experiences. I.Z., who knows me better than the rest, says I just rearrange the truth for more dramatic impact and read all sorts of things not actually present into situations we have seen.

I think he still is smarting a little because I read the Portland whore correctly and he did not. He thought she was cute and waved at her through a restaurant window as we passed. She immediately jumped up from the counter and ran outside to ask where he knew her from. He suavely said he didn't know her, but would like to.

She smiled and without further ado joined us in our walk through the cold night rain. She asked him where he worked and he said you don't want to know, a conditioned response for draftees in the flower-child years. He asked her where she worked and she ducked her head and said *you* don't want to know, which he found charming. But told me all I needed to know.

They hit it off well, I.Z. leaning solicitously toward her short curvy figure like some avuncular caricature in his white London Fog raincoat, New England penny loafers and trademark shades on a dark winter night. I drew him aside and said I will leave you to it, don't let her fish you. That was our term for being taken advantage of by hookers. He thought I was wrong. But I wasn't. He solved his embarrassment for being wrong in his inimitable way: he screwed her on my bed in the double room we shared on our three-day pass. So whenever you tell *this* story, he said with an evil grin, I can always top it: you came in too drunk to notice and went right to sleep in it.

## Interlude Lounge

It was a quiet little Portland bar, dim, and the drinks were good. It seemed to draw much of its trade from hotel patrons who walked in from the connecting lobby door amid a brief blaze of lights from the lobby chandelier.

A woman, nicely dressed, sat on a bar stool, sipping her tall drink. Her back was erect as a drill sergeant. Most men who came through the door gave her the quick–once over, saw her aloofness, and gave her a miss. Not this guy. Suave in his Navy blazer with a phony crest, gray slacks and loafers that almost glowed in the dark he slid right in beside her with a toothy smile.

Her head inclined approximately one millimeter.

He fiddled with the coaster the bartender put down on the way to get his drink. Then he picked it up and read the words.

"These are sayings from Poor Richard's Almanac." He had the studied, mellow tones of a radio broadcaster, and made it sound like a pronouncement.

"How nice," she said softly. "I hadn't noticed."

"Yep, sure are! Look, here's one: 'three can keep a secret if two of them are dead,' what do you think about that?"

"Interesting observation."

She tilted her glass and drank elegantly. Her every movement was elegant. More than one set of male eyes watched those movements more or less covertly. He thought he was making headway. You could almost see his chest puff.

"Benjamin Franklin, you know," he said.

"Excuse me?"

"Benjamin Franklin," he confided. "One of our Founding Fathers. He was Poor Richard, did you know that?"

She tipped off the rest of her drink and stood in one smooth motion. "Yes," she said. "I did know that."

The lobby door swallowed her before his lips could unsmile enough to cover his teeth. The bartender put his drink down on the coaster.

"Say," the man in the blazer said, "couldn't we get a little music in this place?"

## The Frankness of Frankie

So I took the new guy to headquarters to introduce him around and of course the first person we saw was Frankie at her secretarial post out front. She was a cute brunette with wide candid brown eyes and a nice figure. Since skirt hems were migrating upwards, hers ended a couple inches above quite-nice knees. Not that I noticed or anything.

The first time I met her she said *you can turn off the charm, I'm getting married tomorrow*. After I wrote for the fort newspaper awhile she baldly asked why I was so sarcastic and cynical when I wrote about the Army. I am? Frankie: *It's so obvious*. Only to her; she kept you on your toes – or back on your heels. The new guy's tongue wasn't exactly hanging out but close – he'd just spent a year in the Nam. I said she's cute all right but unavailable.

She fixed me with those wide absolutely candid eyes. "Baloney," she said.

"Baloney that you're cute or that you're unavailable," I shot back, thinking myself clever.

"Baloney I'm not available." Her gaze never wavered.

"But I got here one day too late," I said, back-peddling.

"No," she said. "You didn't. You're not too late." She left it at that, watching me for my reaction. My boss the major saved me. He came bustling out of the inner offices – he always bustled – and crooked a finger. *We have to go right now* he said. The commanding general was waiting; some PR crisis looming. I never welcomed one of his peremptory summonses more gladly.

But Frankie protested. "You're not taking him away right now are you?"

"Yes, the general needs us," and that was that.

But as I left she gave me one of those Mona Lisa smiles some women perfect before they get out of high school. Her eyes were still wide and candid, waiting for me to say something. But I didn't. I just had my bluff called in irrevocable fashion – and hadn't even known it *was* a bluff. Only belatedly noticed she wasn't wearing her engagement ring. "What's up with Frankie?" I asked the all-knowing major. "She seemed ... strange ... today."

"Ah, the marriage fell through," he said dismissively. "She'll get over it."

Damn; should have known she wasn't putting me on. Few women matched their name as well as Frankie, candid about everything. Her razor wit – like her remark about my writing – could be devastating. A wit to which no doubt she would subject me if I went back to headquarters anytime soon. I had absolutely no idea what to do.

159

# Chapter 25:
# Greek to Her

TACOMA WAS A GI TOWN, no question, during the Vietnam conflict. Olympia was closer to Fort Lewis, but Olympia was an uptight little state capital that rolled its sidewalks up at dark.

Tacoma came alive at night, topless joints and prostitutes, GIs in cheap PX clothing on the prowl for excitement. Esmerelda's was legendary for the trouble you could get into within its beer-soaked confines. I was once washing up in the Greyhound bus station's restroom while a soldier from the Fourth Division who had overindulged hugged a toilet in one of the stalls, and gave it all back in violent spasms to the city's sewers.

When he finally stumbled out of the stall, pale and shaken, he said to his buddy, "We are shipping to Vietnam day after tomorrow and have a good chance of getting killed. And the last memory I will have of the country I supposedly am fighting for will be Esmerelda's."

"That or the Greyhound bus station," said his unsympathetic buddy. "C'mon, let's go get a drink to settle your stomach. The Mirror Room is hopping."

The Mirror Room, a legendary watering hole in the basement of a local hotel, featured a higher class of skin show than Esmerelda's. Dancers who could actually dance, and from time to time did a pretty good imitation of classic burley-cue fan-dancing and stripping routines. Plus the women were really good-looking. Hand-selected – urban legend said throat-selected – by another local legend. None of us GIs knew about the man behind the curtain. Newspapers reporting on him always appended the description "well-known nightlife figure." Lawsuit-proof code for hoodlum.

Over a decade later, long after honorable discharge, after my faded field jacket no longer zipped, after my last pair of combat boots wore out in grass-mowing, I came to know a lot about this nightlife figure. My writing career had taken a wrong turning. I was a bureaucrat employed by his mortal enemy, the Liquor Control Board. Urban legend was now matter-of-fact grist for confidential enforcement briefings.

To get a job with his "talent agency" that supplied dancers to joints secretly owned by the mob, women had to furnish him a satisfactory oral-sex experience as proof of talent. Purely business, not lechery: easily weeded out undercover cops. The life agreed with him because he lived to a ripe old age.

As the supposed media expert I was consulted when an antic female reporter volunteered her throat for undercover work. She could dance, had a good figure and fairly pulsated with sexual energy. She was not dissuaded by the prospect that public-trial testimony would reveal she sucked off the aging hood to get inside the organization. She wanted on-the-job plainclothes security should things go south, but the risk – and the exposure – was worth a guaranteed exclusive when indictments were filed. The enforcement chief thought it tickled an exhibitionist streak in her; she casually mentioned a sexy book she might write.

Her offer was tempting. Undercover cops were out for the assignment because the defense would plead entrapment, never mind public humiliation for the female cop who provided oral. As working media with her own agenda, she could not be construed an "agent of the police" under entrapment law. The chief would happily nail the old crook but was worried about unintended consequences. So he called me for a consult. My immediate recommendation was drop the idea. Don't know if that tipped the decision but the plan was scrapped.

Thing is, the plan would have worked if she stayed the course. I had zero doubt she would. I knew her. Sexual adventure and exhibitionism and a tell-all book was an irresistible triple whammy. I had wondered what she saw in the stodgy, stick-in-the-mud, often-stuttering reporter she married. One of the most church-going, credulous men to ever man a newspaper typewriter, repeatedly amazed at the wickedness he covered.

His wife had vowed to our chief that he was and would be in the dark until she broke the story. The chief was skeptical. I was not. It was my job to know the media's tangled alliances and hot buttons; I was good at my job. He loved her desperately. She'd keep him in the dark all right. But I pictured his face when the news hit. Pictured cruel newsroom humor with which I was more than familiar. Felt in my gut the sick helpless twist he would feel. Didn't offer my veto for professional reasons but for the peace of my own soul.

As strait-laced as her husband was, he was a competent reporter with good sources. Before a year passed he asked me in his slow cautious stammer about a rumor a newspaperwoman had sucked off the old gangster to get inside the mob. Gave me deep satisfaction to tell him the rumor was crap.

But when I was a GI frequenting the Mirror Room in a rain-logged GI town, all that was the unknowable future. I was just another GI at loose ends, mourning lost loves and looking for a good time to ease the emptiness. Mirror Room drinks were okay, the mirrors were cool, the hectic strobe of black lighting hallucinatory and the bodies very easy on the eyes. You could see them close-up if you bought a dancer a drink between sets. Any further delights were open to negotiation.

Another thing I didn't know was the Mirror Room was managed by the well-known nightlife figure's sister, who had first call on her brother's best-looking dancers. If the girls had kids but no husband – a lot of them did – the sister ran a night-care center, if you will, for offspring. The girls could dance and negotiate in perfect trust their children were safe with a house mother, a reliable older performer off the floor for whatever reason, who had the mob's tough guys on call. Brutal exes and stalkers who did not entertain a death wish left children in Mirror Room night-care strictly alone. An arrangement that earned grudging respect from cops, who hate domestic calls. It made for a well-organized establishment with happy employees who worked hard to keep the customers happy.

All I knew as a young lonely GI was the face – the lovely bodies too – of the franchise. Like many another GI, I entertained a secret hope of finding a dancer not only lovely and agreeable but intelligent enough for a real conversation when they came around the tables. My affection centered briefly on a tall lithe blonde stripper with the stage-name Electra. Her skimpy costume included little colored lights sewn in strategic spots. She said these were cleverly powered by invisible batteries hidden God alone knows where. For her finale, the black lighting would cease its frenetic flicker. The room would go almost pitch-dark. All eyes focused on the bright hallucination-inducing jiggle of her Christmas lights. It was a fine finale to her strip. Then she'd come around to accept drinks, tips and accolades.

In high school, a course I really liked was about Greek tragedians. I saw Greek symbology in her chosen name. Couldn't wait to find out if it was intentional. "So, Electra," I said casually one night between sets, "does your name stand for anything? Like, are you looking for a father figure?"

"It *does* stand for something," she said with a saucy wink. "As for older men, some of them are pretty cool. Especially the ones with money! But you're not an old man, so why the curiosity?"

"I just thought Electra might be indicating your preference."

I could almost see the wheels go round in that pretty head as she tried to figure out what I was talking about. She pursed those lovely lips which – unknown to me – had satisfied the famous nightlife figure of her oral skills. She sipped her whiskey sour, which was probably cloudy iced tea so she wouldn't get too soused to dance. She thought about it.

"I'm a student of the dance," she said finally. "I chose Electra to honor Gypsy Rose Lee's understudy. That was her understudy's stage name, Electra, and I got the idea about the lights from her. Kind of a classic reference, you know?"

I was laughing at myself. She smiled brightly, having made the customer happy. "I guess there are all kinds of classics if you know where to look," I said.

*Sometimes life is merely a matter of coffee*
*and whatever intimacy a cup of coffee affords.*
-Richard Brautigan

# Chapter 26:
# Irish Eyes in Portland, 1966

SHE DIDN'T BELIEVE I was a writer.

In those long-gone days it seemed being a writer was something sexy and men said they were writers as a way to score with women. I met her in The Embers in Portland, Oregon. I was on a three-day pass from the Army. I was still very young toward women, gun-shy after a near-disastrous affair with a married woman. The liquid courage of bourbon propped me up, and I asked almost all the unattached girls to dance. I asked her friend. When we came back to her table, she challenged me about why I didn't ask her first. Sober, I would have panicked. But bourbon answered for me with a courtly bow and offer to mend the oversight immediately. When I led her to the floor she fitted in my arms best of all the women I danced with that night. After that, I danced with only her.

I called her Irish right away.

It might have been the eyes, luminous and lovely in the subdued nightclub lighting. It might have been a vagrant memory that Mike Hammer called a girl Irish in one of those hard-boiled Mickey Spillane detective stories I was reading. She liked the name. And she liked me. I moved to her table.

She didn't believe I was a writer. I wasn't about to tell her I was in the middle of my two-year draftee hitch in the Army. It was not cool to be a GI in the flower-child and Vietnam era. Come back to my hotel room if you don't believe me I said, and I will show you my manuscripts. She had a merry laugh that made her eyes sparkle even more. Nice try, she said. I hadn't meant that at all. Well, maybe I had.

When the lights came up at closing time she left with her friends, with a promise to call me the next day. They lived across the Columbia River in Washington State. The other side of the moon if you didn't have a car. I wandered back to my hotel, disconsolate and alone. This was unsurprising. With one amazing exception in Paris it was how I always returned from such forays. I knew she wasn't going to call me.

But she did. She called me from the hotel lobby. She had taken a bus across the river to see me because her friend with the car had to work. She came straight up to my room, marching purposefully, to call my bluff. In those days a guest in a good hotel could always get the use of a typewriter. I had a big office model to work on, with half a novel scattered all around. I had been pounding away on Chapter 27 when she called. My editor at Doubleday was urging me not to let momentum from sales of my first novel die just because I was stuck in the military.

She handled the typewritten pages almost reverently. She sat in front of the big Royal typewriter and played with the carriage return, reading the interrupted last line I had typed. So you really are a writer she said. I leaned toward her. She stood up into my arms. It was a long, tender kiss. My blood was drumming when she broke for air. Her color was high and her eyes sleepy. By god, I was going to get laid if I could just figure out what to do next. But I hesitated too long.

Long enough for her to say those awful words: "You're so sweet." How could I fondle her breasts then? I didn't think it would be sweet. I was *extremely* young toward women. She eased out of my embrace and examined my battered old B-4 bag, bedecked with torn and stained travel tags, European and U.S. "My, you do travel a lot, don't you?" she said wistfully. "I've always wanted to travel."

My head was spinning slightly. I had a mild hangover. She smiled at me and said something like poor you, and came back into my arms. We kissed some more. Long, gentle kisses that began to heat up. I felt the snare drums in my blood begin their tattoo again. My hands slipped down her back ... She leaned back and put her fingers to my lips. "No. There will be other girls, in other towns."

Not with my luck I wanted to grumble. But she took my silence for assent.

"We can't do this," she said. "You're not looking for permanence. For a" – she hesitated – "wife. Are you?"

That cooled my blood right down. A few sweet kisses and we were talking wedding bells? Hell, I thought this was the era of the Pill and free love. Couldn't we wait to select bridesmaids until after I got laid? But of course I couldn't just out and say that, or anything like that. It would hardly qualify as sweet, would it?

So we held each other and talked. Or she talked. And I listened. The afternoon wore on. I learned about her Dutch ex-husband, and her Greek lover, and the several men since. One of them she had seen walking on the sidewalk in front of this very hotel when she had a car that was running, and she just pulled over and picked him up. She spent the weekend in bed with him. The kind of stories you tell somebody you happen to sit next to on an airplane and know you will never see again. My unworthy, unsweet thought was what the hell's wrong with one more, then?

She fixed me with those lovely eyes. "There's something I must tell you."

Uh oh.

"I'm cold," she said.

I blinked and looked around. She half-laughed. "Not like that, silly. Your arms are warm." She sobered. "I mean I don't like sex."

What the hell was there to say to that?

She said after her last "experience" when she still failed to achieve the elusive orgasm, she decided to just give sex up. Just like that, like she was talking about going on a diet. I was far too young toward women to suggest I might be able to help her accomplish what this coterie of others had not. And forever too young to not give a damn.

I suddenly felt the need for fresh air. She agreed. We walked rain-swept downtown streets arm in arm, heads together. Anyone would have thought us lovers. So much for appearances. She loved to pause and gaze at travel-agency posters in the windows. She yearned to travel abroad, and intended to.

We went into a cafe for coffee and sat a long time, smiling at each other over shared intimacies. It felt comfortable and edgy all in one. She liked the fact I smoked a pipe. "You should buy a pipe to commemorate our day." She talked like that. Maybe she wanted to be a writer too. Though she never mentioned it. "Or to commemorate Portland," she added. "You could have a pipe for every city. Every girl … " Her voice caught slightly. Then she forged ahead. "Every time you smoked your pipe, you'd think about that city."

Before too long she had to go. She worked a swing-shift somewhere across the river. Partings are never easy. The bus was already waiting when we got to the corner. Her lovely calves flashed beneath her dark raincoat as she ran to catch it. She turned at the door and called something out to me, lost in the swish of passing tires.

Then she was gone.

A road not taken. But I still have my Portland pipe, Irish.

# Chapter 27:
# AKA Miss Walter Mitty,
# Part One

WORDS FROM a 1967 army notebook kept for future use by a 23-year-old certain of his destiny as a great writer: *One of the best things about making E-5 within twenty months of being a raw recruit in Basic Training is that there is a Top Five club right across the street from Headquarters Company, decent food and cheap drinks and out-of-the-way tables where I can sit and write and listen to the band music.*

"So studious," a husky feminine voice said at my shoulder one night. "Going to school while still in the Army? Very industrious. But you should put up your homework and live a little." The W's had a V sound, the V's a hint of F; German.

*She said her name was Giselle and offered her hand. If I had to be interrupted in the middle of a paragraph, she was worth it. Long dark hair, lustrous eyes in the dim club lighting, curvy and compact; a teasing little smile. But I have a horror at being thought a student – a strong personal aversion hard to put into words. So I told her the improbable truth: I am a writer ...*

She accepted this without a blink and said perhaps I could write her life story. Not the first time I heard this in the Army. For instance the sad old colonel sidetracked to garrison command in France, who told how his promising career went off the rails in Arabia. As a military attaché, he made the mistake of unpopular recommendations concerning control of desert oil fields. Covert Middle East power plays derailed the career of a top West Point graduate for his prescience. Could have been a hell of a story. He wanted me to write it. But I left France before he did.

*The band struck up a slow moody tune and some guy touched her elbow and invited her to dance. She immediately said she had promised this dance to me, bent to my ear and murmured don't make a liar of me. So I danced with her. As if I already had agreed to be her biographer, she began her life story ...*

A teenage model for Christian Dior in Paris making $950 a week, traveling for shoots to Spain, Italy, and Egypt. Married at fifteen to a GI and lost five children over the course of five years because her husband waited until she was six months pregnant each time and then kicked her in the stomach. Separated from him finally when she was pregnant a sixth time with her son Ernest. And that was just the first waltz.

*When we walked back to my table she asked me why I wasn't writing this down. Well, what the hell? Her tale so far had given me an idea for a short story that I could place in Florida. I took out my notebook and wrote. She ... told me she had been a WAC E-5 and just got out of the Army, which was why she was at the Top Five Club. I didn't follow the logic, but let it go. Another waltz began and she said you must keep dancing with me so those others will leave me alone. I didn't see any others beating a path to the table but again, what the hell? So we danced.*

174

Her next tale: she had gone hunting and killed a black bear that weighed 605 pounds. That sounds like a big black bear I said. She didn't hear the skepticism. Assured me she had enough gun: a .300 Holland and Holland double rifle she purchased in England with her proceeds from modeling. Double rifles by that fine old firm cost as much as a modest family home. But it was her story and I withheld comment.

*She was a marvelous dancer ... wanted to know if I liked her perfume ... told me with a complex smile that it was Tigress, selected because it fits her personality. Then she wanted to know if I was a horseman and had I ever been to Paris. I said I have been on horses and yes. Had I ever ridden from the stables in Paris? No? A pity.*

She no longer demanded I take notes, just her phone number. She said she had a demanding job, no time for romance, but call tomorrow she would take me to lunch. I doubted it, but it was a slow day so I called.

*Her story grew. She thought I was studying because she is always studying; she has studied in Peru, at Bremerton, at the University of Syracuse. Did I read German? No? Too bad, because the German version of Lady Chatterley's Lover is so much more graphic. "The English took out half." She is a fan of Pearl Buck as far as writers go. She owns a Husky pup. Since I mentioned I lived in Florida, she told me she would be in Florida in June "to look at two Arabian horses there I own."*

She said she would be late for lunch but she was right on time in a huge dark Chrysler, and blew the horn. Two MPs stopped to see if they could put the make on her. "Here's my boyfriend now," she said. Seeing the crossed pistols I still wore on my Class As, they said "sorry Sarge," and left.

*She drove fast and erratically but with a sure hand. I was able to examine her at leisure. Her eyes were blue, very pale and luminous, with small very black pupils. She had high sculpted cheekbones, fine flesh taut over the delicate structure of her face, a blade-straight nose and that ink-dark hair, either natural or bottled, piled up in some kind of twist. Her legs beneath a slim skirt were good, shapely and easy to look at. Her breasts were not large but proportional to her five-foot-three inch frame.*

She stopped at Madigan Army Hospital, said she had to get an inoculation for overseas. Madigan meant she had a military connection more concrete than being a former WAC. She walked smoothly and naturally on self-described 3 1/2-inch heels, shoulders back, a subtle roll to her snug hips. Shape, hair, eyes – especially walk – she could be almost Glenda's twin. I tamped that thought away. we walked what seemed like miles of corridors through the sick, the injured and the pregnant.

*All that remains is a blur of blue hospital garments and a succession of men's faces turning to follow her with their eyes. She took my arm, saying she did not want to slip on the glossy, wax-slippery floors. I had one of those errant thoughts: why do they wax hospital floors? We found the office she needed and she got her shot – for some reason she insisted I come into the room with her – and when we started back she just took my hand and held it as we drifted through the clamoring, milling crowds.*

Her small private smile was explained when we got back to her car: she was dating a Madigan doctor. By now the hospital grapevine would advise him she was holding hands with a big MP. I was irritated to be put on display but said nothing.

*We proceeded off-post to a small café that looked sterile from outside but was like stepping into Germany inside, complete to small racks of Hirsch horns on the walls ... She said the Wiener schnitzel was good and it was. She said the soup entrée was terrible and she was right. She dosed her coffee with surreal amounts of cream and sugar and ate as if starved. My magic metabolism that clogs up the minute a girl smiles at me was working, because she was giving me the flirty eyes and the smiles and acting like she was very happy in my company ... she said if I didn't eat she would feed me, and suited action to words, leaning across with forkful after forkful ...*

The spontaneity of the gesture felt intimate. Only later writing it all down did I wonder if it was genuine or affected.

*She drove back to the fort ... and seemed to relish cutting people off on the interstate, forcing them to brake or swerve. Then she blew through the fort as if invisible to MP patrols. Casually mentioned her three sports-car crowns on the European circuit, driving a Jag, which was a lot more fun than this big American boat, but don't look so worried, I won't kill us ...*

I was worried but she missed her guess. She was swooping across Basic Training areas with jogging columns of troops. I could see some dog-tired recruit, detailed out on road guard, more afraid of his shouting drill sergeant than traffic, blundering in front of her. She avoided such horrors without effort and parked outside my office, turned those pale shining eyes on me and announced we now had a date later in the week.

*I pulled her closer across the seat and hurt the arm she'd had the shot in and realized it when she winced but didn't pull away. I traced my fingers along her finely molded lips and when I bent to kiss her she was waiting with parted lips. I kissed her very lightly and her tongue found mine and that went on for a sweet moment and then we broke for air, and she was gazing at me as if trying to see behind my eyes. She took my hand in both hers. I was already very late returning and was afraid she would feel my impatience and evidently she did, but her mind-reading failed. She put fingers to my lips quickly. "There is a time for everything with us," she said. "Everything. But not now. Not here. I have an assignment tonight."*

"Call it off," I said.

She said she couldn't. Asked me to call her later. I called at 7:30 pm. She sounded different – subdued, bellicose – said she had a lot to do. Didn't know if she could keep our date, which irritated me because it had been her idea. Give me a ring when you're free I said. I don't call guys she said. Now I really was irritated. I'm not just some guy I said.

*"I still don't call guys, not even General Pierce. I don't have to run after men. I never have. You call me."*

*"And just keep calling and calling," I said. "Is that the game?"*

*She heard the irritation. "It's traditional," she said in a conciliatory tone. "The boy must call the girl."*

In a way her words echoed instructions from my lost Paris love: *"A woman cannot say take me in your arms and love me. That is for the man to do."* But it sounded more like the high school silliness of call me/don't call me I avoided by never having a teenage girlfriend.

Before she hung up she said she'd meet me at the club tomorrow night at eight. But at eight I was in Seattle with one of my news staff, guarding his bug-eyed Sprite by a fireplug while he ran into a theater to reserve two seats for his upcoming heavy date. Gigi was already consigned to my growing list of near-misses.

# Chapter 28:
# AKA Miss Walter Mitty,
# Part Two

THE WEEK AFTER I STOOD GIGI UP, I had a month to serve on my two-year sentence. I would be going home to face who knew what. Mainly an aborted love affair with a married woman not ready to concede it was over, while the matriarch absolutely opposed resumption. The window was closing for adventures I had – and almost had – in the Army. So when our Saturday shift ended and the Army weekend began, I called Gigi. My notebook: *She ... immediately said she was coming to get me for lunch, but needed to make another stop at the hospital. Once more I figured what the hell? Her officer boyfriend at the hospital wouldn't be able to get a short-timer sent to Vietnam, in King David's Biblical solution to a Uriah problem.*

She launched right into her continuing saga: her real name was Tatiana, a Mongol, heiress to a sweep of steppe and herd of ponies. She worked undercover for the Munich police and was instrumental in breaking a heroin ring. She took a ranging pistol shot along her right rib-cage but "got him" left-handed with her trusty .38, which she preferred to a .45 as "too big." After she was unmasked at trial, she was beaten so badly she was in the hospital a week, and assumed the Gigi alias. While she was being patched up, a visiting sheikh invited her to come see him in Arabia ...

*I was enjoying this now, over my infatuation. I had her pegged now. She was the first female Walter Mitty I ever encountered. I resolved to save all her tales for posterity. Then she threw me a curve-ball: her appointment was at the OB/GYN clinic. Suddenly the slight, tight bulge in her otherwise flat belly took on new meaning. Today she was wearing a loose bright-patterned yellow dress that hinted at maternity wear. "Are you bringing me to have our baby?" she said coyly.*

*"Not ours," I said. "Certainly not mine."*

*"Are you sure?" Her eyes sparkled with her delighted laughter and she was really having fun.*

*"One hundred percent." I couldn't help laughing.*

*"How can you be so sure?"*

*"Because, young lady," I said. "I have never been in bed with you." She shrugged as if that were a quibble and we went into the waiting room. I was the sole male present in a roomful of pregnant women. In my dress greens and eleven-dollar shades that I.Z. got me in the habit of wearing, I played it inscrutable … wandered into another room full of senior lifers who were talking about being on their third or fourth kid and complacent about the whole thing. I picked up an Outdoor Life and joined them until her exam was complete and she was ready to go …*

We ate at the main fort cafeteria. She stopped at the PX to shop for clothes for her two children. She did not look at infant wear. Then dropped me at my barracks to change into civilian clothing so she could take me on a date in Seattle. On the phone then she said her check had not come. She needed money for the beauty parlor to have her hair done before we went. I said hell I'll pay for your hair. She flared up, saying I insulted her. But she would see me at the club.

*She was on friendly terms with Steve, a portly NCO who worked nights as a waiter, and we chatted together that night. But she got restless and wanted to drive. Another mad dash, this time through Saturday traffic; she led me into a department store and homed in on the jewelry counter. She proposed an exchange of gifts ... something with my name engraved on it ... when I pointed out the store was trying to close, she blew up and raced me back to the fort, furious at my "pushing her ... "*

Back at the fort, like a chameleon, she entered another role entirely. Sat in the car talking. Said a car going slowly past in the company street was keeping her under surveillance. Suddenly we were rolling again, onto I-5. She really put her foot down for some fast and fancy driving before ducking into a Tacoma neighborhood and announcing with satisfaction, "We lost them." Professional driver? Who knows? But her driving was impressive.

*She pulled into a gas station and felt ostentatiously in her purse. I waited for her reminder that her mysterious check had not come and could I help out with gas. Instead she said she was just checking to make sure her .38 was within easy reach, handed me five dollars for Ethyl for the big Chrysler, and went to make a phone call. Before I bought the gas I frisked her purse. A female Walter Mitty on a boring Saturday night is entertainment. A female Walter Mitty with a .38 in her purse is something else. But there was no gun ...*

It was quite a night. She raced madly back to the fort and parked outside the MP Stockade. An MP sedan with bubblegum light flashing raced into the night. She instantly took off after it, followed some distance, then cut off and took me back to barracks. Best you not get involved, she said darkly. I am working with them and the FBI, you know, on a big heroin thing. Jesus H. Christ.

*I.Z. was on his bunk reading Camus, one of his favorite writers. He was curious: had I scored with the "clop broad?" He was a big fan of an old TV show, "Boston Blackie," which opened with a man walking dark cobblestone streets, hence clopping. He adapted it to his vocabulary to signify adventure. I told him no, but I had a strange tale to tell. Shit all your tales are strange this calls for drinks he said. So I loaned him my dress uniform blouse with E-5 rank on it; the Top Five Club never checked ID on a man in uniform with the minimum amount of rank. We walked across the street ...*

I launched my tale, waiting for his sardonic humor at being dragged all over the place by an unbalanced broad. But he hunched across the table and said watch your step and sounded serious. He had been in headquarters just yesterday and overheard the Post Sergeant Major and the MP Captain plotting a sting against a heroin operation centered around this club. "They pass the stuff when the lights go out for the black lighting on the dance floor," he said.

"Are you serious?"

"Shit, I'm never serious. But they sure were."

Which recalled what Steve the waiter told me about Gigi. That she first came to the club in the company of a notorious WAC scheduled to go out on a bad-conduct discharge. He was surprised the WAC braved the Top Five, curious about Gigi, then increasingly nervous when she engaged him in banter about being known for serving underage girls with GIs and wondering aloud if he might be up to other "naughtiness."

*It didn't take much imagination to write the scenario: a busted female soldier bringing in a ringer as part of some kind of plea deal for the Army to go easier on her. From there my imagination took wing: had she approached me in the first place because she pegged me as a drug connection? Or decided somebody as gullible as me would make good cover? I dismissed it all. No, she was Walter Mitty in an attractive package, that was all there was to it ...*

I.Z. for once did not accuse me of inventing a story line. We looked for suspicious transactions around the dance floor but saw none. I could write it one of two ways. The surprise about the heroin ring and ambiguity: whether she was Miss Mitty or an actual operative who talked too much. Or pure fiction with gun-battle climax. The real end was more pedestrian – and unpleasant.

*She called to say she needed groceries because the alleged check still had not come. She'd pay me back if I took her to the PX. We'd go shopping and then to a movie; her girlfriend would stay with her children. So they came to get me, the whole crowd. Her girlfriend was a pale slender blonde with bitter eyes and a cruel mouth who radiated protective hostility. Since I wasn't born yesterday, I thought ah, so that's the way it is ...*

The little boy was Gigi's image, sleek dark hair, fine facial features and nose, pale blue eyes. The little girl was dark-skinned. Her hair wasn't quite kinky but tried to;

Africa written plainly in her features. Interracial off-spring were already common in the military.

*It turned out the girlfriend expected me to just hand over money for groceries and they would leave. I said I misunderstood; I thought we were going grocery-shopping together. Her girlfriend cut her eyes at Gigi and her mouth twisted angrily. The silence stretched. Gigi tried to joke with her but she looked about to spit with rage. Gigi had a look I had never seen: trapped, harried, bullied. We need the groceries she pleaded – to her girlfriend, not me ...*

So we went to the smaller of the PXs. Her lover was in a thunderous sulk and refused to get out of the car. Gigi immediately threw a loud temper tantrum, shoppers turning to look while I tried to become invisible in place.

*At that precise moment, the small dark daughter, caught between the quarreling women, looked up at me with a beautiful smile and held up her hand for me to take and walked me into the grocery store. Her tiny hand was steady and confident in mine, as if she had studied me with her small logic and found me acceptable. The adult females followed, slashing each other with bitter sarcasm. Finally Gigi said, "Forget it, just forget it. I won't do it if I will be hearing about it for the rest of my life!"*

She tugged her daughter's hand out of mine. Her daughter didn't want to let go. God help me, I didn't want her to. I wanted to buy groceries so she and her brother – silent and staring – could eat.

*"We'll get it from somebody else," Gigi said, and fixed me with one of those female blaming gazes like it was all my fault. Her girlfriend folded her arms and permitted*

*herself a small vindictive smile. "We'll end it here then," I said. She nodded and they trooped away.*

On my bus ride back to my side of the fort I decided if this was my last Army sort-of adventure, she had given me quite a ride. I.Z. had orders to ship for Vietnam. Our Portland clops were all behind us. I was down to two weeks and a wake-up as they say. Gigi would go on the life-list with Irish. Maybe might-have-been is all I would ever manage. I went back to the club with Portland pipe and notebook to finish this disjointed tale. Steve the waiter came by to say he was sorry to hear from Gigi I was so angry with her I dumped her cold. I didn't know what to say.

*"You're not going to give that gal a break?" he said. "I asked around about her. She's not a bad gal." ... she had never been in the Army though she said she had; she was a lifer's divorcee with post privileges, a regular alimony check, two kids, a big house and the Chrysler. "She has a lot of endearing qualities," Steve said.*

*"You mean the big house and the car?"*

*He seemed shocked and offended. "Give her a break."*

*"I'll pass," I said ... .*

I never saw Miss Mitty again.

# Chapter 29:
# Double Date

A PERSONNEL SERGEANT set me up for a double date with his girlfriend's friend the week before I was due to get out of the Army. His ulterior motive was the friend's Seattle apartment. His girlfriend still lived home with her folks and she refused to countenance a motel as too tacky. He was insistent I had to score with her friend so we could all go to her place and make whoopee. Given my track record I thought his chances slim and none. Right off the bat the tall curvy redhead challenged me: "I understand you've written a few books?" Skeptical head-tilt. He'd been overselling me in his anxiety.

"One," I said. "One book."

"See?" Tom said "A real author. Told you."

So we talked a little about writing as Tom drove us to the main fort Top Five Club. A big swing band like something from the forties was playing. Senior NCOs liked that music. So did I. The place was packed with people partying after the annual inter-service boxing championships, just concluded. Lots of light-moving, well-muscled men breaking training along with their cadres and camp followers, including plenty of women.

Boxers stopped by our table to say hello; I had managed the ringside press table and written dispatches for the worldwide military teletype, my last Army chore. A black Fort Campbell middleweight who liked my description of his knockout punch as a "lethal left hook" looked the redhead over and decided to hit on her. "Gots what you need baby," he said.

She did the head-cock thing, studying a new insect. "You have no idea what I need. And I'm with Ish."

"Ish won't mind."

"Yes, Ish will," I said. "Go away."

It was the Army. Boxer or not, he was far from home base and I was local. And I still wore MP brass. He patted my shoulder and went away. I was glad he knew the rules. And absurdly grateful to her. We danced. We talked. Something she said inspired my ultimate accolade: "You would have loved Paris."

That head-tilt I would come to know so well: "As a matter of fact, I did."

So the City of Light came into our conversation, and her pre-college European tour, including an ocean liner to France. A ship-board romance with a depressed older man, a Greek, that survived until Paris but not beyond. He left her there to go home. Her bittersweet story resonated with my own Paris goodbye. "Little moments of happiness," I said and explained my matriarch's theory. It chimed surprisingly well with her hip sixties thinking: flapper to flower child in three generations.

The part of my brain that never shut up noted she was not the first girl to tell me about her affairs. Not even the first one to tell me about her Greek lover. Irish in Portland had one of those. Damn modern Greeks really got around. I hadn't heard of Zorba. But I had a gripe with ancient Greeks and their outer logic that only permitted one Paris moment of happiness with my Israeli before taking her away. What

I told the redhead was I too loved and lost in Paris. Our affinity deepened. We danced with my engorged cock snug against her belly as if it was the most natural thing in the world. No embarrassment for me; no feigned cuteness from her.

Back at the table, Tom's girl signaled a restroom break and led her away. Tom gave a sly wink. "You're selling it, Dude. She likes you. This is conference-time, plan our night for us."

Looked like he was right when they came back. His girl announced time to go. They led to the parking lot, arms around each other. "That looks like fun," I said. "Shall we?" The redhead slipped naturally under my arm and slid hers around my waist. We were in the back seat maybe thirty seconds before she was in my arms and we kissed. Calming and exciting all in one. The universe shrank to that back seat.

Far away, the couple in front was talking; I heard not a word. All my blood had migrated to my throbbing erection. As the car rolled I nuzzled her neck, her nipples through her top, hard as the tips of my thumbs. Her hands were in my lap.

A sudden wash of coolness. My god, she had me out, in her hands, caressing. Peripherally I saw her friend crane her neck to see, then jerk face-forward as if disapproving. Didn't care. Had my hand under her skirt now, seeking.

A God-damned girdle.

My fingernails scrabbled futilely against nylon armor. Heard that throaty groan of need. Never could I recall such total frustration. My father's admonition against car-sex floated in my brain. I was too addled to figure how to divest that damn girdle. She concentrated on my cock, slick with pre-orgasmic liquid, firm slow strokes ... bending lower to gaze at it in the flicker of passing street lights ...

I was twenty-three. Never crossed my mind she not only was willing to take me in her mouth, she wanted to. I was still very young toward women. A poetic phrase for *abysmally ignorant.* All I could think of was getting her to her Seattle apartment. I sat up and removed myself from her grip. She blinked out of her trance.

"You are too important to me for us to do this here," I said softly. "When I make love to you it's going to be whole-heart. Not groping in a back seat." Writer-speak for I can't figure out the damn girdle. I kissed her some more. She kissed me back.

"Soon," she said. "Make it soon."

"Soon," I promised. But it was not to be. When we turned our attention to Tom and his girl, they were quarreling. I never learned about what. We never made it to Seattle. Tom pulled off at a Tacoma motel and we sat in the coffee shop and drank coffee and listened to him try to placate her and her not be placated.

The car was Tom's girlfriend's; the redhead sold her Fury convertible for college money. Quietly the redhead and I discussed options. I had enough for a motel room. But not enough for a taxi back to the fort. The redhead was visiting her folks in the small town where Tom's girl lived, thirty miles away. No bus service. A taxi out of the question. The redhead and I could take a bus to Seattle – but I would wind up AWOL. Impasse.

Somewhere in there the redhead told me the subject of their powder-room conference at the fort had been her friend trying to trade Tom for me! She gave me one of those Mona Lisa smiles: "Told her I wasn't interested." I wondered if that was why her friend got in a snit when she saw my cock in the redhead's hand. I was never going to understand women.

Tom's girl wasn't mad enough to strand us. She drove us back to the fort – mostly, she said, for my benefit, not his. Just to get the dig in. Her bad humor hung over us like a fog, dousing further amorous exploration. I was so constricted I jacked off in an unoccupied latrine in the midnight barracks. Tom and his big plans for Seattle! Fate had found one more way to gyp me out of getting laid. But I reckoned without redheaded determination.

*She ain't ashamed to be a woman or afraid to be a friend*

*I don't know the answer to the easy way she opened every door in my mind ...*

*But ... lovin' her was easier than anything I'll ever do again*

          - Kris Kristofferson

# Chapter 30:
# Murphy Bed

THE FIRST MURPHY BED I ever slept in scared me. It folded down out of an apartment closet in St. Petersburg. At ten years old, I lay awake waiting for the damn thing to snap up into the wall and imprison me upside down.

The second Murphy bed I slept in was in a girl's apartment in Seattle. I was 23. We tortured it unmercifully but it never once tried to fold up on us. I never would have seen the second bed but for a redhead's determination to consummate our mutual lust.

The personnel sergeant and his girlfriend hooked us up for a double date. Things were good until Tom and his girl quarreled. She dumped us at our barracks and drove away in a huff. The next morning I was having breakfast in a post cafeteria. Here came Tom, grinning like an idiot. "Get an overnight pass," he said. "Right now. They'll be here in two hours!"

They who? The girls of course. He couldn't stop grinning. His girlfriend had called and said the redhead *ordered* her to make peace and drive back here to get us. "You made a big hit, boy! We're all going to Seattle for sure."

I still didn't believe Fate was giving me another shot. But I stuffed cash in my wallet from my wall locker and packed underwear and shaving gear in my briefcase instead of AWOL bag, with some notion of concealing intent. Found out later how amused the redhead was by my transparent subterfuge. This was deep in the sexy sixties, the Pill and free love and flower children, an era I mostly missed. The redhead did not, which eventually led to ambiguous feelings on my part. But that was for later.

It was one of those pellucid spring days people outside the rainy Northwest don't believe really happen. The redhead wanted to show me Seattle Center. I had seen it but wasn't about to argue. I missed signals by which she and Tom's girl communicated it was time to split up. They left with the car. No problem; I had bus fare covered this time.

I liked Seattle Center and its large fountain since I first saw it, usually surrounded by couples lazily making out on benches, or on the grass in dry weather. Reminded me of Paris lovers. Now it was me on a bench with the redhead, fountain spray drifting across us. Unknown to me, we captured the telephoto lens of a news photographer – who happened do be doing his National Guard service as one of my staff in the information office.

The afternoon was one of those timeless happy moments the redhead and I already had talked about. I was strangely unhurried. She mentioned she was supposed to babysit that night, which I took to mean no consummation today. Since I knew up-front, it didn't even bother me. We kissed and told our lives to each other, making out in the spring sun. We took the aerial tram that crossed the whole grounds and held each other quietly. When we disembarked she needed a pay telephone. We found one. She was looking right at me when she told them she could not babysit tonight. Something had come up. Quirky little smile when she said it.

Suddenly I couldn't breathe.

We took the monorail downtown. She led me to a bus stop that took us to the university district. Home to her apartment. And that Murphy bed. My emotions were cycling. Excitement, amazement, doubt – realization I left my briefcase in the car – we sat on the edge of the bed and kissed and fondled and whispered and shed clothing. My cock had been up and down so many times that long afternoon. Suddenly it was limp in her hand.

"I ... need some help," I said. Gasped when she simply leaned over and took me in her mouth. John Thomas responded with alacrity. All turmoil ceased, all doubt banished. I took her shoulders and lifted her. Her lips reluctantly relinquished their suction. Our gazes locked as she lay back under me in that Murphy bed. I entered her simply as coming home from a long absence.

My miraculous Israeli awoke me in Paris to the full wonder of the mystery that obsessed me since I was a child. Later I told my log in innocent arrogance that I required a woman who would measure up. A woman whose sensuality and appetite were prodigious enough to match mine. Consoled myself about missed opportunities by thinking they missed more than I did.

Even before we got that Murphy bed into full cry the first time, such ideas blew out of my brain forever. I'd found her. We spent hours making that poor old bed groan and complain. Resting and whispering. Going again. We did not leave the apartment to eat for twenty-four hours, so light-headed we had to hold each other up. The waitress asked what we thought about some major news event. We were blank. She was surprised – where could we have been not to hear? We found that very funny. "On a very long trip," I said. Could have said *off on a comet.*

Refueled, we went back to it. I was long since AWOL. Didn't care. I wasn't repeating my Paris mistake and leaving my lover. There was no top-secret installation to panic about compromised secrets. With only a week to go, what could they do? We slept. I awoke confused, already on her and in her, moving slow and dreamy. My body sought hers while my brain slept. She was wide-awake, eyes glowing like stars in the dim light, delighted by my sleep-fucking. It felt like the most perfect joining two people could achieve.

Later an apartment resident, maybe kept awake all night by the Murphy bed, banged on the door yelling obscenities about the racket and calling her names. I went from somnolent satiety to instant cold rage. Would have killed him if I caught him. But she held me and gentled me and laughed it off.

"You are sooo fine," she would say in the afterglow, drawing the word out in an indefinable way exotic to my Southern ears. We made love under a shaded lamp. Her sparkling eyes were the center of my universe. Alabaster had only been a word in dictionaries until I saw her nude body in lamp glow on that Murphy bed.

It was very difficult to return to the Army. But I knew I was coming right back to her. The official Army didn't even notice my absence. But my smart-Alec photographer said *we* know where you were; you might even feature in a photo spread. *"Young love at Seattle Center,"* he said with a sarcastic twist. Envious as fellow MPs in Germany when I returned from Paris.

Never saw the pictures. Didn't need them. I cleared post the last time and rode a Greyhound forty miles to Seattle. The longest bus ride of my life. Sat in the coffee shop and waited for the redhead to get off work and come get me. The slant of April light through dusty windows is sealed in memory with the indescribable emotion when she walked through the door. We had a week to do it all again, and we did. Tirelessly, constantly. We were perfectly matched. She skipped most classes but kept her job. I slept then. I loved unpinning her hair when she got home, bobby pins flying, as it fanned like autumn leaf fires.

But I had a job waiting in Florida. Packing before my last night in that Murphy bed, I was nervous and irritable. She sat quietly watching me with wide dark eyes – she'd never seen me like that. I had the awful feeling I was about to lose this girl too, and no confidence I would ever find her again. But I didn't know how to take control of my life and just decide to stay.

That was the last night I slept in a Murphy bed. She accepted my dark mood, loved me out of it and promised I wouldn't lose her. I looked at my packed bags cluttering the room and wished I could understand about choices. I still do. She drove me to the airport in a borrowed car. My last view was her bright auburn hair as the car splashed down the departure lane. The Northwest rains had returned.

# Chapter 31:
## Homecoming

PEACHTREE STREET on an April evening: warm and muggy, bugs swarming in street lights, cockroaches scuttling when I snapped on the light in my hotel room. Black faces crowded the sidewalks. After the lily-white Northwest it was like the heart of Africa. Taxis waited by the hotel; white drivers, solitary women in back, red glow of a cigarette tip limning faces of both colors. Not picturesque as pimps and whores in Paris cafes but the same enterprise with a Georgia drawl.

I was on my way home from the Army. The stopover in Atlanta had been postponed by my week with the girl with the Murphy bed. Walking Peachtree I scanned unconsciously for auburn hair and alabaster skin. *Deja vu:* In Paris I walked the Champs looking for a lithe dark-haired ghost.

The suppressed excitement of the black crowds distracted me. Then I heard a transistor radio: the brand-new Atlanta Braves, late of Milwaukee, were taking the home field for opening day. I was here at an historic moment. The hotel bartender said the game was sold out but I could get it on the radio. I didn't. I had a lot on my mind.

The matriarch had directed me to forget the married woman I was in love with, after the confrontation between her husband and my family. Glenda kept writing. I replied

– but kept my emotional distance. So she sent another photo *"to remember me by"*: wearing a floppy Mata Hari hat and belted trench-coat, lips parted slightly, against a night-dark river reflecting city lights. Could have been the Seine, which felt deliberate. The photographer was a gruff composing-room guy with a camera hobby who liked to shoot her, she wrote brightly. Again deliberate, to make me wonder how *much* he liked her?

She proposed an Atlanta rendezvous to reconnect. Feeling stupid, I agreed. Ten days before ETS I got a letter saying she couldn't get away. When I met the girl with the Murphy bed I sent a telegram that I wouldn't be there anyway. When I signed off post my last day, the orderly room had an answering telegram: reschedule Atlanta and she would be there. So I built in a stopover on my way home. After my magic Seattle week I wished I hadn't. Wasn't surprised but relieved when Glenda didn't show.

My job waited. I shopped Peachtree for summer clothing: gabardine slacks, a Navy double-breasted blazer, shirts, ties in that year's correct width. Flew home. My brother drove me to the Beaches. I told the matriarch I might be in love with a tall Seattle redhead who might come South to live with me. She was not thrilled. Hoped I swore off women after the fiasco with Glenda.

I had my brief moment of happiness in Paris, she reminded me. Best to consider Seattle another such and let it go. Meanwhile, time to re-enter real life: there was mail she held to avoid bothering me. Two letters in the stack beside my typewriter were memorable. One was from "Irish," the Portland girl I failed to bed, enclosing a photo of her standing by the Acropolis. She had fulfilled her dream of foreign travel. If I was ever out that way ... I wrote congratulating her, said it was unlikely I would see Portland again. The second was from a famous author about magazine stories I wrote: *You realize your writing is far too good for newspaper work.*

Since his fame rested on a fictional detective of genius, I asked his advice for finding my lost love in Israel. He wrote back if I really wanted help I would have given him all the details. I didn't *have* details: an address I could barely read, that she had been a soldier and was now a dancer. He said he laughed at my "maudlin sentimentality" – which jibed with the misogyny of his fat detective, but irritated me. What would I *do* if she appeared, he wondered, saying she tried but just couldn't forget me? He implied I would be dismayed.

But I turned his question inside out. Imagined going to Israel and saying the same thing to her after Nero Wolfe's creator found her. Imagined her chagrin, per J. Alfred Prufrock: *"That is not what I meant, at all ... "* Could not bear having so badly misread her interest. So I let sleeping love lie, lest it bite me.

My newspaper had moved to a new building. The newsroom was windowless, carpeted, metal desks in rows like an insurance-claims department. Reporters weren't allowed to bring coffee to their desks! But the biggest shock was above my desk in brand-new offices, a hand-painted banner: *Welcome Home, Ish.*

"Been up there ever since your official separation date," Hollis, now associate editor, said. "She popped in here every day to see if we'd heard anything." He nodded at the editor's office. "He's fuming. But afraid to take it down and seem jealous."

"Glenda made the sign."

"Oh, yeah."

Within ten minutes she came breezing through the door, slipped her arms around my waist. "About time you got home!" A small secret smile curled her lips.

"I'm trying to write a column in here," the editor snarled from his office.

"Hi, Charlie," I called.

"Ish? Ish is that you?" He came to his door. "Thank god! Now we can take down that idiot banner! We're not supposed to clutter up the walls." He shut his door, not gently.

I was amazed. "Charlie, the self-styled maverick, caving in to this new-building nonsense?"

"The shrinks call that displacement," Hollis said from the side of his mouth like a prisoner. "He's just jealous. No woman ever put up a sign for him."

"I was going to show Ish the new building," Glenda said.

"Why don't you?" Hollis said. "Maybe Charlie will be over his snit by the time you get back."

I registered nothing until she led me into a long corridor with windows overlooking the river. She turned, long dark hair up in its office twist, pleated pencil skirt with a peek of kneecap, ruffled white blouse with a hint of cleavage; businesslike and sexy all in one. "Now about that welcome-home kiss," she said.

"In this mausoleum we might get arrested." My emotions were in turmoil.

"So let 'em." She walked into me like she did when I got home from France. The world dissolved. Nothing existed between our first kiss last year and this. When she finally drew back her blue eyes were smoky, lips swollen. She reached into my pocket with perfect familiarity. "You've got lipstick all over your mouth," she said huskily. "I can fix that. Here." She moistened my handkerchief with her tongue, dabbled. "There, good as new."

"You don't have much left on yours." I ran a thumb over her lips. "Most kissable lips in Jacksonville. But I thought..."

"You're home now," she said. "Whatever I said, a girl's got a right to change her mind. I don't care about those other women."

"What other women?"

"Yeah, right – don't care. You're mine now." The door at the end of the corridor opened. "Oops, time for that tour. C'mon, there's new people for you to meet." The woman coming the other way smirked at me.

All I remember of the tour is her proprietary air introducing me. Charlie had gone to early lunch when I got back; in some ways running true to form. I asked Hollis: "Who does he lunch with now Justine is gone?" The previous associate editor, Charlie's main paramour. "He wrote to tell me he was drinking so much it was hard to see the net." Charlie loved tennis.

"That must have been right after Justine gave her notice," Hollis said. "He was hard to be around for a while. Now he's mining talent at his Little Theater group. Has tennis dates."

At quarter till five, Glenda called. "We have reservations at that nice new Howard Johnson's. We have unfinished business. I'm going to make you start forgetting all those other women."

"What about…"

"Downstate fishing with our son. I've got the whole night."

*The line between good and evil is not so different from the foul line on a baseball field ... often made of stuff as flimsy as lime. It ... needs to be constantly redrawn ... if enough players trample on it the line becomes smeared and blurred where fair is foul and foul is fair, where good and evil become indistinguishable ...*

- *The Final Detail,* Harlan Coben

*All things truly wicked start from innocence ...*

- *A Moveable Feast*, Ernest Hemingway

# Chapter 32:
# Failure of Conscience

THE AUBURN-HAIRED GIRL I MET the week before I left the Army was going to follow me to Florida and live with me. *Whither thou goest* – she actually quoted that to me. I was looking at apartments over protest of the matriarch, who saw me repeating blunders of her sons with their women. Even worse, we weren't talking marriage: the redhead had a sixties flower-child's distrust of the institution. We would be *living in sin!* I certainly hoped so.

Then why was I wearing my high-school class ring, reversed to hide the signet and create the appearance of a wedding band to fool imagined guardians of public morality? And checking into a motel right in town? Because the married woman I loved first had summoned.

The motel affected up-scale amenities: sent a kid to guide my car to our room and hand me the afternoon newspaper hot off the presses. The room was spacious and well-appointed and Glenda was excited and happy. No bush-league car sex this time. I checked my doubts at the door, grudgingly acknowledging, once again, my dead great-grandmother's sneer: *a stiff dick ain't got no conscience.*

Soon as we had the door locked we were in each other's arms kissing and murmuring sweet nothings. The matriarch never believed in corporal punishment, but if she knew about this she would want the fire poker with which she threatened misbehaving grown sons.

There was a large luxurious walk-in shower. Glenda decided we should wash work-day grime away together. Her pale tidy little body was just as I remembered. I was immediately at full port arms. What was new was her small hand boldly taking hold. She could barely encompass the girth but her artist's grip was strong. We never turned on the water. Instead she used the convenient handle to lead me to the wide bed. Just as a happy hooker had done in Paris.

"*Now* I start making you forget those other women." Same thing she said at work. I didn't argue. My internal compartments of memory were my own. Each woman unique. I wasn't about to forget. My last cogent thought for a while.

She was active and evidently ardent as we consummated the act interrupted a year ago by possum hunters. *Evidently* because I knew enough to know I didn't know her rhythms. Remembered her evident ardor becoming sobs because she could not orgasm before the possum hunters arrived. I concentrated carefully, wanting this to be special. Wanting to unwind the long empty year believing she didn't want me. To try to make up with my body for humiliation she suffered from her enraged husband.

My own climax was strong and satisfying. Her eyes were enormous and bright in the afterglow. She caressed my face. We snuggled and kissed and touched and I remembered the first time I ever saw her, stunned by her presence in a chair previously occupied by a tired old man. *Retired* old man; she was the new hire. To say you are struck instantly by love's arrow is only a saying until you are. And I was.

One of those random thoughts of mine hit me: my vulgar old wire-service mentor had missed his prediction about women losing interest once one of them got my cherry. I was emphatically no longer a virgin. But she still wanted me. She slipped out of my arms briefly to warm a soapy washcloth in the sink and lovingly clean me. Again the uncanny *deja vu*. The exuberant Paris whore who resembled – and seemed genuinely sympathetic for loss of – my Israeli, and who led me to bed by my handle, was the first woman to apply a warm wash cloth so tenderly afterwards.

No bidet in an American motel. She used the same washcloth to clean herself and lay back in my arms, eyes half-closed, legs parted. I read that as invitation to the cunnilingus she liked during our crazy first date. I nosed in happily. This time she was *very* active, pulling my hair and thrashing her head around and mumbling things. Finally vocalizing plainly: *"Suck my tonsils out!"*

Silly to admit but the crudity shocked me. No woman had used such crude language – unless it was one of the Paris whores, concealed within the sheer eroticism of murmured French. My never-quiet brain pictured the physical impossibility of her demand. The gist seemed to be to suck harder. I intensified efforts, to her shuddering satisfaction. *Evidently* again. I was overthinking this too much; maybe her husband liked crudity during intercourse. Depression seeped into the edge of my thoughts. This was not quite the "glory and the circling of the wings" of someone's romantic description of sublime sex. Which I had experienced with two different women on different sides of the planet.

Still, she evinced continuing ardor. After *evident* orgasm she immediately urged me atop her again. Reliable ol' John Thomas was up to it. Even more durable after the first discharge. I slowed the pace and plumbed her carefully as a riverboat hand sounding the dark waters of the Mississippi. The evening blurred into long, slow lovemaking. Pauses to rest and smoke – she lit two cigarettes at a time and gave me one. Digging in my clothes for a pipe seemed too intrusive, and I wasn't sure I had remembered tobacco. More warm washcloths.

Once she mounted and rode me for a long time, gasping every time I bottomed out. A Grace Metalious phrase from *Peyton Place* floated into memory: *Your nipples are hard as diamonds*. Check. Eventually she dismounted as if sleepwalking and warmed another washcloth. Was fascinated I still was erect after all that. I had achieved what ol' Henry Miller called a "lingering hard-on." She wrapped the washcloth around it and pushed the foreskin down to reveal the bulging head. Her face was close, expression absorbed as a kid with a science project.

I gently pressed her head closer. "Put your mouth on me." She resisted, pushing back. Hell she abruptly was sniffling, almost crying, hair draping forward to shroud her face as she shook her head. I should have wilted at this sudden rejection, but no. Still at full extend. She maintained her grip, continued her ministrations. Not exactly rejection … "What is it, darlin'?"

"Don't you want *me*?"

What the hell? Had I not proved that repeatedly? Confusion warred with frustration. "Of course I want you!"

Almost in resignation, she bobbed down and sucked me in. Crying softly. For me, an indescribable juxtaposition of pleasure and concern. I stopped her and pulled her up into my arms as she sobbed. Petted her and kissed her. Asked how my wanting her to do that made her think I didn't want her. Her answer chilled me. Her husband, she said, made her do that every night because *"a man needs his relief"* and he couldn't maintain an erection and come except in her mouth. For which he blamed her!

Not only a controlling monster, an idiot. If a woman like this could not charge his boilers he must be impotent: oh, the arrogance of a young man with an indefatigable cock.

She apologized! Said she'd do it now she'd got that off her mind. No damn way. I soothed her and kissed her lips and her rigid nipples and fingered her Mons until she stopped crying and caught her breath. Then I applied my lingering hard-on where she really wanted it – what a tremendous sacrifice! Hah. I kept going until she cried uncle. She was eight years older, and had to get some sleep to be able to get up and go to work.

I recognized my own exhaustion and fell asleep with her in my arms. I was still engorged but content. We had no time for morning sex, which I regretted, but my contentment lasted all the way to noon at work. Then she shattered it with a phone call.

# Chapter 33:
# Hodgepodge of Memories

EVENTS AFTER MY MOTEL NIGHT with Glenda raise a hodgepodge of memories. My nineties shrink couldn't even disentangle the Gordian knot, but had empathy for a callow youth's confusion dealing with two diametrically different lovers. One on the Left Coast who offered peace and wonder. The other whose on-again off-again seduction fed off my chaste affection from age eighteen when I first was wounded by love's arrow.

It was helpful to have a Venusian for a shrink. She saw things a man never would. Lunches the cool married woman arranged with a virginal copy boy. Frequent visits to my lowly desk in the wire room, something that did not stand out to me because every good-looking wife on the staff did that. The difference was she never seemed to be laughing at me like the others. Her long serious talks about art and writing impressed me, particularly her self-deprecation, calling herself too shallow to comprehend my deep thinking. Of course I leaped to her defense, projecting wisdom on her. And believed it. My shrink called it a long, careful seduction too subtle for an ignorant youth to grasp. Even with the matriarch's warnings against wiles of designing women.

All this while she never failed to brag how solid her marriage was. Being an inveterate reader, book knowledge finally led me to ask whether she was trying to convince me, or herself: rudimentary psychology. One of the few times I saw her struck dumb. Old Houser called her old enough to know better but too young to care, hot for me, and counseled to let her take my cherry. His heart was in the right place – old reprobate – but I am forever grateful I didn't. If she had been my first I would have been messed up beyond recall. She did a good enough job even after my miraculous Paris *affaire de couer* and my time with the wondrous Seattle redhead.

Glenda initiated correspondence when I went to Basic Training. I was touched, and wrote what I saw there. One exchange stands out: I wrote about GIs sharing pictures of their girlfriends, apologizing for a poor likeness: a bad photo; she looks a lot better in person, stuff like that. And how to a man we accepted the excuses and agreed their girl was a knockout.

Almost by return mail she sent a picture by one of our news photogs: three-quarter profile, hair pulled from her forehead in the exotic twist she wore at work, complemented by a bolero jacket with a collar accentuating her slender neck. A trace of smile at something off-camera. Written on the back: *Don't apologize for me.* I was stunned: did this mean I had a married girlfriend? *My shrink gently shook her head. I could almost see the thought bubble: dumb as a stump. Too professional to say it.*

God, I was ignorant. I wrote candidly to Glenda as I did to the matriarch – including amazement about my Paris encounter. My shrink shook her head again: *Let me guess – after that, her letters became more ... intimate.* I wondered if the shrink was telepathic. *No, she said. But I am a woman.* She wasn't surprised I succumbed to the seduction again when I got home. Gently compelled me to see how my failure of conscience injured a girl who truly loved me. Not fun.

Those insights were far in the future the day after our motel night, when Glenda called in a panic. She had moved to a rooming house to start the separation she tried the summer before. But once more her husband found her and was forcing her to come home. I hadn't known she moved out. But memory of her asshole husband's confrontation with my family was raw. I came to my senses speeding toward the rooming house with my Colt openly in my hand on the steering wheel. Insane. I pulled over, put the gun away, went back to work. In those days a husband had all the rights.

The next few days offer blurred flashes. One: her husband calling me at work, almost apologetic, saying he always liked me and could not fault my infatuation when it was all her doing. Too bad we couldn't clone her and both have one. If not, maybe we could share ... I hung up. I was not wired to share. I was very old before I learned some men *are* wired that way. Makes for sexy pornography these uncensored times. But no thank you.

Another memory: back at work, I was moping around, good for nothing, aggravating my boss. She wanted to talk in the parking lot. Behind black wrap-around sunglasses she told me she couldn't handle a long night of my prodigious sexual appetite. Not only was she painfully sore, I'd hurt her in rambunctious intercourse. A tear leaked beneath the impervious shades. Man oh man. Without my Paris miracle, and the girl with the Murphy bed for a confirming litmus test, I would have been out of business for keeps. Raised by women whose favorite topic was sex, my first thought was to ask family females.

My savvy mother shrugged: *An excuse for going back to the familiar; women never say the real reason.* H'mm. A favorite aunt laughed, her eyes gleamed and she said sometimes my uncle hurt her in his exuberance – but it was exciting and became pleasure. She preferred a little pain to deference. Wow.

I asked the matriarch. I knew she detested sex despite romanticism. She said smugly the old man was rough as they come and twice as strong as me – but she never saw the day she couldn't bounce him all over the bed. Her bald confession to sexual pleasure confounded me because they never slept together; she just vanished into his room from time to time with a towel. I felt betrayed after all her warnings against sex; she lied to me! So she revealed the real reason for her dislike: the old man gave her gonorrhea as a bride, imported from Navy ports of call below the Equator. The disease probably made his bastard on a Central Avenue hussy the brain-damaged idiot he was. Old Doc Mathis cured her, their children were healthy and the old man was a satisfying bull in the sack. But she had a long memory.

Unsettling previously unknown family history did nothing to ease my dismal state. I wrote the Seattle redhead, temporizing about when she should fly South. I wasn't worth the trip, but couldn't tell her why. My editor gave me some days off to get over it – he had a heart after all. At high tide I plunged off the seawall to fight breakers with my fists until exhausted. Saw my boss slip into the liquor peddler's perpetual house party with a new squeeze.

He gave me a man-to-man thumbs-up. On the seawall next day at low tide, I saw a distant female in jeans and sneakers tripping along the tide-line, long hair blowing in the wind. She gave a big wave.

Hell, it was her. She came bouncing up to see how I was doing. Said she was sorry. Said even if I was through with her because she went back to her husband, she wanted to paint my portrait. Jesus. My grace period over, I went back to work. Told my editor I'd made peace with her, incautiously said she wanted to paint me. He leered comically. *"Full-length in the nude no doubt. Say NOW you know what I see in him!"* Newspaperman humor. Got a kick out of my blush. I shrugged it off and wrote a couple not-bad features.

She was always there, sending a fellow artist to pass messages because my editor intimidated her. Soon the messenger said Glenda was moving into her beach cottage, location unknown to the asshole husband. Here were the directions. It was just a mile from my home. Tomorrow was Saturday, come on over.

Well, I went. She was like a different person, feeling securely beyond his reach. Her gal pal was a rock-band groupie immersed in the free-love sixties. Sally said she told her main squeeze when a hot new drummer came along: *Keep him away from me or I will fuck him, he didn't and I did.* Headed off to buy groceries telling Glenda *Don't do anything I wouldn't – in other words, yes, girl!*

Hardly cleared the driveway when Glenda had my pants around my ankles. I learned something then: never wear combat boots if you might get lucky. Damn Levis would not come off over my Army boots as I sprawled on the carpet. She pushed me back, saying *got you where I want you now* – and went down on me. My damn brain kept reciting but you were sore, I hurt you, you associate blow jobs with the pathetic demands of your husband ...

Nothing out loud. I had no wide experience of being orally pleasured – no way to gauge her skill – but I was trapped by my boots so I just laid back and enjoyed it. Never got those damned boots off, never had a chance to reciprocate. Sally came back early and almost caught us, knew she had, and happily congratulated her new roommate, who acted smug and happy. It looked like it was going to be a long summer.

# Chapter 34:
## Mousetrapped

A STREETLIGHT REFLECTING OFF a large gray sedan a block away: I noticed it soon as I turned into the street.

The street itself was only a block long, accessed by short streets at either end. A kind of cul-de-sac, easy to miss out on the main drag. There never had been a big gray car parked there before. Sally's house was halfway down the block on the right. I lost track of happy banter between Sally, in the back seat, and Glenda beside me.

We'd had a good time at the Arts Council costume party on the Navy base. Sally wore Glenda's Mata Hari getup: trench coat and flop hat. Glenda was a gypsy girl. I was being James Bond in a white dinner jacket with side vents over a black turtleneck too warm for Florida but hey, style demanded.

Glenda had been at Sally's several weeks. Her extrication from her husband required subterfuge. Stage one, she just went home from work with Sally one day. Stage two, got him to agree to meet her in a Beaches shopping center with a load of her clothes and belongings, all civilized-like. When he showed up all ready to drag her home again he found Sally with her, ready to get in his face. Didn't know what to do. They stranded him there, taking his car to unload at her "safe house." He couldn't follow. Was fuming when they returned the car. *Pig*, Sally told me with delight, very proud of herself. Every man she disliked, and all cops, were pigs.

The pig's car was a big gray four-door Mercury sedan.

I didn't say anything to question their tradecraft as I turned into Sally's driveway. But I kept the gray gleam down the street in peripheral vision as paranoia seeped in. Glenda sensed I had zoned out. "Where did you go?" she said. Then, "Never mind. You were such a good date I just have to kiss you." A little tipsy from both booze and freedom. She climbed in my lap while Sally giggled in the back seat. As our lips met, headlights flashed on half a block away. The big Mercury appeared in my rear-view mirror, skidding to a stop, bouncing on its shocks. Right across the driveway. Mousetrapping my car.

Marcus came swarming out and marched toward us, highly agitated. So much for the girls' subterfuge. I remember my exact first thought: gonna be expensive to replace my Barracuda's huge back widow. I could already see bullet holes. "Your husband is here," I said.

Sultry seduction to stark terror in less than a heartbeat. Never before, and never since, have I seen such an instant transformation. She slipped away from me, wailing in a minor key like a dying rabbit. She was not tall, or big. But my brain registered the impossible: she shrank to child size and tried – actually tried – to crawl under the low bucket seat. Three inches of clearance, if that.

Time slowed like in a car crash. Marcus yanked open her door, screaming – at *Sally's hat*. Serious nearsightedness plus recognizing Glenda's Mata Hari rig. Feisty Sally screamed right back: *"What are you doing here!"*

Her voice under Glenda's hat threw him. "Sally?" He goggled. I realized his eyesight was too poor to see three people in my car. Why he would think his wife rode in back defies reason. But reason was in short supply that night. For another heartbeat or two it was almost comical. But then he heard Glenda *gibbering in terror*. Only a phrase from books until I heard her down in the floorboards.

He looked down, then stooped like a hawk, grabbing at her. Missed. Came up with her handbag. Ripped it open and started rooting in it. Froze, hand inside.

*"My gun ..,"* Glenda moaned. He required her to carry a Beretta .22 in her purse to ward off men's advances – so if he caught her screwing, she could not claim she was forced. Insane. I had wondered why she didn't just shoot *him*. But a *Burning Bed* defense was in the unknowable future. Maybe she thought him bullet-proof. I did not.

I reached over her and tapped him on the forehead with my Colt. When he looked up into the muzzle, I said, "Enough is enough." His face went blank. He made a funny choking sound. His legs – buckled. He was suddenly on his knees, handbag dropped, clinging to the door frame as he stared eternity in the face.

Remembering he dared to bully Glenda in front of my matriarch and the old man last summer, I was ready to kill him. Coldly furious at him for trying to use his wife's own gun against us. I could call it self-defense. Must have said it out loud as I focused the front sight between his blank eyes. Because, *"No gun in my purse,"* Glenda choked out. *"I left it home."* Well shit. There went incontestable self-defense. Marcus mumbled, *"Why?"*

"The Navy base." Her vocal chords were clogged but she got that out. "No guns allowed ... "

Of course James Bond pays no attention to such rules. Gate Marines didn't bother newspaper visitors. Though still callow and young toward women, I had adopted what became an inflexible rule: when fooling with married women always go armed.

I got out and walked around the car. "Can you stand up?" Silently he struggled to rise. I had to help him. Helping hand for a dead man. He leaned on the Barracuda roof as if tired and old. Almost old as he ever got. "Go home," I said. 'You got something to say to her, call her at work. Or have a lawyer do it. In broad daylight. Like a grownup."

Weak prissy voice: "I have nothing to say to you with a gun in your hand."

B-Grade Western at best. Put down your gun and get shot with a hideout? But tonight I was Bond, James Bond. Maybe a little Gene Autry on the side since my weapon of choice was a scaled-down single-action six-gun. I put my Colt in my belt. Spread my hands.

*"Go away!"* Sally yelled at him. *"You're trespassing! I'm calling the cops."* He flinched. Shambled back to his car. I followed just in case. Learned later he was so angry when he jumped out he forgot the pistol under his own seat. Never needed it to bully her before. Didn't think of a weapon till he opened my door. Bullies are usually cowards. He couldn't go for his gun now. He was beaten, no more thought of gunplay.

He left. I got us in the house, door locked, in case he came back. But what came back were two Beaches cops. Seeking the deranged Viet vet who so terrified a citizen he side-swiped half a dozen cars fleeing town. Was stopped as a suspected drunk driver. Babbled out his lie, barely coherent.

Cops and I had a little dance about whether I had a gun. Perfectly legal those days to have one under the seat, not counting military bases. Didn't like my challenging their demand. My Colt went in Sally's lingerie drawer as soon as cops drove in. Sally the flower child said *show me a warrant*. Knew them from dances they attended where her squeeze's band played. Said *don't act like pigs now*. It calmed things that I went to school with their chief – young as me, but it was a very small town. Maybe six cops. Still more calming, I was a city reporter who knew how cops hated domestics. They didn't arrest Marcus, just got his insurance details and advised him to have his lawyer deal with his runaway wife. In the daytime. I said *Same I thing I told him*. By then it was nearly a love-in; they left with tickets to Sally's guy's next gig. Said they'd tell Billy hello for me.

How had he mousetrapped me? As a wife-tracker he had obsessive talents: noted the odometer before surrendering his car for the possessions handover. Then drove every possible combination of directions from the shopping center till he found Sally's place. Stakeout after that was routine.

The old man was pleased I redeemed the family honor for the previous summer's debacle. The matriarch threw up her hands in horror that I could have gone to jail over *that fickle tramp*. A satisfying postscript for me: the bully's self-image, tough macho man controlling restless wife, blew away like dust in the wind. He had invested so much of himself in that illusion its loss left him bereft. The term of art those days was "nervous breakdown. " His was so severe he was institutionalized and medicated. Glenda truly was free at last.

In Westerns I read as a boy, a kiss and happily-ever-after followed death or final defeat of the bad guy. Of course it being Glenda, and me being me, nothing remotely like that followed. Happily-ever-after never came.

# Chapter 35:
# Summer of '67

THE SUMMER OF '67, GLENDA WAS FREE. More or less. Separated from her asshole husband and rooming with the flower-child artist who worked in the same art department. The bully had become a non-issue with his nervous breakdown after I scared him half to death. I was too young to worry about ramifications to her grade-school son. She dealt with that however she dealt, family, babysitters, school. I was surprised to learn he was in the back seat of their car when his father staked out Sally's house and caught us coming home from a party.

Which meant he witnessed his father's humiliation, was with him when he crashed off several parked cars fleeing the scene and lied to cops about a deranged Viet vet chasing him. Jesus. He was a bright kid; who knew the extent of his trauma? Not a topic I discussed with his mother. She didn't bring it up. She already had said she was leaving him with his father when she planned to run away to the Pacific Northwest. Family dynamics are not for lovers. I knew that much.

I still had difficulty adjusting to the changed environment at the newspaper and my old boss's new prickliness. As if he'd read some supervisor's manual. When I left the Army I had been supervising seven to nine information specialists and photographers, all mavericks. It wasn't rocket science. Charlie had Hollis and me, and rotating layout artists, and acted like Little Caesar. So I largely ignored him and focused my attention on the relationship with Glenda.

Never had a girlfriend before the Army, and only a one-night stand and a one-week stand during. This was new and uneasy ground. My appetite was badly off. I kept forgetting to eat. Still remember one night driving to Sally's when the world went strange and faded away. Came to with Glenda half in my lap driving one-handed, shaking me with the other: *wake up, wake up*! She knew instantly it was low blood sugar from not eating. Took me home and fed me, and muzziness vanished like magic.

Weekends we would leave town for a distant motel. She still spooked at shadows fearing her husband around every corner. Soon as we were on the new expressway headed inland she would relax and turn expansive and happy. Once she was unguarded enough to muse aloud if she could just have these road trips and nights with me she'd be content to stay married. That cut deeply. My turn to ask plaintively don't you want *me*, like she did as I pushed her mouth down on my cock.

She assured me it was just a thought, *of course* she wanted me. That night she was especially ardent as if to prove it. It was decades before other restless wives, more self-aware than she, taught me I should have recognized a Venusian longing for those little moments of happiness the matriarch said are all we can expect in life.

Once at dinner in a nice restaurant, she undertook to teach me *proper etiquette* for opening and buttering a hot dinner roll. I never was a good candidate for being managed. For the first time, I snarled at her. She crumpled like a wet napkin. I instantly felt like a damn bully and tried to apologize. We treated each other gently and carefully the rest of that night.

Good news for me was she no longer complained of soreness or pain, and seemed to relish our weekend sexual marathons. *Seemed to.* I did not question it but lived day to day as in a war. A phrase I picked up from Hemingway. I did not know it would become a sort of mantra in my lifelong Venusian Iliad.

She felt uncomfortable at Sally's since her husband had ambushed us there. I was alert arriving and leaving, though he supposedly was lost in his nervous breakdown. She said it was a good thing his employer had a good insurance plan, a wifely thing to say I did not resent. She found another Beaches apartment he wouldn't know about, because she also was self-conscious about imposing on Sally. I helped her move. We christened the bed within an hour.

In her new bachelor pad she was free and unrestrained as on our weekends. A random memory: I was on the bed fully clothed having just arrived. She sat on the edge with a hand on my chest. Remembering that movie title I said, *What do you think about love in the afternoon?* Her hand moved down. She gave me the most radiant smile I could recall: *Sex with you is all I think about. Anytime!* She loved me slow and tender all that afternoon and into the evening. It was so sweet and gentle any shadow of a doubt I'd entertained evaporated. This was where I needed to be, and with whom.

The matriarch was resigned. *She's like polio,* she said. *You caught it and you're running a fever. You'll either get over it or be crippled.* Her advice concerning the Seattle redhead: *Do not tell her anything. Put her off about coming for a visit. Keep her in reserve.*

Easy orders to follow, because I could not bear the thought of causing her the pain of feeling scorned. I thought of Sally's happy carnality, fucking the drummer in her boyfriend's band just because he was hot. The redhead was a flower child too. But I suppressed such thoughts: the idea of strangers in her Murphy bed made me ill. Illogical, unfair – but absolute truth.

The matriarch had a shock for me. The old man faced more surgery. She was moving the family back to Georgia for its extensive family support. She expected me to go first, secure work while my mother waited for a Post Office transfer. My political uncle had a spare bedroom. And influence with the local newspaper. He'd get me a news job. When the old man bought a new house I could move home. Out of the Army two months, my newspaper and editor changed beyond belief, now this: retreat from Florida. The leggy lady whose seawall code defeated a virginal copy boy had urged me to read Thomas Wolfe. I finally had, and his most famous line was right: You can't go home again.

Surprisingly Glenda endorsed the move. She was ready to get out of town too. She had been ready to come to me in the Northwest. My hometown was a mere three hundred miles north – but still a good distance from her soon-to-be former spouse. Said ask about art-department openings! We'd take this love affair of ours on the road.

I did not like it that while advance-scouting I would be alone. And she would be alone. But her self-confidence grew with every week of freedom. She said she would be fine even without a car, bus service was dependable, shopping nearby. She had this. Go find us a place! Soon as she could get vacation she'd come help me, and look for other work if the newspaper had no artist openings.

So the women in my life had my fate laid out. In July I flew to Augusta, to discover my uncle had entered the newspaper business himself – as a publisher. Partnered with a pawn shop operator of all things. It made my teeth ache to hear they spent a fortune hiring amateurs to start a competing daily – and were predictably plowed under in a brutal advertising war with the established paper.

They made every mistake in the book, ran out of capital and had to cut back to a suburban weekly. All while I was in the Army. I yearned for the lost opportunity. I could have mounted a much better offensive than the amateurs. My uncle said he felt foolish not having thought to ask me, because he thought of me as a famous author, not ink-stained wretch. Newspaper amateur he was, but politically a professional. He carried enough water in Atlanta the executive editor of the paper that sunk his enterprise was happy to give his nephew a shot. Nepotism was well-respected in Georgia.

While this didn't precisely fit the definition, political alliances came close and were equally favored. I'd have a job waiting. I flew home unsure how the change would actually affect Glenda and me.

*We skipped the light fandango*
*Turned cartwheels 'cross the floor*
*I was feeling kinda seasick*
*But the crowd called out for more*
*The room was humming harder*
*As the ceiling flew away*
*When we called out for another drink*
*And the waiter brought a tray ...*

- Procol Harum, 1967

# Chapter 30:
# Georgia on My Mind

I WAS BACK HOME FROM THE ARMY four months when I gave my notice at the newspaper that had changed so much I hardly recognized it. I was following the matriarch's mandate to return to my hometown, preparatory to her moving the family back. The Army had not corroded the matriarch's influence over me, just substituted another authority for two years.

I took the Greyhound north because my mother needed my car for work. The old man's multiplying ills and hospital stays had cleaned out all my book royalties. I was back paycheck to paycheck. My hometown newspaper gave me a nice little raise that put me above a hundred bucks a week, which seemed like tall cotton.

My political uncle met me and took me home. I rented a VW Bug by the week while he worked contacts to find a good used car. I now was the youngest Sunday editor in Georgia, developing a freelance payroll and writing a weekly column, emulating my erstwhile boss. No private office, just a corner cubicle with widows overlooking Confederate soldiers' monuments on Broad Street.

I didn't feel uprooted. The worn newsroom felt like the one I earned my spurs in before it moved to soulless modern digs. Police and fire scanners muttered from the cluttered city desk. Engraving-room chemicals watered your eyes. On the traditional horseshoe-shaped news desk shirt-sleeved copy editors with lead smudges on their elbows smoked cheap cigars and cracked wise.

When Glenda flew up on vacation, she felt right at home, took over a desk and did illustrations for my column. We stayed in a motel for privacy. My uncle and aunt had three kids. One of my male cousins, well shy of puberty but with the familial sexual precocity, confessed fifty years later she rang his chimes and aroused fierce envy of my undeserved luck. In an ancient Polaroid of us together on their piano stool she radiated sensuality. I looked smug. No wonder he was smitten.

Glenda was there when a reporter tipped me to an apartment, helped me move my stuff from my uncle's and christen the bed as I had hers on the Beaches. But there were no artist openings on the paper or elsewhere. Vacation over, she went back to work and I was alone in a silent apartment.

The loneliness could have been worse. The Sunday magazine was part of the morning paper so I worked the night shift like all the morning crew. Night-side was a revelation. I loved it. Between the midnight final and bar closing I became a regular at the table reserved for reporters in a bar run by a local hoodlum. I discovered even in this small isolated city the people of the night occupied a different geography than day people, with its own coordinates, landmarks and icons. It was like stepping into a novel about nighttime Manhattan or Chicago, small-scale. The newsmen were classic ink-stained wretches as immortalized by Damon Runyon or Ben Hecht. When bars closed there were after-hours bottle clubs across the river. I could avoid the empty apartment until the sun came up. Day sleeping was easier. I loved coming in freshly showered and shaved at 4 p.m., looking forward to night like a vampire.

Nightlife was wide-open, women everywhere and available. Not that I was interested, but I enjoyed the show. Watched the up-tight city-hall reporter almost faint when a go-go dancer stripped her top, buried his face in conspicuous breasts and shook him dizzy. Saw another reporter bury his face in a dancer's crotch stage-side until her knees buckled, and come up grinning. Definitely Hecht, if not Henry Miller. Serious drinking and casual sex were drugs of choice for the madcap night crew, whose soundtrack that year was *A Whiter Shade of Pale,* the lyrics antic as our lives. I participated happily in the drinking. *This* was the newspaper homecoming I dreamed.

There were other echoes of early newspaper days – involving women of course. The managing editor introduced a pretty young reporter supposedly interested in writing for me. I waxed poetic about goals for a fine magazine. She smiled and concentrated on every word but left without offering a story. Later the ME said, "Did you score?" and laughed at my blank look. She insisted on introduction because she thought me hot! Nobody else had lucked out with her. But he bet she'd leave me alone if I was *that* obtuse. And she did. When I passed the women's desks, I did not imagine amused looks and giggly whispers. My ignorance of Venusian code made me once more an object of fun to female reporters.

The mobster's bar featured attractive cocktail waitresses in fishnets and quasi-Playboy outfits minus ears. Legs for days. Language like sailors. One blonde vivant joked about fucking a reporter right on the table. Later someone felt her up. A reporter called him on it: *"that's no way to treat a lady."* I was in my cups and brooding. "What lady?" I said. "Ladies don't fuck on bar tables."

Which bothered her worse than the guy's groping. One of our crew came back from the bathrooms saying she was back there bawling because that new guy she had a thing for insulted her. Wait, what? I found her and apologized. She took it graciously, said she always liked my looks and hoped I'd ask her out, that's why it hit her so hard. Holy cow. "How about I take you across the river to the Greek's for breakfast to say I'm sorry?"

She gave me a sad-clown look through runny mascara. "Ask me again when you're sober. If you even remember." Yikes, I believe that was a touché, M'lle. Of course I remembered – I never forget when I've been a jerk. But I never asked her out because I was committed to Glenda. The object of my affections was 300 miles of state highways through darkest Georgia into North Florida. Thirty seconds past midnight shift-end Friday I'd be laying rubber down U.S. 1. Maybe sooner if no one was keeping track.

I was now driving a recycled South Carolina game warden's big Dodge with the police-package 440 Hemi and push-button drive. My uncle scored it for me at auction, said it was the only car he'd found faster than the Olds with which he burned up highways to Atlanta. My best time to Glenda in the Saturday wee hours was four hours flat, an average of 75 miles an hour, pretty good when I had to poke through seven small towns notorious as speed traps. I aired out that old mill on dark empty roads between towns while graveyard-shift troopers cribbed a little sleep or drank coffee at all-night diners.

Glenda would open the door all little-girl sleepy in a modest floor-length gown against the onshore predawn wind. Nothing beneath but the thrilling geometry of her compact curvy body, which I craved with unflagging hunger. Shampoo and scented soap smells would mingle with salt air. Then she would be in my arms, kissing me deep, nipples tenting the gown and burning into me, any resemblance to little-girlhood gone in a heartbeat.

Sometimes she would ruck her gown around her hips and climb me right there against the closed door. She was light enough and I was big enough for that to work just fine. She would search one-handed behind my zipper, find and unfurl me into position. When she fitted me where I belonged she made that sobbing moan of female hunger I had come to know well. I would walk her to the bed, ease her down, all without disconnecting, and we would start our weekend.

I finally wrote to the girl with the Murphy bed about Glenda. I hated that. But she had waited over four months for an invitation I was no longer in a position to issue. She deserved the truth, bitter as it was. I couldn't have them both. Regret for hurting her and a sense of loss that I'd never see her again were the only shadows on my life.

Meanwhile the matriarch was having trouble persuading the old man to put the beach house up for sale. Wasn't that why I was in Georgia in the first place? But my new routine precluded annoyance. I had a pleasant apartment, my newspaper weeks were satisfying and colorful night life assuaged loneliness until dawn. I had all day Monday to get to work from my Glenda weekends. And five short midnight deadlines later I would again be blowing down the aptly-named Woodpecker Trail shortcut to Florida.

I should have knocked on some of that wood.

# Chapter 37:
# Autumn with Glenda

IT WOULD BE DECADES before I saw a movie based on a Sherman Alexie book that featured a car stuck perpetually in reverse. It flashed me back instantly to 1967, the Dodge my uncle found me and the time Glenda and I were eating just south of town before heading for Florida. When I reversed there was a clunk. When I punched Drive – it went backwards. I tried everything, including shutting it off and restarting, but every movement was backwards.

Gave up. My aunt came got us. My uncle sent the Dodge to a garage he said would be cheap. Right; the garage guy had slipped him traffic tickets to fix while he was drinking with roadhouse whores, and he forgot them. A warrant was issued. The guy took it out on me: Four hundred 1967 dollars for an eight-hundred-dollar used car. My uncle paid it when the matriarch yelled at him.

Glenda and I took the Greyhound to Florida. We turned it into a romantic adventure. Cannot recall how she managed so many visits to Georgia. I just liked it. Episodes stand out: being deeply involved in cunnilingus when a motel maid barged in. Glenda said *"Marcus!"* I thought she thought he had found her. But when the maid was gone she said calling his name was ingrained habit from interrupted married sex. A mood-breaker if ever there was one.

Happier episode that fall: we decided to go to Florida down the coast. A storm was rolling in when we hit

Fernandina Beach. They said power was out everywhere south. We checked into a motel. She sent me to the pharmacy for condoms. Don't remember why; maybe she forgot her diaphragm. Palm trees were whipping in the sea wind, broken fronds skittering like tumbleweeds. I chose a box of six. The pharmacist looked out the window with a smile: "*Nice night for it.*" You're right I said. Better take two boxes. He thought I was joking.

Back in the room she couldn't make a condom fit. It split. She tried another, got it on. "You're so damn *big* tonight," she said in exasperation. "Will you fit in *me*?" Despite more broken ones I had plenty. I'd been too embarrassed to tell the pharmacist why I wanted a dozen.

She decided it was time to move in with me. We spent a weekend loading the Dodge. The big trunk held all her stretched canvases and sketch pads, shoe boxes full of paints, brushes and other artist's paraphernalia. We stretched a clothing pole between coat hooks behind the front seat for most of her clothing. I folded her drafting table and leaned it behind the clothes, then back-filled with boxes of romance novels and art books. Loading her stuff was to me a ritual of commitment. I was sure we were forever. She kept enough stuff in Florida to "camp out" until she came north for good.

She found an artist-wanted ad for the Atlanta *Journal.* I made the appointment, thinking the Georgia newspaper connection might help. The personnel guy asked if I was coming with her. Yes. *Great,* he said, *Our managing editor wants to talk to you.* We flew over on a puddle-jumper. Atlanta was cold and windy. I loved walking the streets with her bundled in her winter coat, me in my old clop coat.

The odd things you remember. She wanted to play Parcheesi so we bought a board and played in our hotel. Very domestic. With her stuff in my apartment, I wondered if Parcheesi was harbinger of settled married life. Wasn't sure how I felt. It was fun but it wasn't fucking. Maybe I was incorrigible.

Next day she headed off to her interview. The personnel guy sent me to the newsroom. Four times larger than the *Chronicle* but clearly a newsroom, not an insurance office. The managing editor told me a story, prefaced by saying the *Journal* considered itself the newspaper of record for the entire South. His story: big Yankee dailies stole a major civil-rights scoop right under their nose. James Meredith, first black to integrate Ole Miss, came back to stage a "freedom march" and was gunned down with no *Journal* reporter to see. He didn't want that to happen again.

They were building a flying squad of reporters to hit the ground running anywhere in the South. He wanted a team-leader with both reporting and editing experience, first among equals. *As you must know, reporters don't respect editors without shoe-leather experience.* My being a published author was a cherry on top, meaning team reports would be well-written. Yes of course he knew about me; the *Journal* viewed all Southern dailies as their minor leagues and kept an eye on promising talent. Forty-dollar-a-week raise to begin. When could I start?

Well I couldn't tell him I had to ask the matriarch's permission, could I? Said I'd consider it over the weekend. He thought I was negotiating and said maybe they could do a little better on salary. I gulped and said I'd call him. Expected Glenda to be excited. She wasn't. They found her portfolio wanting – but some idiot said: *on the bright side you brought us your boyfriend and we're hiring him.* She was pretty quiet on the flight home.

Memory blanks on our road-trip back to the Beaches. All I recall is that uneasy quiet. I spent time at the old garage apartment talking to the matriarch. The old man still was hunkered down about staying on the Beaches. My mother's Post Office transfer was hanging fire pending the move. The matriarch was not thrilled about Atlanta. She wanted me to stay where she put me.

My mother said take the Barracuda. *The Dodge will get me to work and your car will make you feel better.* So I drove the Barracuda north like a bat out of hell after delaying departure trying to read Glenda's moodiness. Sports cars with Florida plates were to Georgia troopers like chum to sharks. But he never would have caught me if I knew his radio signal was skipping and he couldn't call ahead. I stopped when I noticed him trying vainly to catch up. My antennae for cops had been blunted by being one in the Army – or maybe lingering worry about Glenda. Something was up with her, but I didn't know what.

So I spent time with a small-town magistrate who refused my personal check until I trotted out my uncle's name. A hundred bucks lighter, I was only a half-hour late for work. Forgot all about the *Journal*.

When I called Glenda at work later that week they said she had quit. I tried Sally. She professed to know nothing. Glenda didn't have a phone in her apartment. I finally called her landlord and asked them to bring her to the phone. They were upset and said never again unless its life and death. She was tense and subdued, said she'd been sleeping and told me not to come this weekend. She couldn't talk freely in front of them but said her dad was coming to drive her down to Ocala for a visit. No she didn't have their number, she was in her nightgown for god's sake!

November was going to be a bad month.

*Did I ever leave you*
*Was I ever able*
*Are we still leaning*
*Across the old table*

*Did I ever love you ...*

*Was it ever settled*
*Was it ever over*
*And is it still raining*
*Back in November*

                                          - Leonard Cohen


# Chapter 39:
## Autumn without Glenda,
## Part One


ACROSS THE RIVER IN SOUTH CAROLINA, the Greek's after-hours bottle club had a Saturday wee-hours steak special with all the trimmings. There was a new comic the Greek imported from the New York borscht circuit. I was going to write a feature about him for next Sunday. The comic scored his final laugh and the jazz combo came back. We finished our steaks and ordered drinks, and the city editor asked me if I was really making a Florida road trip to return Glenda's belongings.

"That ER nurse was all over you tonight on the dance floor," Ribbit said in his bullfrog voice. "If it were me I would be plannin' a cozy winter weekend right here, not drivin' clear to Florida to *not* get laid."

"I've kinda sworn off," I said.

"Not me," Ribbit said. "I have yet to make my mark in darkest Georgia. But I'm studyin' on it. How come you didn't take what was so copiously offered you by that morsel of Georgia womanhood?"

"It's like I've got deep freeze of the genitals. I wouldn't have been able to do her any good, not now." The ER nurses who came across the river from University Hospital at the end of swing shift were dancing with a couple of young residents. Hospital residents were as bad as newspapermen about chasing women.

"I love this song," Ribbit said as the ensemble struck up *A Whiter Shade of Pale*.

"Do you? I think of it kind of as our anthem these crazy days."

"I don't know what the hell the words mean, but it speaks to me," Ribbit said. "I'd like to trip the light fantastic, perhaps with yon nurse." He sighed. "So your Glenda chick has dealt you a psychic war wound, like Jake Barnes in *Fiesta*."

"She's not my Glenda chick anymore," I said. "You're talking about Hemingway. *The Sun Also Rises*. Right?"

"It came out as *Fiesta* in England," Ribbit said. "I am merely demonstratin' my erudition."

"Have another drink," I said. "I am."

"I won't turn one down. But you need to pace yourself if you're really goin' to Florida today." Since Glenda ended it, Ribbit had been hanging around with me demonstrating brotherly solidarity. Almost like my Army buddy I.Z. when I crashed and burned with women. It was strangely comforting.

"Psychic war wound?" I said. "That's pretty heavy for this o'clock. She just put me out of business, that's all."

"A honey badger will do that," Ribbit said. "Before you comment, yes I am now demonstratin' my North Carolina roots by referring obliquely to Robert Ruark's bitter writing about women." He finished off his new drink in one long swallow. "I sometimes think all Southern women are honey badgers."

"Now you're a naturalist," I said. "How about black widow spiders? How about praying mantises?" But Glenda wasn't Southern.

"How about another drink? Honey badgers always go for the groin," Ribbit said. "Ask me: I know."

"I believe I will have one more," I said. "Going for the groin is only bad depending upon the intent."

"Now you're channelin' that nasty Henry Miller," Ribbit said. "Yon nurse looks good for a favorable groin descent. Probably right in the parking lot, she's so ready."

"Get over it about the nurse, okay?" I suppressed a shudder. Fox across my grave the matriarch would say. She had compared Glenda to polio: I'd survive or be crippled. Right now it felt like the latter. "My cannon is spiked," I said. "Sometimes I think it's permanent."

"How he uses cynical speech to hide his bleedin' heart." Ribbit used his voice-of-doom bullfrog voice. "Don't fret, Ish. You're just brokenhearted. Many of us have had it. It will heal."

"I'm not sure I even want it to. Maybe the R.C's have a point about celibacy."

"You are not a priest, Ish. Nor even a penitent. That's just depression talkin'. A natural companion to a broken heart. Shake it off, Ish. Save yourself for a last go at Glenda, just in case. Nothin' like brokenhearted sex. All sad and sweet and final."

My groin shriveled at the very idea. I was finally done with Glenda. More to the point Glenda was done with me. It ached my brain like an abscessed tooth. Ribbit patted my shoulder. "There are those in the newsroom who believe you should just lug Glenda's crap to the dump. But we know that's not you, Ish. By God, all this talk has got me horny. I'm goin' to dance with a nurse and see what develops. Don't wait up for me."

I drove home alone in the first weak rays of November sun. The old Dodge only wandered off the road once, which startled me to cold alcoholic wakefulness. I drove with careful precision the rest of the way. I was drunk enough to stop endlessly mulling Glenda, and slept from 7:30 to 1pm. It was time to load her stuff in the Dodge, which is why I traded the Barracuda back to my mother last weekend. A weekend of no Glenda. Of Glenda's Beaches apartment already rented to someone else, Glenda in Ocala. Her father hadn't driven up to take her for a visit. He'd come to take her home.

She'd never called me back with their number. Finding a listed out-of-state phone number was not an issue for a newspaperman in the good old days of Ma Bell. Her mother answered the phone the first few calls. Glenda was asleep. Glenda was running a fever. Glenda was out. Her mother had a gentle voice that hated lying. Finally Glenda called. Subdued, distant. Sorry, it wasn't going to work. She just couldn't. It was too much sex all the time. She had lied to me; she didn't even like sex. Her mother had prevailed on her to tell me in person. "She said I owed you that."

I scrambled some eggs and brewed coffee for the road. No hangover; I was developing a tolerance for liquor. The stilted conversation replayed in an endless loop. I was disbelieving when she quit her job and gave up her apartment without warning. Then filled with formless fear: what the hell happened? Her bald statement it was over and why, delivered in a flat emotionless voice, couldn't have been better designed to castrate me. I went numb. I stayed numb, as I tried to explain to Ribbit. Psychic war wound was about right.

She hadn't touched her stuff once it was here. I checked carefully to make sure all her oils were properly capped, an old habit from art classes that seemed a previous century. Then reloaded the Dodge. I affixed the clothing pole to the coat hangers and carried out armloads of her clothing. Her perfume lingered, trying to pull memories out of my careful blankness. A folded slip of paper torn from a reporter's slender notebook fluttered out of a fold of skirt. I hung the clothes in the car and picked it up. Her handwriting, a self-inventory:

*"Height: 5' 2 ½*
*"Weight – 115 lbs*
*"Bust – 33*
*"Waist – 29*
*"Hips – 35*

*"Dress size 8*
*"Shoe size 6 ½ AA/B*
*"Bra size – 34b*
*"Prefer seamless demi-toe hose.*
*"Cotton bras – warm socks in winter."*

Who did she write this for? I never saw it before. Her written dimensions blended with her lingering scent, and memory after memory kept trying to form. I refused delivery. Loading only took an hour or so. She had abandoned all her furniture and other encumbrances in the marital home. Including her son. Now she had abandoned me.

The November sun was hiding behind a high speckled overcast. It was so chilly I barely worked up a sweat. I threw a change of clothes and toiletries in an Army AWOL bag, filled my Thermos and took a final look through the apartment. Even with my stuff there, the place looked abandoned as I felt. She had not mentioned her estranged husband that last conversation, but of course he knew where her parents lived. Maybe the cowardly lion was out there somewhere, having regained his bluster. I added my Colt atop the things in the AWOL bag. I was ready.

# Chapter 39:
# Autumn without Glenda,
# Part Two

THE BIG DODGE HEMI SETTLED into a steady purr and ate the rolling hills south on US 1. Traffic was light. I always loved the feeling of a road trip but today the feeling bounced off my bottled emotions. I used to do my best thinking on road trips. Not this one.

South of Lake City, just to top it off, a Florida trooper nailed me, coming out of nowhere in a big black-and-yellow Highway Patrol Fury. I really had lost my nose for speed traps.

"You weren't really doing that much over the limit," he said. "In fact I saw you slow down after I called it in. Wish I'd seen that first, but since I called it in I have to write you." No point telling him I knew better. He had his quota to fill. "Moving day, huh?"

"Breaking-up day," I said. "Taking the lady's stuff back to her place."

"Ah hell," the trooper said. "I'm sorry about that." He sounded like he meant it.

"I guess it comes to us all."

"You got that right, my friend. Take it easy, huh?"

I stopped at a Stuckey's for something to eat and to tamp down irritation at getting stopped. I had forgotten how to pay attention, and the stop proved it. Tension made me sleepy. I kept yawning. When sleek horses showed in pastures I knew I was getting close. The cottage her parents were leasing had been a foreman's house on a large spread. I found it by reading mailboxes along a county highway and turned down an oyster-shell drive past a big horse mansion and white-painted barns.

And there she was, coming off the veranda of a fresh-painted frame cottage on the edge of an orange grove. Five foot two and a half, I recited from the list, 119 pounds. Moves in a kind of skipping glide like a kid about to play hopscotch. Except when she's in heels; then she gets boarding-school regal with that fetching little roll to her hips.

She was in jeans and a sweatshirt and tennis shoes now, long dark hair in a ponytail. She looked like a teenager. She looked happy to see me. She always looked happy to see me. And often a little nervous at the same time, even when we were together. She pointed to where to park. When I got out, she slipped an arm around my waist for a hug, like it was the most natural thing in the world.

"You made good time," she said. "Car running okay?" She was remembering the trip the Dodge dropped its transmission. Didn't seem fair to be playing *do you remember?*

"New transmission's good. Where should I unload?"

"Oh, you can't just start in! You need a break after that drive. Come on out back and meet the folks!" Her chipper tone was just like her, like nothing had ever changed or gone bad. In the circumstances it was surreal.

I had never met her parents. This ought to be something. It was. But nothing I could have anticipated. Mom smiled and said supper was almost ready. She put her hand on my arm for a moment, saying she was glad to finally meet me after hearing so much about me. Dad was kicked back in a glider on the stoop but hopped up to offer a hard handshake and man-to-man look.

"Thanks for bringing our baby's stuff home for her. She always said you were one of the good ones. Want a beer?"

"I'll be driving back after I get unloaded."

"Nonsense! We got our old travel trailer over there in the grove all set up for you. Sleep over, have a good breakfast and go home in the morning. No chance of black ice that way."

"Ice in Ocala?"

"It happens. People get killed because they don't believe it. This winter killed our orange crop in spite of all the smudge pots we put in there."

"Yes, stay," Glenda put in softly. "Come on, I'll show you the trailer."

So I followed her into the orange grove along a thick twisting extension cord from the house. I could smell residual smoke from the smudge pots now and a heavy undertone of spoiled fruit. Felt like I was walking with two left feet. No idea what came next.

There was a little Airstream trailer, burnished silver aluminum, in the grove. Shadows were already thickening under the trees, which made the light in the trailer windows cozy. She opened the door and slipped inside, not having to duck. I did. Before I could straighten, her arms were around my neck. Her blue eyes were enormous, inches away.

"Is it all right to kiss you?" she said. "I've missed you so much."

She kissed me without waiting for an answer. That was Glenda to a T. My arms went around her. Another of those kisses where everything between our last kiss and this one vanished. It was a kiss continued, the same kiss, all our kisses. My head swam as if my blood pressure had dropped. Finally she came up for air, our faces still inches apart, gazing at each other.

I cleared my throat. "Wow. Welcome to Ocala, huh?"

"Your lips are always so warm," she said softly. "Like you're always running a fever. Remember when you used to say I was your fever?"

Okay, that was unfair. "I remember everything." I was thinking about Ribbit's comment about brokenhearted sex. I knew I couldn't. I just couldn't. My lips might be warm but my genitals still felt like they were in deep freeze. John Thomas was not home.

"Let me show you the trailer," she said brightly. She turned loose. "You won't need to use this little kitchen, but you could if you wanted. The little bathroom is behind that door. The holding tank is set up if you need to use it. Past this curtain" – she took two steps and pulled the curtain aside – "is the bedroom. Come look, I fixed it up all special."

There were crisp clean sheets, tight at the corners as a Basic Trainee's, and several colorful quilts folded at the foot of the bed. A small electric space heater stood atop a side table. "It gets cold at night down here," she said. "But you'll be snug under the covers. Say you'll stay."

My head kept spinning. "Okay."

She gave a little happy hop – how many times had I seen that? – and clapped her hands. "Good! Let's go wash up. It's time for supper. Then we can unload."

We had supper – meatloaf with a tub of mashed potatoes and various garden vegetables and home-baked bread. Her dad and I had Busch Bavarian and she and her mom had iced tea. Her dad was a yarn-spinner, laughing about their wandering years in the travel trailer between construction jobs, little Glenda and her sister sleeping on the couch while he and Mom had the little bedroom behind the curtain. Time spent in Arizona, horses they had known and loved, high desert vistas seen. But they were really taken with this Ocala horse country now he was more or less retired.

Saturday-night company conversation with undercurrents: the husband; the absent grandchild. Her abrupt decision to dump her job and move home – the reason I was here in the first place. It may not have been the longest meal I ever endured, but it certainly was one of the strangest.

*Don't look so sad, I know it's over*
*But life goes on and this old world will keep on turning*
*Let's be glad we had some time to spend together*
*There's no need to watch the bridges that we're burning*

*Lay your head upon my pillow*
*Hold your warm and tender body close to mine ...*
*And make believe you love me one more time*
*For the good times ...*

*- Kris Kristofferson*

# Chapter 40:
## Autumn without Glenda, Part Three

IT WAS DARK WHEN I SUGGESTED it was time to start unloading. The folks retired to the TV room to give us space and Glenda came out to help unload. We worked together calmly and quietly, as we always had – for instance loading this stuff to take to my place. I drew a mental blank on her bedroom as she hung up clothes. Like it was invisible. I helped her set up her drafting table by the big window with northern exposure. When we had everything inside, she handed me a flashlight, picked up another and led me back into the grove. "Well," she said.

"Well," I said.

"Well – good night." she kind of bumped me sideways with her hip and went swinging away behind her flashlight.

It was absolutely silent in the grove after I heard the screen door bang up at the house. Silent and dark. Felt like there was cloud cover, probably from the Gulf. It was cold all right, with that smoky defeated smell from the smudge pots. The beer made a light buzzing in my brain. I thought about sitting up to read but was so tired I knew I would be out when my head hit the pillow. That felt odd. This time of night I was usually wide-awake, pushing toward the early downstate deadlines. I slipped off my clothes and got under the quilts. The batting smelled like the matriarch's quilts. Maybe all quilts made by thrifty generations before World War Two smell alike. On that thought, I faded into sleep.

I woke with dawn in the small windows when Glenda climbed into bed. She snuggled into me tightly. Her cold flesh from walking through the cold morning warmed quickly. "How did you sleep?" she whispered into my neck.

"Um. I – okay."

"Were you warm enough? You feel warm enough." Her small hands – I thought irrelevantly she failed to note her glove size on her inventory- – were gentling me like a horse.

"I'm plenty warm."

"That's good." Her lips walked up my neck and across my face. I turned to meet them. I am not awake I thought. I am not here. She is not here. She did not sneak out of her parents' house to bed me in their trailer. This is not happening.

"God I love sleeping with you," she said against my lips. "Sometimes I think that's the best part of all, just sleeping safe with someone you love. Do you suppose it would be all right if we just slept together right here, right now?"

"I'm not sure I woke up," I mumbled.

"Good. Don't wake up. I could go to sleep so easily here in your arms. Who knows when I'll ever get another chance?"

Another chance? I left that strictly alone. As young as I still was toward women I knew I could not handle on-again, off-again. Not even for Glenda, though my emotions ached to have her so relaxed and comfortably in my arms again. I felt a kind of nervous dread she was sneaking up on asking for sex. Once we were together a while, she had a very direct way of asking when she was in a certain mood, and like quicksilver her mood could shift that way in an instant.

I dreaded it. I couldn't. I just couldn't. There was no there-there anymore. Maybe Ribbit was right; maybe she gelded me with the equivalent of a Jake Barnes war wound. Not by ending it, by the words she used to explain why. A stiff dick might have no conscience but maybe a flaccid one had a sense of self-preservation.

"Are you asleep yet?" she said under my chin. Her hands drifted lower, exploring. Was she curious about my first-ever lack of reaction?

"I will be if you will hold still," I said.

She giggled with delight. "Ah, okay. Then I better hold still."

I breathed a sigh of relief. *Hell hath no fury like a woman scorned.* I thought that probably applied doubly to a woman who was the first to scorn. That wasn't close to logical. But degree by painful degree I was learning these creatures I came to call Venusian.

She tucked her hands on my chest and squirmed into the curve of my arm and laid her head on my shoulder. There's a song about this I thought. Probably more than one. Probably country, but maybe blues. Maybe when I hear one of them I will remember this. I listened to her breathing deepen, achingly familiar. She was asleep. I didn't think I would be able to sleep for nervousness, but I did.

Her dad banged on the door a couple hours later. "Rise and shine in there, breakfast is ready." He had a laugh in his voice. He seemed to like me, and clearly doted on his daughter. Maybe he thought everything was going to be all right after all, since she slipped out to the trailer to be with me. The futility of that thought brought up a lump in my throat. I felt a sting in the edges of my eyelids.

Glenda stretched lazily. "The best sleep ever. I haven't slept like that since, well – you know since when. Can I borrow a shirt to put over my nightie to get back inside? I don't want to scandalize mom."

I handed her my shirt from the day before. She kissed me once, lightly, and was gone, skipping through the heavy dew on the grass like a teenager in a man's shirt, nightie and tennis shoes. Sockless in winter I noted, thinking of her inventory again.

She was very decorous at breakfast. Her dad was smirking like an old goat. Her mom was the gracious Southern hostess doling out fried eggs and grits and red-eye ham with the efficiency of a short-order cook. Breakfast went a lot faster than supper. Glenda made me a pot of coffee to fill my road Thermos while I went back to the trailer to freshen up and shave. They all stood on the porch waving goodbye after Glenda dived up on tiptoes and planted one final kiss.

I still was in a daze, still feeling that kiss, the one I absolutely knew was the last one ever, a hundred miles later when another god-damned Florida trooper got me on the northbound at twenty-five over. He was a smart-ass, and asked me what the hell I was running away from – there were no hurricanes this time of year.

"You just never really know, in Florida," I said.

# Chapter 41:
# Poignant Thanksgiving

MY APARTMENT ECHOED. My typewriter gathered dust on the dining table surrounded by untidy pages of what was supposed to be my second novel. I had not touched it all summer. Now it was almost December. I had stacked my little black loose-leaf notebooks from the Amy, stuffed with stories, beside the German-built Schreibmaschine purchased with book royalties. I still corresponded with my New York editors. They were growing impatient. Secretly I wondered if I was a one-shot wonder with nothing else to write.

Glenda had always been on my mind since I first saw her when I was eighteen. Now there was a vast echoing hollow in the middle of my brain. When Glenda thoughts tried to form, a curtain of blankness fell. Efforts to use writing to fill the hollow were feeble. Before I moved to Georgia I had finished one short story begun in Germany on an MP typewriter. My New York magazine editor liked it, but wanted me to turn it into a novel. He sent pages of ideas to lengthen it. He was a legend, mentoring a lot of famous authors that way, and treated me as their equal in chatty letters with news of them, including me in his magic circle. His ideas for the German story were sparks from a perpetual dynamo. But I could not catch fire through the sieve of my heartache.

He was writing to the virginal boy I'd been, with a writing discipline that logged hours daily. When work stalled the boy spent self-assigned hours retyping chapters to prime the pump. That boy was gone. I couldn't put in the hours. Couldn't even sit still. The apartment was so empty I felt like screaming. Glenda was gone. Ignoring the matriarch's sage advice I had not kept the girl with the Murphy bed in the dark. She was gone too.

No way could I take up the challenge of the Atlanta *Journal.* Taking the lead among a crew of fiercely competitive reporters to cover the entire South would require focus and dedication, and all my talent. Such as it was. Focus and concentration were out of the question. I wrote an essentially incoherent letter admitting a love affair ending badly had damaged me, thanks for the offer but no.

*We here understand the situation*, the managing editor replied. *Please think of us when you regain your equilibrium.* A classy response proving I had missed a call-up to the majors. I'd always be bush-league now. Which dovetailed with regret I no longer considered myself an author.

But small-city night life still throbbed. After deadline the newspaper table at the bar was always jumping, wild tales and rude jokes and amiable insults flowing like the liquor we consumed. The colorful Greek's after-hours joint was my refuge from the empty apartment until daylight. Women still were flirtatious, hinting interest. My magazine was a success thanks to a stable of free-lance writers willing to accept twenty-five bucks for a full-length feature. Editing and page layout and headline-writing I could do by rote.

I volunteered to cover beats to give other guys a day off. Police beat for one. The night a family was wiped out by a drunk on U.S. 1, the ER nurse who liked me was impressed I didn't get ill from the smell when they brought the bodies in. Gurneys backed up in the hall. She flirted with me above the gray deflated corpses, one svelte white stocking exposed as her uniform rode up when she cocked a foot on a chromium gurney rail: just another late shift at the butcher shop. She wanted me to take her to the Greek's later. I made some lame excuse. In a curious way I felt as finished as the corpses. Her vibrant aliveness could not penetrate the bell jar around my emotions.

The night shift filled the night with activity that overrode my drab interior monologue. The bars and after-hours clubs supplied liquid anodyne for loneliness and helped me through the night to safe daylight, when I could finally sleep.

The matriarch didn't say I told you so. Didn't have to. Said file Glenda under lessons learned and write when I could, until lightning struck again. She had a lot on her plate. Still hadn't persuaded the old man to move back to Georgia. Second leg gone, he was proving an unpleasant invalid. She was exhausted catering to his every whim. Meanwhile her new obsessive worry was my brother's stark tragedy, beside which my Glenda trauma was trivial.

Home from the far Pacific, he was stationed at a local Naval station. Too late for the heartrendingly beautiful girl who said she'd wait for him. She was killed when the car she was in flipped, threw her and landed on her. The rest of the story was as heartrendingly ugly as she had been beautiful: she was riding with a boy known for his sexual conquests and drunk driving. Everybody gossiped that she was fucking him. Nothing exposes secrets like death.

Assuaging loneliness because my brother left her for an aircraft carrier off the coast of Vietnam? Or just moving on? My brother blamed himself. Believed if he hadn't joined the Navy to avoid the draft, his presence would have delivered her from temptation. But he surely would have been drafted, so the result would probably have been the same. Imponderable, essentially irrelevant.

She had been the matriarch's favorite of all his beach bunnies. A serious girl, raised strictly, deeply in love with my brother. The matriarch always said a girl can get kind of crazy when her man is at war. She never explained her remark about craziness, but her first fiancée had been killed by Bosch mustard gas in the First World War. Taken with her remark about crazy, I sensed a dark undertow: perhaps remorse about dallying with a certain rum-runner before news of her doughboy's death came. This time death had stalked the home front, and exposed a girl's craziness for all to know.

I went home for Thanksgiving. By unspoken consent the family did not talk about my brother's dead girl. But her ghost haunted the feast. I saved a striking photo from those he was discarding. She was leaning against my Barracuda – of course he used my car to court her. A gorgeous blonde in sweater and skirt, one loafer off, tickling with her stocking toes the belly of a beautiful German shepherd lolling like a ninety-pound puppy. Movie-star radiance in her smile. Dead and gone. The matriarch decreed we honor his private grief and not hover. A poignant day of thanks.

At the end of the day she and I were alone in the TV room. She dipped some Butternut and said, "Now what about you? You been moping around like the last rose of summer hit by a hail storm." One of her favorite phrases for the blues. "He can't do anything but hurt. But you need you a girl."

I said I was out of the game. If I had been thinking in terms of a sexual Iliad at that age, I would have said mine was over already.

She never said "Pshaw!" But her eye roll said it. "Why don't you call your girl in Seattle?"

My gut knotted around my heavy Thanksgiving meal at the memory of that sweet lost time, and what I'd done to her by taking up with Glenda. I thought I might throw up. "She wouldn't want to hear from me. Not after I told her about Glenda."

"Glenda!" She lifted her spit can and spat. Her wordless opinion. "Forget Glenda. Call your girl in Seattle."

"She's not my girl. She could have been."

"You didn't give her a chance."

"I hurt her so bad she'd never want to hear from me."

She rocked in the old rocker and lipped her Butternut. Her vivid blue eyes that could be ice-cold and disdainful were twinkling. "Think you know it all now, don't you?" Suppressed – something – in her tone. Mirth? My situation might not be tragic, but it wasn't funny.

"I know she doesn't want to hear from me," I said.

"Wellll." A beatific smile broke through. "That's not what she told me. She said she'd be glad to hear from you."

Flabbergasted is too mild a word. "She called you?"

She lifted her spit cup. "I called *her*. You ain't got the brass. And she was too busy *honorin' your wishes* to call. Told her your wishes have changed. She'd like to talk about that."

*"When I saw my wife again standing by the tracks as the train came in by the piled logs at the station, I wished I had died before I had ever loved anyone but her."*
  - Ernest Hemingway, *A Moveable Feast*

*You have put a circle of castles*
*around my penis and you swirl them*
*like sunlight on the wings of birds ...*
  - Richard Brautigan, *Poems*

# Chapter 42:
# December Reunion

THE LOCAL AIRPORT WAS SMALL. Arriving airliners parked out from the terminal on the concrete. Steps were wheeled out. I waited at the gate as people from the Atlanta Delta disembarked beneath December storm clouds. She'd had to change in Chicago first and then Atlanta. All flights South came through Atlanta.

She was about halfway back in the straggling file across the pavement. I stood behind the gate as greeters swarmed awaited travelers. Others rushed into the gap. She stood back to let them go. Our gazes met and locked. She seemed faintly amused by the noisy greeting rituals. To me we seemed separated by antic pygmies. It was cold but she had no coat. Her auburn hair blazed under the gray sky. She wore a Kelly green dress that hugged her curves and had a strange wide green satin band along the hem. A scoop neck showed elegant collarbones beneath the pale column of her neck. Finally she stepped through. Handed me her old Pan Am carry-on.

I remember the diffidence with which we came together and turned toward the terminal. Nothing else. Did we hug? Did we kiss? Did we claim her checked bags? We must have done. All I recall is walking her toward the Barracuda. I was going to unlock the passenger door when she said "I'll get in this side," and dropped gracefully behind the steering wheel.

She braced against the floor, lifting her hips and reached with her right leg to slide across the bucket seats. The green satin hem rode above her knees. Her calves and quads defined themselves and I thought *my god, those legs!*

She was here. She was in the Barracuda. It seemed like a miracle. She actually had taken my call as the matriarch said she would. We talked a long time. My frozen emotions thawed. It felt so perfectly natural. Until I idiotically said something like you always knew we'd be together again.

The pause before she answered was a knife slicing through euphoria. *Did I? Well, we have a lot to talk about. But not on the phone ...*

It was almost Christmas. The day before or after the shortest day of the year. My whole being was aware of her beside me in the car, overlaid by that ... diffidence. She was here – but was she really? How strange that, for all my prodigious feats of memory and the alleged "photographic" nature of that memory asserted by grade-school testers, the ride to my apartment remains a blur.

We must have parked on the street like I always did, and walked down the drive to my apartment in back of the landlady's house. Did Grace come out puffing on one of her unfiltered Camels to say hello? Grace approved a young man's having girlfriends. After I rented the place the matriarch grimly told me Grace had a fling with the old man back in his firefighting days. My hometown was full of complicated associations as a Faulkner novel.

Anyway, somewhere in there we kissed. Really kissed. Once she was in my arms it wiped the slate clean of everything since April in Seattle. As if we were back in the apartment with the noisy Murphy bed. Her girdle offered no difficulties in my apartment. The marks it left on her alabaster flesh filled me with aching tenderness.

We made love in a much quieter bed. The bed I had shared with Glenda. I don't believe that even crossed my mind. All of that had been packaged up, tied off with my sexual numbness and put away. Far away. Along with any lingering doubt the numbness would last. My vigor was back as if it had never been gone.

She never mentioned Glenda being here first. Her personality expanded to fill every corner of the place until there was no room for ghosts. It really was a miracle. One I was pretty sure I didn't deserve.

By the time I finished my final shifts that week and we headed to Florida for Christmas, we were together as we were in Seattle. Though there still were conversations she said we needed to have that I dreaded. The matriarch had personally invited her for Christmas, having weighed her up in their telephone talks – there had been more than one – and found her worthy.

It was a happy Christmas in that crowded old beach house, gift-giving and merriment, my brother holding his grief for his lost girl privately, and the rest of us saying nothing to rouse the specter. My mother immediately bonded with Chloe, affirming the matriarch's judgment. The old man liked her and drove her around to see the Beaches in his Mercury, now equipped with hand controls since he had no feet. His oldest son, a Pentagon functionary bucking for his first star, had worked bureaucratic magic for prosthetic legs despite the old man's ancient BCD. They enabled walking with crutches but not driving.

I actually had pangs of jealousy about her being off with him. She liked him and felt sorry for his handicap, and the old man never needed much time to capitalize on a woman's sympathy. One-legged, he had fucked the nurse from across the lane married to the radio exec, right in our living room that was now his bedroom. The matriarch almost caught them *in flagrente* and said *Better you than me, the old goat.* When I warned Chloe, she laughed at me: *That sweet old man?* She didn't know the family history yet.

The thing that most annoyed me that Christmas was the matriarch's insistence on separate sleeping arrangements for Chloe and me. Didn't want the redhead's folks to think us trashy! She refused to believe her mother brought extra pillows for my Seattle week in Chloe's apartment. Called me a liar. Refused to ask the redhead. We drifted around in sexual frustration. Considered slipping into the Barracuda across the lane in the neighbor's garage. She was willing but we finally decided no.

I was in a state. Which led to my most vivid memory of that Christmas. I had told Chloe about my teenage spying on Blondie from the upstairs bathroom, and my ignorant fumbling toward masturbation. It was still the sixties. We were practicing full openness and honesty. Something I would come to regret, but not yet.

She quietly drew me into that bathroom one afternoon and closed the door. We made out like teenagers. Then she put down the toilet seat, sat, pulled out my furious erection and whispered, *time for a new memory here*. She engulfed me with her warm mouth. I halfheartedly resisted; no room for intercourse. She shook her head – pulled back – *this is all for you*. Then she took me deep. It was her first full-on fellatio in our time together.

I erupted. She drained me without spilling a drop. Had to help me hobble out. My legs had turned to India rubber. She had a little smile. *That should hold you till we get back to Georgia.*

Rightly or wrongly that fellatio, in the bathroom where I made the first ignorant steps on my sexual Iliad, became my most enduring recollection of how 1967 finally wound to an end. Almost as vivid was the image of her in that green dress, meeting my gaze above the scurrying pygmies at the airport, and the strange diffidence with which we closed the distance. Everything between remains a sensual blur of the time we reclaimed our Seattle moment of happiness before the first shadow fell.

*I haven't read Tennyson, but the Lees means the Yeast at the Bottom of the Glass or Bottle of either Wine or Beer ... I suppose (he) meant Drink Life to the Full, do not Hold back but Dive Straight in ... Grab Life with Both Hands, do not Hesitate.*

-Blog entry, *Yahoo Answers*

# Chapter 43:
# A Brief Shining Time

IN AN OLD MAN'S MEMORY my time on the night-side *Chronicle* sparkles like a small perfect jewel, a stage-set where I lived life to the lees, in Tennyson's old phrase. In a way it was my brief shining time, my Camelot. I loved deeply, suffered deeply, lost one woman and gained another. Through it all there was the *Chronicle* and its antic crew of newsies – Ribbit, Brush, Lightnin' Man, Charlie Brown – like a Greek chorus for my star turn. Supporting cast: the genial mobster than ran tabs for us at his Magnolia Club, the manic Greek whose bottle club across the river was a refuge till dawn; gamblers, crooked pols, go-go dancers, ER nurses, whores and barflies.

Characters in the story were larger than life, led by my political uncle who as a teenager taught me my first word: *touchdown.* A yellowing Kodak print shows a lanky kid wrapped all around a chubby grinning toddler clutching a football. He was my favorite tall person. He smoked a pipe, Mixture 76. As soon as I was a teenager I smoked a pipe. As a politician he ignored rules prohibiting relatives visiting Basic Trainees and my captain – no political fool – opened the day room to give us private time. He hosted steak cookouts for Military Police classmates of mine they remembered fondly fifty years later. He was a political maverick who ran as a Republican when the Southern Democrat machine would not give him a shot – and won. GOP functionaries in awe of his charisma rode his coattails into Atlanta.

On the matriarch's orders he sat with me and the *Chronicle* executive editor and materialized my job there. He welcomed Glenda to his home while we were together despite the matriarch's misgivings. When she left me, he commiserated as only he could: arranged in Atlanta for a cheerful Negro whore to defrost my frozen genitalia. Being me, I worried my size was inadequate, given those salacious books about *Mandingo*. Never forgot her happy chuckle as she paraphrased Hemingway's advice to Fitzgerald: *"Baby, it ain't the size. It's what you do with it. You got nothing to fret about!"*

When Chloe came back to me, my uncle approved. For decades she kept the autographed photo he gave her – *"Hurry back to Georgia"* in his distinctive scrawl – when she left after Christmas to close her Seattle life and return. My uncle's charisma so impressed my friend Bradley he said there was no political office he could not win.

That was saying something. Brad was a former radio newsman from DC and GOP stalwart who had managed House and Senate campaigns. Canadian-born, I never quite got how he wound up drafted and stationed at the local fort. He came into my life as a freelance writer for my magazine, and worked as a nightside disk jockey. Being in the Army seemed to sit very lightly on his shoulders due to his undoubted political connections. He said he would kill for a candidate like my uncle up north.

Brad was one of my stable of talented writers who made the magazine so popular advertisers demanded space in it. He drew me into his social circle of college professors and race-car drivers and entertainers. He exercised an almost godlike power over the night people of my world when he took to the airwaves to spin platters on the midnight-to-dawn show. He called it *Night Sound* and was all alone at his control board, horseshoe-shaped like a news desk, in the deserted station. Surrounded to the ceiling by hundreds of racked records, from worn wax 78s to the new hi-fi vinyl LPs, he used them all in eccentric combinations to weave a spell across the night.

Bradley's show could take whores at the Magnolia Club from a sensual sentimental swoon to sad talk of suicide in three songs and several dozen velvet words. He had the same effect on bar girls, emergency-room nurses and insomniac housewives. He knew it, too. Sisters under the skin, he liked to say. He had an intimate, husky, honeyed voice matured thousands of miles from the South that he tuned with deadly accuracy. Every woman seemed to think he spoke exclusively to her. A lot of men felt like he spoke *for* them, shaping inarticulate longings into words. They discussed things he said with the gravity later reserved for doomsday-radio hosts.

I never met a woman who listened to Bradley that didn't have to be careful not to want him. Never met a male listener who didn't fear letting his woman be around

Bradley. Chloe found my belief amusing. Said she liked him and admired his guitar play at parties he was always organizing so he could have an audience. But she was done fucking other men.

Would have been done before, if I had not abandoned her for Glenda. I knew nothing about Venusian revenge fucks back then. Even if I had, the number would have seemed excessive. I needed to man up to the much-touted sixties honesty and accept blame for her looking for love in all the wrong places.

But my unstated fear was she was a true sixties flower child to whom serial fucking was no big deal. The fear gnawed at me, given the long list of girls I never fucked but wanted to. And the injustice: I resented that females always had the upper hand to say yes or no. Old Houser had warned me as a virginal copy boy I would bump up against that inequality once I knew what I'd been missing. And I had.

Chloe was the first American girl to say yes. To me our Seattle time was magical. And my forsaking her for Glenda guilt-inducing betrayal. She said she played sad love songs by Barbra Streisand interminably after she knew. But she also kept saying yes and bringing men to her Murphy bed. Six she admitted to, before the matriarch called her. Men in Georgia were attracted to her looks, and to my jealous eyes acted overly familiar, as if they could smell *yes*. But she assured me *yes* was off the table, there was nothing to worry about, even with attractive men like Bradley.

Despite my sexual angst, I lived those months with gusto. Chloe and I were regulars at Bradley's Tip Top Inn table, along with formula-V drivers and college profs. We double-dated with Brad and Cyndi, his latest squeeze; saw *The Graduate* with them. Mrs. Robinson reminded me of Esther Jacks and the long-legged woman whose seawall code I failed to crack.

Cyndi was a go-go dancer, a slim blonde, ridiculously good-looking, who alluded darkly to her checkered sexual history. Bradley urged us to forgive her sexual trespasses ordinary people could not even imagine. Chloe smiled her enigmatic smile. I thought *if you only knew, my friend.*

When he was out in public Bradley was pursued with equal gusto by Central Receiving nurses, bar girls and insomniac housewives who loved his radio show. But despite abundance of opportunity and the dreamy sensuality of his show, Brad was not a player. In those halcyon post-Pill, Playboy-key days, while ragamuffin Boom children played sexual musical beds in VW buses, muddy fields and crash pads, Brad – like me – was looking for his one true love. Each time he was with a new woman he was sure she was the one. Each time she moved on, as women tended to do those days, he was disillusioned and then depressed. I empathized. Cyndi was his latest.

Cyndi and he were good together and she seemed happy, if bemused she had captured the affections of this local celebrity. An Army lieutenant obsessed with her had tried to pull rank on my enlisted friend to chase him off. Given Bradley's political clout a couple of phone calls brought the bewildered officer to heel, which impressed Cyndi. She liked strength. But I feared his devotion, his unspoken plan to make her an "honest woman," was doomed.

All against the beguiling backdrop of night-side newspapering and Chloe's presence. Life lived large in the dark watches of the night. I was so happy I should have seen it could not last.

# Chapter 44:
# Knee-High Snow Frost,
# Part One

HUNTING DAWN; it trembled in my deepening awareness like the first pink flush of shooting time. Wings on the upland or wings on the marsh, waiting beyond our warm old homemade quilts where we slept side by side on the upstairs porch. I had dreamed the smell of baking biscuits. Dreamed I heard the matriarch downstairs in the kitchen. Dreamed the ocean down the lane was quiet, no loud surf. My right arm moved to shake my brother awake.

Soft arms around my shoulders, warm yielding breast beneath my slack mouth. Slumberous female heat curled along my body. This time I really woke up. The matriarch still was in Florida trying to get the old man to move home. My brother was in the Navy. I was in Georgia in my own apartment. Biscuits and our old beach home faded with a pang of loss.

This was home now, sleeping in Chloe's arms after the *Chronicle's* midnight deadline. She was back to stay. The period of her absence after Christmas, while she was in Seattle packing up her life, seemed to last forever. In her absence women came out of the woodwork to test my fidelity. The first test came after a late-night- final deadline, when the managing editor and I were having breakfast at a diner. A hot blonde dragged her equally hot blonde friend to our table and hit on me with zero ambiguity.

While the ME – a considerable horn-dog – chatted up her friend, she wanted me to take them dancing across the river at the after-hours clubs. Just like that. She laughed at the expression on my face – whatever it was. "*You don't remember me, do you? How's your grandma?*" Married to a son of the matriarch's South Carolina niece, she saw me when I drove the matriarch out for a visit and liked my looks. But I went down in the oak bottoms to target-shoot and we hadn't met. How lucky to find me tonight when she was on the loose!

The ME was amused. And unhelpful. "Ish has a nice apartment. A stereo. Lots of records. We could go there and dance." The blondes happily agreed. All I could think to say was my place was too messy for company. "*Typical bachelor,*" the second blonde said. "*We can work around it. Got anything to drink?*" The ME chimed in he had two bottles in his car. Damned unhelpful. I could not bring a party home with Chloe's things there. Just couldn't.

They eventually accepted I wasn't inviting them home but were undeterred; left saying they'd meet us later at the Greek's. I wasn't going there, so that worked. The ME called me an idiot. "*Shit, they both wanted some of you! I was a consolation prize. Not that I mind. Coulda been hot.*" My brain was in free-fall. All those years of near-misses, now I was throwing it away? My second-cousin's wife – wasn't that like incest? She didn't care. *Both* wanted some of me? He had to be kidding ...

"*You been married long as me, you'll repent this night,*" he said. "*Mark my words.*" Which resonated with old Houser telling a virgin copy boy to grab all he could. I just wasn't cut out for the sexy sixties. That was all there was to it. Being committed to a single woman was equivalent to virginity in an odd way.

Then Janine came along. I was at one of those private Sunday parties *Chronicle* men held every week since the madcap governor shut down Sunday liquor sales. Lots of free booze and pseudo-intellectual conversation; college professors, graduate students, young doctors, a smattering of Army officers. Brush, the New Jersey copy-desk guy, was hosting this one. I got involved in one of those silly debates about literature, championing Harold Robbins against the shouters of some new thin-blooded "literary" writer all the rage that winter. Robbins is plastic, just plastic, phony intellectuals from the college said. Well-poured plastic endures better than most steel, I said.

The tall curvy girl with strange large violet eyes and silken helmet of short fair hair dropped into the argument from time to time, remarkable eyes focused on me, nodding solemnly as if she agreed with my every point. She was obviously sleeping with the crew-cut liberal with the cutesy bow tie and sleeveless sweater, so I thought nothing of it.

Brush's guest of honor was an 80-year-old Botswana journalist touring the States by Greyhound. Brush and I enjoyed his travel tales. He financed his travels with freelance work. I'd put one of his African stories in my Sunday magazine. Oxford-trained, closest thing to a Victorian gentleman we ever met, we liked him a lot and admired how he put away the Scotch. Janine flirted with him and he handed it right back with a twinkling eye. A man to emulate.

When the party broke up Brush told me Janine was a Midwest newspaper heiress stopping with friends on her way to Miami to plan an elaborate wedding to an Annapolis grad. He handed me a slip of paper with an address. *"She told me she plans to fuck you before she leaves. Just helping out."* Waggled his eyebrows. I laughed him off.

Monday night at work he had a phone number. *"I promised you'd call. Don't be rude."* For crying out loud. But I called. Janine's hostess invited me right out for a drink. I went on my lunch hour. An upscale condo done up in stark-white-and-mahogany that reeked big bucks. Janine was off on a date. The wife smiled a secret smile. *"Stick around. She'll ditch him and come back. Her radar is locked on you."* Yeah, right. But I stayed for drinks to be polite. Interesting woman, married to a local power broker. *"Writers!"* she said. *"I was married to one. Couldn't take the mood swings. Got a solid boringly reliable guy now."* To my surprise I knew her ex through my New York editor. *"Small world,"* she said. *"I'm cured but Janine needs a writer fix. She'll be back before you finish that drink."*

As if there was some feminine telepathy at work in the Georgia night. At 25, I thought myself worldly. Still didn't have a damn clue about Venusians. Janine was back within the hour, full of sophisticated banter about Oklahoma City and San Francisco and Manhattan and Miami; led me into the night saying *"Now show me your Deep South."*

I was reluctant to take her to the Magnolia Club since I was supposed to be working. It would be hours before the Greek's started hopping. We stopped at a tame piano bar for a few slow dances and got acquainted. I was embarrassed at the paucity of nightlife I had liked fine until she asked. She had a solution: *"Why not take me to your place so we can screw?"*

But Chloe's clothing still was there. Packages she shipped had started arriving. I was emotionally raw over all the men she admitted fucking the summer I was with Glenda – trying to suppress suspicion she might indulge a farewell fuck or two before returning. She was far more in tune with the sexual sixties than me. Damn it, this fidelity thing was heavy going. I used my messy-apartment excuse again, and deflected, asking her about the bow-tie prof and her supposedly pending marriage.

She had newspaper blood all right – simple declarative sentences: *"The bow-tie as you put it is a latent queer. The marriage is to tie two family fortunes together. Just say you can't, if you can't. You'll have a good reason, because I know you want me and you know I want you. I don't need to know your reason to respect it. Our timing just sucks."* An intriguing woman, out to sow wild oats before nuptials. Who even knew women thought like that? The ME was right, I was going to repent Janine.

But not yet, not warm in Chloe's arms. Icy wind slid a preying paw through the window above the bed. I listened to her peaceful breathing, felt the humid rise and fall of her breast beneath my face. My guilt-free reward for fidelity. But why the dream about biscuits and bird-shooting? Now I could actually smell Hoppe's Number Nine lacing the warm musk of our lovemaking. Woke all the way up.

Across the room, the canvas sheath of my old Winchester pump gun glowed orange in light from the gas log. My faded canvas shell vest and leather-fronted birdshooter pants were folded on the dresser beside Chloe's jewelry box. Two fresh cardboard cartons of sixteen-gauge shot shells on the vest. Gun oil must have triggered the biscuit dream from teenage hunting mornings when the matriarch made us breakfast. I was going bird-shooting today for the first time since the Army, with the *Chronicle* sports editor. A quail preserve up in the South Carolina piedmont, classic Havilah Babcock country.

Prentiss and I admired the smooth-writing college professor with a literary passion for bobwhite quail. For me it would be a visit to farm fields and thickets where my matriarch as a young girl visited country relatives. Got in trouble for pampering bird dogs with too many table scraps, so lean she thought they needed fattening. A different world from bottle clubs across the river growing rich off refugees from Georgia blue laws.

I slid out of bed allowing the bare minimum of chill room air to displace warmth. Chloe stretched extravagantly like a large silken cat, then settled into whatever dream made her lips curve softly at the corners. I doubted it included biscuits and bird-hunting. I went into the bathroom to relieve my bladder and brush my teeth. When I came out, flushing and splashing had awakened Chloe. She watched me step into cotton waffle-weave long underwear. When I put on my faded corduroy shirt she sighed. "So you're really going outside. And at this hour."

"Yep."

"You remind me of Ralf." Her mother's Swedish boyfriend, a building contractor, hunter of big game in high mountains and high latitudes, including polar bears on the ice. A far cry from bird dogs and eight-ounce bobwhites.

Evidently a satisfying lover for her sensual mom – and fully prepared to protect her daughters when needed.

One of Chloe's unsettling stories about her summer of fucking involved a possessive guy furious when she refused him fellatio. Said she reserved that for me even though I was gone. Pretty to think so; it was sick-making enough to imagine him in her Murphy bed thinking he had a right to demand.

She called Ralf. I knew Ralf from my Seattle time with her. Bald, deeply tanned and muscled, his black Swedish temper could match my old man's. Unlike my old man he didn't destroy the presumptuous asshole, just kicked him out. Good on Ralf.

In that magic Seattle interlude after the Army, Ralf promised to teach me the mountains when – not if – I returned. In my euphoria with Chloe, I had joked his offer as guide was almost equal to her sexual attraction. But I didn't return. She admitted fucking six men before the matriarch called her …

# Chapter 45:
# Knee-High Snow Frost,
# Part Two

AWARENESS OF ALL CHLOE told me about that summer clotted under my heart like a cancer when I let the thoughts intrude. She had been with a damned Kikuyu university student when the matriarch called her. I knew more about Kiyukes than she expected: they mutilated their women's' Mons to remove the pleasure centers and traveled abroad to fuck and dominate white women. Goddamned Mau Mau in waiting was my thought.

He made her walk paces behind him in the street and sit in the car waiting while he partied with friends. I could not grasp her putting up with it – a submissive side I never saw. I hoped tough Kenyan settlers Robert Ruark wrote about in *Something of Value* killed a lot of his relatives in the race wars ...

I pushed all that down deep; didn't belong on a hunting morning. Pulled on my pants and took wool socks from their perch on my rundown combat boots. Got socks and boots on, cold inside leather warming quickly. "You went somewhere," Chloe said quietly. "I can read you pretty well, you know. Bad thoughts?"

"Just wishing I came back to Seattle. Before ... everything. So Ralf could take me elk hunting. To be with you too, of course."

Her smile was sad, hearing the unsaid things. She read me, all right. "Ralf likes you. So does Mom. Maybe you can get a job on a Seattle paper."

"Maybe I can. One of the GIs who worked for me got on at the Tacoma paper. Another one already was a Seattle photographer."

Her smile brightened. "The one who took pictures of us at the fountain that day. Did he ever send you one?"

"I never asked. I don't need a picture to remember our first day." I went to her, tipped her chin up and kissed her lightly. "I will remember every detail till my dying day."

"Where's your pipe?" she said against my lips.

"What?"

"The bed frame's metal. The wall is some fake particle something. Your pipe is real wood. Knock on wood!"

"My family has infected you with our superstitions."

"Just do it. Please?"

I walked across to my Winchester and peeled the sheath down partway. "Genuine American walnut. I'm knocking, see?"

Her thoughts turned practical. "Do you have time for breakfast? I could scramble eggs, make some toast." Not biscuits. I dismissed the mental quibble and said okay. While she was in the kitchen I got my sweater and ski jacket out of the closet. White Stag skiwear from Portland for quail-shooting in South Carolina; strange enough for a short story. Maybe I would write it one day. Maybe I'd make it about Janine and what might have been. The bow-tie liberal and the Botswanan. No Kiyukes. Definitely no Kiyukes.

Prentiss was right on time. I grabbed my stuff and gave her a burdened hug. "It'll be good to see a light in the window coming home." The cold air seared my lungs. I left footprints in the frost. Cars on the street were iced over. Prints got his station wagon rolling almost before the door closed. The heater was on high. We picked up Danish at a cafe full of yawning white-collar day workers. I filled my Thermos with hot chocolate for later. Then we were across the river. South Carolina closed around us. We were riding the clock at sixty miles an hour toward a nine a.m. rendezvous.

Prints talked about playing basketball in college. About how he met his wife, how she enjoyed fishing and camping, made more money than he did. He wasn't always going to be a rim man on a Podunk daily's sports desk, taking Friday-night high school football scores over the phone. He was going to be an outdoor writer famous as Corey Ford or Ted Trueblood, learning the trade one column at a time. One day he would do nothing but fish and hunt and get paid to write about it. An enviable dream.

A stand of pecan trees came up on the left that Prints said marked our rendezvous. He pulled in behind two pickup trucks under winter-bare branches. Two men leaned on the one with dog boxes in back, peacefully smoking. Two bird dogs with happy active tails toured frost-killed ground cover, doling out urine that steamed. We stepped out for ritual amenities. "Might be a good day," Prentiss offered.

The older of the two chewed his foul-smelling cigar stub. "Had us a knee-high snow frost this mawnin'. Hit's gotten to be like wintertime. Birds will sit tight."

The younger man, Frank Carswell, was opening the preserve. Newspaper publicity would help. We didn't need hunting licenses because it was a private operation with pen-raised birds, open months longer than state bird season. They provided dogs for apartment dwellers with more money than time, no space for their own dogs and a hankering to play country gentleman. We listened politely, then loaded our pump guns. Prentiss handed his Remington to the old man, Ike, and unlimbered his old twin-lens reflex camera. "Keep my buddy company on the covey rise. I need pictures."

Ike sent the big young English setter out with a wave. We lined out across a rising field, Prints and Carswell lagging in deference to the guns. When we walked up behind the first point, quail flew in a brown-feathered bomb burst. I missed three straight times. Ike shot once but nothing fell. "Those must of been wild birds," he said. "They flushed wild."

"Then you must be a wild man," offered Carswell. "You shot wild."

The liver-colored pointer bitch kept coming back to where the covey jumped. The big setter worked high sedge a hundred yards away. The lemon-and-white blur of his coat slammed to a halt. Ike hefted the gun. "Them's pen birds I know. Put 'em down this mawnin'." We each missed three times. "This gun gotta be choked down like a rifle," the old man grumbled. "I was right on them birds."

"It's bad to frustrate the dogs thataway," Carswell said.

Prentiss was itching to get in on the action. Carswell held his camera. Prints missed nine straight times on the next three covey rises. I was warming up; I grassed two.

Carswell and Ike led Prentiss after the big setter off across a steep meadow. That left the liver bitch with me to work a thicket of berry bushes. She hunted up three singles. I shot into a tree behind the first and had no clear shot on the second. The third sprayed feathers and glided out of sight, the liver bitch right behind it. When she didn't come back I followed her soft whimpering down to a shallow creek.

She was half pointing the dead bobwhite cradled in a tangle of briars just above the water. She sampled the dark water with a paw and shivered. "I don't blame you," I said. "I'll get it." I laid the little Winchester out of the way and got down on my knees. Heard a truck coming to the right, easing along, men talking above the engine. The bitch forgot the bird and bounded behind me, nudging me with a careless flank. I just had time to grab the bird before I went in the creek up to my armpits. The cold was a profound shock. I yelled and bounced out and flopped on my back. The truck stopped. Doors slammed. They called out, sounding concerned. Prints and Ike.

"I'm all right," I yelled. "Damn dog ducked me in the creek."

I peeled off shell vest and parka. Shucked sweater and corduroy shirt and long underwear shirt. Frigid air bit. Used dry shirt-tails to dry myself. My trunk was covered with gooseflesh. Ike came through the brush. The bitch followed, looking guilty. "Sorry, mister," Ike said.

"It's all right. I got the bird." I was wringing out the wool sweater. I wiped the ski parka dry. "This'll keep me warm enough – " I stopped. Ike was staring. "What's the matter?"

"You must not of shot in a long time for that little sixteen-gauge to chew up your shoulder like that. Looks like the rats been at you." He began to grin. "Wait. You ain't left-handed." Grinned so hard his eyes vanished in a skein of wrinkles. "Guess the gun didn't bite you. Not the gun."

I looked down. Little overlapping purpling half-moon bruises stood out on my left shoulder and chest. Chloe had marked me pretty good. My right shoulder was clear; I still knew how to cradle recoil. I pulled on the sweater and parka. Clammy wool warmed quickly. Stuffed wet shirts in my game bag. Ike picked up the wet bird and smoothed water from its feathers. Still grinning. "What's so damn funny?

"Nothin' at all." he handed me the bird. "It's jest kinda nice to see a young man these days keep things in balance. I ain't so old I cain't remember the way a woman's mark feels when it's fresh. Or what it's like to know she's waitin' for you to get on home to start markin' you up agin."

Felt myself try to blush – odd sensation on chilled flesh. "A kid now, "Ike said, "gets along fine jest going' huntin'. So can an old fogy like me. But a man now, a man's gotta have balance in his life or he'll get all messed up. Desperate, like. You need the balance. So when the birds don't fly right there's the woman to go home to. If the woman don't do you right there's always the birds."

We walked back up the hill and shared my hot chocolate. Carswell invited us to supper, but we were due back for the night shift. Halfway back to the city, Prints recounting every hit and miss, me half-listening, I finally absorbed Ike's simple wisdom. When Glenda nearly castrated me, it never crossed my mind to go hunting, though hunting was my teenage passion. I had things out of balance when I thought I had things straight: women and work, in that order. But Glenda had proved how quickly a woman could turn on you, and work was a poor salve.

I was sure as I had ever been of anything Chloe would be home with the light on. But if things ever went bad again there would always be the birds.

*Take the grand look now; the fire is burning*
*Is that your reflection on the wall*
*I can show you this room and some others*
*If you care to see this house at all ...*
*Careful up the stairs a few are missing*
*I haven't had the time to make repairs*
*The first one is the hardest one to master*
*The last one I'm not really sure is there ...*

- Waylon Jennings, *The House Song*

# Chapter 40:
# Night Sound -
# Third Intermezzo

ON HIS NIGHTLY RADIO SHOW Bradley sometimes played a strange song. I knew nothing about it other than it was strange and mournful and no other station seemed to play it. Bradley didn't play it much. As with all his music he chose his spots. I came to believe it signaled some watershed in his mercuric moods. Since he was a friend I paid attention.

This one night I was filling in for the *Chronicle* police reporter, driving his VW because he had a police-band radio under the dash. I muted calls for service when Bradley spun up the house song. He hadn't played it since he and Cyndi had become an item. His cryptic words when it was finished made me U-turn from Fifteenth, park the Bug at the Krispy Kreme next door to the station and grab two black coffees. I punched the side-door button that lighted a blue bulb above Brad's board. He came back to let me in. "Thought you'd be about ready for some coffee."

"You thought right, thanks!" He grinned and beat it back to spin up the next record. I came in and leaned in my favorite corner. Brad introduced a new record and shut off the mike.

"You played that house song tonight," I said.

"How's ambulance chasing?" Brad said.

We spoke at the same time, laughed, sipped coffee. "Ambulance chasing is slow. A fatal out on U.S.1. That's it so far."

"I've played that song ten times," he said. "Once on the air."

"You having trouble with Cyndi?" That was why I was here.

"Not a bit. Cyndi is wonderful. She's everything I've ever wanted in a woman."

"A natural-blonde go-go dancer with legs up to here, and a Mensa? What's not to want?"

He smiled fondly. "She's home listening now. Called after her last dance-set at the club."

"Then what brought on the house song?"

"It just felt right." Brad could freight the simplest phrase with a Barrymore's worth of drama.

"Those words," I said. "A house goes on sale this morning. Taken off the market in the afternoon. Be careful up the stairs a few are missing ... Do those words speak to you?"

"Don't they speak to you?"

"I hear despair. A world of despair. Kind of a rough song to turn loose on young lovers and barflies out there isn't it?"

He shrugged, keeping an eye on progress of the needle across the record of the moment. "Young lovers don't feel the despair. They're immune. They think they are. They probably feel an emotion they can't identify and think it's pity. They won't feel the words until they're not lovers anymore. Or just not young."

"That's a lot of bitterness," I said.

"Mine, or the song's?" He put his finger to his lips, flipped the switch and leaned in murmuring to his faithful.

"Let me ask it, Damon Runyon-like," I said when the mike was cold. "This song you refuse to give up, it brings you back no fond or not-so-fond nostalgia? It was not, once upon a time, yours and someone special's special platter?"

Bradley cocked his head professionally at my attempt to sound Broadway. "Crackers should stick to typewriters. Trying to sound like Runyon in that drawl ought to be against some kind of law."

"A nice avoidance. Why not answer the question?"

"The reporter bores in. No, it's too new to have been our song."

"Ah," I said. "*Ours.* But it triggers no memories?"

"Just a very strong sensation."

"A sensation of what?"

"Pain. We never had a house together. We could have." He spun another platter, slowing the mood to sentimental. Said maybe I was right; he shouldn't inflict personal pain on the audience. He was making up for it the only way he could, smoothing out the night.

"Personal pain sounds bad," I said. "Did I know this one?"

"It was before the South. Back when I was headed for the big markets. When Claudine and I were together"–his smooth voice roughened – "all songs, *all,* had a special meaning. And the meaning was we were forever. That's how I know lovers out there are immune. We were immune. I was sure we were. But we weren't."

He said this like a veteran of a bad war speaks of combat but doesn't want to. It's hard to imitate that knowledge of mortality. "She told me to stop being afraid to love. "He gazed up at the stacks of records. "She was everything I ever wanted in a woman. So I stopped being afraid. And loved her. Completely. I had dreams, plans. Such plans! I was going to be" – he broke off to insert an eight-track cassette with a commercial for pickup trucks, introduced with a cleverly ironical twist.

"Going to be … " I prompted.

Bradley cupped his pasteboard coffee container in both hands, reading the dark liquid like a reverse crystal ball into a dismal past. "A major success." His lips twisted the words. "This was before politics. I sing, you know. I did once. And play. And wrote my own songs."

"For god's sake. Is this house song one of yours?"

He shook his head. "It could have been. If I used the pain when she left me instead of going to pieces. And the thing is – anything I wrote truly would have been as successful as this one. Which is to say no success at all. The music scene is changing, Balkanizing, getting rock-n-rolled to death. I guess I play the house song out of solidarity with the man who had guts enough to write it. In ten years – less – it won't even find rotation space on a country station."

This was strong stuff. I drained my coffee. "How do you decide when it's time to play it?"

"I just go along and don't even think of Claudine very often. Off somewhere globetrotting like she did before we met. She won't have been without male companionship long. Not her." He scrunched up his eyes. I saw it, and felt it, with my raw knowledge of all Chloe's men. "Think I should play *Smoke Gets in Your Eyes*?" he said.

"Sure," I said, "since you're in such a sentimental mood."

He blinked. "Tough guy. Wait until it's your turn."

"It's been my turn," I said. "You know some of it."

Bradley nodded. "It speaks to everybody who's had their turn. Tells you to own your pain, grow big enough to grow around it and make it part of you forever, stop fighting it."

"The Zen of broken hearts," I suggested.

"Damn. You are cynical for one so young and Southern. This has nothing to do with metaphysical Hippie bullshit. This is a lacing of tears in your wine of life. Tells you drink it down and don't flinch."

"Pretty good for this time of the morning."

"It is, isn't it? Maybe I'll work it into the broadcast."

"Say hello to Cyndi." I tossed my cup in the wastebasket.

"Time to get back to work?"

"Yeah, Police blotter, fire dispatch, stop by the sheriff's office about the drunk who killed the guy on the highway. You know the drill."

"Say hi to Chloe. We should get together again soon."

"Chloe likes Cyndi. So do I."

"Cyndi is fine isn't she? Everything I ever wanted in a woman." That again, three times in the same conversation about two different women. "Brad…" I stopped. Didn't really want to say it.

"Yeah?" He caught my tone in one word; we knew each other pretty well.

"Brad, three months ago Joan was everything you wanted in a woman. Then the crash. You played that house song a lot."

His expression went flat. "Joan is a world-class bitch. You're welcome to her. I know you had the hots for her."

That really hurt, because it was true. I liked her a lot, jealous of the way she couldn't keep her hands off him. My affair with Glenda was falling apart. But no way I would hit on a friend's forever-love. I kept my feelings to myself. Thought I had. Should have let Brad have the last word. But hated seeing him running his emotional life off a cliff over and over. And he pissed me off about Joan.

"Before Joan," I said, "Susan was all you ever wanted in a woman. Joan helped you get over Susan. Joan was everything you wanted in a woman. Tonight it's Cyndi. Before Susan – before the South – it was the mysterious Claudine."

"You leave Claudine out of this!"

"Hell, leave all of them out of this. Just maybe be a little cautious." I left with tension still between us. Didn't know how to fix it. Felt rotten. Wished I hadn't stuck my nose in.

A week later Cyndi ran away with Brad's roommate, a *Chronicle* sports reporter whose dad owned a Kansas City trucking firm and offered her an office-manager job if she would marry his son and drag him out of the benighted South. Far as I know Bradley never played the house song again.

*I cannot speculate on what our cluttered mind will save – sleepy Sundays, or a nosebleed after love. I know only the dying heart needs the nourishment of memory to live beyond too many winters.*

*- Rod McKuen*

# Chapter 47:
## Rod McKuen's Fault

CHLOE LIKED ROD MCKUEN'S treacly love poems and played his "spoken-word" records on my old stereo while I worked nightside. We still were new together, and I was too absorbed in lust and angst-filled love as we sorted emotions about having screwed others, to notice our conflicting biorhythms. She was the quintessential lark. My joy in nightside newspapering confirmed me a true night owl.

She would have been asleep for hours by midnight-final deadline. So I was guilt-free about the two hours to bar-closing I spent with other newsies at the Magnolia Club. Going home to wake her with lips and fingers was infinitely more appealing than after-hours clubs across the river. Didn't see how life could get much better.

One of those nights at the Magnolia I found Janelle back in town, snuggling in a booth with Brush the slot man. She immediately took her hand out of his pocket and confronted me. *"Why do you have an unlisted phone?"*

What the hell? I sat with them. The waitress put down my regular bourbon.

"Thought you were in Miami," I said.

"Well, I'm back. Where the hell were you tonight?"

"She came by the paper," Brush said. "Told her you were out on a story."

"I just bet," she said. "Like the story you were on with me that night?"

I could not keep up. I knocked back the bourbon and called for another. It developed she had put her engagement to Annapolis on hold. Why? Because she had unfinished business in Georgia. With me. Had been trying to reach me since she hit town, getting frustrated and now clearly angry. Jesus. I was glad she didn't know where I lived and my number was unlisted.

"It's your fault I'm with Brush," she said.

Brush looked pained. "Said I'd keep her company till you showed up."

She eyed him. "Men! You promised more than that, Brush."

He wouldn't look at me. "Yankees are opportunists, like buzzards," I said. Knocked back my second drink. Hard to put a name on my emotions. Relief Chloe wouldn't know about this. Regret: Janelle was an impressive woman. Disbelief she came all this way to see me – when she already her hand in Brush's pocket. Awareness I would never, ever understand women. My third drink arrived. I downed it, felt the buzz start.

"I'll leave with you," she said. "Right now. Sorry, Brush." She was dead-serious. Couldn't happen. If it had been going to happen it would have happened while Chloe was in Seattle. Janelle was a road I'd never take.

"Stick with Brush," I said. "Brush will give you a good fuck." Tough-guy parting line. Walked out trying not to register the shocked hurt on her face. Knew Fate would get me for this.

Fate didn't wait long. My nightside news career came to an abrupt end within weeks. I was fired without ceremony by the egomaniacal executive editor who hired me on my uncle's say-so. Looking back, I see how my subsequent fear of being fired lay at the root of many poor work decisions over the years.

I had known I was in the asshole's cross-hairs because of a simple act of loyalty. The asshole – we called him Captain Queeg – summarily fired my friend the managing editor. Word flashed through the newsroom; everybody lived in fear of Queeg's tantrums. My friend was well-liked but they turned their backs on his walk of shame to get his belongings from his office, escorted by an armed security guard. Like Kipling's poem about the regiment turning its back as death drums played for hanging a deserter. The ME was no deserter. Just a victim of Queeg's fear his competence showed the old fraud up.

I went over to help him carry his cardboard boxes to his car. Took him for coffee at Snappy's downstairs to vent humiliation before facing his wife. "You know your days are numbered for this," he said. "No matter how much water your uncle draws in Atlanta, that crazy son of a bitch will find a way to fire you."

"If not turning my back on a friend gets me fired, then I don't want to work here." Words I would remember in unemployment lines.

I went right on putting out my magazine with work from underpaid freelancers. My uncle recruited me for PR for a special sheriff's election; said my brochures tipped the scales. We elected a former city cop, pal of the old man's in his firefighter days. *Le bon temps* rolled on. Then Chloe's poet, McKuen, got involved.

Not just Chloe's. In those strange sixties, *The Times* of London called McKuen *"one of the most riveting performers of his generation."* Allegedly the most-widely read poet of his time; which I thought more a commentary on the times than his talent. His songs reportedly amassed millions in record sales. The year I was fired his *Lonesome Cities* won a Grammy for best spoken-word album. He began reading poetry with Jack Kerouac and Allan Ginsberg in 1950s San Francisco. In the Bay City it was a hop and skip from Beats to Hippies. McKuen skipped nimbly.

So how did he figure in a Georgia newspaper firing? Well, young lovers across the land emulated his saccharine verse. Including a lovesick infantry captain at Fort Gordon. Bradley, my freelancer, DJ and – it seemed only incidentally – a GI, introduced the captain, whose hobby was photography. His passion was a slender good-looking girl in the Sears, Roebuck credit office. He combined the two in a sequence of photos of his lady-love bundled in winter clothing at a reservoir, and McKuen-style blank verse. Brad recommended it for my magazine.

The photos were dramatic: close-up of a curve of cheek beneath dark fall of hair on a sheepskin collar; strolling across stubble in a dead corn field. A wide-legged stance on the lake shore, slim jean-clad legs, curves hinted under her car coat, gazing at her reflection. Subtle sexuality in stark winter. His poem began: *Anyone can love in summer – in winter, I love you..."*

I bought it all for forty dollars for a winter center spread: six pictures, his verse, lots of white space. Put her lakefront photo on the cover. Public reaction was quick. Memorably a colonel's wife, for whom I published a story about fort life, calling to say her husband sat with the spread in his lap all morning, gazing out at the weather. *"Remembering somebody ... It wasn't me."* She reminded me of Penelope's plaint in *Ulysses Returns*, a poem by a Georgia poetess less famous but more astute than Tennyson. Another woman wrote she never hoped to see anything so romantic in the newspaper. All letters and phone calls were favorable; readers loved it. Captain Queeg did not.

He stopped by my desk to grumble. "You could have written a whole feature about this young woman in the wasted white space. Where's your newspaper sense? What's her name, how old is she, does she live here? What's her life story?" He flourished the magazine. "And what's this cover photo? It looks like somebody peeing in the lake!"

"It's her, studying her reflection."

"For God's sake. Who is this poor child?"

To my eternal regret I named her. A couple of days later the captain called ready to go to war: Queeg had approached his girlfriend at work and made a hard pass. She was outraged, said she would see I got him fired for his impertinence. Old man with a prominent wedding ring trying that crap with her. The captain asked if I *could* get him fired.

"That was my executive editor," I said. "Think commanding general."

"Oops," the captain said. "But still..."

"But still, he's an asshole. This is a new low." Within two weeks the acting ME had my marching orders: His Nibs had decided the magazine wasn't a sufficient challenge. I would spend two days on general assignments and a day as business editor to keep me out of trouble. I demanded a pay raise for additional jobs and was forthwith summoned and fired.

"Your uncle can't help you this time," Queeg smirked.

It hadn't crossed my mind he could. But since he raised the issue: "Why is that?"

The asshole was too happy to explain. Said you know he's part-owner of that weekly, all that's left from his big plan to build a daily to compete with us. "I'm president of the state newspaper association," he said. "I refused to allow that cheap little rag membership. I don't consider it a real newspaper."

Such membership would earn a share of advertising revenues from national companies that relied on the association to spread small ads through a state's small papers. Revenue to cover production costs and give a fighting chance to turn a small profit. Queeg twisting the knife to ensure the upstart publication's defeat was total. He admitted – it pained him – he had to get the publisher's permission to fire a member of a family nobody liked to cross. "He told me reverse my position and let your uncle's paper join the association before I fired you," he said. "Done deal. You're history in this town."

And so ended my all-too-brief nightside Camelot. The matriarch blamed my uncle for betraying me to save his little paper. Asserted he was too enthralled by his affair with an Atlanta heiress to a meat-packing fortune to take care of business. When he divorced and remarried, it was to that woman. Her sons never stopped disappointing her in their choice of women. But at the end of the day, fairly or not, I blamed Rod McKuen.

# Chapter 48:
# First Deep Depression

WINTER WEEKS AFTER I WAS FIRED were grim. The unemployment agency denied me benefits. There was an appeals process – but you had to show up at 7 a.m. one day a week to file. The line formed by six. Just to make it more humiliating they only took ten appeals a week. I got the message and gave up. Had no clue an appeal denial would qualify for court review – they felt no need to advise us. A rough introduction to ranks of the unemployed in Darkest Georgia.

The agency's Atlanta HQ was apologetic to my uncle but said the local office followed proper procedure; sorry, sir. Didn't advise him about the court option either. Chloe wanted to go to work. My uncle worked contacts for a telephone-company operator interview. She was turned down – first time not getting a job she applied for. My uncle raised hell. The PR guy said she was overweight by operator standards. Ma Bell wouldn't waive rules even for his Yankee slut; didn't he normally fuck less-plump chicks? Chloe was humiliated about the weight issue. I didn't tell her the rest.

My friend Bradley had heard her play the piano. With years of lessons, she was good. Brad set up an interview for a piano-bar gig. I scotched that. Given Chloe's disclosures how easily men picked her up and fucked her that summer, I was far too insecure to expose her to Georgia lounge lizards. Brad didn't get it. I didn't tell him why.

My uncle gave me a nightlife column in his weekly to keep my byline out there, and annoy Captain Queeg. The sheriff I helped elect fed me exclusive crime stories that scooped the daily. Friends at the newspaper said Queeg almost got down and gnawed the rug like Hitler. A nice image, but my uncle wasn't paying me a salary. A few twenties here and there; a power-bill payment. At least we were eating and had shelter. He invited us to all his social doings.

It was at one of these his asshole pawn-shop partner cornered Chloe, gazing into her eyes, hand splayed on her back, rubbing. She was frozen, a trapped look on her face. My rage was instant. Took his wrist and rolled the bones together. He tried to jerk away. I bore down. *Geeze* he said, *I was just bein' friendly.* Maybe I wasn't even seeing him, but the parade of strangers through her Murphy bed. *That kind of friendly can get you dead.* I threw his arm against his belly.

He was a big tough blowhard skating the edge of the underworld. But he backed down. I was convinced he got fresh because he figured me impotent after I was fired. Illogical; he was just an opportunistic asshole. But her paralyzed reaction underlined*: no piano-bar gig.* My uncle supported my anger, blood thicker than money. But we stopped going to his social affairs.

When the matriarch yelled at him for letting me get fired, he tried to deflect by telling her about the Chloe incidents. She had the answer to nip such nonsense in the bud: get married. Then he would have been recommending his nephew's wife. Georgia always bent rules for nepotism. No sleaze would attempt to poach a family wife: too dangerous. Living in sin, she said, was not an option in Darkest Georgia. She didn't say darkest but that's what she meant.

Chloe was so reluctant I asked if she wanted to go home. *Not until you come with me*. I didn't have money for such a trip. What the hell would we live on once we got there? She said the doctors she worked for would take her back instantly. I could look for a newspaper job. But I just couldn't see it. It was decades before I recognized I was in the grip of my first immobilizing depression. Or that being fired would sink deep hooks of insecurity into my psyche that would surface every time a future job offered difficulties, resulting in some bad choices.

The older women in our lives in Seattle and Florida thought marriage would fix what ailed me. So her mother sent Chloe the wedding ring her father bought when they were married and posted an engagement notice in Seattle papers. I bought a pawn-shop men's ring for five dollars. On the appointed day – April 1, because getting married was a fool's game – we went to a Justice of the Peace. His wife was witness while he said the requisite words.

For our wedding feast we went out to East Boundary, Greene's Drive-in, staffed by Negro car hops in immaculate starched-white jackets like some fading whisper of Tara. Greene's made the best chocolate milk shakes on the planet. Their giant hamburgers were legendary. Then we went back to bed and didn't come out for several days. A reprise of our Seattle magic, fueled with Greene's calories and whatever we could find around the apartment.

When need for supplies drove us out, the significant news we had missed was murder in Memphis of Dr. Martin

Luther King, Jr. Cities were starting to burn in paroxysms reminiscent of the Haitian and Nat Turner rebellions of other centuries. The city hummed with tension. We didn't understand until I stopped at a hardware store to buy .22 ammunition to teach her to shoot out on the levee, where the old man taught my brother and me. The clerk said ammo sales were suspended under ancient Reconstruction law.

My old man's old buddy the sheriff gave me some ammunition. Grumbled the old law was written against Confederate veterans by occupying Yankees. Used now, it was meant to apply only to blacks, belated payback for an ancient grievance; the Old South had a long, long memory. Denying a white man .22 ammo, the sheriff said, meant this color-blind equal-opportunity shit was getting out of hand.

The world had gone crazy while we weren't looking. The matriarch had an answer for that, too. Her plan to move the family back to Georgia had fallen apart, so bring Chloe to the Beaches and start over. I got a hitch for the Barracuda, rented a U-Haul and we went home. The old man's upstairs bedroom with his old steel-frame bed was ours now we were legal. The boom of home surf down the lane as we made love was a wonderful tonic for depression.

Florida came through in many ways. My mother, with years of waitressing and periods of unemployment between, was angered by my Georgia experience. Said check with Employment Security. *Like schools,* she said, *Florida is better.* She was right. The intake person rolled her eyes when I told her what happened. *Georgia will pay,* she said, *when Florida bills them. Back to the date you were fired.* And that's what happened. The back pay helped a lot. Her attitude, in a way, helped more: unemployment was just a fact of life in a seasons-based economy, no reason for shame.

There were no newspaper jobs. I interviewed for strange positions: apprentice in a chemist lab; a debt-collection agency. None wanted to hire a newspaperman, fearing some sort of expose. They actually said that. Chloe insisted on looking for work. First time out she was hired for a hospital medical-records office; went a long way toward erasing her telephone-company humiliation. It took me longer to find work. A Navy civil-service writing job required exams and interviews that dragged through the summer. Meanwhile I was her chauffeur. And we wore that old bed out. Liberated by Florida, our energy seemed boundless. Sex was the perfect anodyne for depression. I was determined to be everything to her.

There was only one dissonance: remembering a famous hippie poet's dictum – not McKuen – that a woman's body is a closed piano awaiting your finest concerto, I held her and stroked her and tongued her and would not relent until she shuddered into semi-consciousness. Coming out of her trance, she said it felt as if I drained her soul from her, and she fell into a dark place she did not understand. The event proved even lovemaking could deepen depression, but never was repeated.

It would be thirty years before I learned the reason:

Childhood sexual abuse buried so deep she didn't remember.

But the dissonance could not stand against our happy lust. Nor could my depression. When we were in bed, the entire drab world went away. We got creative. We got a little kinky. She had me tie her wrists to the bed uprights so she could not escape my caresses. Which seemed odd to me – tempting that darkness again – but she wanted it. Instead of fading into a trance, she went so wild I really got into it. Her orgasms intensified until she broke the steel posts out of the bed frame to grab me. My silk ties bruised her wrists. *Last time for that* I said.

So she said her queer brother, explaining to their mother his ecstasy beneath his macho partner, was stunned when Mom said any good wife expects back-door visits from her man. He just had to tell his sisters. Hell, they talked sex obsessively as the women of my family. *Shall we?* she said.

Man alive. She learned she liked it. I learned a woman who likes it *really* likes it. I just *thought* she was wild tied-up. Never heard her so gutturally vocal. It's a wonder the bed stood. Hell, a wonder the *house* stood. Of course, it withstood hurricanes. But still. On the Beaufort Scale we created an indoors Force Twelve event. Lay spent in each other's arms. My brain was scoured empty of depression. It would seep back – it pervaded my life until I finally found work.

But every time we made love, it was like hitting reset. I would be at peace, secure in her affections, safe from the outside world. This married life had a lot going for it.

# Chapter 49:
# Married Life
# and a Failed Novel

MY BROTHER WAS GETTING MARRIED, finally having put away grief about his girl's tragic death. Elaborate August wedding planned; I was expected as best man. The matriarch approved his bride-to-be as she had approved Chloe.

His wedding confirmed my dislike for elaborate social occasions. They had a damn *rehearsal* the night before, and a crowded sit-down dinner. Tallahassee heat and humidity were in perfect sync for maximum misery; I damn near suffered heat stroke in a long-sleeve white dress turtleneck with a heavy medallion on a chain – embarrassing *de rigeur* fashion. Chloe hated hats; the church required them for women. Her rebellion was an outlandish Arabian Nights turban a black Baptist church lady would love. I was strapped into a monkey suit, aka formal morning tux, for the wedding. Overheated again, nearly as bad as Basic Training. Looked like a ponce – as if turtleneck-medallion attire didn't! – but my brother was happy.

The heat killed my mother's old game-warden Dodge. She came home with us while it was fixed. The Navy job had come through; I went to work, and she and Chloe took the Greyhound back to bring the Dodge home. A road trip and bonding experience. We found a roomy garage apartment on the west side of the city, eye-level with merging expressways where traffic noise was constant as surf. I could drop her at work and head out to the Navy base and my new job editing a weekly military newspaper.

Like the Fort Lewis newspaper, it was published by a private business that made its money selling ads directed at military personnel. The editorial hole belonged to the Navy – to me. Like editing a small community newspaper whose neighborhoods were hangars and flight-lines of jet squadrons home from aircraft-carrier deployment.

We still were adjusting to married life. Chloe was no cook, so her mother taught her to fry chicken; I was a Southerner, right? The matriarch rolled her eyes and gave her recipes, including one for the best macaroni pie in the world. She vowed to try it.

Meanwhile, the civilian publisher of all the Navy-base newspapers was a curly-haired handsome womanizer who took his Navy-base editors, civilian and sailor, on the town to celebrate each weekly deadline. He knew all the city watering holes. Women gravitated to our group, and the nightlife resonated seductively with my *Chronicle* days. Full-size phone booths with real doors still existed, even indoors. I saw our handsome guide sit in one with a cutie on her knees blowing him, while he mugged and winked out the glass door. The sailor-editors scored a new woman every week.

I did not partake, but being free one evening a week enabled me to renew acquaintance with a good-looking daily-newspaper librarian who had been new when I returned from the Army. She had used her connections to *bolita*-runners to place bets for a story I wrote about the numbers racket. Which was alive and well despite police assertions they wiped it out. Won thirty bucks on a one-dollar bet, while learning how runners moved invisibly through the community. Took the librarian to lunch on the proceeds. She led me to the grounds of an abandoned mansion, a favorite hideout. The sexual tension was there, but I was too in thrall to Glenda to act.

She was glad to see me when I returned to Jacksonville and showed me her favorite nightspot, a jazz bar featuring an old black pianist who doted on her. He assumed we were an item, even played us the *Casablanca* theme. We never took it further – I was with Chloe now. Since Chloe was a pianist, I took her to hear him. The night we went he closed his keyboard abruptly, grumbled he was taking the night off. The librarian told me later with a rueful smile Cat Man thought I was two-timing *her*. Oops, time to stop tempting fate. I went back to the weekly Navy outings.

The horn-dog publisher was amused when I shied away from casual fucking my one night of freedom. Said I was too newly married; I'd get over it. Sounded like the *Chronicle* ME before he was fired. Still, I enjoyed the nightlife and it was easy to lose track of time. Got home so late one night Chloe was ready to call hospitals.

When she understood I was just partying, she tremulously showed me what had been a perfect macaroni pie until she burned it as worry grew. The blackened congealed lump came out of the pot with a thud. *"Good for a doorstop now,"* I said; liquor-fueled humor.

Oh, the redheaded fury! She raged as freely as she made love. I found it cute, went to hug her. Man, she had a mean right hook. I only slipped it thanks to faster reflexes. Held her while she struggled and ranted. Eventually coaxed her out of her mad and made up. But it was years before she made the matriarch's macaroni again.

Young sailors I worked with reminded me of horny-GI days. A Vermonter, my staff photographer, rented a cartop boat and motor from Special Services. Mounted the boat on his rump-sprung Chevrolet, and traded me for the Barracuda opening weekend of duck season, so I could hunt and he could chase girls. Chloe and I sweated blood getting the old Chev to the Beaches. The boat walked on the racks. We had to reach up both sides to hold it still. The car drank quarts of oil. Had to stop frequently to top up the cracked, leaking battery. We overnighted in the old man's steel bed. The matriarch got us up and fed us breakfast. Chloe was going with me, a first.

We arrived at my favorite lake's Six-Mile Landing 6 a.m. – so many cars there was almost no place to park. We were unloading the boat when a guy in a frogman's suit drove up, took a surfboard off his roof rack, grabbed a shotgun and paddled into the dark lake. Chloe gave me a look: *Does this happen all the time?* I pretended not to notice. God knows what she was thinking.

We made the middle of the lake before guns cut loose as if war had been declared. The sky was suddenly full of hurtling coots, 70,000 at last newspaper report. Ducks finally flew about eight. I missed a couple over my decoys, more upset by the minute. "Thomas Wolfe said you can't go home again," Chloe said. "I guess it's true."

A redhead who would hunt with me, and quote literature against my rising frustration? How lucky could one man be? The subdued morning light on the water, old Spanish plantings long gone wild, formations of ducks – I saw it all again with teenage eyes. "There's still the water, and the clouds, and being out under the sky," I said. "And there's you. I *am* home."

With that sort-of epiphany my aim improved. We had several ducks when we got back to the beach house. My brother and his new wife were there for dinner. He helped me dress ducks and seemed wistful for our teen years. Maybe I was projecting.

Finally finished that second novel. My New York magazine editor turned it down and insisted I focus on expanding a short story he liked. My hardback publisher gave me an advance and a contract. Using Author's Guild guidelines I edited it, signed it and sent it back.

The newspaper owner threw a big Christmas party for Navy people and his employees. I killed a fifth of Jack Daniel's before Chloe and I left for the Beaches. We got in at 1:30 a.m. Got up 3:45. I declined the matriarch's breakfast offer. Chloe ate toast and drank coffee with her. My breakfast was tomato juice, Excedrin and Alka-Seltzer. We rented a boat and motor at a fish camp and fought shallows to a lake blind. I only put out twelve decoys.

Ducks were scarce, my reflexes slow. I vowed to nail the next one. Wings; reflex; dead. A coot. Wings again; reflex; splash. Coot *again*. My brother liked shooting coots. I didn't. Rain, plunging temperature. Hunters quit in droves. Ducks gone. *Coots* gone. Alone with wind, icy rain, the incredulous wife: "*You can't tell me you enjoy this. You just can't!*" I did, but we went in, shivering and soaked.

Back at the beach house I was finally dried out and warm, fed and sleepy, when the matriarch said I had a phone call. Took it in the TV room upstairs. It was the new editor at my New York hardback house. My original editor had been promoted. The new guy was huffy about my contract changes. In retrospect, he was negotiating. But I was too damn sleepy to be polite. Perhaps more to the point, his attitude reminded me of depressing events around my firing. When he said *"We're not going to give away the whole store,"* I snapped.

"Send the book back," I said. "I withdraw it from consideration." Had one chance to retreat from my kamikaze decision: my old editor called to smooth the waters. He had shown many kindnesses to the matriarch while I was in the Army, little notes and holiday cards, special checks against royalties when the old man's hospital bills poured in. Mailed me boxes of books to encourage me to keep writing even in the Army.

But it felt like he was supporting the new guy's hard-nosed attitude – granted, in softer language – and therefore disrespecting mine. I said my decision stood. Rex Stout, president of the Author's Guild, wanted me to write a Guild expose about my publisher's reaction to a model Guild contract. I passed, fearing publishers already saw me as a problem child not worth their effort.

Easy years later to see my attitude as undiagnosed depression. Even easy to see how weak the book was, forced to completion under pressure of depression triggered by unemployment. It would be thirty years before I published another novel.

*Blake Alphonso Higgs (1915-1986) Matthew Town, Inagua, Bahamas. Better known as "Blind Blake" ... best-known performer of goombay/calypso in the Bahamas from the 1930s to the 1960s ... For several decades arguably the most important figure in the Bahamian tourist-entertainment industry.*

- Wikipedia

# Chapter 50:
# Nearly Abroad

CHLOE AND I ENTERED THE BAHAMAS as tourists. The customs guys didn't bat an eye at the exorbitant amount of baggage we brought in; tourists were sacred. Blind Blake was on his banjo with steel-band backup, playing welcome music in the terminal amid the waft of clove cigarettes meant to mask Mary Jane. Hollis was waiting, relaxed and a lot happier than the last time I saw him in Jacksonville. Insisted we have Planter's Punches to celebrate arrival before loading our stuff to take us to our hotel. Hollis drinking alcohol was new; island life agreed with him.

We checked into our hotel. First night the shower curtain crashed in on me. I couldn't get the damned rod to stay in its socket. It was about one thirty-second of an inch longer than the space it spanned. Third time it came down I started to blow. Then did what van Vogt called *a Null-A pause* to let my cortex take over from the thalamus. Told myself this is Nassau, you are now an expatriate writer, and shoddy island design merely confirms this. The first night felt like vacation. We made love like we invented it to the sound of trade winds whistling in balcony bannisters, and German sailors chanting drinking songs downstairs. We were *abroad*. Nearly.

Hollis had gone straight to executive editor in Nassau from his Sunday Magazine job, and offered me an out from civil service drudgery. Next morning he took me to work at company offices in Oakes Field, inland a ways. The publisher's small children romped through the halls dragging an exhausted nanny in their wake. Employees affected casual attire – one wore no socks – and laid- back attitude. The whole place moved at a slower RPM. Most of the art department was off to one side of editorial, visible through wide windows.

Glenda sat at her drawing board inside editorial, fifteen feet from what would be my desk.

Chloe and I talked about this a lot when I said yes to Hollis's job offer, after he revealed he already had hired Glenda. Chloe wasn't thrilled. But said go for it, to escape stultifying civil service. The idea of facing Glenda again was abstract until I walked into editorial. Now it wasn't. I felt Hollis grinning off to one side, sly devil. Last time I saw her was in Ocala when I returned her stuff from my Georgia apartment. Lot of water under the bridge since then. Now I was married, and she was not.

She was pouring coffee from a Thermos. Perfectly steady hands. Stood up and came to me smiling, carrying the cup. "Welcome to Nassau, stranger. Long time no see."

"Hi there."

Why did I think everybody in that art department stopped what they were doing to peer through the glass? My vocal chords felt tight. She handed me the cup. "This is for you. Just the way you like it, strong and black as a woman's heart." Hollis chuckled. She smiled at him radiantly. "The old team, back together again. Trust Hollis to make it happen."

"Bring your coffee," he said. "People to meet. You two can catch up later."

"Don't forget and leave my cup somewhere," she said. I nodded. Full of snappy comebacks, this new expatriate writer.

I have no clear memory of people he introduced me to, just a general sense what they did. In subsequent weeks their names stuck. I left Glenda's cup with the receptionist. Hollis took me to the airport to rent a car. A TR Herald convertible with tyres and a windscreen, not tires and a windshield, but steering wheel on the American side. Driving on the English side of the road was odd, but at least the car arranged itself around me familiarly.

We met back at the hotel restaurant, owned by a German married to the woman who owned the hotel, and got the sailors singing Oktoberfest songs last night. Hollis wanted to brief me on the work situation without being overheard. Things were not as tranquil in paradise as its appearance. The publisher's wife, a J-School grad, had imposed herself between the publisher and Hollis as final editorial authority, despite his title.

The company's Cadillac publication was a thick annual tome sold to libraries around the world as the final authority on everything Bahamian. With a fine disregard for deadline, she had assigned a slew of new stories with the book already in pre-production. Completed stories already in type were to be discarded to make room, requiring a whole layout shift. She was roosting on the new stories, nitpicking. He planned to miss the deadline by *three months*. Or more accurately was resigned to it.

He shrugged: life in the islands. The office had been quiet because everything was on hold. We would focus on the lesser publications while I began research on the new book he'd hired me to write. Meantime – he grinned – Chloe and I were guests of honor at an upcoming party hosted by – who else? – Glenda. It would be well-attended, he promised; no secrets in a small company. Everybody hoping for fireworks between the two women with separate claims on the famous author.

There was so much wrong with that I didn't know where to start. I chose the famous-author bit. "One book when I was twenty," I said. "Nothing since. Not very famous."

"It's still selling, Ish. The local bookstores have the British paperback. That impressed the boss – chance to scarf off a famous author to write the new Bahamas tour book."

I dropped it. "Did you put Glenda up to this party?"

"C'mon, nobody puts Glenda up to anything but Glenda. You of all people know that. She wants to get a look at the competition."

"Dammit, Hollis, there *is* no competition. I'm married!"

"Tell Glenda. As I recall she was the married one last time."

"You're having way too much fun with this."

"Me?" He grinned. "You're the famous writer with women fighting over you. Maybe. Nah, it'll be civilized. Both of them are too classy for that." He'd met Chloe when we came back to Jacksonville before he left for the islands.

"Can't get out of this, huh?"

"None of us has TV here. We need the entertainment."

So I spent the next several days writing a story about the famous Mermaid Hole and new housing developments crowding its small patch of reserved ground. Hollis shot some nice photos of a woman's lovely bare back from the hips up against the pool; sleek dark hair, sexy. He never had trouble finding women to take their clothes off for his camera.

Chloe found a real-estate company offering what they called a "bed-sitter," a one-bedroom flat around the corner from the company on the grounds of a defunct Playboy Club. Promised we'd clean it up if we could get out of the hotel quickly. The company gave us a nice break on the first month's rent for that. She did most of it while I was at work. I drove the Herald to the docks to pick up our library, shipped in trunks.

The dock layabouts didn't believe a white man in coat and tie, even one my size, could shift those heavy trunks. Being me I suspected they'd rip me off. So I removed coat and tie and muscled the trunks to the car. Then they didn't believe they'd fit. They did, putting the little car right down on the springs. The customs guy just waved me through; the Mets were beginning their march to their first World Series and he was glued to a game on the radio. I felt smug until Hollis said he hired some of those guys and a truck for his stuff; why raise a sweat? I thought that defined the difference in our personalities.

The flat had wall-to-wall bookshelves that held the whole lot. It was looking like home when we attended Glenda's party. There was a table loaded down with food contributed by guests. The two women sized each other up; Chloe with her trademark cocked eyebrow and Glenda a little too obsequious. Closest thing to fireworks was when Glenda told Chloe to help herself; others were already eating. Glenda was preparing a laden plate. Chloe gave her the cocked eyebrow, like how could someone so small have such a large appetite?

*Oh,* she said, *this isn't for me, it's for Ish. I know everything he likes!* Was it my imagination or did the assemblage hold its breath?

Chloe smiled. *So I've been told. I'll bring his iced tea.*

The party was a success. Everybody said so.

*Almost everyone who has visited the Bahamas will tell you the same thing about my people; Bahamians are very friendly, open and honest, always smiling and eager to please. Indeed, all of the travel guides depict Bahamians ... as being amongst the most beautiful people of earth ... the typical visitor might honestly believe that this nation of islands is at least a close approximation of Eden ... The Bahamas, however, is not quite paradise ... there are ... often below the surface, aspects of Bahamian culture (barely hinted at in the travel guides). For instance, we are a little bit too willing to ignore rules that don't quite suit us ... Serial adultery, which is euphemistically called 'sweetheartin,' is something of a national pastime ... ."*

*- Virgil Henry Storr, Journal of Caribbean Literatures*

# Chapter 51:
# Nassau Memories

NASSAU LIKE PARIS WAS ONE of those cities that stayed with you always. Over the years, saying I lived in Nassau seemed to create a pause in conversation, as others re-calibrated their view of me. Usually they expressed envy. Uniformly said I was lucky. I agreed. It was interesting how many women asked me if it lived up to its billing as Stud Farm of the Western Hemisphere.

Evidently the Venusian telegraph was not deflected by tourbook rhapsodies about white sand, blue-green water and trade winds. Focused instead on island sex and the alleged prowess of young Bahamian males. I admitted witnessing them slip over the fence onto the private Sheraton British Colonial beach downtown, shucking shoes, shirts and pants to reveal Speedos, inviting themselves onto the beach blankets of pale Northern girls. Sometimes they got run off, most times they got lucky and left with their new friends. Women hearing this story professed shock at their presumption – but sometimes with a covert gleam in their eye.

Virile native studs were not the only ones island languor and a supposedly aphrodisiac conch diet energized into serial "sweetheartin.'" The expatriate community played too. But our publisher, near as I could tell, was locked in his travel-guide world view with no interest in glorifying sexual riptides in Bahamian culture. He liked, for instance, Hollis's suggestion to expand the line to include a children's coloring book, and a collection of West Indies folk tales. Glenda already had the coloring book underway, more confident than when she did one about St. Augustine on the mainland.

The publisher still was dithering about the book I was hired to write, so Hollis took me along to research folk tales. I had traded the TR Herald for a Fiat 850; we took two tape recorders, a raincoat and umbrella in case of squalls, and drove out to Adelaide Village. He had located two storytellers, 65 and 71, to spin B'Boukee and B'Rabbi tales. Told me B'Rabbi was Bahamian for the same Br'er Rabbit that Joel Chandler Harris made famous. B'Boukee was

B'Rabbi's perpetual fall guy. We convened beneath cedars on the lee shore. Light surf piled up on an offshore reef, a light hiss on the tape beneath their melodic accents. They did not confine their yarns to those two, spreading out to lie about encounters with mermaids – probably too sexual for the publisher – and an African tale about how dogs lost their tails.

Hollis loved that stuff, and still was optimistic about new ventures. We ran out of tape before they ran out of stories. He gave each a dollar for beer. Back in the village the Fiat refused to start. Laughing boys too young to chase tourist girls circled us, offering to fix it for a dollar. Hollis told me to pop the hood, and re-secured the distributor cap. The boys were unembarrassed he knew their trick. Our second visit, it was just the spark-plug wires. Twice irritated me but Hollis thought it was fun. The weeks slipped by. The main book, the fat annual, still was not cleared for publication by the publisher's J-School wife. Even Hollis's patience was wearing thin.

Nassau was a party town. Employee parties would start with island conviviality but devolve into wickedly sarcastic jokes about the publisher's indecisiveness. Frequent expat-community parties included natives, boyfriend or girlfriend of an expat. Not infrequently the Bahamians would score an additional fuck off compliant foreigners. Skin tones from Abaco-white to Gold Coast-black and all between, males upheld their stud-farm legend. The legend was silent on island women – a form of gallantry? – but on party evidence, they were no strangers to sweetheartin.'

The running expat joke was no one drank the water, substituting gin. Tanqueray, my favorite, was almost the official lubricant. Bourbon was too heavy in the heat. Expats shared a wealth of arcane knowledge over endless drinks. A Dutch engineer confided for really long road trips English drive is better than American: you can rest your gas-pedal foot against sidewall to avoid cramps.

Two drinks and Chloe would be dozing. If she pushed it she would sick up. Expats, observing me holding her hair away from her face above a Bay Street trash can after a Blackbeard's Tavern night, steadying her with my other hand, said it must be true love. Hard-drinking women showed mild contempt when she nodded off at parties, and closed in on me. One voluptuous English blonde sat close to describe being raped by several Haitians who broke into her place. Her description was more reminiscent than traumatized. *"They were gentle when I didn't argue ... didn't hurt me, though some were quite well-endowed ... .they were just lonely. Didn't even steal anything. Would you think me a slut to say it wasn't that bad?"*

Peculiar form of come-on but damned if she didn't seem aroused. Abruptly seized my arm, said, *"Take me dancing at Charlie-Charlie's!"* An Over the Hill nightclub that didn't open till two a.m. I said Chloe's too drunk. Instant reply: *"She can sleep in the car ... "* She later told Hollis I was *a real man, worth getting to know.* We did eventually dance at Charlie-Charlie's on other nights, but I avoided sex with her. A non-Bahamian thing to do. My Augusta ME and the Jacksonville Navy publisher would have shaken their heads. Hollis just grinned and shrugged.

Chloe, with her Seattle knowledge of queers, said there was more than heterosexual attraction around. A little Welsh guy was a party regular with his male partner. When

I questioned her dancing with his English roommate Chloe said, *"He's doing his duty so his macho partner can hit on you."* Which amused her, as women hitting on me did not. The Welshman volunteered to guide me bird shooting on various Out Islands for my putative tour book, just us. I avoided that but attended a stag "smoker" featuring 8mm pornography.

Even in Nassau they weren't bold enough to invite women. The Welshman told Chloe lots of men affect a drunken doze to pretend disinterest, *"but you can see light on their eyes under the eyelids. They're looking, all right. Not Ish – he really was asleep. Head turned away."* I was a fraud. The porn was heterosexual and so arousing I had to keep my eyes off to avoid tumescence in an all-male setting. Chloe thought that funny.

Hollis and I flew to Long Island, Columbus's second landfall in 1492, just across the ocean from Watling's, his first. Watling's was said to have excellent duck shooting. Never found out; we didn't go across. Hollis had his Hasselblad for advertising-spread photos of the posh north-end resort built by our hosts. The German wife was our pilot in a new, comfortable Piper Cherokee. I went to take notes for the tour book. Lodging, meals, drinks were on the house. The rich and colorful guests, the clubhouse, the cottages, were something out of Somerset Maugham, *"South o' Cancer."*

We took a long drive down the island in a whirring Austin jitney, natives waving and smiling. From two white churches Friar Jerome built in Clarence Town near the mail-boat landing, one Anglican, one RC, we counted 34 churches back up the island to the resort. Then there were the signs: *Joe and the Girls Grocery; Jean's Cold Drinks and Dry Goods Store; Kentucky – Club No. 2;The Pink Elephant* – Hollis said such names would never ring true in fiction.

One of us – I don't remember who; Hollis said me – compared our jaunt to road trips Hemingway and Fitzgerald took in Europe. I was larger, but Hollis had the jaded world view of a Hemingway. I was the naive one. Proof of which was not long in coming.

The resort owners' daughter, a Montreal advertising executive, dark, intense, vivacious, lobbied her parents in support of my suggestion that *"game-bird-shooting at Columbus's landfall"* would make their resort even more attractive to certain rich patrons – like her Irish friends who flew to Quebec each fall to shoot.

Over drinks in the clubhouse, she related her surprising plan to live on an Israeli kibbutz. I asked if love led her so far from her Montreal-Bahamas axis. She wondered why love was my first thought and I told her my Israeli story, which absorbed her. We talked writing, from books to newspapers to advertising. She seemed to like me. Hollis took her away to shoot photos for the resort ad. I saw them in Nassau: curvy and smoldering in a swimsuit, wading in a beach cave. *Look what you turned down,* he said. That night when he returned to our guest cottage, I had mentioned I was sleeping without Chloe the first time since marriage.

*But not necessarily alone*, he said. *Our new friend is taken with you. Gave me her cottage number. Go on over for drinks and whatever. By yourself. Three is awkward for that. I concede the field.* I was nonplussed and reflexively declined.

Like the Augusta ME and the Navy publisher, I finally had Hollis shaking his head. The simple truth was that I feared rejection, and didn't want to make a fool of myself. And wasn't sure how I would feel if I *wasn't* rejected. In an island environment where philandry ran rampant, I was uncomfortable. To save face, I spun a rationalization for Hollis: just the fact a woman like that thought me more wildfowl than tame barnyard rooster was enough. Worldly-wise Hollis was kind enough not to call me a chicken.

*In 1682 Brandenburgers, with a lucrative slave trade in West Africa, began building Gross Fredericksburg 36 miles up the Gold Coast from Taboradi and needed a receiving base in the West Indies, which led to disputes with Danes and English. Then in 1713, the Elector of Brandenburg died. His successor had no interest in overseas trade, withdrew Brandenburg claims for West Indies islands and gave the African fort to a celebrated chief called John Connu. The Bahamian holiday festival stems from this chief's ascendancy per Sir Allen Burns, History of the British West Indies ...*

-Ish's Nassau Log

# Chapter 52:
# Junkanoo and
# Fear of Firing

THE FESTIVAL WAS JUNKANOO, a carnival-parade-frenetic celebration reminiscent of Rio's Carnival, The Big Easy's Mardi Gras, Germany's Fasching. Hollis hired me to rewrite an old Bahamas tour book that was skimpy on history. Which led me to the Old Jail Library on Shirley Street, a remarkable three-story octagonal structure, old cells crammed with bookshelves. Of all the libraries I ever used it was my favorite. I could lug historic tomes to a window seat and read, listening to steel-band music across the street in a hotel garden-restaurant favored by

Confederate blockade-runners, later by Prohibition rum-runners. History on the page, history out the window, history in the very walls.

After Hollis secured me a press pass for 1969 Junkanoo, I saw little changed from Junkanoo descriptions in a 1929 book by an Englishwoman, copied at the Old Jail: *The weird monotone of rhythmic drumming and of a curious tune played upon a tin trumpet, or with a large cowbell ... was unvaried, and might have been played by the same person ... but for the fact that I could locate the sounds now far, now near.* "Are you gwine down to market in de mornin to see dem keepin de Lawd's birthday?"

*"About what time?" said I.*

*"About two or three o'clock," she said solemnly.*

*"But it's dark then!"*

*"Oh yes, and de masquerade done look wonderful fine in de dark ... " In the uncertain light, mysterious shadowy men rushed up and down the street – a weirder crowd than any I ever imagined ... beating of the drums and all the sounds of the previous night were concentrated now ... you might walk the whole length of the street and hear no variation in the rhythm, which everyone kept perfectly, without any general conductor. The dances varied slightly ... .*

Histories said the African chief John Connu "required" white slavers to permit Africans in the West Indies a Christmas celebration of old tribal rituals. No single reference as to *how* he required it. In the library, steel bands tinkling, Obeah or other dark magic seemed implied. I followed his name book to book.

He morphed into Johnny Canoe, substituting an Arawak word, then Junkanoo. No cross-reference to the ancient Prester John of papal legend, who wielded remote power with his magic far-seeing mirror. If Johnny Canoe was his descendant, slavers would have been smart not to cross him, as an ancient Pope hoped Genghis Khan would fear crossing his namesake. The Pope threatened to unleash the African wizard's dark magic, and regiments of huge black Christian soldiers, on the Mongols if they didn't back off. History says Khan died suddenly, Mongols retreated, Europe was spared ... and centuries later, Johnny Canoe became Junkanoo, and Bahamians danced.

An excellent fantasy novel I never wrote. Meanwhile, the M/V *Buccaneer* out of Jacksonville, Barracuda aboard as deck cargo, was delayed again by bad weather. Renting a car was getting expensive. The New Zealand secretary transcribing our B'Boukee and B'Rabbi tapes loaned me her Flower Machine. This was a Capri with large flower decals pasted all over it and an odd four-speed shift on the column, not floor.

The decals I suspected were inspired by her first U.S. landfall among '60s flower children on the West Coast. She cohabited with a red-goateed hippie from the art department, and a Robert Heinlein cat, in refurbished slave quarters downtown; wore translucent blouses sans bra. The car was a piece of work: one tire went flat immediately in the garage under our apartment. I couldn't work the European tire jack. Glenda drove over with her American Ford jack, then showed me how to use the European one. Small smirk: *Wasn't Chloe in Europe? Too girly to know from cars?* She drove me to the Gulf Station on the roundabout to get a patch. Chloe*: Tomboy ex-lovers useful to you, huh?* Neither in the other's hearing of course.

After their vorpal-blade snick-snack, Chloe and I went out for an evening paper in a cloudburst. Hit a puddle, damn car stalled. Probably wet spark plugs. I could not find the hood latch. Chloe steered while I pushed toward the Gulf station. Bahamians whizzed by, staring in horror at a bare-headed man being rained on. The company's native accountant had explained natives really did catch pneumonia that easily in winter rains. The slope up into the station defeated me. The young attendant danced beneath the roof over the pumps, terrified of the rain, then ran with a bumbershoot – to push one-handed under its shelter. Bahamian stud material for sure was my private thought. He couldn't find the hood latch either.

That required a suave PLP man in a Saville Row suit to remind me the Flower Machine was at base a *Ford,* with a "bonnet" opening from the firewall, not the grill. But he declined a curvy little black woman's plea to push-start her TR convertible. Not in the rain! So did the attendant. Her starter was fried; only a push would get her started. I couldn't get wetter. While the kid dried my plugs I pushed. No go. Pushed her back. Tried again. Still no go.

Her canvas top wouldn't go up either. Gave up and drove her to her hotel, the Dolphin, wet as me. She invited us to her suite, poured Cokes and gin, all she had, and changed into a bathrobe. Offered me her shower. The shower in our flat still wasn't working. Fed up with washcloth baths, I accepted. Lord, what luxury. Steaming Niagaras of really hot water. After a long delicious shower I wrung out my clothes, let the shirt hang to dry, socks and underwear in a puddle, and went barefoot in damp pants to drink with her and Chloe on her deck.

She was some character, telling Chloe she was lucky to have such a brawny man. Topped up our drinks. Said I should stay till my clothes dried. Chloe said later she wanted to play. Play what? *With us, Ish. Play with us.* Laughed at my expression. *Didn't you get the hint when she put on that MoTown music and wanted to dance? With me, when you turned her down?* My flower-child was amused at my shock. We left, my wettest things in a bundle, shoes without socks – the Bahamian way – and damp shirt. She was dancing by herself. Never did get a newspaper.

Glenda had offset plates from composing cut about eighteen inches square, and loaned me black paint and a brush to paint them. I used her white acrylic and Chloe's mascara brush to paint my license-plate numbers and print *Nassau Bahamas*. The license-division guy assigning numbers said there were so many cars on the island he expected it to sink. Island humor. Charged $B25 a year and you letter your own plate. Expatriate humor: *making license plates is beyond the skill of inmates at Fox Hill Prison.*

When the Barracuda was on the dock, the customs man smirkingly announced $B300 import duty. Accepted my Royal Bank of Canada check after tedious paperwork. Finally I was free of the Flower Machine. Rolling down Bay in my Barracuda, the hood now wide enough to land a helicopter, I had to strain to hear eight-cylinder purr after the sewing-machine clatter of Continental cars.

The New Zealander who loaned me the Flower Machine liked to frequent beaches without her boyfriend to check out the Bahamian studs. She lured Chloe along. Chloe's ear for speech patterns had her sounding like a Kiwi when she alluded, smiling, to preening males whose skimpy suits displayed large bulges. I called a halt to beach excursions, fearing the New Zealander's sexuality would stir Chloe's flower-child licentiousness. I wasn't going to play, and by god I didn't want her playing either. She acceded with good grace. At drinking parties where sex was always the topic, no expat or native moved on her. Hollis said they were afraid of me; good.

But I never wrote the new Out Island tour book. The publisher changed his mind when he saw the budget needed to send me to all the islands. I experienced a surge of unease about whether my employment would continue, since the main reason for my hire had evaporated. The Bahamian publisher was kinder and gentler – if wacky as a Lewis Carroll character – than the Augusta asshole who fired me. But I'd quit a tenured civil-service job for this uncertainty. Fear of being fired again ate at me. Firing would cause residence-permit revocation. Chloe and I could be kicked off the island with little time to pack, let alone reship the car.

Hollis said relax. The publisher liked having an author on staff – I was safe. Loaned me his Honda motorbike to go downtown for ministry press releases – easier to park. Hadn't been on two wheels since my motor-scooter, but my balance was okay. Just had to remember to ride on the wrong side of the road. Crisp winter sun, pretty girls on the sidewalks and laid-back ministry people were a nice diversion. But I started reading *Editor and Publisher* classifieds.

*Please, Mr., please, don't play B-17*
*It was our song, it was her song, but it's over*
*Please, Mr., please, if you know what I mean*
*I don't ever wanna hear that song again*
                    - Welch and Rostill, *Please, Mr., Please*

# Chapter 53:
# Lunch Downtown,
# Part One

THE SOON-TO-BE FAMOUS SIXTIES ended for me in Nassau. The first big winter Northeaster of 1970 roared down out of the North Atlantic, ricocheting off the Gulf Stream that blocked it from the mainland, and chilled "the eternal isles of June." My wife was off the island. I was going to lunch with Glenda. "God, this old thing is big," I said, as we climbed into her enormous black '58 Ford.

"Oh, it is *not*," Glenda said. "You're just getting used to these little windup toys the Brits drive here."

She keyed the rough idling eight-cylinder to life, dropped the stick shift in gear. We rumbled out of the company parking lot. The salt air of the trade winds must have eaten through the muffler to give it that throaty roar. When we cleared the overhanging canopy of casuarina trees, the big sea wind caught us and rattled the windows in their rusting channels.

"Christ, I hate the cold weather," she said.

"You always did. But it's only about forty degrees."

"Forty degrees in Nassau! The tourists probably want their money back this week."

"I always loved the cold weather. But here cold weather seems irrelevant."

We rolled down the block to the stop sign and took a left toward Bay Street downtown. The Ford's wide nose came around like an aircraft carrier nosing into the wind to launch planes. Riding as a passenger in a giant American Ford on the English side of these narrow Nassau streets made me nervous.

Nassau was more suitable for Morris Minis with sewing machine engines and the steering wheel on the wrong side. But it cost less to import my Barracuda than to buy, even with the piratical import duty. Without a British car I still could enjoy penny candy from glass jars in Bay Street stores with wooden floors and slow big-bladed ceiling fans. Smell raw conch from fishing boats tied at Government Wharf, and winter-damp straw on the waterfront where the straw dollies wove colorful palm baskets for tourists. Strong rum just about everywhere. Downtown on the simplest errand, the smells reminded me I was an actual expatriate, even if only a short plane ride from the U.S.

My friend Hollis slyly had not mentioned he already hired Glenda until I was committed to come to work. I had lost track of her after our painful breakup, back when I had been quite sure she was the love of my life.

Now she was a divorced mom living the expatriate life, whose looks attracted a variety of men. Soon as she knew Chloe was off the island she suggested lunch. I could not ignore the memory that was how she commenced seduction of a virginal copy boy eight years ago. But I agreed anyway. "I'll never know why you had this beast shipped over here," I said.

"Because it's mine and it runs good," she said. "Same reason you shipped the Barracuda." She had a history with the Barracuda. "How much import duty they get you for?"

"Three hundred Bahamian."

"Highway robbery."

"More like island piracy. They can get away with it."

The old office clichés of away-from-home Americans fell into well-oiled grooves. I began to relax a little. This wasn't going to be a problem after all. It was just lunch. First lunch alone together since we parted. For keeps I thought.

It didn't work this way in the movies. Especially not movies about expatriates who led glamorous and exciting lives outside any conventions, maybe starring Richard Burton and Elizabeth Taylor. This was just lunch in downtown Nassau in the tourist season while Chloe was home on the mainland. Maybe Nassau was too close to Florida to be that glamorous. I was taking a lot of notes and thought if I ever wrote about living in Nassau I would name the book *Nearly Abroad*. Hollis said I had a way with titles. So far the title was all I had.

If I wanted to be a real expatriate I should have tried to get back to Paris where I never got to spend enough time in the Army. Or Israel, home of the woman who made me a man in Paris, but whom I never had the courage to seek again. But Nassau is what I had.

The thought that the bonnet of Glenda's Ford resembled an aircraft carrier probably occurred because the Navy job Hollis rescued me from was at a home base for carrier-aircraft squadrons. Hood, I corrected myself; bonnet was too cutesy-British to say about a '58 Ford V-8, even if it was accepted Bahamian usage. I was scheduled to take the lighthouse tender down to Crooked Island the day after tomorrow to do an interview with the longest-serving lighthouse keeper in the islands. Took Chloe to the airport yesterday. Last night slept alone for only the second time since we were married. The empty bed brought back a sharpness like the hunger of bachelor days in an empty apartment.

I had lived too long with how it ended with Glenda not to be nervous about even lunch. The pain after she left was part of me, sad story of a broken heart safely in the past. Until suddenly she was in my present again every day, her desk not fifteen feet from mine. As soon as she knew my wife was off the island, she made her first overture. I dodged instinctively. Then was afraid she wouldn't ask again. As if I forgot everything I knew about her: she never took no for an answer. When she asked again I hadn't hesitated. It was just lunch after all.

The Northeaster had rolled over New Providence Island last night. It rattled jalousies dangerously and made unheated flats miserable, especially if you were sleeping alone. The wind was cold and full of strong salty odors. You could almost hear sounds picked up a thousand miles away if you listened hard. A Northeaster had a different wildness than tropical storms, a threat of real cold on its winds. It made me homesick for cold weather in a way Glenda never understood.

She knew a private place to park around the corner from Bay Street. A major perk for lunch downtown in the tourist season. We walked two blocks to the imitation British pub, jammed with pale old white tourists in bright clashing colors and svelte Bahamian secretaries who ranged in skin tone from French roast to cafe au lait. We found a table. I looked the crowd over.

There weren't a lot of white expatriate girls in the steno pools anymore, with the black-power party having seized control from the Bay Street Boys on the strength of promised jobs for the native-born. Expatriate work permits had been squeezed to a trickle. Many were amazed even a writer could get one under the present regime. But our publication's native owner loved American newsmen. Even married an American woman with a Columbia J-School degree. That's why he hired Hollis and why Hollis' recommendation prompted him to call in a favor for one more American employee.

Chloe had not been amused at my sharing an office with Glenda. Didn't really believe I had her out of my system after she patched my broken heart back together. But a tax-free salary, escape from boring civil-service, a chance to write feature stories, maybe write fiction again, was too good to pass up.

All of the Americans in the pub had the unmistakable look of tourists. Not all were old; that had just been the first impression. Some were young and beautiful, some had the stamp of idle money. Young or old, they looked windblown and a little dazed, taking refuge from the weather. So much for eternal isles of June ...

*First the tide rushes in*
*Plants a kiss on the shore*
*Then rolls out to sea and the sea is very still once more ...*
*I can tell, I can feel*
*You are love, you are real*
*Really mine in the rain, in the dark, in the sun ...*
- Sigman and Maxwell, *Ebb Tide*

# Chapter 548
# Lunch Downtown,
# Part Two

GLENDA FOUND US A QUIET CORNER like she did back when we were a going concern. Where surrounding conversation took on a seductive purr and you could hear sweet Muzak tunes clearly. I had forgotten we shared simple joy in piped music of which everyone else made fun.

I glanced at one of the young tourist women who bore the stamp of serious money. Lean and dark and Semitic, awakening bittersweet Paris nostalgia. She wore a form-fitting white jump suit with a golden zip that could bare her from collarbones to crotch with one healthy yank. The big golden ring of the zipper glowed between the double swell of olive-skinned breasts.

"She does have a gorgeous shape," Glenda said.

"What?"

"The woman in the white jump suit. That zipper is just begging to be pulled, isn't it?"

"And he's no uglier than I am either. I don't understand it." She laughed intimately, in the old way. It pulled me back from Paris without even trying. "It doesn't really matter," I said. "I'm a bystander these days. Maybe I always was." There, that was good enough for at least a television soap opera.

"Aren't we all," she said. I admired the deft way she handled it into the even blander form of everyday office yak.

When the Bahamian waitress finally got all of her compatriots served, and all the tourists including latecomers, she finally turned to us. The serving class had built-in radar for expatriates. We learned to crack jokes (*"You can tell a tourist from an expatriate easily – the tourist looks happy"*) and wait them out. It was a badge of pride not to be mistaken for a tourist. We gave our orders. Our voices moved easily into routine expatriate jokes after the waitress left. As a very young man ages ago my words had followed one another cautiously into careful sentences as I tried to very hard to impress her.

Our very first lunch together in another country was at her instigation. I never would have mustered the nerve. After that, lunch together became a ritual, words circling each other with the cramped sensuality of that T.S. Eliot poem about lives measured in coffee spoons. When I was drafted she gave me an engraved coffee spoon to remember her by. God, I was so very young toward women. Never dreamed I was being seduced. She was the one married. I was a virgin quite sure she was the love of my life. Hadn't even kissed her.

When I finally got around to that part, after I was no longer a virgin, I was secretly stunned how deftly she divested herself of a lime-green frock and came into my arms, burning like she had a fever. In the same Barracuda parked under my Oakes Field bedsitter – I resolutely put that vivid image away. Tried to keep my face unchanged by it. We talked about nothing in particular.

"Well," I said into a pause after the waitress finally got around to bringing the food. "Have I changed all that much? I don't *feel* changed."

"Oh, yes. You've changed." She spoke as carefully as we did long ago.

"How, exactly?"

"You're more assured. More at ease. Quite the expatriate man-about-town."

"Is that good?"

"It's ... different." She paused. "I've changed, too."

"Have you?"

"I've cried up all my tears."

What the hell was this now? "Have you?"

"Long ago. Now when I cry it's just dry sobs. They hurt."

Oh no you haven't changed. I was looking at two young Bahamian secretaries flirting with a young black athlete in a Carnaby Street suit. Life looked simple over there.

"I don't feel changed." I wasn't going to ask her why her tear ducts had run dry. Not a chance. That wasn't even television-rerun material.

"You are, though," she said. "You're so much easier-going. Not so uptight." Amazing how she could charge such banal words with meaning. The message was if I just hadn't been so uptight in the old days ... I blinked. I felt curiously light-headed. Her face floated in the gloom of the pub, clear and flushed. Her expression was half-open to me, suggesting – what?

I couldn't meet her gaze directly but saw her clearly enough. Too clearly: a thin ghost of a twenty-year-old's nervousness awakened just beneath the surface of my skin, trembling with all my callow vulnerability to her moods. I was suddenly parched. I gulped some of my pint of draft John Courage. We ate for a while in relative silence.

"Of all the places in the world," I said finally, "that I used to think of us having lunch, the Red Lion in Nassau wasn't even in the running. I didn't even know where Nassau was. I thought it was up where Bermuda is."

"Life is full of surprises," she said. "Light me a cigarette, will you?"

I tapped two Canadian Rothmans out of the box and seated them side by side in my mouth, like a double-barreled shotgun to hold her at bay. Our eyes touched and slid away. I was lighting them with my old Zippo with the German mark welded on the side when the song stroked out of the Muzak, soft and mellow. I took her cigarette out of my mouth and handed it to her. She smiled, listening to the song, and said nothing.

That's awful I was thinking. That's not fair. It was probably inevitable that particular song would be on the tape. Muzak kept on with a song long after everyone was sick of hearing it. I heard it plenty of times since we parted without this reaction.

I should say they're playing our song. If I had any guts at all I would say it. I could see her like yesterday, combing all that long black hair out in the sunlight, singing it to me with the radio. It's ours, all right. Her hair then was black and lustrous as a Labrador's coat thanks to beauty-parlor magic. It still was.

She drew the smoke down deep. When she went to take the cigarette out of her mouth, she fumbled momentarily. I felt a tremor in my own hands. The song went on and on. The other noise in the place seemed to fade away. We smoked the cigarettes completely down without speaking as if waiting for the thing that came up between us to ease. Just for once in my life I would have liked to know what she was thinking. Just once. Just for the sake of knowing, because I hate not knowing things.

"I wish ... " she said.

"What?"

"I wish we had time for coffee ... "

She never made a move to leave first. She never had. A simple but effective tactic. I looked at my wristwatch. "We do have to start back."

"I guess we can brew a fresh pot at the office," she said.

"I'll get the check, if you'll make the coffee."

"My treat next time. Your wife wouldn't like you spending too much money on other women."

There was nothing to say to that. The wind seemed colder when we came out onto the street. I was so lost in the past I almost put my arm around her. Remembered in time that when we were together she liked walking free beside me. Unlike Chloe, who liked my arm around her and was tall enough to walk in lockstep. It was too blustery to talk on the walk back to the car. Isolated within the running wind I could not escape the notion that phantom loves past and present, and perhaps yet to be, walked with me down the windy pavement.

When she cranked up the Ford, the roar of its rusty muffler shattered uneasy ruminations. She ripped the big car backward into the street and bullied her way into a gap in the traffic. I was suddenly too busy for further melancholy, looking everywhere at once. Bracing for collision, trying not to act tense. She always drove like this, even in America on the correct side of the road. She drove like a Frenchman possessed, one in command of a runaway aircraft carrier.

We were only ten minutes late getting back. People at the office said we set a new record for lunch downtown in the middle of the winter tourist season.

# Chapter 55:
# Fourth Intermezzo –
# Out Island Fantasy

From my Nassau notebook: *Yesterday we flew with Hollis and his wife aboard an old Bahamas Airways DC-3 to Andros Island, largest of the Out Islands. We took turkey sandwiches and Cokes in a soft-sided cooler. I took my shotgun in its factory carton and leaned it against the dogged-back door on the firewall behind the flight deck. Unthinkable in the United States these hijack-crazed days ...*

WE WENT AFTER BOXING DAY of the last Christmas of the '60s and the new year ushering in a new decade. We had been in Nassau since October when my Bahamian work permit finally was approved. It was a happy Christmas facing a bright new decade full of promise. I was writing again, for real. Had an actual literary agent in Manhattan. Already had short stories in the mail.

There was an English stewardess on the flight, trim and curvy with sleek brown hair in a bun. I thought she was wasted for the short hop. Maybe she had been demoted for sitting on a BOAC pilot's lap; there had been news stories about something like that. The Andros airport was smaller than the Waycross, Ga. Greyhound depot. No tower, just a short-wave radiotelephone.

An islander drove out from the harbor town to receive the flight and used a lone baggage trolley to move luggage to waiting resort vehicles. Hollis went to see about arranging a hire car. The wives talked. I sat to write in my log. What flowed out of the ballpoint was completely unexpected, my first attempt at sexual fantasy.

*The fire was flickering through the trees, and her face was very close to mine now. We lay together in the back of her old VW bus – she called it a lorry – with hay all over the floor like somebody had a stable. Hay makes me itch, I said. Her face had that look, that open, slack-lipped look. Bastard, don't lose my panties in the hay she said, and kissed me hard, holding on around my neck and squirming her hips up to give me access. I got them down and off her ankles.*

*What are you doing with them, she said.*

*I put 'em in my pocket.*

In my mind's eye it was the svelte stewardess. The words flowed as if dictated. It was a singular composition in my checkered writing career. *Her hands returned to my opened fly, pushing impatiently until there was room. I felt, dimly, the harshness of strands of straw pressed in her palms. Then I hitched the uniform skirt over her hips and moved over her and into her in one smooth gesture, like sheathing a machete. Cutlass I remembered; in the Bahamas we call them cutlasses.*

*Steel band music tinkled in the night off near the bonfire, and people were laughing and chattering happily. Her arms went back around my neck and her breath was hot and wet in my ear.*

*Oh God you feel good, she said, in that plummy English accent, and did something that squeezed me deep inside, her knees coming up into my short ribs. I moved a little and my knees slipped on the straw in the bed of the truck. I lost some ground and had to hunch forward in small little jerks to re-establish full contact. She chuckled and caught her breath at the same time and moved both hands to my rump to hold me in her and just like that we were into it, slow and deep and strong and tight.*

I have read that entry from time to time over the half-century since with a certain bemusement the stewardess inspired such a full-blown fantasy. The constant undertone of island sexuality must have been getting to me. The damn story just flowed.

*She threw her head back and I could see her in the reflected firelight and she was breathing as hard as I was and my heart was trying to kick out of my ribs, and she started saying now, now, now, over and over again. I didn't think so. But she was moving under me, clamped to me and bucking, we were sliding sideways on the straw, and just like that I realized she was right and went off so fast it startled me and I almost yelled. Then I hung on while the aftershocks piled through me into her and were magnified by hers back into me until I didn't see how she could hold me in, but she did.*

When I finally decided to commit the notes to type, I sternly resisted the urge to edit, to smooth, to improve. That long-ago spasm of creativity was too pure to adulterate.

*Then the long slow glide and I could hear the music again over my heartbeat as I eased down on her and she dug her fingers deep in my rump and murmured M'm,*

*M'm, M'm in my ear, like a Honda motorbike at idle. Sweat dripped off my face into her eyes and she blinked, then smiled and reached up left-handed to stroke my forehead. Wow, I said.*

*Uh-huhhh, she said, still smiling. Then we both tensed. I could hear someone crunching along the crushed shells in the parking lot. I rolled to one hip, so she could straighten her legs, and tugged her skirt down. By the time whoever it was walked by, I had her head cradled in my shoulder and her stewardess jacket spread over her legs and my butt. Whoever it was didn't even look in. He paused further on and we heard a steady stream as he made water in the shrubbery and then crunched back to the fire. For some reason she found that funny ...*

The detail was precise as if I lived it. I saw the stewardess. I saw an abandoned VW bus in the parking lot. Everything else was pure imagination.

*She stifled her giggles against my shoulder until he was gone. Then I put a cupped hand under her chin and kissed her.*

*I'm Muriel, she said. Fly me.*

*Yes ma'am, I said. Clear around the world.*

*She pushed at me. Don't be vulgar!*

*Me?*

*Yes you, you big lug. Not so soon anyway. She patted me on the cheek. Let's get ourselves sorted and go find something to drink, h'mm?*

*Okay, I said. You want your panties then.*

*Silly! I'd just gum them up now. You can give them back at the hotel. She must have seen the crestfallen look on my face, because she laughed softly and said don't worry, Hon, I'm not through with you yet ...*

End of the entry. Hollis showed up with a local citizen willing to drive us down the island in his big yellow American pickup. He already had one passenger, a Peoples Liberation Party candidate standing for office in a by-election. My notebook filled with conversations with the politician. I never had occasion to snap my Spanish double-barrel together. I was supposed to write about shooting and fishing for the publishing company, but our guide didn't know much about where good wild-pigeon shooting was. My warm little Out Island fantasy story just – stopped. The stewardess who inspired it was not on the return flight to Nassau.

*I knew I must write a novel. But it seemed an impossible thing to do when I had been trying with great difficulty to write paragraphs that would be the distillation of what made a novel. It was necessary to write longer stories now as you would train for a longer race.*

*- Ernest Hemingway, A Moveable Feast*

# Chapter 50:
# Winter in Nassau
# Part One

THE TWENTY-SIXTH JANUARY of my life was drawing to a close. I was almost halfway to twenty-seven. Twenty-six was my personal deadline for publishing my first serious novel. Hemingway published *Fiesta* at twenty-six. He was living over a sawmill in Paris. I had been sidetracked for a year into a stultifying civil-service job but escaped to Nassau and lived next to a lumberyard. Close, but no cigar. I knew I wasn't going to make it.

It was cold by Nassau standards. The wind had backed into the north and came whistling in off the sea. It rattled jalousie windows and crept through cracks into our unheated flat. Electric guitars and Bahamian voices carried on the wind from dance clubs out by the harbor. Moron dogs the islanders called potcake hounds barked and barked beneath our windows. I thought hunger made them bark all night. Like people at the clubs talking under the heavy goombay beat, trying to say something meaningful about other kinds of hunger.

There the dogs went again. Maybe the throb of island drums in the distance set them off. Here came that song again about where had all the flowers gone, long time passing. I wished Bahamian musicians would stick to island music and leave political folk songs on the U.S. mainland where they belonged.

Chloe told me today I had what her mother called the mollycoddles, a form of depression that was fitful and clinging. Sleep, lovemaking, conch fritters at the yacht-basin restaurant and a drive around the island lifted the edge. But by the time we strolled Government Wharf to watch weekend cruise ships leave for America, the depression came back. It clung.

Chloe had a very good female barometer when it came to cold weather; she had to snuggle. Cold burrowing woman-flesh turning warm in close contact was marvelous for holding back the mollycoddles. Lovemaking left her in deep tranquil sleep in the tangled bed-covers. But it brought me hard-edged wakefulness, depression just around a lighted corner in my mind.

I pulled on clothes and unfolded our brand-new electric blanket over her. Last electric blanket in stock at the Shirley Street Ironmongery when islanders grabbed every other one in Nassau's unseasonable weather. I stroked her forehead while warmth spread through the blanket. "I love you," she said, little-girl sleepy, half-waking up. She sounded like Shirley Temple when she was sleepy. Little Shirley Temple in a black-and-white Late Show movie, not Shirley Temple the lady politician who came later. Then she was back asleep. The harbor music was going to wait till the midnight hour when its love came tumblin' down, with steel-band rhythm.

It seemed strange and lucky to have charge of the sleep of this softly breathing creature of so-pale Nordic skin and lustrous dark red hair while the sea wind prowled and distant guitars suffered. But women could be victim to the mollycoddles too. Of course they could. Chloe said recently the only reason I married her on the rebound from Glenda was because she made herself so available as soon as she knew I was alone again.

She knew damn well I married her on the matriarch's orders, because she didn't want us "living in sin" in the uptight Georgia town of my birth. Chloe was reluctant with her sixties flower-child distrust of marriage. I missed the musical-bed sixties – she didn't – but understood her distrust and even shared it. We compromised and married on April Fool's Day.

Last Sunday I hadn't been depressed about missing my self-imposed writing deadline, or obsessively worried because my publisher had canceled the tour book I was hired to write. We had a pleasant day at home with late breakfast, then each with a good book, when Glenda came knocking on the door and caught us unprepared for company. Nobody telephoned ahead in Nassau. Almost none of us had a telephone. It was too costly and complicated to get one.

I was reading Hornblower. Mister Midshipman Hornblower in the West Indies. Hornblower read very well in Nassau with trade winds making up. Chloe was reading one of those big thick novels by some South African writer about voortrekking and British versus Boers. One of the most interesting interviews I had for the *Chronicle* was an eighty-year-old journalist from Botswana traveling America by Greyhound to sell stories about his homeland. Eighty years old, still writing, still going walk-about. An admirable man.

I couldn't get into the books Chloe liked. All I knew about South Africa, besides the Whistling Women of Nzadzu, an African Christmas story the Botswanan sold me for my Sunday Magazine, was stories the old writer told. Memorably, that Boers gave the British Army as much grief as Francis Marion did a century earlier – a parallel the Oxford-educated Botswanan drew. That Boers used 7mm Mausers effectively as the Swamp Fox's Carolinians used squirrel rifles. Chloe's books had none of that.

We were perfectly comfortable reading authors we liked without trying to evangelize each other. I thought that might be a pretty good basis for a happy marriage. We were reading in companionable silence when Glenda knocked. The flat was a terrible mess. Without discussion, with hand signals, we chose to sit very still and pretend not to be home.

Her eight-year-old boy said my Barracuda was in the garage under our flat, I must be home. Glenda knocked several times, but gave up. Her big old Ford roared to life and crunched down the crushed-shell drive past the defunct Playboy Club. I started scrambling to get presentable. "She won't come back," Chloe said. "I want to keep reading."

"She'll come back."

"Why? We're not here!"

"She'll be back. Listen: do I know my Glenda, or don't I?"

Probably shouldn't have said it just that way. But it got her up to dress and straighten a little. They were back in less than thirty minutes knocking on the jalousie again. I remembered now Glenda said she might stop by today. Forgot it in the peaceful relaxation of the weekend. We had picked up just enough – the flat just stale enough – for Glenda to take one sweeping look and think she knew what we were doing when she knocked the first time. Chloe saw the look and the conclusion easily as I did. It gave her a kind of sadistic kick.

We had missed the damp washcloth draped over the back of a dining chair. Chloe had it over her eyes to ease the strain of too much reading. My wallet and car keys and pocket change and wristwatch and wedding ring were in the same chair. There weren't many places to put things. Glenda chose that chair.

She carefully transferred to the table the same wallet, car keys and wristwatch she moved from similar perches when she and I were together. The spare change had been American not Bahamian. There hadn't been any wedding ring. She moved that last of all, held delicately between thumb and forefinger. "Men!" she said to Chloe with a small smile.

"You're pretty good at picking up after them," Chloe said softly.

"Well, I've had practice here and there..."

Standing in front of the mirror combing my hair, still wet from a hasty shower, I could have sworn they just fired warning shots across each other's bows. Maybe the Hornblower influenced my thought.

The only ring I wore with Glenda was my high school class ring with the face turned in to resemble a plain gold wedding band. I was so young I feared an eagle-eyed guardian of public morality behind every motel registration desk. Glenda on the other hand didn't wear her wedding ring, which exposed a pale circle on her tanned finger.

Chloe knew pretty much my whole history with Glenda. I knew her history with serial men when she thought me gone for good because of Glenda. That touted sixties honesty was overrated. We both had our emotional wounds. She was secure enough not to object to me sharing an office with Glenda. I was mostly secure she was done fucking other men. Love would see us through. I hoped. Even through Glenda visits I forgot to tell her to expect ...

# Chapter 57:
# Winter in Nassau,
# Part Two

WHEN I TURNED AWAY from the mirror, Chloe's smile was a Cheshire-cat simper as she watched Glenda steadfastly not-look at the damp washcloth on the chair she chose. "You were going to take me out to Franz's yacht today," Glenda said. "Remember?"

I hadn't really agreed to do that. At the office she just said maybe I would take her because Franz was selling his boat. I had been talking about buying a boat to live on. But I had given up on the notion and told her so. Thought that was the end of it, but no point in arguing. "I did forget," I said. "I'm not really in the market for a boat anymore the way things are shaping up with the government."

Franz's invitation of course was for Glenda alone. Why get the exotic artist lady with long dark hair and deep blue eyes and sexy lips on his boat if there was a crowd? That would cramp his style, and Franz was stylish. A pit boss at Paradise Island Casino, much taken with a sketch of him Glenda did for a gambling feature. Even more taken with Glenda. Glenda always had the gift of misunderstanding interest her looks attracted from sudden kinds of men like Franz. Men with a dangerous edge. She included her son in the outing without asking. I was pretty sure Franz didn't expect a 200-pound chaperon either.

The boat story was complicated. My father flatly refused to loan me his 32-foot *Maverick* to bring across the Gulf Stream and live aboard. Hemingway didn't get a boat until he sold a couple of novels. But this was the buy-anything-on-credit age. I discussed financing with Royal Bank of Canada on Bay Street. But the Bahamian government was in the hands of the black-power party, Bahamas for Bahamians, and no expatriate's work-permit renewal was automatic. I dropped the idea.

Same reason Franz had his boat up for sale. Preparing to cut his losses if he had to go back to Continental casinos. The international gambling press was in speculative frenzy about potential nationalization of Bahamian casinos and replacement of professional European dealers with surrey drivers and conch fishermen.

But Glenda always moved in her own orbit. She fully expected me to go with her to Franz's boat. It had a certain flavor of expectation from when we were a going concern, but I was not her protector anymore. Maybe I was mistaken and she didn't want a protector, just remembered my interest in a boat. But if she was writing me back into her life in that wonderfully unconscious way she wrote us into an affair to start with, failure of memory was prudent.

She was running away from a violent bullying husband of whom she was deathly afraid when I became her protector. She needed something to run toward. Like all bullies her husband had flown into a towering homicidal rage when he saw her slipping away. Even in his fury he understood, as I did not, I was irrelevant to his loss of control. That was the year I almost shot him, and broke his hold over her. Then she dumped me, having borrowed my courage until she found her own, I suppose. She needed me gone before she could believe she was truly her own person.

I was back with Chloe when Glenda wrote to thank me for giving her space to sort her feelings, and invited me back into her life. As if her emasculating departure were just another lover's spat. Her letter conveyed she now *was* her own person and wanted me back. It reflected the same sort of amazing unconsciousness as her Franz invitation. For the first time since I knew her I was immune to the siren call in her letter, inoculated by Chloe's love. I still was. Said I'd give Franz's boat a pass. Then we sat making polite conversation waiting for her to leave.

The damp washcloth on the chair transfixed Glenda. She knew what that had been used for. She did like hell. But she sure thought she did. She looked everywhere but at the washcloth. Chloe sat at the other end of the tiny table like a cat watching a mouse. "Where does Franz keep his boat, Glenda?" she said, all brightly interested. "Over in Hurricane Hole, I bet."

"He says whoever buys it can keep the same slip," Glenda said.

The boy said, "Are we gonna go out with Franz on his boat today, or what?" He fidgeted in the third kitchen chair. I was in my writing chair. He liked me well enough. When he knew things were going bad he said, not without sympathy, *Won't work – you're ten inches taller than mom and she's eight years older than you.* The wisdom of a child.

I could work comfortably with Glenda. We talked candidly about everything but shared romantic history. Glenda had a knack for totally blocking out as if it didn't exist anything she didn't want to talk about. That suited me fine. She also brought a Thermos of strong black coffee every morning, just the way I liked it. I didn't mention this to Chloe because it felt too intimate. But I drank the coffee.

She was opening herself meagerly to new men, even confided in me like a Dutch uncle about the rake-hell Abaco conch fisherman who fucked her almost before she knew what was happening. Or as she put it. *Suddenly I realized he was making love to me – and not badly!* There were other men like Franz her looks had always attracted, to whom she seemed perfectly oblivious on the mainland. Now she allowed herself to acknowledge their interest. A Kraut doctor who liked to discipline the boy a little too Teutonically could mean she was succumbing to a domineering asshole like her ex. Not my business.

I loved her extravagantly in that other country without counting cost to myself or others, from the matriarch to Chloe. But that love was cauterized by the way she ended it. No faintest ghost of old passion could be allowed to threaten Chloe's belief in me. But I felt a peculiar need to free Glenda from her fixation on that washcloth. I recalled with perfect clarity the times she used a warm soapy washcloth to lovingly clean my privates after lovemaking. So I got out of my writing chair, plucked the washcloth from behind her and pressed it to my jaw.

"A tooth came out in a sweet roll this morning. Hurts like hell and aspirin doesn't even touch it."

"Really?" Glenda said.

"He's such a baby about *anything* the least bit uncomfortable," Chloe said, with that Cheshire simper. "Aren't you, Ish?"

I went back to my chair with the washcloth. I was going to get a hellacious razzing from Chloe when they left. The boy's face fell. "I know what this means. Now we don't get to go out on the boat with Franz." I hadn't even thought of that.

"Sure we will," his mother told him. "Maybe not today…"

Glenda was too preoccupied to notice he knew she was lying, caught up in my lie about the washcloth. She would expect me to receive such ablutions from my new woman and lie about it to protect her feelings. Proof we were fucking when she knocked the first time.

That was last weekend. Chloe was surprisingly gentle when she jibed me. Now this: the mollycoddles because I was never going to be a famous writer. I got up and heated water for instant coffee on the gas ring in the postage-stamp kitchen. Live blue warmth of the flame broke the chill momentarily. Then I sat with a heavy book Hollis gave me to read the closing chapters of the most authoritative Hemingway biography.

The way he ended was very bad, despite everything the last woman of his life did to fight his depression. Electroshock treatments, trips to the Mayo Clinic. Disoriented and paranoid he wandered backwoods roads near his mountain-valley home, suspecting the FBI had him under surveillance. So he wrote his own final thirty.

I had sold one short story to a down-market imitation of *Playboy* for a lousy hundred bucks. I thought the story was okay and had three more in the mails I thought were okay. I was using short fiction between efforts on my first serious novel. The one I meant to finish my twenty-sixth year. Now it was January and I was preparing to face defeat. It didn't matter. It didn't matter because it all came out the same in the end. Despair now or despair in forty years. Famous and celebrated or unknown, it ended the same.

Last Sunday when Glenda went out the door there had been a rectangular spot from the damp washcloth imprinted on the back of the chic pale-yellow frock she chose for a day on a boat. She could have moved it as easily as she moved the wallet and keys. But she couldn't bring herself to acknowledge its existence. I wished I had just explained about the Hornblower and Chloe's South African eyestrain. But no explanation was better than any explanation, truth or lie. Because that came out the same too despite the details.

I closed the book and turned off the lamp by my chair. The sea wind was colder through the jalousies, distant electric guitars and steel drums were louder. Potcake hounds still barked incessantly. My coffee was cold.

# Chapter 58:
# Leaving Nassau

SPRING CAME TO NASSAU. Every payday after depositing our checks Hollis and I ate at the downtown Burger King, to talk about the job without being overheard. The publisher's wife still had not cleared the big guidebook for publication. Even Hollis's patience had worn thin and he was seriously considering pulling up stakes. I said I'd go with him; couldn't face dealing with the goofy publisher and his up-tight wife without Hollis to intercede.

This Burger King, first one I ever saw without a parking lot, sat right on Bay Street like a sidewalk cafe. Its windows gave us throngs of colorful tourists parading by in search of island color, not interested in a car-less anomaly from American suburbs. Burger-flippers were all Haitians, studying English texts between customers; Haitians took all the menial jobs Bahamians refused.

One Friday I told him my *Editor and Publisher* reading produced a lead, not in help-wanted classifieds but the news columns. The Augusta managing editor fired so summarily had landed on his feet as assistant executive editor of a large Pennsylvania daily. When I wrote to congratulate him, almost by return mail I got a job offer for general assignments. So I had a possible exit strategy. Hollis said his own exit was looking more complicated but he was working on it. Advised me keep my plans quiet to avoid a flap with the publisher, he would cover for me if I decided to bail.

One night a few days later, things unrelated to work got strange. Chloe and I heard footsteps racing up the stairs to our bedsitter. Loud knocking before I could reach the door. It was Hollis, tense and skittish. "I need to borrow your shotgun."

"What?" Last thing I could have expected. "Why?"

"I need to kill a sonofabitch." My usually unflappable friend was deadly serious. Someone had driven up to his remote inland house, fired a couple shots, and beat it. He drove to the constabulary where a CID man suggested he "get a shooter" since he had no phone. I had the only gun he could think of. I didn't know his experience with firearms. Didn't want to embarrass him by asking in front of Chloe. So I got my Spanish double and shellbelt, we left his wife and son with Chloe, and I checked him on loading and safety on the deserted rural road before we got to his place. Surprised he knew shotguns from hunting as a kid because we never talked hunting.

We cruised back roads and chatted with uniformed constables looking for the gunman. They seconded the CID man's suggestion but disrespected my bird gun. Said they'd smooth paperwork required to buy a pistol, and train him on the police range. His status with the publishing company made him part of the privileged class so handguns were available. Working stiffs need not apply. I kept my opinions about anti-gun hypocrisy to myself; the U.S. was going the same way with the infernal '68 Gun Control Act. He dropped me home, got his family and took my 16-gauge with him.

Chloe suggested the real reason I went with him was not firearms safety. It was in case I could get the shot: most dangerous game and all that. Hell, even she was buying that Hemingway crap about me.

Soon Hollis had the blood-warming satisfaction of seeing his would-be assailant above the barrels of my gun, and seeing him crawl. As with Glenda's ex, shooting was unnecessary. The idiot had a starter pistol (*never bring a starter pistol to a gunfight*) when he showed up to threaten my friend.

Sounded dangerous in the night, fired only blanks. A cuckold metaphor if ever there was one. Because this idiot was the crazily jealous boyfriend of a sexy little blonde who liked leather mini-skirts – and Hollis. One more married friend who had kicked over domestic traces for "a bit of the strange," as the British style it. Not too surprising in the Stud Farm of the Western Hemisphere, where sex simmered everywhere and of which a Bahamian scholar wrote "*Serial adultery, which is euphemistically called 'sweetheartin,' is something of a national pastime … .*" When in Rome, as the saying goes.

Evidently I was the only expat in our circle who had not gone native in this respect, and didn't plan to. As the allegedly famous writer drinking morning coffee brewed by his former lover, walking home for nooners with a sexy redheaded wife, I could not imagine straying. Not after passing up a chance at the beautiful advertising exec on Long Island.

Through Hollis I knew an island farm family that lived as far from urban buildup as you could get on a 7x21-mile island. Just like Georgia farmers except Mr. A. was white and Mrs. A. was black. I was interested in Bahamas bird-shooting to compensate for a missed season at home. Their son promised to show me a hidden pond Bahamian pintails used; Hollis had acquired a Winchester 12-gauge as more useful than a pistol, and said he'd like to go.

Junior wasn't home but we followed vague directions from Mrs. A. No pintails on the pond, but we kicked up wild pigeons, doves and woodcock from the adjoining bog. I missed a couple. Hollis didn't shoot. We even flushed a covey of bobwhites; I hadn't known the island had quail. We got our Clark chukkas and pant legs wet before the bog gave way to untended banana-tree plantations.

Ambled and talked about escaping the island, and lovers and hopes for the future, more freely than if constrained by wife-and-walls. Walked as far as the Bacardi plant on the edge of tidal marsh, closed and dark on Sunday. I noticed his yellow nylon windbreaker blended better with island vegetation than my canvas shooting vest.

My friend from Augusta had had *his* boss, the Pennsylvania executive editor, issue me a personal invitation. Payback for walking out with him the day he was fired in Augusta, all the sweeter since I did it for friendship, expecting nothing in return. Hollis still was piecing together his own plan. As to the future, I said if I ever found a pond and bog like this, screened from salt wind by pine and hardwood, insulated from the ocean by wide gamebird-filled marshes, I would be content to call it home. Hollis was doubtful. What about women like the Montreal ad exec? Like his leather-loving blonde? What about living in London, knowing exotic women, taking them on the ferry to the Continent for holiday road trips in a Porsche?

When we got back, our wives had been to Burger King to get Whoppers, mundane comedown from flights of fancy. The burgers were cold but we were hungry, and hunger made a better meal than proper temperature. His questions had raised memories of France and women I failed to sleep with, a kind of nostalgia for a life I never lived. But the pleasure of living as an expatriate in Nassau had been dimmed by recurring fear of unemployment, which shaded any prospect for further adventure. And would for the rest of my life.

A newspaper in Rio had offered me a job, contingent on learning passable Portuguese within six months of hire. German was also prominent, and they liked it I had a head start on Deutch from Army days. A tabloid in the English Midlands said all I had to do was show up and I would have a job. Both papers took my presence in Nassau as evidence I was a seasoned expat.

But the dual security of a friend at the top, and a Newspaper Guild contract firmly in place, made Pennsylvania my hands-down choice. As spring blossomed in Nassau, I followed Hollis's advice and kept quiet as we got ready to go. We shipped our trunked library and all else we could; loaded the Barracuda down with the rest and put it back on the *Buccaneer*. Pirates serving as customs officials laughed at my petition for refund of import duty. I rented a car and drove Chloe and her new kitten, with necessary feline-immigration paperwork, to the airport. Saved for myself one last night in Nassau at the Paradise Island casino, which by law was off-limits to a resident.

I dressed up in my one Nassau-tailored suit by a refugee from London's Savile Row: charcoal with a chalk stripe, three-button front, high side vents *a la* James Bond. (Thirty years later, John LeCarre's *Tailor of Panama* made me wonder if my tailor was SIS man in Nassau, like Graham Greene's vacuum-cleaner salesman in Havana.) Ian Fleming's exotic old Bahamas Club from *Thunderball* was defunct; Paradise Island was anticlimactic. Patrons wore garish tourist clothing, Bermuda shorts and flip-flops, for god's sake. Croupiers were better-dressed; two separate pot-gutted Hawaiian-shirt loudmouths took me for a pit boss. I made a hundred bucks last all night, not counting Havana cigars I would miss Stateside. Saw one elegant woman in a silk sari lose five grand at Blackjack without a flicker of emotion.

Zero romance; zero sexual tension. Every woman, stylish in silk or silly in pedal-pushers, was focused on cards, the wheel or the slots. I was an overdressed clown. Didn't even get drunk; boring end of the grand expatriate adventure. Slept in the stripped apartment, left early for the airport, and slipped out of the Bahamas without further ado.

Thank you for reading.
Please review this book. Reviews help others find
Absolutely Amazing eBooks and inspire us to keep
providing these marvelous tales.

If you would like to be put on our email list to receive
updates on new releases, contests, and promotions, please
go to AbsolutelyAmazingEbooks.com and sign up.

# About the Author

**William R. Burkett, Jr.** is an acclaimed sci-fi writer, listed in the *Science Fiction Encyclopedia*. But his "straight" writing is a well-kept secret, until now. A product of Georgia and Florida, he now lives in the Pacific Northwest where he can enjoy the fishing and duck hunting. He was once described by author Frank G. Slaughter as a "natural-born storyteller." After a Quixotic career in journalism and public relations, he's now turning his attention back to his trusty typewriter, uh, we mean computer. "Times change, but good storytelling goes on forever," he says.

# The New
# Atlantian Library

NewAtlantianLibrary.com
or AbsolutelyAmazingeBooks.com
or AA-eBooks.com

www.ingramcontent.com/pod-product-compliance
Lightning Source LLC
Chambersburg PA
CBHW060813030726
47503CB00002B/471